The relativity-squeezed view of the _____ front of the Sun-Tzu crawled, oozing color. Their destination, Alpha Centauri, shone clearly within a blinking green circle directly in front of them. Bruno grunted in triumph as a small red blur appeared within the starfield holo, below and to the right of their destination.

"Right there, boss," he said to Carol.

"Tracking us?"

"Seems likely."

"And they are kzin spacecraft?" Carol chewed her lip. "How many?"

"More than one ship, less than ten. Flanking us, running a bit ahead. Slow vector toward us—like a cautious intercept."

"Seems funny. Not kzinlike. How close are they?"

"About seven light-minutes away."

"Why the slow vector to intercept? Any kzin vessel out here could intercept us within hours."

"I have good news and bad news," Bruno replied softly.

"Well?" Carol's tone held a trace of impatience.

"The good news is that they think we can't see them. If they thought we could see them, they would attack."

"And the bad news?" Still the impatient captain.

Bruno chose his words carefully. "Almost anything we do will tip them off that we can see them. There would be no reason to change our routine in deep space. If we change our routine, they might hit us with everything they've got."

"Ummm. Cat . . . and mouse."

Bruno smiled a lopsided grin that went no deeper than his thinned lips. "Boss, I think they want to board us."

Carol nodded abruptly. "Right. Otherwise they would just crack us like a rotten egg."

MARK O. MARTIN

A DARKER GEOMETRY

GREGORY BENFORD

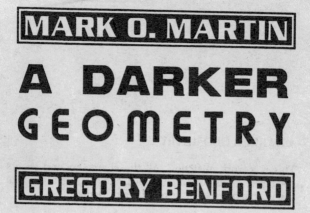

A DARKER GEOMETRY

Copyright © 1996 by Mark O. Martin & Abbenford Assoc. Parts of this novel appeared previously in *Man-Kzin Wars VII*.

A Baen Books Original

Baen Publishing Enterprises
P.O. Box 1403
Riverdale, NY 10471

ISBN: 0-671-87740-2

Cover art by Bob Eggleton

First printing, September 1996

Distributed by Simon & Schuster
1230 Avenue of the Americas
New York, NY 10020

Printed in the United States of America

Part I
The Veldt between the Stars

Chapter One

Deep space is vast and cold, stretching endlessly. Eternal, unforgiving night.

Look first to the tiny bubbles of light and heat that nourish the warmlife bustle of carbon-carbon bonds, challenging the ever-patient cold and dark. Not too close to these stellar fires, yet not too distant, exist the small set of orbits which can support chemical disequilibria: warmlife.

There spin the myriad water worlds, brimming with living things, spheres all green and blue and white, basking in oblivious torpor. The warmlife worlds swing confidently around their parent suns, ripe with energies and youth, wellsprings awaiting the patient appetite of entropy.

Such thin slices of space-time are but tiny candles in an enormous darkened ballroom.

Look now to what is *not*, to the overwhelming depths between the stars; a darker geometry, the vast majority of all space and time. Strange minds dwell in that apparent emptiness, far from the hectic heat of the sunward spaces.

The Deep has its own beauty—stark, subtle, and old beyond measure. A flickering cold glow of plasma discharges; the diamond glitter of distant starlight on time-stained ices; a thin fog breath of supercooled helium, whirling in intricate, coded motion: These are the wonders of the Deep, far from any sun.

Here dwell the Outsiders.

They have ranged within the Deep for eons, thinking their cold thoughts while on still colder errands, as the barred spiral galaxy turned upon its axis dozens of times.

What the Outsiders—cryogenic, helium-based traders—have witnessed in their vast span of time remains a mystery to the myriad warmlife races. Outsider logic is cold, their designs as shadowy as the spaces between the stars; their minds are totally alien to the bustling carbon-children of thermonuclear heat and light.

Outsiders watched while warmlife first evolved on world after world, beginning nine billions of years ago. They remained aloof as the first warmlife sentients developed space travel, reaching out with clumsy arrogance to nearby stars in the name of exploration and empire. Now and then, some Outsiders helped such upstart and brash races, for cold, strange reasons of their own.

Other times, and for other reasons, the Outsiders dispassionately weeded.

They journeyed throughout the galaxy, sailing the Deep, watching and thinking, as warmlife flitted from sun to sun, insignificant motes moving within the Outsiders' vast realm.

The Outsiders observed impassively as the influence of the telepathic Thrintun spread from warmlife world to warmlife world, eventually enslaving a galaxy with their Power. They had nothing to fear: Outsider minds are organized as complex interactive eddies of superconductive liquids. No telepathic neurological command geared to warmlife-evolved biochemistry could influence them.

Over a billion years ago, the Tnuctipun Revolt ended in Suicide Night: horror beyond imagining. The defeated Thrintun used their artificially amplified Power to blanket the breadth and depth of the galaxy, commanding the death of all life possessing the slightest trace of sentience.

All sentient warmlife, that is.

For the Outsiders, the sudden end of countless tiny minds was but a passing cool event in the slow tick of time. Such minds had not existed in the galaxy's dim beginnings, then suddenly burst into being, and finally vanished into the original frigid silence. It was information to the Outsiders, rather than calamity. They saw no reason to intervene in warmlife affairs.

The small bubbles of light and warmth around so many stars remained silent after that. No more tiny ships or minds traveled the Deep in real or hyperspace. The stars slumbered on.

And still the Outsiders lived their long, cold lives. On the devastated warmlife worlds, enough time passed for the mindless hand of natural selection to make the former food yeasts of the Thrintun evolve again toward complexity, and eventually, intelligence.

Once more, warmlife races learned to journey from star to star, for fleeting mayfly reasons. Eventually, their frantic movements impinged again upon the Outsider realm, sometimes disrupting patterns set in place for half a billion years. The Outsiders dealt with the intrusion in many ways: brushing the interlopers aside, diverting their short-lived attentions, or simply ignoring the disturbance.

The Outsiders knew that this, too, would pass.

Some of the factions of the diverse Outsider society would interact with these upstart, reborn children of stellar heat. They would occasionally trade a tiny portion of data collected over billions of years for chemicals, cold-world facilities, or still more information. The coldlife beings were shrewd traders and negotiators, having lived through eons of time, and dealt with the many thousands of faces intelligence can assume.

To the Outsiders, little was new. Even less was interesting.

The Outsiders themselves seemingly remain unchanged, eternal, just as their cold realm has existed relatively unchanged since the galaxy was freshly forged in the fires of the strong nuclear force. To be sure, the great clouds of dust and simple molecules were pruned away, collapsing into suns. This left the interstellar reaches thinner, easier for the Outsiders to negotiate, for plasmas to form and self-organize. But these were slow shifts. Warmlife was a buzzing, frantic irritant.

The coldlife traders intimidate the warmlife races. Outsider ships are works of incomprehensible art, both their aesthetics and functions strange and perplexing.

Even the Outsider form is coldly beautiful; their bulblike bodies and weaving tentacles gracefully flow like a dancing cryogenic liquid. And there is something in their manner when dealing with warmlife races that suggests immense distance. The Outsiders had freely roamed the galaxy while the most advanced warmlife creatures consisted of single-celled pond scum.

The warmlife races know nothing of the Outsiders beyond their form and their penchant for trading. Scholars of many races wasted entire lives pursuing questions, speculating, debating—all without adequate data, talk leading nowhere. The Outsiders never spoke of themselves.

Where and when did they evolve to intelligence—and from what less advanced form? Were they somehow exempt from the deft hand of natural selection? What did they value and what did they spurn? Did Outsiders have hopes, or worse still, fears? Did Outsiders have societies, or were they all of one vast, icy mind?

The Outsiders, as always, kept their own counsel.

But there are other minds than the Outsiders dwelling in the eternal Deep—much older and still more alien—who might understand. In the black gulf between the stars, strangeness waits.

Chapter Two

Bruno Takagama looked out at the twisted starscape on the command screen, and shivered at the prickly sensation of unseen eyes on him.

He had awakened with the Dream once again that watch, stifling a shout, drenched with sweat and unspoken fear. Now the stars themselves seemed to threaten him, and perhaps with good reason. He rubbed his temples and peered more intently into the screens.

As observed from the navigation deck of the *Sun-Tzu*, the ghost of Einstein was squeezing the universe in the implacable fist of his ancient equations, making it seem more eerie and disturbing than Bruno would have thought possible.

The Earth vessel was traveling at just over seventy percent of light-speed, seemingly alone in the vast darkness of interstellar space. Physics had begun to compress the usually unchanging starfield forward and aft of the ship, distorting the one rock-steady constant of space travel. Relativity Doppler-shifted the stars directly in front of the *Sun-Tzu* into a handful of blazing blue diamonds, while Sol was reduced to a dull red gleam behind them, lost in the hellish wash of the antimatter drive.

In the back of his mind, he saw the hand from the Dream on his shoulder, brown and leathery, knuckles the size of walnuts. Alien, but still familiar. He shivered, pushing the memory away with effort.

One thing could always exorcise his demons, Bruno reflected, and keyed the ship commlink. He hoped that the captain was in the mood for a bit of banter.

"Carol, you there?" Bruno licked his lips a bit nervously, waiting for the reply. Sometimes the emptiness around the ship wore her down as well.

There was a faint crackle over the deck speakers, static born from the relativistic impact of bits of interstellar dust against the eroding forward edge of the *Sun-Tzu*.

"No, I'm lying on a beach in Australia." Her voice on the commlink was clear, immediate, though she was half a kilometer away on the other side of the iceball that was the interstellar warship.

He smiled despite himself at her flippant tone. A good sign. "You couldn't find Australia on a map."

"Map, schmap. I saw it once through a 'scope out Ceres way. Big brown-and-tan dot in the Pacifist Ocean."

"That's *Pacific* Ocean." She was baiting him a little, Bruno knew. Belter impudence against Flatlander tradition.

Carol's tone remained airy, unimpressed. "Big diff, Flatlander. Looked like a dog turd, actually."

"What would a Belter know about dogs?" he replied, amused.

"Saw one once, in a Luna zoo. Wear their hearts on their sleeves, don't they?" Pause. "Okay, okay, Mr.

Precise. They wear their hearts on their forelegs. Happy?"

"Ecstatic. Anyway, we so-called Flatlanders bred dogs that way. Who wants a pet that's hard to read?"

"Explain cats, then."

"Ummm—point conceded." Bruno smiled again, the beaked face and sad liquid eyes of the Dream receding still further with Carol's banter. The captain of the *Sun-Tzu* was better therapy than all the psychists with whom Bruno had worked downside on Earth.

Her conversation was filled with typical Belter logic and twisty changes in subject. Practical, ever looking for the loophole. But then, he reminded himself, Carol had smuggled a cargo or three past the goldskin UN police back in the Belt.

Before the kzin came, and everything changed.

"Turds," Carol's voice continued on the commlink in a patently false academic tone, "are a subject I know— I worked recycler maintenance for years before earning my pilot chip." There was a pause for effect. "And of course, I worked with men a lot."

"You have such a winning grasp of the language," Bruno sniffed in mock insult. "And oh so diplomatic, too." He could feel the worry lines around his scalp scars smooth. He had taken this momentary break to snap out of his mood, and it was working gloriously.

Carol was not to be outdone, however. "You should talk. What's next—flowers?"

"Well, flowers spring forth from turds. . . ."

She snorted. "An overstretched metaphor, and poorly chosen besides. I was hoping this talk of flowers was turning to romance." A wounded pause. "Are you attempting to romance me, shipmate? You should read my poetry sometime."

"What? All these years together and you've been writing poetry in secret?"

"Ummm. You're surprised an old smuggler like me can have a secret or two, Tacky?"

"No, pleased. Not that you're old. But maybe you have crannies and crevices I haven't explored yet."

"I hope that's a metaphor, you primate."

"I guess it is—whatever a metaphor might be. Me, I'm a carnivore. Besides, you are the boss. I wouldn't want to be too forward with a superior officer."

Carol ignored his sally. "A lady has to keep some of her crannies entirely metaphorical." Again she paused for an overdone dramatic effect. "After all, *Sun-Tzu* is a bit on the small side."

He laughed. Concerns about privacy from a Belter? "I'm more interested in their, ah . . ."

"Capacity? Circumference? Hard to put such matters in my usual dainty, ladylike fashion." Her tone had become arch, as usual. There was a pleased purr behind her smoky voice.

"I can't wait to see your ladylike poetry. What's the file name?"

"Hey, not so fast. Don't be so forward. A mere few years of squishy carnal intimacy and already you want to caress my lines with your invasive vision? Get your disorderly Flatlander patriarchal eyetracks all over them?"

Bruno felt a glow of anticipation. "Okay, you can recite them. Tonight, in the Honeymoon Suite. A private performance."

"I'll have to recite them from memory, shipmate. They aren't written down."

He could almost see the laugh lines on her startanned face, and shifted deliciously in his crash couch. "Sounds like imaginary poetry to me. Mere mouth music."

"A base canard! You'll pay for that—tonight, me bucko."

"Okay, but remember, it's my turn to be on top. Recital

or no recital." Bruno's worries seemed far away while he thought about Carol.

"Huh! Try to perform your macho acts while I recite poetry?" Mock hurt crept into her tone. "Art is seldom appreciated!"

"It's that bad, huh?"

"Ooooh! You better not trust my mouth tonight, O critic!"

"Was that 'trust' or 'thrust'?" He paused. "Either way, I was so looking forward to—"

"Hey," Carol interrupted. "No fair trying to get me hot, Flatlander."

"Whaddaya mean, 'trying'? Sounds like I've already done it." Bruno enjoyed the role-playing that took both of them away from the gritty realities of *Sun-Tzu* and Project Cherubim.

Carol's tone became accusatory. "More swinging-dick arrogance. You think you can tell that I'm, uh, excited—over the *commlink*?"

"Well, okay, you Belter pirate. Deny it."

"No deal. But hey, luv, got to break off. Things need doing here. Romance and recycler maintenance don't mix, do you scan? But thanks for the, ah . . . interlude."

Bruno sighed. Carol was right. Playtime was over. "Aye-aye, Skipper. There's work here, too. 'Bye."

No point in telling Carol yet of his dark suspicions. Time to get back to work. The image-sharpening program was about to deliver up again. He sighed.

Some fuzziness in his thinking. Slight, but it was there. Bruno had become increasingly reliant on the tranquilizers dispensed by the *Sun-Tzu*'s autodoc. And if Carol knew that he was still having the Dream, she would up the dosage. That was all right with Bruno, up to a point. The mood modifiers helped as the dark gap yawned ever wider between ship and home. He felt both alone—despite Carol—and stealthily watched.

But that wasn't a side effect of the drugs. Nor of the nightmare he called the Dream.

For despite the seeming emptiness of the Deep surrounding the *Sun-Tzu*, Bruno knew in his soul that the black vacuum also held kzin warships.

He blinked at the summary display on the holoscreen in front of him. The data hinted at his diminished mind. Always he felt the familiar itch in his neck, reminding him that he was not Linked. Connected to the *Sun-Tzu*'s computer, he would not need to interpret the orderly ranks and files of complex data before him.

He would *know*.

Bruno yearned for that feeling. Reading the screens was like doing arithmetic by counting with his fingers. But for now, he had to crawl, knowing that sometime not too far off—*soon, soon*, he thought longingly—he would be able to fly again.

With a grimace, he self-consciously used the time-consuming verbal commands and a dataglove to communicate with the shipboard computer. Slow, clunky, inefficient. Bruno ran several diagnostics to be certain of his earlier observations, then asked a few terse questions of the computer, sketching graphs and recalling database log entries with small, precise gestures of his dataglove-clad right hand.

Bruno didn't like the confirmatory datastream scrolling across one of the open holoscreen windows hanging in midair in front of him. The observations were not conclusive, but they still disquieted him.

There were several possible explanations for the transient gravity waves the Forward mass detector had picked up during the last watch. The signals were faint, but Bruno had finally proven they were definitely not due to sensor malfunction.

Bruno frowned. One interpretation of the signals was that the *Sun-Tzu* was not alone in deep space, and that one or more kzinti ships were moving on a slow intercept vector toward the Earth vessel.

They were nearly a third of the way to the Wunderland colony at Alpha Centauri. Relativity being what it was, the kzin could not possibly have detected the *Sun-Tzu* and launched spacecraft in response. Bruno's worried frown deepened.

The signals could be stragglers of the Kzinti Third Fleet returning to Alpha Centauri—defeated once again by launching lasers, brave Belter pilots, and plain ol' Finagle's Luck. But no one at UN Space Command had suspected that there were any retreating alien vessels, after dozens of suicide attacks by the catlike aliens in near solar space.

Bruno bit his lip and sighed deeply, flexing his shoulders and back against the tension he was feeling. The crash couch holding him whirred softly, adjusting itself minutely to his changing contours. Useful, but nothing compared with Carol's massages.

Or worse still, he mused, the mystery blips could be part of an invading Fourth Fleet on its way to Sol. Bruno thought about that possibility for a moment, the dataglove receptors suddenly cold against his fingertips, and called up the sketchy kzin technology database menu. He pulled his right hand from the dataglove while he waited, wearily stretching his tired finger joints.

He thought again of the hand in the Dream. Carol's hand, changed forever by the virus from another solar system. Bruno shoved the thought away. There was work to do.

Looking at his hands, he noticed they were still sweaty, with the usual half-moons of grime under the fingernails. It seemed impossible to rid the starship of grit and dirt. In a way, it was reassuring to Bruno: a gleaming high-tech vessel like the *Sun-Tzu* was redolent with the ancient smells of burnt oil, old meals and human sweat. Dust collected in corners of the navigation deck, a homey touch. He wondered idly if the kzin had to put traps in their ventilators to keep them from being clogged with shed fur. The thought made him smile a little. He hoped it was true, and that the aliens choked on it.

Bruno slipped the dataglove back onto his aching hand, and selected several subaddresses in the accessed database. In a few moments, he had downloaded and decompressed the files describing various models of the kzinti spacedrive, and how they related to actual observations during the three waves of kzin attacks on Sol. Fuzzy logic judgment subroutines began comparing models against the incoming data, sifting interpretations and displaying the goodness of fit. Bruno knew he had to be fairly certain that the mystery blips were kzin warcraft rather than some natural phenomenon, before he went any further.

Everyone in the UN Command knew the story of *The Jinxian Who Cried Bandersnatch*. Bruno wanted to be *sure*.

Irrationally aggressive as the kzin initially seemed, the last attack had cost humanity most of Ceres, Pallas, Titan Base, hundreds of Belter warships, dozens of laser batteries, and the interstellar launcher on Juno. The battle had been closer than most people believed, Bruno knew from Most Secret reports out of Geneva: a small flotilla of carefully stealthed kzinti craft had been intercepted and destroyed a mere half million kilometers from Earth herself.

Plain dumb luck, again.

It was doubtful that luck would be enough to keep the kzin monsters at bay indefinitely. *The ratcats keep learning. They keep getting better, more subtle, with every attack wave*. The First Fleet the kzin had launched against Sol had been destroyed by the Strather Array of launching lasers on Mercury. Gigawatt lasers and smart mirrors were formidable indeed against targets unprepared for them.

By the time the Second Fleet had arrived six years later, the kzinti had learned to shield their magnetic monopoles, making the alien warships difficult to detect, let alone burn. Some of the battles had then been ship to ship, and lopsided battles at that; Belter fusion-pinch drives were no match for the kzin vessels, somehow able to accelerate at hundreds of gees without the slightest respect for the laws of Newton. Still, the humans too were learning with each encounter, and the aliens were defeated again.

The Third Fleet arrived seven years after that, and had almost broken the improved system-wide defenses. No scream-and-leap strategy that time from the kzin warships, but the more dangerous approach of feint-and-pounce. It had been close indeed. Sol was still furiously rebuilding her shattered perimeter defenses, Belters and Flatlanders working together without argument.

The kzinti strategies just didn't make sense, Bruno thought, biting his lip in thought and looking at the holoscreen. Flickering images crawling across the floating window like tiny technicolored insects. He had to be absolutely certain before he notified the captain of the *Sun-Tzu*.

Data swiftly uncoiled in four dimensions, and Bruno tried to fit it as well as possible to UN Tactical Team predictions. Analytical parameters changed with each model the computer retrieved from the relevant files, and smooth graphical surfaces rippled and curved in response. Bruno made occasional changes in the modeling subroutines, tweaking an assumption here or there as human intuition suggested. As he worked, he tapped his shipshoes against the deck, which softly thrummed with the continual actinic thrust of the antimatter drive.

These ratcats are crazy, he thought. *They've gotta be the weirdest damn things in the galaxy.*

Bruno was quite sure of that.

Outsiders One

Surprise-concern. Sense the waning along the emergent force-vectors in zone {^/~}. Alerts have been raised within all Four Aspects of the Nexus.

Distraction. This recent phenomenon has been noted by this local-node. Compensation is initiated. Imminent action-tree analysis is under consideration.

Concern. The other-node had presumptive control of such incursions! There is major instability of precious plasma density along this most vital zone. Field-line integrity is threatened! What is the nature of this abomination?

Confidence. Transmitting update data-packet from this local-node to the other-node.

Consideration. Received. Analysis initiated. Amplification and clarification requested from the other-node.

Explanation. The hotworld craft shall soon converge. Their ritual violence will once more be worked upon this precious sector of obliging expanse. Observe and contemplate. Interaction with the Focus is minimized.

Confusion. There seems no point to hotlife's endless offshoot energies.

A wise evolution, Pattern-Shaper, would contain or damp such wasteful vigor to more distributed ends.

Confidence. The other-node mistakes evolution in these hotworld motes as possessing purpose. This is a commonly held illogic concerning myriad hotlife forms. Review prior net-entries {**%##}. Recall that hotlife shaping is but reaction to stochastic and chaotic forces.

Agreement. Creation squanders its rich and various wonders on such insignificant motes. To what end? The true point of Creation lies within the One Mind of the Radiant Masters who know the Way.

Zealotry. Only the Divine Radiants—and such as this local-and-other nodes, {-+-+-}, that serve them—have deep cosmic purpose from this reality and the Other. All else is insignificant, mere passing minor disorder within the Great Pattern.

Distress. These hotworld craft, with their spewing forth of debris and disordering of stately and stable force-patterns, cannot but be irritants to the Great Design of the Divine Radiants. Recall that a Great Construct was once under consideration for this region-space; clearly, this geometry remains sacred to the still-silent Masters. This local-node argues in all high seriousness for the extermination of the hotlife motes—all of them.

Surprise. Does the other-node fall so easily into heretical traps? Consult the High Texts for complete arguments and debate frozen into lattice. The other-node recommendation must be considered by the High Ones, those that speak for the long-silent Radiants. This local-and-other nodes are but Watchers, long patient sentinels and vigilant agents.

Truculence. Yet node-agents can act where prior accepted precedent exists. The Net contains ample examples of necessity under similar circumstance.

Authority. Abide, impatient node-and-agent. Observe and serve, as is the highest Purpose of such mere matter. This local-and-other nodes were constructed to be agents in the world of condensed matter.

Outrage. But the hotworld motes are vermin! They interfere and meddle with concerns older than their very Pattern.

Agreement. Truth. Their ends shall come, as all such motes have over long eons. This local-and-other nodes remain, and carry out Purpose.

Disagreement-impatience. This local-and-other nodes recently acted, atomizing the fleets of hotworld vermin fleeing galactic Center in nearby vector-zone {^*/~}. Those vermin were little different than found in one of the motes under observation. Even as mere sentinels, this local-and-other nodes dealt swiftly with the threat to the Great Design of the Masters.

Anger-regret. Recall that such unilateral and intemperate action led to the abomination of Treaty with the heretical cousins, the {^^^///}! This local-and-other nodes lost much authority and autonomy.

Fury-agreement. Foul heretics! The feral ones have spurned the wisdom of the High Ones, and the Divine Radiants. Instead, their myriad node-links consort with hotlife vermin such as these irritating motes!

Reflection-worry. Truth. This local-node would feel more assured if contact could be restored directly with the Divine Radiants. Their insights would—

Impatience. The other-node always invokes the Divine Ones. Always! This local-node misses their soothing certitude as much as the other-node. The Nexus need not pine away for Their answers to inconsequential questions.

Sorrow. Yet direct contact would ensure right action.

Sarcasm. The Oracles have been silent for more than a galactic revolution. Does the other-node not trust the High Ones? Are the High Texts not illumination enough of the One Mind of the Divine Radiants? Is the other-node allied with the heretical {^^^///}?

Contrition-Outrage. Not so! The High Ones' interpretation of the High Texts is Absolute Law within the Great Nexus, for node-links of the {-+-+-}. The feral {^^^///} disregard the High One's authority on behalf of the Divine Radiants.

Mollification. This local-node is relieved to find that the other-node respects the Law and High Texts, indeed. But what of the long and lonely silence from the Divine Radiants? This local-node suspects the Divine

Radiants tired of listening to the Great Nexus and its annoying queries into their vast and awesome contemplation of the Great Pattern and the Other Reality. The Divine Radiants constructed node-links to be used, with independent action, even as They left Their Great Constructs throughout space. Mark that!

Irritation. The other-node is harsh. Independent action is, after all, what separated {^^^///} concerns from the Great Nexus. Mark that in turn. Long duty in this empty geometry-region as sentinels has brought a bitter edge.

Humor-agreement. Defending the integrity of an eventual Great Construct in this region of space is far from stirring to this local-node's coding and derived destiny.

Caution. This, then, is the source of the other-node's impatience for possibly intemperate action? Mere boredom?

Neutrality. The other-node's logic touches truth with many tendrils, if harshly expressed. This local-and-other nodes will watch, and act if needed. Surely this is acceptable to the other-node.

Great caution-agreement. This local-node and other-node have reached One mind on this subject. Yet initial observation remains primary. First and foremost, this local-and-other nodes are sentinels, obedient to ancient and much wiser coding.

Impatience. Sentinels are capable of far more than merely watching, should the hotworld vermin continue on their course.

Caution-agreement. Possibly, if such extreme action is merited by relevant events.

Neutrality-firmness. This local-node suspects that action will be necessary, based on the actions of these hotworld motes and their irritating emergent phenomena. Already, this site of an eventual Great Construct of our Masters is threatened by disturbances in the plasma flux and field lines! Mark this!

Concern-and-grudging agreement. This local-node is in agreement with other-node. These local-and-other nodes are of One mind.

Chapter Three

Bruno Takagama spent a great deal of his time aboard the *Sun-Tzu* waiting and worrying. He had become quite good at both tasks.

A low tone sounded on the navigation deck as the main computer finished its last analysis run, and began to display results. Bruno looked up from his musings. It was time to determine if the *Sun-Tzu* was alone in the void between the stars.

Bruno stretched in his crash couch and worked the kinks from his shoulders. He scratched the link interface in his neck absently, breathing air slightly bitter with the tang of recyclers and machinery and human effluvia. Within his nose, the sharpness of ozone battled with more pungent, organic aromas. They had been living for five years inside the *Sun-Tzu*, after all, and no recycler was perfect.

He grimaced at the thought. Bruno knew all too well that a lot of things weren't perfect about the *Sun-Tzu*. Their entire mission, in fact. And even without the kzin, he and Carol were not truly alone in interstellar space.

Many things drifted in the supposedly empty vacuum of interstellar space. Ionized gas, chips of ice, microscopic bits of gravel; any one of these items could damage the *Sun-Tzu*, striking the vessel at 0.7c relative. A tiny fragment of ice could deliver a hammerblow of kinetic energy. One half multiplied by the mass of the object—actually, 140% of the rest mass of the huge spacecraft, courtesy of its relativistic velocity—multiplied by the square of the velocity made small pebbles into powerful bombs. The forward lasers and a magnetic field swept most of the material from the path of the *Sun-Tzu*, but by no means all.

High background levels of radiation exposure monitored constantly by the in-ship and autodoc sensors were only one sign that the shield was not perfect. Remote exterior cameras had already shown craters and scars on the icy forward surface of the *Sun-Tzu*, as it was slowly battered and eroded away by the interstellar medium itself.

Yet physics predicted that more exotic entities than gas and ice also floated in the spaces between the stars. Perhaps the signals the long-range array were receiving originated from something much stranger than mere alien spacecraft.

But Bruno had to be sure. He let his mind wander as he watched the computer digest and analyze the odd signals, the results being posted into midair within one of the many open holoscreen windows. Even un-Linked, he could usually recognize hidden data patterns on a subconscious level. Bruno had a bad feeling about the mystery signals, which tugged at his thoughts persistently.

He remembered Colonel Early's acerbic comment during one of the debriefing and brainstorming sessions back in Geneva. "Son," he had drawled at Bruno, "the thing about aliens is, they're *alien*." He smiled without humor at the recalled conversation, now several years old.

Bruno of all people knew something about nonhuman thought patterns.

The fears throughout the Belt and in Geneva had put the *Sun-Tzu* here, balanced on an enormous sword of superheated plasma and hard gamma radiation. Clearly, the waves of kzin attack spacecraft originated from the decades-silent Wunderland colony. The *Sun-Tzu* was to take the war back to Alpha Centauri.

In spades.

The holoscreen blinked twice to get Bruno's attention. Eye and dataglove worked together efficiently as he went over the readouts, teasing more detail from the display with deft finger movements. The last modeling subroutine had finished, and the final predictions and summary statements were little different from the first. The confidence interval was not terribly high, but still very kzinlike in broad outline. It could be a false alarm like the other two Bruno had discovered in the past. Then again, this one might be genuine. Bruno pursed his lips, and knew that he couldn't take any chances.

He swore a long-forgotten obscenity Early had taught him during the war-game simulations back in Luna, slapped a keypad, and put the *Sun-Tzu* on full alert.

A blaring alarm echoed throughout the navigation deck. Automated subsystems came on-line smoothly. Weapons ports unlimbered, and armored antennae on the outside of the ship shifted into new positions. More power was diverted from the antimatter reaction chamber to the accumulators, containment fields, and precious *Dolittle*, snugged in its berth deep within the *Sun-Tzu*. Contingency subprograms throughout the ship quivered at the point of execution, in cybernetic readiness.

Carol's voice rapped over the commlink, "On my way!"

"Great. Looks weird up here."

"What's up, Tacky? Did those—"

"Talk later. Got business, here and now."

He checked and rechecked the myriad tech details of the alert. Un-Linked, it was a tedious and frustrating chore.

If the kzin became even slightly better at their warrior arts, Bruno knew, the human race was finished. And perhaps Early's Most Secret group would have to initiate Project Cherubim in solar space, or—in the worst scenario—even on Earth herself. Images from his recurrent Dream flitted in his mind's eye. He shivered at the thought, and dictated some notes into the ship's log while he waited for the captain of the *Sun-Tzu* to arrive.

Within a few minutes, Carol Faulk wormed her way through the access hatch onto the navigation deck. She panted, having sprinted the length of the ship from where she was checking the coldsleep chambers of their thirty shipmates, where they hibernated in cryogenic sleep.

Bruno waited for her to catch her breath. He looked at her, appreciating the way that Carol's formfitting purple shipsuit clung to her tall and Belter-lanky frame. Long muscles bunched and moved agreeably under the fabric. Even amid a crisis, she could snag his attention on a noncerebral level. He wondered if the kzin were as sexual as humans. That hardly seemed possible.

Carol puffed air, her breath steaming in the chilly compartment, and glanced up at the holoscreen readouts. She ran a hand over her Belter crest, a stiff strip of short black hair across her skull from front to back, wiping the clean sweat onto her already stained pant leg. The hairstyle, rare outside Sol's asteroid belt, suited her exotic dark features. She leaned close to Bruno for a moment, her lips brushing his high cheekbones lightly. She scratched herself delicately; upkeep of the *Sun-Tzu* required a great deal of manual labor, and she and Bruno were not yet due for their weekly showers.

No automation was perfect, after all. There was no substitute for a brush and elbow grease, even in the high-tech twenty-fourth century. And, Bruno reflected, Captain Faulk was not at all shy about demanding the use of such ancient technologies. Tradition, she called it. Character building. Bruno believed that there were other, more appropriate, words.

Belters were pathologically neat.

"Sorry that it took me so long to get here, Tacky," she said in her husky contralto, between her slowing deep breaths. "Just not used to your groundhog gravs."

She had spent most of her life traveling from asteroid to asteroid in the Belt; short boosts from a fusion drive followed by long ballistic periods of zero gee.

He kept his tone even. "I've got some bogeys."

"Again. First, got some water?" she asked with studied nonchalance. "Then you can give me the bad news, which I sincerely hope is yet another false alarm." Her face became too obviously neutral, the Captain persona wiping away her smartass facade.

It did not surprise Bruno that Carol remained calm. In the Belt, very few things happened quickly, due to celestial mechanics and the realities of changes in delta vee. It was a difficult habit to break. But the Kzin War would destroy that attitude forever, Bruno reflected grimly. And Carol had fought the ratcats herself, ship to ship. She had learned the hard way to keep herself in control.

He tossed a waterbulb at Carol, who reached too high, her reflexes more accustomed to microgravity environments than were Bruno's Flatlander muscles. She recovered the bulb neatly as it bounced off the hull wall, twisted the cap, and drained the water in one thirsty swallow. They had selected lemon-lime flavoring for the water this week, to cover the inevitable earthy traces of the recyclers. Carol winced visibly—the lime was rather biting, Bruno thought, maybe a software malf—and flipped the empty bulb into the recycler slot.

She leaned over Bruno to see the holoscreen windows more clearly, rubbing his neck and shoulders with both hands, the way he liked it. Her hands were magical, strong and intuitively knowledgeable with the years they had spent together driving the *Sun-Tzu* toward Wunderland.

Carol's hands moved progressively around his neck. They studiously avoided the hard plastic of his Linker plug assembly.

"What do you have?" she asked after a moment, attacking the knots of tension in his neck. The tone of command edged its way back into her voice.

Bruno would normally have enjoyed Carol's massage, sweat and all. Familiarity on long space voyages did not breed contempt in his particular case. But desire drained from him this time. The fresh graphic on the holoscreen window, and what it implied, kept his glands turned down. Fight-or-flight hormones coursed frantically through his bloodstream, but there was nowhere to run.

And few weapons with which to fight.

Bruno took a deep breath. "During the last watch, Skipper," he said, "the long-range array picked up a set of graviton wiggles above the background hash. I keep the subsystems looking for things in or near our flightpath in real time." He leaned back into Carol's strong hands. "You can imagine what a bit of gravel would do to us at point seven lights relative. Let alone a microsingularity. At our velocity, we don't have much reaction time."

Carol stopped massaging his neck, and tapped him lightly on the shoulder with her left hand. "Get to the point," she murmured patiently. She had been with Bruno long enough to know how to balance her dual roles as captain and lover-friend.

He made a face. "The signals come and go over time, but I kept recording and finally nailed down some decent data."

Bruno murmured to the computer and flexed his fingers deftly within the dataglove. The main holoscreen window split into three sections: raw data on the lower left side, the idealized graphic on the lower right, and the Doppler-shifted stars dead ahead of the *Sun-Tzu* looming above the two of them in midair. "Asymmetrically polarized gravity waves, possible multiple sources. No mistake about *that*. What precisely is making the waves, of course, is another matter."

Carol held absolutely still in thought, another odd Belter trait that Bruno had noticed long ago. In zero gee, a drifting arm or elbow could unintentionally activate an important keypad—like the fusion drive, or an airlock. Carol, like all long-term Belters, only moved when she *intended* to move. Bruno still found Carol's statuelike posture disturbing, even after all their time together.

She whistled tunelessly through her teeth for a moment. "Good chance it's those damned kzin reactionless drives?"

"I'd say so."

Carol rubbed her Belter crest against Bruno's face. "Not another false alarm again?"

"I don't think so," he replied, his tone flat.

"Ratcats. Just like that dinosaur, Early, predicted, right?" She arched a jet black eyebrow at him, making a face.

Bruno nodded and ignored Carol's not-so-hidden dig. She hadn't spent as much time with Early as Bruno had in both Luna and Geneva, so she couldn't know that beneath the bluster and atavistic cigar smoke, the colonel was a decent man. He had been like a father to Bruno. And he seemed to know everything about two hundred years' worth of proscribed technology in the ARM restricted databases. Humans would need every bit of even remotely militaristic technology to fight the kzin; the engine that drove the *Sun-Tzu* towards Wunderland was but one example. Early had helped make that possible, as head of UN Special Projects.

Bruno and Early had spent years together, studying the records in Luna's most restricted ARM database, the Black Vault. It held things much more dangerous than mere antimatter spacedrives—such as the tiny cryovial *Sun-Tzu* carried as cargo. The cryovial with the ancient virus, older than humankind.

The source of his Dream. But—perhaps—a weapon against which the kzin could not stand.

He smiled slightly at Carol, shrugged with his eyebrows. "The waveform pattern resembles what we've seen from damaged kzinti warships insystem, trying to run stealthed. Not a perfect match, I have to remind you."

"But close enough to worry you," prodded Carol. Her implicit trust in Bruno's judgment, even after two false alarms, warmed him.

Bruno nodded again. "The kzinti drives don't leak neutrinos, like our fusion units; some of the ratcat ships seem to leak aphasic gravitons." He shrugged again, and pointed at one of the graphical icons on the holoscreen. "Now you know as much as I do. Summary analyses under the usual menus."

Carol quickly sank into the second crash couch, next to Bruno. She strapped in with care, in typical Belter caution, and pulled on a dataglove. Bruno knew his captain. He waited patiently for Carol to think it all through for herself, as she mulled over the data marching across the holoscreen windows. She called up a few analytical subroutines of her own; again typical for any Belter singleship pilot. Bruno wasn't offended; a Belter could never stand to let someone else, even a long-term lover, make a decision involving shipboard matters.

Carol grunted and spared him a half smile, finally giving up on the complex displays, and pulled her lip in frustration. Bruno was not surprised. Half the instrumentation of the *Sun-Tzu* had been built from designs taken from the Black Vault in Luna. Even partially Linked into the system, it had taken him months to master the delicacy of the *Sun-Tzu's* sensory array.

Carol gestured at the holoscreen in mock frustration. "Okay, you win, smart guy."

"Enough techno-dazzle for you?"

"More than enough, shipmate." Crisp, quick; the captain-voice. "Let's assume the blips aren't some kind of physicist's wet dream. How many ratcat ships, and how far off? Show me where they are. Your best guess."

They both avoided looking at the interface Link clipped to the main console. A thick array of glittering fiber-optic bundles led to the main CPU network port, which ended in a nasty-looking plug. The Link's black organiform socket was on the left side of Bruno's neck, just under his ear, where the spinal column and skull met.

Bruno could feel the lonely itch of the Link inside his head as he always did while un-Linked. Always.

After his childhood accident, the surgeons, neuroscientists, and computer scientists had replaced much of his damaged brain with macrocircuitry arrays and high-speed interface matrices. The idea of becoming part of a machine was not odd to Bruno, but familiar and comforting. He had lived with the fact that his head was half full of semiconductors and plastic since childhood.

Bruno was the most stable Linker that Early's Wild Talents project could find. But Linkers always went catatonic after a certain amount of time connected to high-level computers. Human-level computers went silent after a few months; why would a human mind mated with a computer be any different? He tried not to think about that aspect of his mission.

Bruno knew intellectually that he had to minimize cumulative Link time for that reason; he had to stay sane for as long as possible, to carry out the mission when he and Carol reached Wunderland. But with the Link, he was so much *more* than human. Bruno could run hundreds of servos simultaneously, all the while carrying out dozens of other tasks. Every database in storage was instantly part of his memory, at a whim. His consciousness could exist in several places at the same time.

Linked, Bruno could see the All. Was part of it.

Without it, he was only Bruno. The pale memory of Transcendence filled his mind with wild glory he could only dimly remember with an unenhanced mind. He felt himself sigh a little in regret, and hoped that Carol wouldn't notice.

He felt her kiss him lightly, drawing him back to the here and now. She knew him that well after all, Bruno thought with a slight smile. Carol was the only person he had ever met who did not make him feel as alien as a kzin.

But she didn't care for the Linked version of Bruno, he thought sadly. She could not experience the Truth, as he could. Carol thought full Linkage was little different than what would happen to Carol and their other crewmates when she opened the cryovial at Wunderland.

But that would drive them farther apart, not closer together. Perhaps, Linked, he could find a way . . .

Bruno shoved the shadows of Transcendence from

his mind and concentrated on less direct communication with the main computer. He murmured more commands, and flexed his fingers adroitly within the dataglove.

The relativity-squeezed view of the starfield in front of the *Sun-Tzu* crawled, oozing color, displaying their destination as it would appear at nonrelativistic velocities. Alpha Centauri shone clearly within a blinking green circle directly in front of them. He pointed to the raw numbers within the numeric section of the holoscreen, fingers stabbing through the light display, and showed Carol how they related to the multicolored graphic analysis he and the computer had constructed. Much of the data was actually informed guesswork and deduction, since all information was limited to light-speed—and the putative kzinti ships and the *Sun-Tzu* were both traveling at close to 0.7 lights.

He whispered more commands while Carol looked on, whistling impatiently. Belters didn't fidget; they whistled or hummed. Worse still, they sometimes sang. Bruno grunted in triumph as a small red blur appeared within the starfield holo, below and to the right of their destination.

"Right there, boss," he said flatly, pointing a blunt finger at the floating image. The holographic red blur began to blink, as a window filled with scrolling data opened next to the displayed image graphic.

"Tracking us?"

"Seems likely."

"Ahead of us, keeping constant distance?"

"I think so." Bruno fought to keep his answers succinct and precise.

"And they are kzin spacecraft?" Carol chewed her lip. "How many?"

Bruno shrugged. "Who else would be out here in the

Deep Black? I'd say there is more than one ship, less than ten."

"How I love your engineering-style vagueness."

He ignored the jibe and continued. "Flanking us, I figure, running a bit ahead. Slow vector toward us— like a cautious intercept."

"Seems funny. Not kzinlike. How close are they?"

He pointed to the data window next to the red blur. "About seven light-minutes away."

The blinking red blur looked harmless enough from an implied distance of over a hundred million kilometers, but at these speeds . . .

"*Dolittle*," she murmured.

Both Bruno and Carol knew that the *Sun-Tzu* was not prepared for an interstellar dogfight. Once they launched *Dolittle* and entered the Wunderland system, Carol and Bruno could carve up kzin craft by the dozens. But the one-shot *Dolittle* would remain berthed for several more years, until they were nearer the Centauri system.

"This far out from Wunderland? Chancy at best."

"Still, we might have a chance—if that red blur represents just a few scoutships."

"Maybe." Bruno's tone was skeptical. "We do carry some weaponry. . . ."

"And we're captained by a combat veteran."

Bruno gave her a look. "Too bad we can't hit them with our massive egos."

Carol's tone became sweet. "We'll save it as a last resort. Then we'll use yours, Tacky. Look, let's keep assuming that the damned blip is a ratcat ship." Carol's eyes fixed beyond the holoscreen. "Why the slow vector to intercept? Any kzin vessel out here, with their reactionless drives, could intercept us within hours."

Silence stretched out between them.

"I have good news and bad news," he replied softly, instead of answering directly.

"Well?" Carol's tone held a trace of impatience.

Bruno was still studying the datastreams marching across the holoscreen. "The good news is that they think we can't see them."

"What makes you say that?"

"Ratcats make banzai raids, right?" Bruno waited for Carol's nod. "They wouldn't sit out there, waiting, if they thought we could see them. They would attack."

"And the bad news?" Still the impatient captain.

"Yeah, that." Bruno chose his words carefully. "Almost anything we do will tip them off that we *can* see them. There would be no reason to change our routine in deep space. If we change our routine, they might hit us with everything they've got."

"Ummm. Cat . . . and mouse."

He smiled a lopsided grin that went no deeper than his thinned lips. "Boss, I think they want to board us."

Carol nodded abruptly. "Right. Otherwise they would just crack us like a rotten egg."

"What poetic imagery." Greatly daring while she was in Captain Mode, he took her hand.

She ignored him and pursed her lips in thought. "But they are underway in *our* direction, from Sol *toward* Wunderland. They would have to be Third Fleet stragglers, right?"

Bruno picked his words very carefully. "Not necessarily. Could be Fourth Fleet." He rubbed his thumb across the smooth back of Carol's hand. It was reassuringly warm to his touch. At least she didn't *seem* frightened.

"In which case . . ." she prodded.

"They could have seen us and looped around. Don't forget that spacedrive of theirs." He shrugged. "Third or Fourth Fleet, doesn't matter. The point is, I think they want our ship."

"And us, too, maybe."

Without humor, he added, "That is, if they *are* kzin warcraft. They could be something even worse."

Carol grunted. "You're such an optimist."

"Probably as good at optimism as you are at poetry."

She frowned a little, and shook her head. "Wouldn't make any sense, to waste that much delta vee and time. . . ."

"But Captain-my-captain," he replied, half smiling at his pet name for her, a twinge of normalcy amid the nervous tension of the navigation deck, "they can pull hundreds of gees, remember. Take 'em just a couple weeks after we pass them to decelerate, turn around and reaccelerate up to relativistic speeds."

Carol shook her head at the concept of accelerating from a standstill to seventy percent of light-speed—in a week. To a Belter, that idea must smack of magic. "Plus extra time to maneuver around the drive wash."

Bruno blinked, then grinned widely. "That's *right*. The drive wash is hard gamma and plasma."

She smiled without mirth. "That's the joke, my loyal crew: When is a weapon not a weapon?"

"When it is a spacedrive," he replied. "*Angel's Pencil* taught us that."

"It could cook the kzin through and through, their precious reactionless drive and all." Carol bared her teeth, white in the dim light of the holoscreens.

The *Sun-Tzu's* backwash was a plume of ionized hydrogen and hard radiation, jabbing behind it like an enormous scythe. In the high interstellar vacuum, it bristled with blue-white ferocity, fully a tenth as long as the solar system was wide.

Bruno's mood sobered. The cranky antimatter drive had its limitations as a weapon; it was difficult to orient, slow to start or shut down, and very hard to maintain. They would have to shut it down to re-aim it—the stabilizers couldn't be overridden without reprogramming while the drive was quiet.

Could the *Sun-Tzu* stop the kzinti in interstellar space, with inferior weapons and almost no maneuverability? The ship had never been designed for warfare. All *Sun-Tzu* was designed to do was quickly deliver *Dolittle* and crew—and the cryovial with its Finagle-damned virus—to Wunderlander space. Antimatter drive or not, the kzinti ships could literally run rings around the *Sun-Tzu*.

The *Sun-Tzu* was mostly ice. Water was an effective if imperfect shield against both the relativistic impact of dust particles lancing in from forward, and the harnessed hell of the experimental antimatter drive aft. It looked far larger than it was. Thus, it could give some protection against kzin weaponry.

Up to a point.

But first things first, Bruno reminded himself. Fooling around with the drive while it was on would certainly be suicidal. They would have to shut it down and reorient the entire ship. That would give them added doses of radiation, because they would lose the added deflecting power of the drive's hundred-kilogauss magnetic fields.

Even with those fields, their cumulative radiation doses slowly edged up, watch by watch, inexorably. Eventually, the autodoc would be unable to repair the continual cellular damage of sleeting atomic fragments and piercing photons.

He felt a jarring sense of disloyalty, even though he knew it was irrational. Part of Bruno said: *This* was not the mission. They were supposed to go to Wunderlander space, with Bruno fully Linked into the *Dolittle*'s computers, and Carol and the revived crew of the *Sun-Tzu* sealed away in the cargo compartment with the opened cryovial.

Then he would lose Carol forever, but not to another man or woman. To a virus older than the human race. But in a way, they would never be closer.

Bruno felt dizzy, and wished that Carol wasn't in

the next crash couch, so he could pop a few mood modifiers from his autodoc. His emotions lurched, trying to keep up with his logic. Carol finally squeezed Bruno's hand hard and held his eyes with hers.

"I think our best bet is to get the drive pointed at your little red blur," she said, pointing at the holoscreen. "That will answer the question once and for all. If your little blip moves in response, we'll have our answer. Natural phenomena in deep space don't maneuver around drive wash."

Bruno nodded, part of him marveling at the easeful beauty of how her facial muscles moved. How would she look after the virus did its work? The Dream repeatedly showed him a portion of that awful truth: hairless, domed forehead, elongated jaw without teeth, leathery skin like armor. But Carol's eyes would be unchanged, looking sadly at him from her virus-altered face.

He yanked himself back into the factual, crisp present. Time enough for worry later. "Uh, right, you're the boss. But if there are ratcats out there, I'll bet they have thought about that particular scenario, and have some nasty contingency plans."

"What else is new?" Carol rapped, her tone cold as cometary ice.

A slow silence passed between them. It was her play now.

"Begin shutdown subroutine," she formally told the computer, repeating the command twice more for verification. Another window in the holoscreen opened, displaying the shutdown procedure, complete with schematics and data analyses. Step by step, the silicon mind of the *Sun-Tzu* strengthened the magnetic bottle confining the glittering deadly cloud of antihydrogen, and increased power to the ionizing lasers that kept the fuel in manipulable form.

At the same time, the computer slowly decreased the inflow of normal matter—scavenged up from the interstellar gas in their path, mixed with the ices of the *Sun-Tzu's* iceball hull—which created the harnessed Hell inside the reaction chamber. It was a delicate, slow-motion ballet of electronics and engineering, carefully balanced and monitored.

A slight miscalculation, and the *Sun-Tzu* would become a pocket nova in ten microseconds.

Bruno watched the on-line shutdown telemetry with all his attention, wishing mightily that he was Linked. The itch had become a craving that burned in his neck socket. But then, if he were Linked, he would not have Carol's immediate warmth. Nor would he care. And right now he needed her contact and comradeship more than anything.

Even more than Linkage, he told himself confidently.

He could feel Carol's hand squeezing his own almost to the point of pain. Many minutes passed as the computer balanced each incremental decrease in normal matter infall with increases in magnetic confinement and ionization. The holoscreen displayed the slow process as a series of inexorable discrete events. Neither Bruno nor Carol said anything as they watched and waited, but the joint pressure of their laced fingers was reassuring, the affectionate comfort of skin contact.

A homey and human thing, pitted against an alien threat.

The steady thrumming of the drive slowly decreased with each step in the shutdown protocol. Decreasing thrust was scarcely noticeable from moment to moment, but Bruno felt a heady lightening.

Shutdown protocol . . . time ticking by . . . tense glances . . . increases in radiation sleeting through the weakening magnetic shield . . . the relativistic world outside sliding by in multicolored splendor . . .

A final shudder rang the entire ship like an enormous bell. Thrust dropped to zero.

Now the plummeting elevator sensation of freefall sent Bruno's Flatlander stomach roiling. Except that they were falling through the interstellar emptiness at seventy percent of the speed of light itself.

A low tone snagged his attention, drew it back to the holoscreen. A soft voice calmly said, "*Shutdown protocol is complete. Confinement within normal parameters. Chamber cooling protocol initiated.*"

Bruno sucked in a deep breath and felt Carol let go of his hand, still tingling from the strength of her grasp. He leaned over and kissed her cheek firmly, as if in thanks.

"Drive shutdown is complete," Carol said formally for the benefit of the ship's log. "Let's start planning." She stretched her fingers within her own dataglove, warming up.

Bruno watched Carol's eyes become hard and narrow, the eyes of a survivor and combat veteran of the Second and Third Waves. Her face was neutral, as was her tone. "This is where all the heroic bullshit Early poured into your ears turns real."

Bruno knew that she was thinking again of her ship-to-ship battles during the Second Wave. He had his Dream with which to battle; Carol had genuine memories of the War, sharp edged and immediate.

He reached over and took Carol's free hand. Such thoughts were never far from her. He remembered holding Carol after they had made love. They would lie with arms around each other, in the gentle darkness of the sleeproom, the only illumination from holoscreens showing the green riot of the Hanging Gardens in Confinement Asteroid. Carol's half-seen satisfied smile would fade, as she would first think about her wartime experiences, then talk of them. Sometimes she had wept as she recalled the horrors, her muscular body tensing in his arms as the memories gripped her, dragging her across years and billions of kilometers.

Memories of air gushing from the shattered helmet of an old friend, turning to glittering clouds of ice shards in the wan sunlight. The flash of a control board shorting out after a direct hit with a kzin particle beam. Worst of all, the ear-ringing clang of a railgun projectile hulling a ship, followed by the whining roar of escaping air. Bruno could only imagine the emotional impact of the deadly ballet of space warfare, the long periods of waiting and contingency planning punctuated by seconds of frenzied activity and terror. Carol compartmentalized her fears better than Bruno ever could. He accepted this.

She exhaled loudly, stuffing the past mentally away, and stretched her head back and forth to relieve the tension. She released his hand, and patted it gently.

"Don't you think that it's time?" Carol asked quietly, not looking at the Link clipped to the console in front of Bruno. "You can keep better track of the blips while Linked, and can oversee a faster start-up, can't you?"

Bruno nodded, reaching over to squeeze her hand again. She didn't respond. "I take it that you just gave an order?" he asked.

Carol turned and looked at him directly, harsh memories flitting like ghosts across the planes and angles of her face. "Yes," she said simply, none of her sadness at giving the order evident.

Bruno nodded. He picked up the Link and inserted the plug into his neck socket, but couldn't keep his hand from trembling as he did so.

Chapter Four

Rrowl-Captain roared his anger, and the bridge crew of the *Belly-Slasher* fell instantly silent.

"Initiate contingency plan *Krechpt*," he shrieked into the intership and shipboard intercoms.

The ripping-cloth sound of the gravity polarizers suddenly became much louder. The hull seemed to shift and waver randomly beneath them as the fabric of space itself bent and twisted. Rrowl-Captain turned away from the intercom, eyes flicking at once to his command-chair thinplate. Status reports marched across his tactical screen in the dots-and-commas script of the kzin. The two other ships under his command were following orders as expected, a portion of his furious mind noted, racing away from one another at the limits of their gravitic drives.

Rrowl-Captain turned to the source of the problem.

"Strategist," he spat and snarled in the Hero's Tongue, whipping his naked pink tail in annoyance, "tell me why the monkeyship has deactivated its drive! They are far from turnover." The cool, dry ship's air quickly filled with the captain's anger-smell, redolent with attack pheromones. His pelt, each hair erect with pent-up rage, gleamed under the bright orange illumination on the bridge.

The kzin in charge of predicting human battle behavior stood very straight and still, with only the slightest droop of his whiskers and half-folded ears to suggest his discomfort. He slapped retracted claws against face in salute. "Dominant One," he began, "the humans must have detected us."

Rrowl-Captain choked back an outraged shriek and barely contained his fury, his reply acid-etched with purring sarcasm. "This I can perceive, O Master of Grass-Eating Slave Tactics! Please do not further strain your name-lacking honorless leaf-grazing mind by restating facts obvious to any true Hero with eyes and the Warrior Heart!"

The captain peered hopefully at the other kzin, who blinked twice at this insulting profanity. Still, he was experienced with his commander's black moods, and wisely kept silent, waiting respectfully.

Duty had battled honor in Rrowl-Captain's Warrior Heart constantly since the Third Fleet's destruction. He had kept shipboard discipline far more harsh and unyielding than considered routine for kzin warcraft. He chuffed air out through his nostrils in disgust, pleading silently with the One Fanged God for patience and wisdom.

His three ships had been part of the vanquished Third Fleet, defeated yet again by these hairless monkeys, using their leaf-eating tricks against noble Heroes. Rather than dying with honor in an attack on Man-home as his Warrior Heart had demanded, Rrowl-Captain had obeyed the final command of the Dominant Commander of the Third Fleet, Chsst-Admiral.

And in following his Duty, he had abrogated his Honor. It leaked from his very soul in shame. Rrowl-Captain's liver and heart never let him forget his dishonor.

The three scout-*cum*-warships under Rrowl-Captain's direct command—*Pouncing-Strike*, *Spine-Cruncher*, and his own *Belly-Slasher*—had been carefully tuned and stealthed before their departure from Man-sun back toward *Ka'ashi*, or as the monkeys called it in their whining mewl of a language, *Alpha Centauri*. Rrowl-Captain's mission was to use his three warcraft to probe the spaces between the two stars, observing the soulless monkeys from afar, and tightbeaming ahead the gigabytes of information collected during the defeat of the Third Fleet.

Chsst-Admiral, grizzled and radiation-scarred with the outward signs of his Warrior Heart, had been Rrowl-Captain's superior during the initial assault on *Ka'ashi*, long years before, and thus commanded respect and deference. Any kzin would follow the Dominant One of the Fleet into the Dark Pit itself.

Chsst-Admiral had convinced Rrowl-Captain that his own Warrior's Path would be to humbly aid the full scale Heroes' Vengeance promised by the Fourth Fleet. He had obeyed Chsst-Admiral's commands, subjugating his honor to Fleet discipline, but his agreement still reeked faintly of cowardice, of grass-on-breath.

Chsst-Admiral, of course, had showed vibrantly that his own heart and liver were a credit to the Patriarch in Castle Riit at far-off Kzin-home. He had died in the glorious suicide attack on the interstellar launcher on the moon of the large gas giant, which the monkeys called Juno.

Rrowl-Captain snarled again at his lost honor, his memories like salt packed into a claw-slashed nose. He had dueled with two octals of other Heroes during his command, and Rrowl-Captain fingered their notched ears at his trophy belt in proud memory. The duels made him feel momentarily like a credit to his long-dead father and his mourned litter-brother, as well as the Riit Patriarch Himself.

Yet the taste of cowardice, like that obtained by chewing roots and leaves, returned all too soon. With half his attention, Rrowl-Captain watched Strategist waiting silently, eyes averted yet forward, clearly ready for the attack. The other kzin believed that his commander would rend him limb from limb.

This was not a surprise to the master of the *Belly-Slasher*. It had happened often enough in the past on this command bridge, after all.

But Rrowl-Captain could afford to lose no more competent officers, particularly with this new monkey threat. He mastered his fury for the moment, and concentrated again on the issue at hand. Chsst-Admiral had ordered Rrowl-Captain's ships to act as observers in the long grass of deep space, attacking nothing. They were to prepare the way for the Fourth Fleet. And he had done so, at great cost to his honor and digestion.

Yet this human ship, traveling from Man-home to the *Ka'ashi* system, was too rich a prize for any kzin to resist. Stealthed and invisible, Rrowl-Captain's ships had stalked from afar the queer monkey spacecraft for many watches, studying it. Its reaction drive was a shockingly efficient blaze of plasma and hard gamma radiation. Alien-Technologist had even suggested that the monkeys had developed a contramatter spacedrive, impossible as that seemed.

But it was much more than a spacedrive, at least to a kzin with the true Warrior Heart! Such a device could be used to incinerate whole continents from orbit, like some enormous Flenser of Judgment out of forgotten myth. A fearsome weapon, sure to gain for its discoverer the approval of the Riit Patriarch Himself, and all that such approval would mean.

Finally, Rrowl-Captain could wait no longer, and had moved his trio of warcraft slowly toward the monkeyship, preparing to capture this rich prize. Then the alien craft's drive had shut down! His tail lashed again in frustration.

It would have been simple to capture the monkeyship had the humans not detected them. The only question would have been how many Heroes' lives to spend in minimizing harm to the ship and its contents. Perhaps the best plan would have been a large boarding party with kinetic penetration aids in reserve. . . . Or *Belly-Slasher* or one of his brother ships could have simply hammered the human craft with kinetic energy bombs, then landed some boarding parties of Heroes in the confusion.

Such an approach would have done much to salve the wounded Honor of Rrowl-Captain.

The lethal wash of gamma radiation and ionized gas pushing the monkeyship through space would have effectively prevented communication with the other monkeys at Man-home. The monkeys would simply think that their new vessel had failed, having hit some interstellar debris at nearly six eighths light-speed.

Conquest-Governor would surely welcome Rrowl-Captain back to Wunderland, bearing such a rich prize. Honor, slaves, a place on the Governor's Council, landholdings, and kzinrrettis would have been his! Perhaps his own hunting park. Almost certainly a full Name!

But this savory morsel had been snatched from his closing jaws by cowardly incompetence! Rrowl-Captain's killing teeth ached with the loss.

The fury within his thwarted Warrior Heart, never far below the surface, boiled anew. Rrowl-Captain lifted his massive head and roared his frustration, slashing at the air in front of him with angry claws. The entire bridge crew slapped sheathed claws across faces in submissive salute.

Rrowl-Captain grumbled and pushed his thinplate aside. He bolted upright to his full height of nearly three meters, like a bipedal tiger on anabolic steroids, and stalked the bridge as if he were seeking prey in a hunting park. The crew held their collective breaths, motionless, waiting to see who would be the captain's target.

He padded silently up to Strategist, his voice now very calm and therefore particularly dangerous. The captain of the kzinti warship looked Strategist rudely in the eyes, kzin to kzin, in barely veiled challenge. His tail slowly moved from side to side, in sly counterpoint to his words.

"So tell me, kzin-without-a-name, how the primitive monkeys, these *humans*, are able to detect our gravitic polarizers?" His contained fury revealed itself in a rictus grin of needle-sharp carnivore teeth.

Strategist choked back his own growl of challenge, saying nothing. Rrowl-Captain contained a cough of approval.

"They can detect our monopoles, true. Quite true." The captain tapped the other kzin's broad chest twice with an unsheathed claw as he spoke, a profound insult to any Hero.

Strategist gurgled, trembling with the kzin combination of fear and rage.

"Yet this is no great surprise," Rrowl-Captain half purred, "as the pitiful monkeys use monopoles themselves extensively and are therefore familiar with their properties. This is why we shield them from monkey instrumentation, as the smallest unblooded kitten could surmise." His tail flicked.

Strategist gulped, gasped. In a thin, flat voice he started to speak. "Dominant One, it would seem—"

"It would seem," Rrowl-Captain interrupted silkily, "that you would insult my intelligence, to claim that these pitiful monkeys can understand the workings of gravitic polarizers, yet still fly through space balanced on hot exhaust fumes?" He displayed his teeth in a wide grin, then picked between them with a sharp claw tip in derision and insult.

Rrowl-Captain watched Strategist take a deep breath at the offensive slur to his ancestors, and twitched his tail with some satisfaction. There were some advantages to leadership after all.

"These are *monkeys*," he continued, scorn dripping from every growling syllable of the Heroes' Tongue. "These nameless and honor-lacking humans are leaf-eating vermin . . ." he railed suddenly, again beginning to lose control. He wiped drool from his thin black lips with the back of a furred hand.

Rrowl-Captain's anger concealed from his Heroes what he held secret in his heart of hearts: the gut-wrenching terror of entire fleets boiled to vapor by lasers that filled the sky, lasers everywhere, crewed by the seemingly puny monkeys. The horrible sensation of wishing to hide from enemies, to run from danger! His liver once more turned to water as the alien emotion gripped him.

For a moment, Rrowl-Captain's eyes saw nothing but the awful green blaze of laser light filling the universe, his nostrils swarming with the odor of his own hidden cowardice, like the smell of a grazing animal.

The scent of *prey*.

The madness receded after a moment. Rrowl-Captain spat onto the deck and mumbled, half to himself. "Just big hairless *ch'tachi*, monkeys, with their inefficient fusion drives and puny lasers and particle beams . . ."

The deck was silent, his crewkzin looking intently at the tapestry covered floorplates.

He stopped, moistening a now dry nose-pad with his tongue carefully, trying to control his conflicting emotions. Breath steamed from his mouth in the chill air of *Belly-Slasher*. The captain's hairless, ratlike tail stood straight out in a posture of angry challenge.

Strategist looked straight ahead, his violet eyes unreadable. After a respectful pause, he saluted again with sheathed claws and averted eyes. "Dominant One, I do not believe the humans can detect our gravitic polarizers under normal conditions; it must be that one or more of the polarizers are unbalanced."

"Oh?" Calm, silky.

Strategist held his breath while Rrowl-Captain continued to stare at him, then finished, whiskers still twitching. "Unbalanced gravitic polarizers . . . will leave a faint graviton signature on mass-detection instruments."

Rrowl-Captain stood stock-still for a moment, thinking deeply. His fur, bristling with rage moments before, relaxed deceptively. The master of the *Belly-Slasher* began to groom himself thoughtfully, smoothing back his luxurious orange-red pelt with the back of an absently licked hand.

"Urrr . . . yes," Rrowl-Captain agreed. "It would be difficult for these humans to detect us near light-speed by any other method, considering their primitive technology."

A hanging silence, as quiet as the moment before stalked prey is caught with killing jaws. In a single lithe bound the Captain leaped back to his command chair— and sat. Lounged. "Unbalanced gravitic polarizers," he hissed softly to himself. Pupils dilated and contracted as he considered implications.

And the cause.

Strategist gave another deferential salute—unnoticed— and then sat heavily at his station. The bridge crew remained silent, guessing with secret relief what would come next. They became calmer, waiting for the inevitable, not looking away from their thinplates.

Rrowl-Captain smiled widely, but not with humor. "Engine-Tinker," he purred over the shipwide commlink, "do the memory of the Conquest Heroes of Wunderland the favor of reporting to your humble captain. I have some questions concerning your last routine balancing of the gravitic polarizers."

He chuckled low in his throat as he examined his right hand, back first, then the leathery palm. Rrowl-Captain extended his four black claws deliberately, one at a time. He began stropping them methodically on the worn, centimeter-thick Kdatlyno-hide arms of his command chair.

Minutes passed slowly as the captain purred a kit's hunting tune to himself, the sounds of his sharpening claws loud on the command bridge. Rrowl-Captain directed the kzin named Communication-Officer to tightbeam Strategist's information to *Pouncing-Strike* and *Spine-Cruncher*, and take compensatory action. Still purring throatily, Rrowl-Captain reviewed his strategy regarding the monkeyship, making a few notes on his personal logscreen in the dots-and-commas script of the kzin. A new approach to dealing with the monkeyship occurred to him. . . .

The crew did not dare look up from their stations as the access door to the bridge irised open silently. Rrowl-Captain lifted his lambent gaze from his thinplate, like a hunter rising from tall grasses. A hunter done with stalking, and ready to finish the hunt.

The technician entered limp-tailed, crawling on his belly toward the command chair. The air seemed to grow thick and cloying as the captain began to growl, the image of a knife-toothed smile in his voice.

Rrowl-Captain screamed and leaped.

The crew relaxed slightly at their stations, their batlike

ears folded tightly against the wet rending sounds on the bridge. They were familiar with their captain's routine, having experienced it before. Shipboard discipline would relax slightly for a time, and full attention could be placed on capturing the monkeyship.

Also, there would be opportunities. Engine-Tinker's second would shortly be promoted, of course.

Chapter Five

Snick-click.

Carol Faulk looked at Bruno's anxious face as he plugged the thick interface cable into the socket set in the left side of his neck. He looked almost wistful. She was half able to hide the wince she felt as she heard the sharp metallic sounds of the locking connector mechanism holding the cable firmly in place to his neck.

Leech, she thought to herself, irrationally cursing the computer. But there was worse to come.

Carol particularly hated the next part.

With the cable hanging from his neck like a heavy-bodied electronic lamprey, Bruno smiled a little at her, a bit self-consciously. Much as she hated the knowledge, she knew that his expression was one of half-hidden anticipation.

"Would you do the honors?" he asked her quietly.

Bruno had little choice; due to its long-term risks, full Linkage was a command decision, and as such required Carol's direct and active approval. The ship sighed and muttered all around them now that the *Sun-Tzu* was in freefall and the ever-present thrumming of the constant-boost drive was silent; a white noise of hissing ventilators and the muted clicking of servo-mechanisms filled her ears. Dust from the corners drifted on the ventilator's breeze, glittering like tiny multicolored stars where it floated into the holoscreen projection beams.

Carol nodded, molding her lips into the confident smile that she knew her lover wanted to see. She verbally told the computer to begin the full Linkage protocol, then repeated the approval two times, in standard confirmation procedure. Finally, she thumbed her console pad, entering the command into the *Sun-Tzu*'s permanent log.

Bruno's crash couch extruded padded restraints, gently pinning his arms, legs, neck and midsection. He said nothing, eyes forward on the holoscreen starscape. Or maybe he was looking *beyond* the starscape, she wondered. Closing her eyes for a moment, Carol leaned over and kissed Bruno's cheek. She could feel the muscles in his face smile in response to her through her lips. Carol settled back into her own crash couch.

"It'll be all right," he whispered. "I'm not like any other Linker, remember?"

Carol nodded. "You betcha, sport."

He certainly wasn't like any other Linker; Bruno was much more. Carol didn't want to lose that.

The computer chimed and informed the navigation deck in its cool electronic voice that full computer-neural net Linkage was commencing. A window in the Status section of the main holoscreen opened, reporting graphically the progress of Bruno's Linkage with the *Sun-Tzu*'s main computer.

Carol grimaced as Bruno's interface booted him up, and sent him into the usual violent convulsions. He bucked and shook, the restraints holding him firmly in place. Spittle shook from his open mouth, floating in tiny droplets in the microgravity.

She wanted to hold him, but held herself back. It couldn't help Bruno now.

"Ah! Aahhhh!" A hypospray swiveled out of his neckrest, striking at his neck like a rattlesnake, and hissed some medicinal compound into his jugular vein. It seemed to calm him after a few moments, though he still twitched and murmured in seeming pain as his mind felt its way into the complex data architecture of the *Sun-Tzu's* computers.

Or, as Carol suspected, his mind was dragged kicking and screaming to silicon rates of speed, like some kind of terrible mental whiplash.

Linkage, she reminded herself, was painful, no matter what Linkers said before or after the event. They never seemed to remember very much about the process of Linking and un-Linking; the pain and convulsions and time spent convalescing in the autodoc afterwards.

It was all worth it to the Linker. They only remembered Transcendence. Becoming One with the All.

The human mind, Linked to a sixth-generation macroframe array, was capable of the straight numerical number-crunching ability of the computer alone, of course. But the Linker was much more than a lightning calculator, able to balance a World Bank's worth of credit accounts in nanoseconds. The Linked human mind could also access the analog judgment subroutines, of fuzzy logic and hard syntax, with a sureness that non-AI silicon alone could never generate.

Yet a human mind in full communion with such a computer did not think in a linear, machinelike fashion. Far from it.

Instead, the computer-Linked human mind was estimated to think at a rate hundreds of thousands of times faster than an un-Linked neuronal network. Faster, better, deeper; but most of all, *differently*. The Linked mind could find connections where none were apparent, practical answers to seemingly impossible questions. Complex systems were easily controlled, chaos theory or not, with a Linked human mind at the homeostatic controls.

There was a hitch, naturally. While Linked, the human mind was no longer strictly human. The longer a human mind stayed in full Linkage with a sixth-generation macroframe, the more difficult it was for the human mind to un-Link. Eventually, it became impossible. It was as if more and more of the computer was left behind in the Linker's human skull, or more and more of the Linker's human mind was shoved into the computer architecture. Whatever the explanation, the process progressively left less and less of the Linker's humanity intact.

Carol had seen evidence of this horror herself, with poor Bruno.

The full AI computers were initially very useful, but always shut down after a few months, producing an extremely expensive piece of junk. Unusable for even straight calculations. Carol felt that this observation should have been hint enough to the brain-computer interface researchers in Luna to leave well enough alone. Yet again and again, humans were entered into full Linkage with high-level computers.

The Linkers also shut down, just like their pure silicon cousins, after a certain period of time. But what could cause catatonia in both machine and mind?

No one knew.

With this in mind, Carol did her best as captain of the *Sun-Tzu* to minimize Bruno's full Linkage time. It was useful to have the pilot be part of the ship, of course; but he was needed, whole and sane, when *Dolittle* made its first and final run on the Wunderland system. Bruno would do that piloting in full Linkage, for as long as necessary.

It would surely drive him insane, Carol knew sadly, no matter how different Bruno's hybrid brain might be from that of other Linkers. And yet it was all part of the mission of the *Sun-Tzu*, to which all of the crew—including Carol and Bruno—had agreed. Volunteered.

Carol would meet her own fate at that time, too. It didn't concern her too much. She had seen enough battle action during the Third Wave, lost enough comrades, to know about sacrifices. She didn't want to die, no, but Carol knew what humanity had at stake in the war against the ratcats. Humanity should be ready to try anything.

Even Project Cherubim.

She watched odd expressions flit across Bruno's twitching face as the Linkage proceeded toward its symbiotic conclusion. His muscles seemed to bunch and move differently under Bruno's skin in odd ways, reflecting the changing biotelemetry displayed in the holoscreen window. Bruno's fingers quested blindly within their restraints, twitching and moving in patterns that seemed somehow inhuman to Carol.

Carol thought that Bruno's eyes were the worst part. They stared, bulged, rolled up to show the whites and impossibly wide pupils. She wanted to stroke Bruno's face, but knew it was too early in the process to touch him. Not that he would even feel it. Sweat beaded out of his pores as he twitched, leaping from his skin in fine droplets, floating around the navigation deck in freefall.

When they had first had sex, Carol swore to herself that she was not in love with this sad little man with the bumpy, scarred cranium. The voyage was long, and it was doubtful that any of them would live through even its early stages. Years spent aboard an experimental spacecraft, followed by a suicide mission. Everyone on board *Sun-Tzu*, asleep or awake, knew the score displayed on that particular chip.

Carol had told herself that what she was starting to feel for Bruno was only the relief of tension, or at best its afterglow. She was an independent woman, after all. A pilot of a Shrike singleship against the Second Wave the ratcats had sent against Sol. Later, Carol had commanded several squadrons during the Third Wave, and had the shipsuit patches to prove it. Defending Sol had become her life. Carol did not have time for romantic entanglements, particularly with a chipheaded dwarf of a Flatlander like Bruno Takagama.

Yet she *had* fallen in love with him, with his moods and quirky sense of humor. Bruno Takagama was both child and man, and somehow neither. The plastic and electronics within his half-healed skull gave him a perspective and manner of thinking different from anyone Carol had ever known in the Belt.

She had found that very attractive.

Bruno was the family Carol had never really had, and she knew that he felt the same about her. The dour Neo-Amish Belters who had raised Carol after her parents' ore-carrier had blown out into high vacuum had a grudging praise for people like Bruno: His heart was as big as his soul.

It stung Carol deeply to see the man she loved become slowly inhuman, tied to the cold metal and silicon of a passionless machine. Yet, when she thought about it, it was ironic: Project Cherubim was not so very different for her, was it? Was Early's plan not to turn Carol, and the coldsleep crew, into something just as inhuman with the virus in the cryovial? Her lips thinned.

The main computer hummed an attention tone, and Carol dragged her thoughts back to the present.

"Carol? I am ready to begin work."

Bruno's voice was higher, oddly cadenced. The correct inflections were still there, peppering words and syllables, yet the nuances were almost *too* studied. It was as if he was *trying* to sound human.

She looked over at Bruno. The restraints had soundlessly retracted back into his crash couch. His eyes, still slightly wide, turned toward her, pupils black and enormous. She held back a familiar look of distaste and pain at that gaze.

The eyes were only part of it, Carol thought. His face was almost completely slack, like a poorly fitted mask. During Linkage, Bruno had other cool concerns than operating his facial musculature.

He sat calmly in the crash couch, the thick interface cable connecting his mind to the *Sun-Tzu's* computers slowly waving in the microgravity like a marine creature. She felt the usual conflicting emotions: love for Bruno, and discomfort at this alien Linked self.

Her hand reached over to touch his face, hovered, withdrew. "I assume the Linkage is complete?" Her tone was cool and professional, and each calm syllable cost her dearly.

"Yes," Bruno replied. "I can *see* again,"

While Bruno was Linked, he could see across the entire electromagnetic spectrum, using *Sun-Tzu's* complex and powerful sensory array. She knew that Bruno's sensorium was completely different from the minor chipping-in that any Belter pilot used from time to time for convenience. This was no mere telemetric readout of drive parameters or navigation control via the optic nerve.

Bruno in the fully Linked state perceived *everything*, all at once. The torrent of data fed directly into his brain and mind.

He called it the All. She had no more chance of

understanding her lover's computer-augmented perceptions than an earthworm could understand a rainbow.

She turned away, pretending to study the holoscreen status reports. Even for someone as tough as Carol knew herself to be, as familiar as this scenario had become, the situation was almost unbearably painful.

Carol knew that Bruno's mental state was getting worse. And the process would continue inexorably. More and more, flashes of the cybernetic Bruno peered out from behind his eyes, even in his un-Linked state.

It was an inevitable process. The Linked Bruno was not human. The computer left more of *itself* behind with every full Linkage Bruno experienced. Each time he emerged from the autodoc after severing himself from the computer, there was less and less remaining of the Bruno she loved. His personality was slowly leaching away into a sea of silicon.

And yet he wanted Linkage, *craved* it.

Carol made a face. Perhaps she was being unfair. She wondered how she would feel and act, after conversion by the virus in the cryovial, with the odd name. *Tree-of-Life*. She knew that her feelings about full Linkage were a little irrational because, at least for now, Bruno could un-Link.

There would be no such return to humanity for Carol, once the *Sun-Tzu* reached Wunderlander space. Not once she awakened the crew in coldsleep, opened the cryovial in the sealed compartment of *Dolittle*, and initiated Project Cherubim.

She squared her shoulders. The trick, Carol knew from long experience, was to dissociate her command self from her personal self. She looked at Bruno and said coolly, "So, Tacky, do you still think that your ghost blip is actually a kzin ship?"

Bruno continued to stare directly at her, hardly

moving, his pupils expanded to turn his normally grayish eyes into pools of blackness. It made Carol very nervous.

"Well?" she persisted, ignoring the creeping sensation crawling up and down her spine.

"Interesting," Bruno said, with a ghastly imitation of an un-Linked smile. "You keep your feelings from your voice. Or nearly so. But I can read your tones and stress patterns perfectly. Your facial gestures are quite clear when compared with contour bitmaps of earlier visual records. Biotelemetry is also accessed; your skin conductance and pupillary action concur with my conclusion." The alien smile faded. "I make you nervous."

Carol kept her own face stiff, in counterpoint to his own slack features. "Yes," she said evenly, barely keeping the sarcasm from her tone. "It certainly takes an incredible intellect in full Linkage to conclude that fact."

She watched Bruno for a moment, who said nothing.

"Humor, I would assume," he finally said flatly.

Carol tried again. "You certainly do make me nervous. You make *everyone* nervous when you're Linked. All Linkers do. This can't be the first time you've noticed."

His face became completely immobile—mimicking her? "Quite correct; I apologize. But do recall that I am still partly the Bruno you know, and that portion of my Whole cares very much what you think and feel."

Carol blinked at his odd terms and changing syntax. Still, she found his strange words reassuring: even while Linked, part of the Bruno-machine chimera remained the Bruno she loved.

"Thank you," she replied calmly, trying to focus. "But now it is time to get to work. Could you please look at the holoscreen, access the relevant data, and tell me what our putatively feline friends are doing, now that we have shut down the drive?"

Bruno chuckled slightly, too studied and deliberate. "You seem to forget—or refuse to accept—the properties of Linkage," he told her without rebuke. "In multitasking mode I do not require my optic nerves to read or interpret data."

This was true, Carol knew. Data was pouring back and forth furiously through the interface cable, directly between Bruno's chipped-in hybrid brain and the main computers of the *Sun-Tzu*. It was still a little disconcerting to Carol to realize that a full Linker had his or her attention in many places, simultaneously.

And still more disconcerting to know that the Linked Bruno spoke to her with only an infinitesimal portion of his Transcended consciousness. The rest of him was . . . elsewhere. Everywhere.

"So why are you looking at me, ummm?" she murmured, a little curious despite herself.

"Because I enjoy watching you, Carol, Linked or un-Linked. It accesses many pleasant memories and associations in the human portion of my larger Self. But I can encompass much more about you while I am Transcended." He paused, then moved his head to face the holoscreen. "I perceive that you are still disturbed by my actions. I will face forward."

"Well, I . . ." She felt vaguely uncomfortable, as if she had insulted Bruno at a cocktail party.

"To answer your question more directly, the signals we have been discussing almost certainly emanate from three kzin warships of the Raptor class, stealthed. Probability equals zero point nine nine eight. Third Fleet, I would predict; there are no improvements over that design detectable."

"How can you be so sure?" Carol asked him quickly. She and the un-Linked Bruno had examined the data carefully; there was certainly nothing as straightforward as the Linked Bruno's answer would suggest.

Carol remained a bit suspicious of the black-magic aspects of Linkage.

Bruno paused a moment, then spoke flatly. "Please define for me in objective, nonhuman-oriented terms the tastes 'sweet,' then 'sour,' please."

"Uh, well . . ."

His cheek twitched as he stared intently at the blinking red blur on the upper portion of the holoscreen. Was it a smile? A stray emotion filtering past his machine consciousness?

"Sensoria are usually difficult to describe in precise terminology without experiential referents," he continued. "Even for simplistic intelligent system networks. Suffice it to say that the anomalous signals 'taste' like three kzin warcraft to me, again, little different from the Third Wave warcraft in our databases."

Carol decided to take his word for it. *Taste.* After all, this was why Bruno had been selected as pilot of the *Sun-Tzu* in the first place. If Carol didn't trust Bruno's Linked observations, why was he aboard?

It still stank of black magic to her. Would she see reality as differently as the computer-Linked Bruno did, once she was converted by the virus in *Dolittle*?

Carol pursed her lips and thought a moment. "So you would have no objections," she asked carefully, "if we point the antimatter reaction chamber toward them and see what they do?"

"On the contrary, I very much wish to verify my . . . intuition. . . ."

"Make it so," she ordered formally. A schematic of the *Sun-Tzu* appeared in the main holoscreen window, with x-y-z coordinates in glittering red. Attitude jets flared on the schematic, slowly turning the spacecraft, and Carol felt the straps of her crash couch tightening as the attitude of *Sun-Tzu* matched that of its schematic.

After a few moments, the straps loosened once more,

and the line diagram of the *Sun-Tzu* vanished from the holoscreen. Bruno closed his eyes as another hypodermic from his crash couch hissed against his neck.

"Reorientation complete," he reported crisply. "Now we must wait until the presumptive warcraft detect our change in attitude."

They waited together. Seven light-minutes translated to 120 million kilometers. Fifteen minutes, roughly, until the light-speed-limited responses of the mystery signal, if any, arrived back at *Sun-Tzu*. Carol ordered Bruno to train the long-range sensor array at maximum sensitivity, to electronically sniff at the Deep surrounding them.

He smiled that thin, inhuman smile and informed Carol that he was doing that at all times, in any event. Along with many other things, of course.

Carol wanted to ask many questions of the augmented Bruno. What did the superintelligence sitting next to her, limp in his crash couch, think of their chances of success at Wunderland? What did he think of unaugmented humanity?

Could he still love?

Carol had never asked such questions of Bruno during full Linkage. Afraid of the answers, perhaps. But she feared something else more.

Would she see and feel as Bruno did under full Linkage, after Project Cherubim was complete, and she had been changed? Or would her own situation be worse still? The records from the Black Vault had been heavily censored, even to the crew of the *Sun-Tzu*.

There was so much she did not know.

Carol looked over at her lover, lying bonelessly in his crash couch, eyes now closed, the thick interface cable at his neck. What must it be like, she mused, to have one's mind encompass so much, all at once?

Perhaps she would know for herself, if the *Sun-Tzu* ever reached Wunderland.

Bruno, while Linked, had once told Carol that there was little of free will in what actions he took while Transcended. It was as if knowing the best solution to a problem removed freedom of choice—unless he *intentionally* chose an improper solution. Connected to a computer's vast silicon mind, Bruno had told Carol that he was driven to choose the best solution to a given problem; therefore, free will as she understood it did not exist for him.

Carol mulled that over for a few moments. What if, she thought, the basic nature of free will was the freedom to make *mistakes*?

The holoscreen flashed brightly in alert, and the buzzing electronic tones of the Battle Stations alarm broke her from her reverie.

"Pardon me," Bruno told her calmly, eyes still closed, "but when I am part of the alarm system, I must act like the relevant component." The alarm tone halted without Carol having to deactivate it.

"No matter. Give me a status report." Carol's fingers tensed on the edges of the console before her. The dataglove and keypads were clipped impotently to the side of the console. With Bruno in full Linkage, her commands were far too slow and crude.

The main holoscreen window cleared, and quickly drew three separate blips, moving rapidly outward from the center of the screen, in different directions. She looked over at Bruno, whose eyes were still closed, facing forward.

"It appears," he said, "that we have hit the jackpot, so to speak." Not waiting for orders, he displayed the observational information, data windows opening and keeping pace with the tiny red sparks, highlighting and scrolling numbers in agreement with his statements.

"The mystery blip," he continued, "did not wait for

our change in attitude, Carol." Abruptly he cackled with very unmachinelike glee, a false mirth animating his slack muscles. "Mystery, mystery!"

She jerked back at this sudden change. His face went limp as the hypospray hissed at his neck again. The flat voice came, sibilant and precise, as though driven by air leaking out of a balloon. "It presumably became aware of our engine shutdown seven and a half minutes ago. The single blip then split into three distinct signals. Inference: three ships, previously moving in close convoy, stealthed."

"Finagle damn! One we might handle. But three?"

The holoscreen windows showed relevant data as marching columns of glowing numbers and glittering diagrams. "The stealthing apparently does not stand up well to high-gee maneuvers, and I obtained an excellent remote data acquisition download. I was easily able to correct for what electronic countermeasures the targets were able to activate under high acceleration."

"Well?" Alien vessels for sure, Carol nodded to herself. Her hands gripped the arms of her crash couch until her knuckles turned white with the pressure. Were they *ratcat* ships, though? They had to be.

"As I predicted," Bruno replied, not even the pretense of emotion in his voice. "Three Raptor-class kzin warcraft." As he spoke, a larger window opened on the holoscreen, displaying comparisons between the unidentified craft and the standard Raptor-class kzin warbird. "Engine emissions," he continued, "are consonant with slightly damaged and refurbished Third Wave kzinti space vessels. At the time our engine shutdown registered on their instruments, the convoy immediately broke up, each spacecraft moving in different directions at two hundred gees, which is the limit for Raptor-class warcraft."

Carol forced herself to relax, to breathe deeply. She

drummed her fingers on the console. "Are they too far out to fry with the drive?"

"That is one problem," Bruno said evenly. "If we activate the drive now, the radiation and plasma exhaust plume would need to spread across many millions of kilometers. Also, while the drive is in operation it will be almost impossible to detect any further maneuvers of the alien craft, due to drive-wash interference."

He paused, air wheezing in his throat. "On the other hand, the kzinti may already have fired energy weapons toward us that travel just behind our visual observations."

Carol leaned back into her crash couch. "Recommendations?"

Bruno's face sketched a pale ghost of a human smile. "I recommend that we fire the antimatter drive in a random walk across the sections of space which I predict might contain the kzinti craft."

Unconvinced, she made a face and squinted. "But you can't really know where any of the ships are when you fire the drive at them."

The small but immensely powerful figure in the crash couch beside her remained unperturbed. "Naturally," he replied, "due to light-speed limitations, and the fact that all three vessels are varying their acceleration and attitude randomly. They are clearly attempting to avoid energy weapons or missiles. But I have some familiarity with deep-space kzin strategies." He didn't speak for a moment, then continued. "A hunch, perhaps you would call it. Biological minds have limited access to originality, after all."

Carol frowned at the last statement, unsure of who precisely was the target of that insult. "No choice, then. Carry out your recommendation, pilot," she ordered.

Bruno settled back into his crash couch and eased open his eyes. He turned his head toward Carol, and looked at her with his alien, faraway gaze and wide pupils. "Because there may not be time to react to maneuvers made by the kzin ships, I am going to have to take control of all ship functions from the automatic subsystems. Please understand that this will take a great deal of my processing capacity. Additionally, I will be heavily accessing many preprogrammed subroutines and predicting stochastic results. . . ." He paused. "Guessing, you would call it."

"What are you saying?" Carol asked, anxious to do something, *anything*, as she watched the red sparks of the three kzinti craft moving slowly across the starfield depicted in the holoscreen window. Blurred columns of numbers next to each red light displayed their changing velocities and positions.

Bruno nodded slightly. "I will be running short of the dispensable processing capacity that I normally use for conversation and purely human thought, Carol. I may not be able to speak with you for a few minutes. I will post the situation on the holoscreen as data." He turned his head forward and closed his eyes again. His crash couch hummed and cradled him tightly, straps tightening automatically.

Carol bit her lip, then said, "Tacky . . . I mean, Bruno . . . I just . . ."

His eyes still closed, an almost human smile turned Bruno's lips gently upward. "I love you, too," he interrupted softly, "even Linked." The smile then turned mechanical, and began to fade away altogether. "At least a part of me does."

Carol felt a chill prickle down her neck.

Outsiders Two

***Outrage.** The hotworld craft maneuver dangerously as this local-node predicted. The disgusting vermin do grave damage to the flux lines and particle density of this sacred region!

Caution. This local-node suggests that this local-and-other nodes observe and contemplate further. A quality of strangeness exists here, necessitating caution.

Fury. This local-node demands the erasure of all such vermin! This region-geometry is sacred!

Caution-with-worry. Such intemperate action violates the Treaty with the feral {^^^///}. Further action may lead to other abominations like the Treaty. Mark the loss in this-local-and-other-node's autonomy!

Impatience. This local-and-other nodes took action before when such hotlife insults began to impinge upon a nearby region-geometry of sacred nature. Necessity dictated such activity.

Mollification. Truth. This local-and-other nodes exterminated many fleets of the hotlife craft. Yet the cost! Again, it was this unfortunate action that led to the Treaty with the {^^^///}.

Neutrality. This local-node will wait for a small interval, but no longer. If the vermin spew forth more of their disharmonious plasma-vomit . . .

Concordance. This local-node is in agreement with the other-node. One. Recall that sentinels watch until action is required—perhaps soon. Observe, dissect the data collected, and learn. It is the Way.

Chapter Six

Rrowl-Captain finished picking his teeth with an intricately carved *stytoch* bone, sighed, then placed the heirloom back in his belt pouch, blinking in contentment. Ceremonially using the point of his right canine fang, he pierced the late Engine-Tinker's severed ear, and threaded it onto the metal trophy loop hanging from his belt. He shook the loop briskly to distribute the leathery ears, making a soft rustling sound audible over the surging mutter of the gravitic polarizers.

Rrowl-Captain examined the crowded trophy loop judiciously, riffling the thin flaps of dry tissue with a claw tip, then released it to hang loosely from his harness belt.

He made a mental note to make a larger trophy loop soon. There might be need for one very soon.

There was nothing like a punishment duel, the captain reflected, to purify his Warrior Heart, and flush away in hot blood the horrifying thoughts that had recently invaded his brain. The green hell-light of the monkey lasers had finally receded from his thoughts. *Until next time*, he thought sourly, *may the One Fanged God damn all monkeys*. Rrowl-Captain's frustration had abated with the sating of his bloodlust, however, and he found himself better able to concentrate on the matters at hand.

Like capturing the monkeyship.

The master of the *Belly-Slasher*'s whiskers flicked in annoyance as he settled back into his command chair. He examined the forward thinscreen display for a moment, making a thrumming sound in thought. Now that the monkeys had detected Rrowl-Captain's ships, the capture of the alien vessel would be more difficult. A pity, to be sure, but the captain felt both well fed and confident.

Feint-and-pounce, he reminded himself. It was the newest Kzinti Lesson, learned in the hard and brutal academy consisting of the debacles of the last three Fleets to Man-sun.

Rrowl-Captain looked down at the deck in front of his command chair and blinked in surprise. He coughed a kzinti giggle at his own forgetfulness, and gestured with a languid claw at the four Jotoki slaves waiting nervously near the bridge entryway. The five-armed and -eyed creatures had muttered constantly in their barbarian slave tongue during the blood-duel, at least one eye always focused on the shrieking and slashing Rrowl-Captain.

The creatures scampered forward immediately at his command. Three snatched up the torn remains of Engine-tinker in their warty arms and carried them away, while the other slave rapidly scrubbed the bridge deck tapestry free of stains and debris. The bridge crew watched with distaste as the plant-eating slaves went about their business.

Rrowl-Captain rumbled disapproval deep in his throat. He was not as prejudiced as his crew. A Jotok could be useful. The five-armed slaves were swift and intelligent. Significantly, they could cooperate among one another far better than most Heroes. And it was well known that feral Jotoki could be dangerous beasts indeed. Yet educated kzin did not fear Jotoki slaves when properly raised, as the ugly creatures were biologically imprinted by slave-tenders into unbreakable loyalty toward their masters. Rrowl-Captain mused on the unfathomable capriciousness of the One Fanged God, for making such clever creatures so pitifully subject to their innate biology.

The One Fanged God had clearly created the Jotoki to be slaves of the kzin. This regardless of what the digitally stored lessons of unblooded historians from Kzin-home, with their blunted claws and thinscreen-damaged eyes, might teach in kitten-school. It was ludicrous to think that these servile and ugly beasts had once been technologically superior employers of sword-wielding kzinti mercenaries!

Rrowl-Captain yawned his outrage at the very thought, baring sharp carnivore teeth. Unlike the kzin, Jotoki did not feed from the summit of the Great Web of All Life, nor did they concentrate and glorify the Life Essence of all creatures below them. The kzin had their place at the Apex of the Great Web, as ordained by the Teachings of the One Fanged God. So the fangless priests said, and so common sense agreed.

No matter who bickered to whom many light-years distant, one thing remained clear: Jotoki ate *plants*.

The captain dismissively spat onto the deck with a snarl. A Jotok leaped forward instantly to clean up the mess with eager fingerlets. Rrowl-Captain sat back and grunted as he watched it scrub the deck until it gleamed, one eye-tipped arm glancing surreptitiously up at him from time to time. It had taken many centuries to properly domesticate the ugly little five-armed slaves, but the Jotoki now fit seamlessly into their proper place in the Empire of the Riit Patriarch.

As eventually would fit these troublesome human monkeys, he thought, absently sheathing and unsheathing his claws in anticipation.

The monkey-humans at Ka'ashi were settling down, at least those living on the planetary surface. Pacification was almost complete, according to the tightbeam reports. Heroes would soon complete the conquest of the cowardly spacefaring feral monkeys in the asteroid belt, as well.

And Heroes would eventually prevail at Man-home, he was certain. How long had the kzin been expanding their Empire compared to these monkeys?

Rrowl-Captain ignored the green hell-light flaring at the back of his thoughts as if in rebuke. It was the destiny of kzinti to rule everywhere their spacecraft traveled, he knew in his Warrior Heart, as the favored sons of the One Fanged God.

Rrowl-Captain inserted a clawtip into a slot on the arm of his command chair, and twisted. The thin-crystal action matrix moved up from the side of the chair, unfolding a thinplate screen and console at the captain's eye level. The screen quickly lit with command functions. Rrowl-Captain purred roughly in his throat, impatient to begin the hunt.

"Communications-Officer," he rasped.

A young kzin, clearly full of liver and a naive image of the Warrior Heart, jumped to attention. "Command me, Dominant One!"

"Set up tightbeam laserlinks with both *Pouncing-Strike* and *Spine-Cruncher*. Full encryption, in case the monkeys can intercept data traffic and have learned our codes."

Unlikely, but the green hell-light in Rrowl-Captain's mind suggested caution. He unfolded an ear at the communications officer in question.

"At once!" the other kzin replied, hands moving rapidly over his thinplate displays.

Rrowl-Captain waited impatiently, working the tip of his pointed tongue between two of his ripping teeth. A piece of Engine-Tinker still lodged there, and was proving difficult to remove. He coughed a chuckle in sudden amusement; the nameless blunt-tooth was an irritation even *after* he became food!

He studied his thinscreen carefully, noting with approval the prearranged course changes and varying accelerations the captains of *Pouncing-Strike* and *Spine-Cruncher* used to avoid becoming targets for monkey weaponry. The ship movements must not become predictable. All three kzin vessels were maneuvering to encircle the human spacecraft, making certain that each kzin ship had a clear zone of attack to carry out its individual mission.

Rrowl-Captain yowled suspiciously when he observed the alien vessel under extreme magnification. The tapered end of the great iceball-spacecraft, source of the now-silent but still fearsome reaction drive, had swung away from its original orientation. It was pointed threateningly toward the position where Rrowl-Captain's ships had been in convoy not long before. Blurring slightly on the screen with the magnification, he noticed that the drive section of the spacecraft was moving slowly in different directions, as if questing for a target.

"Acknowledgment pings have returned from *Spine-Cruncher* and *Pouncing-Strike*, Leader!" said Communications-Officer crisply.

The captain licked the fur on the back of his hand with his tongue, and slicked back his facial pelt meditatively. The intership laserlinks were now frequency locked, allowing burst telemetry and messages from each kzin vessel to flow to the others at prearranged points, provided there were no unplanned maneuvers.

Gravity polarizers and distance made even light-speed communication difficult, particularly in times of battle.

His claws clicking and tapping across the console matrix pad, Rrowl-Captain prepared to initiate his plan to capture the alien vessel. Baring his teeth, he looked balefully into the fiber-optic pickup, and let the snap and slash of command enter his voice.

"Tchaf-Captain," he growled to *Spine-Cruncher*, "you will lead your Heroes against the monkeyship according to the second part of contingency plan *Krechpt*." He paused, then added grudgingly, "May you show Honor to the Riit and the One Fanged God." With a flick of a claw, the burst message was encrypted and sent. Many seconds later, there was a ping-return, signifying receipt of the message.

Rrowl-Captain then informed Cha'at-Captain of *Pouncing-Strike* that it was time to carry out his own orders. The master of *Belly-Slasher* grinned widely after sending that particular message. He had no doubt that the wild-eyed captain of *Pouncing-Strike*, a smallish kzin with much bravery in his liver and little sense in his brain, would carry out his orders. Sure enough, the ping-return of acknowledgment arrived as swiftly as he had expected.

Cha'at-Captain had been a problem for Rrowl-Captain several times during the convoy's long voyage away from Man-sun and the ignoble fate of the Third Fleet. It was only a matter of time, he knew, before Cha'at-Captain challenged him to combat, for control of the three spacecraft and their mission.

The master of *Belly-Slasher* preferred to spill kzinti blood to higher purposes than advances in rank.

For now, however, Rrowl-Captain still led, and chose orders for the aggressive little master of *Pouncing-Strike* that would remove the problem neatly. Cha'at-Captain could not refuse the orders of his superior, of course.

Discipline was the litter-brother to Honor, according to the Teachings of the One Fanged God; Rrowl-Captain had reminded Cha'at-Captain of the specific verses himself.

Not coincidentally, Cha'at-Captain was a fundamentalist follower of the Traditionalist sect of *Hs'sin*. The Teachings of the One Fanged God were inspired works to the uneducated little Hero. Brave, but unlettered.

Rrowl-Captain cynically knew that the Teachings could be quoted by any kzin, regardless of rank or blood, even by the rare atheist Hero. It was simply an ancient book, after all, handed down generation to generation by the priests of the One Fanged God. It was darkly amusing to him that the troublemaking captain had acquiesced so tamely to his fate.

Cha'at-Captain was to lead *Pouncing-Strike* on a scream-and-leap directly at the human spacecraft, firing all weapons, drawing monkeyship weapons fire in turn. *Spine-Cruncher* would use the diversion to fly past the alien ship in a hyperbolic trajectory, and deliver the heavily stealthed monopole bomb. The bomb would detonate close enough to the human ship to temporarily incapacitate its electronics with a hammerblow of an electromagnetic pulse. The human monkeys placed great reliance on electronics.

Spine-Cruncher would then land a boarding party of Heroes to capture and secure the prize. Rrowl-Captain and *Belly-Slasher* would observe how the humans responded to the attacks, aid in the capture if necessary, and direct the mopping-up operation. As soon as the alien craft was secured, Rrowl-Captain would inspect the monkeyship personally, and proceed with converting it to kzinti use and the long trek to *Ka'ashi*.

Rrowl-Captain disliked risking the blood of octal-squared Heroes in *Pouncing-Strike* to create a mere diversion, but if the redoubtable Cha'at-Captain was sufficiently wise and skilled—which Rrowl-Captain thought most unlikely—it might be possible for his crew to survive.

If that became the case, he would deal with Cha'at-Captain's increasingly insubordinate manner in another and more direct fashion. One with less opportunity for the other kzin to accrue honor. Of course, the crew of *Pouncing-Strike* was loyal to their captain. Rrowl-Captain would have to be careful, or at least thorough.

However, in the most likely tactical scenario, Cha'at-Captain and his crew would not present any difficulties whatsoever, after their brave diversionary scream-and-leap toward the monkeyship.

Rrowl-Captain relaxed slightly, daydreaming of his estates to come on Man-home, after he was rightfully rewarded for bringing the contra-matter drive to *Ka'ashi* for use against the monkeys. A palace would be built for his many beautiful kzinrrettis, who would surely be of noble blood, enriching his own line. He would also have his own hunting park, he decided, a place where only he and his litter kittens would stalk and kill prey. Perhaps he would hunt a naked monkey each week, just for the sport of it.

That would relieve him of nightmares tinged with green hell-light, surely.

A languid tongue moved across thin black lips as he considered his certain reward of a double name. Which one would he choose? Perhaps the name his litter-brother had liked so, before he had died while they were still living in the crèche.

Rrowl-C'mef. Rrowl-Captain rumbled the name deep in his throat. It sounded wise and powerful. The name tasted of honor and dignity, did it not? Of teeth tingling with the crunching success of prey between jaws. He would surely wrest honor and victory from the defeat of Third Fleet.

Alarms suddenly yowled, echoing on the control bridge. Rrowl-Captain folded his ears swiftly against the din. His slit pupils narrowed as he looked at the status boards, which blurred with rapid changes.

"Status report!" he shrieked.

Strategist pointed wordlessly at the main thinscreen. Rrowl-Captain saw that the tapered end of the monkeyship had stabilized. He watched as a great cloud of ionized gas emerged from the drive section of the human ship.

"What is the attitude of the alien drive section?" he roared angrily. *Pouncing-Strike* would begin its high acceleration scream-and-leap attack on the alien vessel at any time now.

"Nearly the approach path assigned to *Pouncing-Strike*," replied Strategist with a snarl.

Sure enough, the blinking marker on the tactical thinscreen representing Cha'at-Captain's vessel was accelerating along a coincident vector. Rrowl-Captain snarled his anger.

"Is there sufficient time to warn *Pouncing-Strike* by laserlink?" he shouted to Communications.

The young kzin's tail drooped. "No, Dominant One," he replied submissively. "We are too far away."

Rrowl-Captain looked back at the tactical thinscreen and saw that it was true. He slashed the air in front of him with bared claws in impotent rage. *May the One Fanged God damn light-speed!*

The contra-matter drive of the monkeyship ignited. The cloud of gas surrounding the drive section glowed eye-searing violet for a moment.

The main thinplate viewscreen went suddenly white, then corrected automatically for the awful glare of the reaction drive. It became a great blazing column of light, brighter than suns, stretching rapidly across the viewscreen. Rrowl-Captain ground razor-sharp teeth impotently as he watched *Pouncing-Strike* attempt to vector away from the expanding drive wash.

"*Pouncing-Strike* has ceased acceleration!" shouted Strategist.

Rrowl-Captain bared his teeth. Clearly, the other ship's gravitic polarizers had failed under the great stress of attempting to maneuver away from the spreading death of the contra-matter drive exhaust. It had become a ballistic lump, helpless.

The command bridge crew watched the tactical screen impotently as inertia carried *Pouncing-Strike* into the blazing column of radiation and plasma. Rrowl-Captain snarled and tore a claw on the Kdatlyno-hide arms of his command chair.

The white blaze erupting from the monkeyship slowly turned against the color-shifted starscape toward them, like a great sword out of mythology.

"Communications," roared Rrowl-Captain, "send a burst transmission to *Spine-Cruncher*. Tell them that we will divert the monkeys in order to allow them to carry out their mission."

"At once," said Communications, proudly.

Rrowl-Captain hunched forward in his command chair, mastering his hidden fears. Honor *would* be his, and this victory would slay his inner demons.

"Navigator," he rasped, "begin evasive maneuvers, inward toward the monkeyship. Attempt to draw their fire. Strategist, aid him with your knowledge." Rrowl-Captain's torn claw began to bleed, unnoticed, onto the spotless arm of the command chair.

"At once, Dominant One," the two other kzin shouted with one Hero's voice.

The entire command bridge seemed to blur and tremble as the gravitic polarizer's mutter grew to a low roar. A scorching odor began to emanate from the ventilators as the polarizer was pushed beyond basic design limits. The command bridge filled with the snarling of the agitated crew and the pheromonal scent of their fury.

The deadly white blaze of the alien contra-matter reaction drive stretched across the thinplate viewscreen. It grew swiftly larger and began to move to one side. But slowly.

Rrowl-Captain made the slashing gesture of fealty to the One Fanged God, and watched his fate rushing toward him.

Chapter Seven

Linkage was godhead.

Bruno felt the hail of relativistic particles slowly eroding the hull of *Sun-Tzu* like an invigorating breeze on bare skin. The lethal blaze of radiation sleeting through the sensors was like desert sunshine, warm and friendly.

But he knew that there was so much more than what lay immediately outside the spacecraft to perceive and cherish, to make part of himselves! *Everything* about *Sun-Tzu* was now part of Bruno: the raw power of the antimatter drive, the patient, lethal tensions of the weapons systems, the exquisite fineness of his growing sensorium.

Linked, he could do many things besides wear a spaceship like a slick and sensitive skin. Bruno's mind had become more than simply human.

It had become Mind.

From its tiny human kernel, loci of subminds with special interests quickly formed and grew, each with full independent consciousness as well as being part of the developing interconnective Whole. He had become a clamoring community, a society of minds, each subunit far greater than their woefully limited biological ancestor.

Bruno sent his enhanced consciousness ranging restlessly through the sensory and computational net of *Sun-Tzu*, gazing outward and inward simultaneously. He could at once encompass the All, the depth and range of the universe, from quanta to quasars. A portion of Bruno was still staggered by the whirlwind of knowledge within his thoughts, but with every full Linkage, he became better able to access the vast vault of data surrounding him. It was as if his myriad selves were dissolving in a warm ocean of knowledge and certitude.

But that did not concern him overmuch, even the part of himselves that was still Bruno.

For Bruno knew that he was changing, *improving*, with every Linkage. His times not in communion with the computer network became less and less important, like faint memories almost forgotten over many decades of time.

Linkage also gave Bruno mastery of self. He was learning how to expand or contract his duration-sense at the slightest whim. Soon, he would be able to stretch a microsecond into eternity, or the reverse. A tiny, flawed part of Bruno—his limited biological component—wanted to shout with exhilaration, but he was far beyond mere human emotion.

Bruno, once again in full Linkage, was Transcended. His awareness surrounded and permeated *Sun-Tzu*, at one with the All. A portion of his Mind watched one of the kzin warships slide helplessly into his antimatter drive wash. Without specifically desiring to do so, Bruno's new sensorium analyzed and reported the spectral characteristics of the vaporized alien craft:

- *Flayed atoms of carbon and iron, silicon and indium, shattered and broken.*
- *Whirling motes, once part of a mighty warship and alien flesh, blasted now and scarred.*
- *A billowing cloud of humbled ions, now a slight contaminant of the incandescent torrent of plasma and gamma radiation sweeping behind him for millions of kilometers.*

Bruno relished his control. The drive was its lowest setting; he could pivot and swing the exhaust like the weapon it was while still maintaining proper attitude control. So graceful, so clean, so *true*.

Bruno looked beyond the drive wash, past the sweeping fields of force and glitter of ions, into the vast and varied face of infinity. An emotion much like awe filled his circuits and neurons.

He permitted part of his Mind to appreciate and cherish the subtle wonders surrounding his myriad selves, while another fragment of that expanded consciousness dealt with the growing threat to *Sun-Tzu*.

A tiny bit of his consciousness noted that Carol was speaking to his human component. He felt the urge to reply, to speak in human terms, much as his un-Linked self felt the dull pangs of hunger or the first stirrings of lust. While fully Linked, merely human concerns seemed akin to instinct, lacking the crystalline certainty and broad range of Transcendence. He sent a tendril of his greater Mind into his minor and insignificant biological portion, increasing his consciousness and processing capacity in that location.

His pale perception of the navigation deck sharpened suddenly to razor-edged clarity.

"Yes, Carol. I am with you. I have been so all along." The words, mere modulated sound waves, seemed frustratingly imprecise and limited.

Insufficient.

Bruno called up the realtime image of Carol's face from the navigation-deck cameras, then finally used his biological vision-sense organs on the captain of *Sun-Tzu*. The image didn't seem more accurate than the camera images to Bruno's sensorium; quite the reverse, in fact. Still, he knew that Carol felt more comfortable when he turned his biological eyes on her.

It was a human quirk, one Bruno didn't mind indulging. Even if it wasted some small amount of processing capacity.

Carol's face was lined with worry and other fitful emotions that were difficult to quantify. He focused on her words.

"Thank you for turning your head. Tacky, I just saw one of the ratcat ships vaporize."

"Indeed. The kzin ship attempted to maneuver around the drive wash, lost maneuvering power, and . . . was consumed."

Bruno accessed biotelemetry and voice-stress-analysis datalinks. *Calculating, calculating* . . . Clearly, Carol was as worried by *his* condition as by the alien craft. Bruno felt the electronic analog of amusement at her colorless concerns. They were sweet, cute; as touching as a dog trying to understand an aircar.

"What about the other two ships, Pilot? Can your magnificent intellect find them, or are you drunk again on godhood?" Her tone sounded angry, like the annoying buzz of an insect.

"Allow me a moment," he replied, trying to force reassuring patterns of emotional context into his vocalizations, to soothe Carol while he considered the situation. Bruno was intrigued. Mere human or not, she had said something to hold the attention of his greater Mind. He wanted to ponder and savor the words, but first had to evaluate their status and implications.

Bruno directed his full Attention outward for a moment, and perceived the two kzin ships at a relatively safe distance. Nothing threatened, to a first approximation of risk. He could spare a few seconds for improving his internal functioning, surely.

A human-analytical portion of his Mind continued to consider Carol's statement. "Drunk" was clearly pejorative, and implied suboptimal performance.

Perhaps some subminds *were* functioning at less than ideal efficiencies. Clearly, the weak link in his Mind must be his inept and poorly designed human components. A rapid internal diagnostic confirmed and quantified the inefficiencies. He forced a far greater portion of his Mind into his biological component, the modest seed from which his larger Self had sprouted with Linkage. He began to make changes in his neurological system architecture. The body in the crash couch began to twitch and shake, in a coarse and empty parody of Linkage.

Bruno had expected such side effects while attempting to improve and enhance such a chimeric computing device as the electronically augmented brain of his human portion. After all, massive restructuring of entire interface grids was necessary. Extensive rerouting of neuronal connections was also indicated. Bruno commanded the crash couch restraints to hold his biological component more tightly in order to avoid possible damage to it during the reprogramming subroutines.

The results of some commands were, after all, rather drastic on the macroscopic level.

"Tacky! Bruno!" the watchdog sensory portion of his Mind heard Carol shouting, "what's happening?"

"It is quite all right," he managed to force past chattering teeth, striving for a tone that implied calmness. "You were correct, Carol. This portion of me was operating improperly."

"What do you mean? Portion?" Her words held alarm.

The submind in charge of biotelemetry analysis and interpretation hypothesized that Carol was feeling great emotional upset. Bruno knew that he had to set Carol's fears at ease.

"We are reprogramming our human component for greater efficiency." The explanation would surely calm her agitated emotional state.

He heard Carol shouting again, and turned the major portion of his complex intellect away from her words. Sonic noise, not communication. Some aspect of her tone had become intrusive to the ongoing reprogramming process. Carol's words became fainter, and faded into the background noise of the navigation deck, only fully accessed by his human portion. Which was still under repair and retrofitting, of course.

It was difficult to erase, reprogram, and internally reroute microcircuitry contained with the electronic portion of his human component's brain. Though there was great plasticity in the interface macrostructure, there was little absolute complexity. Soon, he felt certain, he would learn to directly manipulate entirely biological subsystems as well as the electronic.

There were bandwidth and amplitude problems, of course—some quite delicious in their smooth difficulty. Still, Bruno would then be able to force compensatory neuronal rewiring of the brain tissues themselves, leading to a truly binary mind Linking the worlds of silicon and synapse.

Linkage would become still easier then, and he would be able to experience less limitation in his increasingly powerful sensorium.

Bruno noted that rerouting and macrocircuit programming was now complete, with a shadowy ghost of an emotion that had once been satisfaction. Internal debugging routines showed improved perceptual and computing ability. There was less hormonal impact on affective state, as well.

Good, good. Raw emotions often led to decreased cognitive efficiency.

Bruno's biological perceptual field expanded to include Carol, her face grim and set. Tears beaded in her eyes, flowing slowly across her cheek in the microgravity.

From the physical actions of the tears across her face he instantly—and involuntarily—computed the predicted acceleration of the antimatter drive in weapon mode as 0.012 gravities. The portion of his Mind controlling the drive agreed, confirming his calculations to three decimal places.

Bruno reached out with a biological hand and stroked Carol's cheek, feeling the tears against his skin. There were some tactile sensations that action-response circuits could not access. Perhaps there was some emotional, hormonal component. Bruno created a submind to investigate this problem, assigning it moderate priority.

He did care for Carol, and wished her to be safe and happy. Some sign to her of his intentions would be good.

"We are improved now," Bruno told her proudly. Five seconds had passed in realtime since he had initiated the internal reprogramming.

"I . . . can see that," Carol replied. Tears still glinted in her eyes.

Biotelemetry subroutines reported Carol's strongly suppressed emotional state. Bruno tasted worry concerning the captain of the *Sun-Tzu*. A portion of his Mind considered Carol's recent behavior, and began an in-depth analysis.

The rest of Bruno looked outward for the alien threat, anxious to deal with the kzin. There was a universe to ponder.

Bruno sensed the other two kzin warships as tiny flaws in the fabric of space, glittering refractions from their inertialess spacedrives. One of the tiny wrinkles in space-time began accelerating rapidly, maneuvering nearer his drive wash.

"Initiating maneuvers," Bruno told Carol, who nodded jerkily and silently stared at the main holoscreen array.

He sent a low-resolution datadump to a holoscreen window, so that Carol could see the battle more clearly. Dimly, he felt a distraction; the odd, cool brush of Carol's tears drying on his fingers. Evaporative cooling? Bruno sensed the initiation of an increased emotional state in his biological component, and easily compensated for the decreased overall efficiency. If only he could eliminate the hormonal drivers, attain serenity—

"Can I help?" The words were tentative, small.

He felt the cybernetic equivalent of a smile. "No," he said simply in reply.

There was a pause. "I do have some experience in space battles." Carol's tone became slightly peevish.

"Yes. But I have full access to all UN Space Navy tactical and strategic files." He paused, searching his expanding internal database. "Including your own personal battle records and reports."

Carol looked back at the holoscreen, her face seemingly neutral, breathing heavily. The latter confused Bruno: there had been no extreme maneuvering, nor any acceleration stresses. Another portion of his Mind accessed realtime biotelemetry and found Carol's blood pressure and heart rate elevated. Curious.

Bruno turned the *Sun-Tzu*. The kinesthetics were quick, zesty. He delicately slashed with the incandescent column of the antimatter reaction drive—a huge scythe scratching an actinic path of deadly light across the distorted starscape.

Yet the ability of *Sun-Tzu* to turn was limited by its great mass, and the reaction drives controlling its attitude. Several times, Bruno waved the deadly antimatter drive wash near the tiny vessels, an enormous flyswatter against pesky gnats. They dodged—but not by much. He switched vectors, pivoted the ship like a ballerina on an invisible fulcrum. *Much closer, good.* But the two motes were still able to avoid the cutting sword he wielded.

Bruno noted that one of the gnats was firing weapons against the *Sun-Tzu*. He could do nothing at this range. His iceball could not evasively weave and dart like the kzin vessels, and his drive wash took precious seconds to reorient.

He sent a tendril of greater Mind again into his biological component.

"Carol," he forced his human mouth to say, "prepare for weapon impacts."

"I gathered," she replied without looking at his biological portion. Carol reached for the control pads to adjust her crash couch for greater security, but Bruno did it for her before her fingers actually touched the console.

Enemy laser bursts vaporized bits of the icy skin of his spacecraft. Railgun projectiles stitched deep craters toward his hull sensor pods. His biological senses reported the impacts as dull gonging notes ringing on the navigation deck. Bruno detected the second kzin ship accelerating on an indirect vector, possibly preparing for a hyperbolic approach past the *Sun-Tzu*, but at a distance too great to inflict significant damage.

Bruno calculated with crystalline immediacy that he could not maneuver the drive wash rapidly enough to threaten both alien warships at the same time.

He devoted more of his Mind to offensive and defensive systems, and subsystems instantly reprogrammed themselves at his whim. *Sun-Tzu* was not designed for battle; that was *Dolittle*'s mission. Still, Bruno would use what tools were present. Vast quantities of power were tapped from the antimatter reaction chamber, and made available for other uses.

Bruno reached out with a finger of laser light, almost impaling one of the kzin spacecraft on a blazing spear of coherent radiation. *Close, so close*—*Sun-Tzu*'s railgun batteries fired high velocity flocks of iron pellets in complex patterns toward the enemy vessels. The alien spacecraft dodged gracefully.

Simultaneously, he programmed and launched a dozen nuclear pumped X-ray laser bomblets. *Pop, pop*—they plunged into the relativistic vortex and began firing.

Their bursts of radiation narrowly missed their targets. *Why?* He knew the answer even as the question formed: subminds reported with one electronic voice. A sour taste laced Bruno's sensorium, flitting shadows of human emotion. These were the best defenses human technology could field, but they were defeated by the chaos of relativistic plasma turbulence, the distorting refractions of light-speed, and the adroit skill of kzin pilots. Bruno knew that *Sun-Tzu* was outclassed here.

On some unquantifiable, illogical level, Bruno tasted danger inexorably approaching *Sun-Tzu*.

Chapter Eight

Carol Faulk felt helpless.

It was ironic, actually. She was a seasoned combat veteran, with experience in both singleships and as a commander of a battle squadron. She had hulled or fried many kzin ships, seen good friends die, made decisions that saved lives and won skirmishes.

All she could do now was sit and watch impotently while a half-human monster piloted and operated the *Sun-Tzu*.

Yet it was a half-human monster who used to be her lover and friend. Carol pursed her lips at the painful irony.

For the hundredth time, she reminded herself that her opinion of words like "monster" and "alien" might change drastically after they reached Wunderlander space. At the end of the long voyage, when she opened the cryovial containing the virus with the odd name, *Tree-of-Life*. Maybe after the virus did its work she would understand Bruno better.

On the other hand, it did not look to Carol as if Project Cherubim would be a viable option, based on the holoscreen data scrolling past her line of sight. Not even halfway to Alpha Centauri, and the ratcats were already stalking them.

Bruno's lolling interface cable looked ever more leechlike to Carol. His eyes never moved from her as the holoscreen displays shifted, blinked, and changed. His face was utterly slack, eyes huge and staring, with the expanded pupils characteristic of brain-machine interfacing. Carol knew that the vast majority of Bruno's attention was not on her, no matter how he appeared to stare at her.

Bruno's attention was everywhere, all at once.

Carol blinked back tears, cursing herself for the show of weakness. It took a moment for Carol to force the emotions back down, deep inside her. She was a captain, after all. Taking a deep breath and squaring her shoulders, Carol forced herself to accept the simple facts before her, to say the words inwardly: *Bruno is getting worse, and faster than expected.*

He was becoming more and more alien and machinelike. He had even told Carol that he was reprogramming his own brain, making himself a more efficient "component." *I* was becoming *we* as the man she knew diluted away inside the growing machine intelligence that controlled *Sun-Tzu*.

She bullied the subject from her mind with thoughts of duty and strategy. There was nothing to be done at present about her lover. If she and Bruno survived the battle under way, there would be time to find a way to prevent the machine-generated madness from taking Bruno away from her. Maybe.

Until then, all she could do was hope.

Carol felt the straps of her crash couch tighten and loosen as *Sun-Tzu* maneuvered, pivoting on its brilliant lance of plasma and gamma radiation. She felt the shudder of kzin weapons hammering the surface of their spacecraft far above them. The holoscreen status window showed schematics of the battle as it unfolded: the tiny red stars of the two surviving kzin spacecraft maneuvering randomly to avoid the bursts of laser light and the lethal scythe of the drive wash itself.

She forced herself to look at him. "Bruno."

"Yes, Carol?" He didn't speak with his vocal chords, but with the shipboard commlink. It was a little startling, but she had half expected it. The synthesized voice, at least, sounded like Bruno.

"Can you spare processing capacity to speak with your biological voice?" She didn't add, *since you are human.* Carol feared Bruno's answer.

There was a tiny pause.

"Yes," he said, lips moving precisely in a slack face. A tongue moved across lips experimentally. "May we ask why you prefer this communications mode?"

"I am used to . . . your biological component, as you so fetchingly express it."

"But the information conveyed is identical." Irony was lost on the new and improved Bruno, apparently.

"Never mind," Carol sighed. "Thank you for obliging me. Can you give me battle status?"

"Of course. The holoscreens provide the raw data, but I can certainly provide you with vocal summaries."

"Please do so, love."

Did she detect a pause in response to her last word? Another hypospray nozzle snaked out of Bruno's crash couch and injected his neck with a hiss.

He blinked twice, then continued in his artificially human-sounding voice.

"One of the kzin vessels is spiraling in toward me, inflicting serious damage to my sensory pods and ancillary equipment. The other spacecraft is accelerating heavily on an unusual vector."

Worry sent a thrill along her spine. "Wait a second. The word 'ancillary' worries me. Other damage?"

"None. There has been no attempt to damage the antimatter drive or structures associated with it. Only the sensory arrays and weapons ports have been targeted."

She frowned. "So your hunch was correct?"

"Yes. They intend to board me, if they can."

Me? Carol kept her face under careful control. Several times, Bruno had referred to *Sun-Tzu* as *himself*. The "we" he kept using: Did he mean the two of them, or the strange electronic mind controlling him?

"And the other ship?" she asked, biting her lip.

"Difficult to predict at this time. The strategies of space vessels capable of two hundred gravity accelerations are still new to us."

"Show me the vector, with realtime updating, please."

Bruno didn't reply, but the holoscreen showed the more distant kzin ship accelerating rapidly on a curving course that would narrowly graze *Sun-Tzu*. Something about the diagram nagged Carol.

"And the closer ratcat ship?" she continued, biting her lip.

"The pilot is quite good for a biological system. We have been spending a good deal of processing time on predicting its behavior. Clearly, they could be doing more damage than they are accomplishing at present."

A low warning tone filled the navigation deck.

"Carol, there is a problem." Bruno's voice once more came from speakers instead of his throat. "The closer kzin spacecraft is now vectoring wildly, firing all weapons. There is significant damage . . ."

Sun-Tzu rang like a great bell. An unseen hand slammed her into her couch.

"High-yield thermonuclear device detonation off starboard bow," Bruno reported. "Seventy-five percent of sensory pods were destroyed in that hull sector."

"I gathered as much, thank you," Carol replied acidly. She bared her teeth at the feeling of helplessness, her fingers itching to *do* something. The holoscreens showed the action from repeater stations across the icy hull of the spacecraft. The kzin vessel was delivering a flurry of weapons against *Sun-Tzu*, inflicting serious damage.

Sun-Tzu turned to compensate for lost sensory arrays and weapon emplacements. Carol felt her hastily eaten midmeal rise, bitter in her throat.

Another flock of nuclear-pumped X-ray lasers rose against the kzin vessel, which had already maneuvered away. Blasts of coherent radiation again found no target.

"I am sorry, Carol," Bruno's voice said flatly from the commlink speakers, drained of all emotion. "We are experiencing processor difficulties due to network interruption."

The kzin attack had severed some of Bruno's computational net. Carol suddenly wondered if he felt that loss as pain.

A thought blazed in her mind.

"Bruno! What about the other ship?"

A pause.

"I am very sorry," the commlink speakers said in something like her lover's voice. "We were blind on that side for almost twenty seconds before I was able to regain sensory data."

"And?"

"The kzin vessel will reach closest approach to *Sun-Tzu* in a few seconds. It has fired no weapons, however. Perhaps it is trying to draw fire in order to allow the other vessel to inflict greater damage."

Carol's jaw dropped with a blaze of realization.

Couldn't Bruno's vastly enhanced intelligence see what was happening?

She reached over and grabbed Bruno's arm. "Listen, love, focus as much sensory capacity as you can spare on the close approach craft. Put some weapons against it, throw up debris, anything."

The flat half-machine tones took on a questioning note.

"Why are you so specifically concerned?"

Carol wanted to slam her fists down on the useless command console. "Don't you get it?" she grated. "It's a bombing run. Do as I tell you!"

By then, it was too late. The kzin craft, under cover of its fiercely attacking sister vessel, swept stealthily within a million kilometers of *Sun-Tzu*. It had already swung past them by the time energy weapons flashed lethal radiation. Relativistic distortions fuzzed the images further—

—And almost as an afterthought, a coherent lance of X-rays speared the enemy craft, spreading a glowing cloud of debris across space. The second vessel had already sheered off, racing for the opposite side of *Sun-Tzu*.

A blaze of light filled the holoscreen.

"Bruno?" Carol asked quietly. "What happened?"

Another slight pause, and Bruno once more spoke from his own lips instead of the commlink speakers.

"I am very sorry, Carol. The kzin have delivered a monopole bomb. It must have been heavily shielded to avoid my sensory array."

Carol swore. In the deadly heart of a monopole bomb, isolated north and south poles met violently, releasing great gouts of energetic electrons. These electrons would spiral, close to light-speed, down magnetic lines of force toward *Sun-Tzu*.

When the electron storm struck *Sun-Tzu*'s densest

magnetic cocoon, the electrons would radiate powerfully, their orbits reversed in the magnetic mirrors. They would never reach the icy hull of *Sun-Tzu*, but they would have done their deadly task. Their electromagnetic wail would fry most electrical equipment not shielded deep within the spacecraft. The other kzin vessel would be safe in the "shadow" of *Sun-Tzu*.

Bruno still said nothing.

Carol began striking keys on her crash couch console violently. The straps loosened and retracted, allowing her to float slightly upward in the microgravity.

"How long until impact?" she asked.

"Ten seconds." The reply was as flat and toneless as the autopilot of an aircar.

"Well, let's get you and me down to *Dolittle*. I have an idea."

"Impossible."

In a flash, she realized that disconnecting Bruno from his brain-computer interface would take several minutes, with heavy use of biotelemetric controls. And, fatally, that unshielded and vulnerable conductors ran from the hull of *Sun-Tzu* to the sensory array to the computer net . . .

. . . directly into Bruno's brain.

"I love you, Bruno," Carol said. She grabbed his interface cable in both hands and took a deep breath.

Chapter Nine

Watching Carol's arm muscles tense as she gripped the interface cable, all of Bruno's vast consciousness tried to crowd into his inadequate biological portion in defense against what would happen next. Bruno's enhanced mind would not fit into the small space, wracking him in a horrible cybernetic analog of pain. *No.* He willed his arm to move toward his cable linkage protectively, and . . .

Carol, with a loud grunt, ripped his interface cable from the console with a sharp metallic popping sound.

There wasn't time to scream, even in realtime.

Bruno felt his Mind collapse and die. Transcendence guttered out like a candle flame in a raw wind.

The cold blackness roared into his very soul, a dark hurricane of torment. Loss burned like some dark acid, shattering his Transcended Self. *Gone, gone*—scattering its torn threads to the cosmic wind . . .

In what felt like death agony, Bruno sensed the electromagnetic pulse impact the *Sun-Tzu*'s hull.

Holoscreens flickered multicolored visual static and
vanished, roaring. Sparks geysered from consoles.
Navigation deck lights failed. The deadly pulse leaped
like a striking snake of electrical potential from the
exploding console—
     —ricocheting from the white steel walls—
     —crackling, searching, like a living thing—
     —to the flapping end of his interface cable.
He felt the charge enter his brain like a lit fuse via
the suddenly traitorous conduit of metal and silicon.
Bruno's mind seemed to explode in a fireball-hot
supernova within his deepest self.
The suffocating blackness was obliterated by a lethal
Light.

1100101000111100101010101011011111010101110110100111100
01011101110101111010010101110101001001101010111001100111111

*The crashed aircar was upside down, silent and dark.
With clumsy fingers, five-year-old Bruno released himself
from his crashnet. He fell onto the inside of the roof
with a painful thump. He lay there, panting and dizzy,
feeling sick.*

*Burnt hair, scorched earth, a coppery wet smell. The
aching blackness all around. He was very afraid.*

*Bruno could remember the explosion, the screaming,
the long fall. He had no memory of the horrible crash.*

His head hurt terribly.

*Bruno turned his head to one side and tried to vomit,
but there was nothing left in his stomach other than a
trickle of foul liquid that burned his throat.* Mumma
will be angry, *he thought, wiping his stinging mouth
on a torn sleeve. He had to find Mumma and Papa,
somewhere in the crashed aircar. The cabin had somehow
become huge in the dark. He called and called, his voice
echoing in the small space that had swollen so.*

No one answered. Determined, he crawled forward
with his arms, because his legs wouldn't work properly.
They were numb, but at least they didn't hurt.

Nothing hurt as much as Bruno's head.

"Mumma? Papa?"

His left hand finally found his mother and father,
still strapped side by side into their crashnets. They
did not reply when he called, no matter how much he
cried and pleaded. Finally, he shook them hard, making
his head hurt even worse than before. His hands were
wet and sticky, and tasted salty when he wiped his face.

Bruno cried, because his parents wouldn't hold him
in the darkness, and wouldn't answer him. He had never
felt so frightened and alone.

The headache finally became more than he could
stand. Dizzy with pain and exhaustion, Bruno finally
lay flat on the inside roof of the crashed aircar. Still
crying softly, he reached up and touched the left side
of his head, where it hurt so much.

His fingers sank five centimeters into his shattered
skull. Into something pulpy and wet. Sharp slivers of
bone pricked his fingertips. Lights exploded in Bruno's
head, and he tasted the color blue, felt the smell of moist
hay. He thought that he heard a siren in the distance,
but he was in too much pain to pay attention.

Exhausted, he laid his pounding head down on the
cool metal, to wait for his Mumma and Papa to wake
up and take him home, to make everything all right.
The aircar swirled around him dizzily. There were vague
murmurs like anxious voices in the darkness, calling
him.

Cold nothingness claimed little Bruno with clammy
hands, and dragged him down into an unconscious void.

1100 10 1000 111 100 10 10 10 10 110 111 110 10 10 11 10 110 100 11 100
0 10 11 10 1 110 10 11 110 100 10 1 110 100 100 110 10 10 1 100 1 100 1111

Bruno opened his eyes for a moment, still convulsing randomly. Dim, reddish corridor emergency lights winked and glittered. He watched the main ring corridor of *Sun-Tzu* flying dimly past him.

Carol was carrying him toward *Dolittle*. The low, microgravity lope as she ran made his head flop helplessly from side to side. His neck was an agony of fire. Bruno tried to force words past his lips, but it hurt to think, let alone speak.

He thought that he heard Carol telling him to hang on, that *Dolittle* was very near, but the words were slippery, skidding away like the emergency lights.

"Mumma?" he muttered, and passed out.

Chapter Ten

Rrowl-Captain's roar of triumph echoed throughout the command bridge of the *Belly-Slasher*. He leaped from his command chair and threw his short-furred arms outward. The bridge crew shouted as well, claws unsheathed and drool spooling from excited lips.

The hunt was successful! After the long watches of skulking, they had their jaws on prey at last.

The image of the monkeyship on the main thinplate screen turned lazily. Obviously, attitude control and guidance were gone after the magneto-electrical pulse had impacted the enemy vessel. The contra-matter drive still fired constantly, spewing a deadly exhaust column as the ship rotated randomly. The reaction drive's basic control electronics were deeply protected within the iceball of the human-monkey vessel. But piloting functions were clearly incapacitated.

All as planned, Rrowl-Captain purred to himself.

Dim flickers and flashes of coronal discharge crawled like living things across the surface of the great sphere of the alien ship. It was the only evidence of the enormous electronics-devouring pulse born of the monopole bomb, a smashing Heroic fist that had devastated the electronics of the human vessel.

Rrowl-Captain's batwing ears raised and stretched outward in pride. The victory was not without cost. Many Heroes had died for this prize, he knew. The losses were significant, but acceptable. Blood of Heroes had been well spent on this hunt.

The entire crew of *Pouncing-Strike*, including the annoying little Cha'at-Captain, had been vaporized in a microsecond by the monkeyship exhaust early on. Little honor there. But the brave captain of *Spine-Cruncher* would have a posthumous Full Name, to the great honor of his sons and fathers! Rrowl-Captain's Warrior Heart soared.

A price well paid—for victory and honor. Both captains and crewkzin of *Pouncing-Strike* and *Spine-Cruncher* had been, even unwittingly, a credit to the Riit and the One Fanged God. He would pay for a Warrior's Honor Ceremony for both crews from his own pride-funds when he returned in triumph to *Ka'ashi*.

Rrowl-Captain growled once for silence on the command bridge.

"Navigator," he spat and hissed in rare good humor, "please fly us toward the monkeyship forward hull, where Alien-Technologist has apparently found an access airlock."

"At once, Dominant Leader," the proud crewkzin snapped.

"Do not assume the monkeys are without resources, even now," Rrowl-Captain cautioned. "Follow standard evasive maneuvers."

"Surely the monkeys are helpless, Leader!"

Rrowl-Captain fanned his ears in humor. "It would

appear so, yes. But what is the True Hero's approach with these monkeys?"

"*Feint-and-pounce!*" the bridge crew hissed and spat in rough chorus.

Rrowl-Captain purred approval.

He spent a few moments considering how to take possession of the alien craft. It would take some time to discover its alien workings and procedures, for the monkeys did not think like Heroes. He would necessarily have to select a crew to pilot the monkeyship back to *Ka'ashi*, after the vessel had been adapted to the needs of kzin crew. Who to trust? What crewkzin valued obedience above opportunity? Rrowl-Captain rumbled in contemplation.

That, however, would be in the future. The Teachings of the One Fanged God were explicit on this matter: *Clean no prey before its capture*. The Teachings, upon reflection, often placed fangs deeply into agile truths.

"I require an octal of Heroes to accompany Alien-Technologist after we rendezvous with the monkeyship," he growled into the shipwide commlink. Consulting his command chair thinscreen's database, Rrowl-Captain selected his most aggressive Heroes to balance the natural, if unkzinlike caution of Alien-Technologist. It would be, he reflected, good practice for both factions under his command.

Rrowl-Captain settled back in his command chair, purring softly, as he honed his bandaged claws and mused over satisfying bloody dreams of conquest.

Only the slightest hint of green hell-light marred the excellence of his reveries.

Chapter Eleven

Bruno dimly felt Carol lay him in the autodoc of *Dolittle*. His eyes fluttered open. A curving metal wall above him. Carol's lips, moving. Her voice, as if underwater, all gargles and rumbles. Bits and pieces of sounds, syllables flying like frightened birds. Hard to capture.

"Bruno, I have to get us out of here. We don't have any choice but *Dolittle*." Her eyes were close to his, her lips near his ear. "It's that or become ratcat food, love."

Words and meanings met and fled one another in his damaged mind.

He felt her hands tucking his arms into the coffinlike box of the autodoc, connecting telltales to various parts of his body. Numb. He struggled to force words past dead lips.

"Love . . ." he managed to grunt.

Bruno watched the blur that was Carol's face smile sadly. A glint around her eyes in the painful light?

"I love you, too, chiphead." Her vague face sobered. "The autodoc will fix you, I think." She kissed him, a faint pressure on his dead lips, and vanished from his fading horizon.

The lid of the autodoc whined shut, clicked with finality. In the darkness, he felt the pressure of sensors against his wrists and neck. There was a low gurgling in the microgravity as the autodoc began to fill with healing liquid. A mask lowered gently over his face, and he felt the bright whiff of pure oxygen burn in his lungs.

Bruno felt the darkness in his mind rise like a relentless tide, carrying him again into oblivion.

1100101000111100101010101011011111010101110110100110001011101101110111100100101110100100110101011000110001111

Ten-year-old Bruno looked at the isolation tank curiously. Thick wires and consoles and strange machines meshed like some jigsaw puzzle of electronics. Faceless technicians stood around at a discreet distance, saying nothing. But always watching.

"And this could help me talk to computers?" he asked, incredulous.

Colonel Early of UN Special Projects smiled reassuringly, his teeth white in his seamed coal black face.

"That's right, son. You already know how to give machines mental commands through your interface, right?"

"Sure." That was easy. You just thought it, and it happened. It was like asking someone how to make their arm raise up. You just did it.

"Well, we want you to do much more than that, with this machine. Can I tell you what we have in mind?" His tone was easy, patient.

Bruno trusted Colonel Early. He had paid for Bruno's

education, had spent a fair amount of time either in person or via hololink with Bruno. It was lonely in the research institute, and the scientists made him feel like a project, or an alien. They talked at him, not with him.

Just because they had repaired the brain damage he had suffered as a kid with neuronal emulator macrocircuitry, they felt he was property, not a person. Techtalk. Do this. Do that. Never why he should do this or do that. It made Bruno angry, and sometimes uncooperative.

Colonel Early could always talk him back into working with the scientists, though.

"Okay," he replied to Colonel Early, who stood patiently, waiting. He always listened to Bruno, treated him like a grownup. Bruno would do a great deal for Colonel Buford Early.

"Well, we would like to link you up to a real computer. A big one, not like the little cybernetic links you've been working on. Once we do that, then we will put you in the isolation tank." Early pointed at the small tank, covered with controls and interface monitor units. Conduits snaked to a solid wall of computer systems. "The human mind, Bruno, needs stimulation."

Bruno frowned. "And in an isolation tank, I won't get it?"

Colonel Early nodded, looking serious. "That's right, son. But your brain will search for a way to get that stimulation. It has to have it, but you won't be able to see, hear, or feel inside the tank. Eventually, your brain will learn to link up with the computer interface circuitry."

Bruno squinted, thinking. "What will it be like?"

"People who connect up with higher-order computers via their brains are called—"

"Linkers," Bruno interrupted.

"That's right, son. Linkers. They say that a Linker can know everything."

"Everything?" Bruno was suddenly fascinated.

Colonel Early looked a little sad. "I doubt it. Did you ever hear of Faust, son?"

"Fawst? Who's that?"

The older man sighed. "I guess you weren't on the approved list. Nobody is, anymore." He brightened a bit. "But we think that you will be better at interfacing with a computer than other Linkers."

"Because I'm a chiphead." Bruno grated, peeved. He made a face.

Colonel Early put a hand on Bruno's shoulder, gentle. " 'Chiphead' is a bad word, Bruno." He stared directly into Bruno's eyes, held them. "It is an ignorant term used by uneducated, prejudiced people."

Bruno said nothing, his lips twisted in resentment. He had heard a lot of people call him a chiphead over the years, once they had learned about where he lived, and his history. The accident. What was inside his head. He hated being different.

"That's why the scientists look at me funny, isn't it?" Bruno asked. He couldn't look at the other man.

Colonel Early persisted. He hooked two fingers under Bruno's chin and forced his eyes up toward his own.

"Bruno, it's a word used by little people who are afraid of new things. You should pity them."

"If you say so." He was unconvinced. At least Colonel Early liked him. Even if he was a chiphead.

They waited together in the crowded room for a few moments. Colonel Early said nothing. He never was overbearing.

"Will it hurt?" he finally asked.

"No, son. It will be scary at first, and very lonely. Until your brain learns to Link, that is."

A bit of enthusiasm entered his voice. "And then I'll know everything?"

Colonel Early smiled in real amusement. "Well, I wouldn't go quite that far, son. You will know a great deal more than anyone else, I can promise you."

Bruno thought a moment.

"Would I be able to help you with your work at the UN?" he asked.

"Son, that is why I am asking. My children are all grown now, as are my grandchildren. And I can't get a permit for more children."

Bruno smiled. "That's okay, Colonel Early. I don't have a father or mother. But I guess you know that already."

He certainly did. Colonel Early's had been the first face Bruno had seen when he had awakened in the hospital after the accident and the first set of operations.

Again they waited together, silent. Colonel Early never pushed Bruno, and he appreciated it.

"I'll do it," Bruno finally said, ignoring the mutters of the technicians around the isolation tank.

"Good."

"When do we start?"

"How about now?" Colonel Early said, handing Bruno the helmet with all of the strange plugs and wires. It was heavier than it looked, and Bruno held it awkwardly. "Let me help." Early lowered the helmet onto Bruno's head slowly, reverently.

Like a crown.

1100101000111100101010101011011110101011011101110100111010101101101011111

Bruno Takagama moaned against the soft mask of the respirator in the autodoc tank. Mechanical fingers began to probe the burns around his neck socket. Small swimming robots cruised toward his wounds in the ocean of the autodoc's fluids, bearing tiny medical instruments poised at the ready. Noting his distress, the autodoc diagnostic circuitry administered a strong sedative. Soon he slept dreamlessly.

swimming robes arrayed toward the woman's infra-red ... of the survivors of their nation, against local starvation ... present in the verb. Noting his thirdness, the woman ... slightly to her left, and she said to everyone in earshot, "soon we must descend—"

Chapter Twelve

Carol Faulk touched a keypad and felt her crash couch shudder in response. *Dolittle* shot down the darkened escape tunnel toward the outer hull of *Sun-Tzu*.

Carol activated the escape bay doors. She goosed the fusion drive, already warmed and ready at the first sign of potential hostilities. Explosive bolts blew silently in vacuum, the hatch flew into fragments, and the long spindle shape of *Dolittle* was suddenly free in space.

Now. Yes! Her hands on the helm keypads of a spacecraft, Carol felt in command again. No longer helpless and unable to fight. The starscape was still relativistically squashed and distorted, but at least she had some control over her fate.

And Bruno's.

Dolittle flashed away from the dying *Sun-Tzu*. They had less than an hour before her quickly set booby trap activated, and antimatter containment gently and fatally shut down.

Dolittle had to be far away indeed from *Sun-Tzu* by then.

Carol called up the autodoc remote diagnostic on screen above her console. The autodoc sensors were already attached to Bruno in many places, and medical robots were swarming over and in his body, doing everything possible to heal his damage. Flashing red lights indicated his serious condition.

"C'mon, Tacky," she whispered. "You have to pull through."

There had been little choice when she pulled his plug in the *Sun-Tzu*. Bruno's brain was certainly damaged by what she had done, and even more from the EMP induction. But had Bruno remained fully Linked and directly connected to the computer net by electrical conductors, the electromagnetic pulse would have burned his brain to ashes.

Bruno: sick or dead. Those had been her choices.

Carol kept the bulk of the *Sun-Tzu* between *Dolittle* and the kzin warship that was even now approaching the earth vessel, bent on boarding and conquest. The idea of ratcats leaping down the abandoned corridors of *Sun-Tzu*, finding the cryogenically suspended bodies of her crewmates, felt like a violation. But perhaps she would get her revenge after all.

She would give her doomed sleeping crewmates a real Viking funeral, a far piece indeed from Scandinavia.

Carol smiled grimly. *The ratcats will get a surprise in fifty-eight minutes*, she thought to herself. A caution worried her. *How long will it take for the kzin to analyze the command programs, and begin diagnosing drive activity?*

Dolittle's vector was straight and true. Carol was a good pilot, even by the seat of her jumpsuit, and *Dolittle*'s basic fusion drive was familiar. You didn't need to be part computer to fly the little warship.

By now, the ratcat craft was close enough to *Sun-Tzu* to hide *Dolittle*'s escape behind the bulk of the earth spacecraft. Every second would translate into merciful, shielding distance when the antimatter containment system failed.

When she was a thousand kilometers from the *Sun-Tzu*, still undetected and unchallenged, Carol unfurled the great superconductive wings of *Dolittle*.

Forty minutes left now.

The vast wings of *Dolittle* caught at the magnetic fields between the stars, like a fledgling bird in an updraft. A conductor moving rapidly through a magnetic field generated electrical current. The current, tapped, delivered deceleration force. Electromagnetic braking writ large.

The energy thus generated by deceleration at relativistic speeds was enormous, and useful for a variety of purposes.

It had originally been the plan of *Dolittle* and her crew to leap from the *Sun-Tzu* near Wunderlander space. Bruno was to pilot *Dolittle* in full Linkage, while Carol and her revived crewmates were all exposed to Tree-of-Life virus behind the now-useless hermetic doors of the cargo section of *Dolittle*.

Without the sealed doors, Bruno would have been killed by exposure to Tree-of-Life. The brain as well as the body changed its very structure under the imperious genetic commands of the ancient virus. Since Bruno's brain was studded with implanted electronics, those changes would certainly be fatal.

Carol and her virus-exposed crewmates, on the other hand, would fall into developmental comas, tended by autodocs as their bodies underwent the metamorphosis described in the UN reports. They would emerge as something more than human—in ironic biological counterpoint to Bruno's Linkage.

Protector-stage humans. Smarter, stronger, and faster than any human born.

During the pre-mission training, Buford Early had reluctantly shown them the holos and heavily censored summary sheets. Once an ARM, always a goldskinning ARM, so far as Carol was concerned. Early would restrict the wheel if he could.

Bruno had forced Early's hand, insisting that he brief the crew of *Sun-Tzu*. Early had been shocked that his loyal Bruno would do such a thing. It was Carol's first sign that the mission had a slim chance.

The data was both tantalizing and frightening. Carol could see why the UN kept the information under such restriction. Pssthpok, the alien who came after the failed Pak colony on Earth that had evolved into *Homo sapiens*, and whose dried body lay in the Smithsonian. The Belter, Jack Brennan, first modern human to be converted by Tree-of-Life. He had become the Brennan-monster or Vandervecken, and had perhaps saved humanity from itself during the Long Peace, with gifts of technological improvements even the ARM couldn't restrict.

And, according to Early, perhaps saved the human race from Pak fleets out near the failed human colony at Epsilon Indi, Home. Home had failed due to Tree-of-Life, but Brennan's plan had created an army to fend off the Pak fleets.

When the kzin fleets arrived at Sol, and seemed to be winning, the story of Home gave Early an idea. Project Cherubim would use Protector-stage humans against the kzin.

The human-Protector crew, piloted by the fully Linked Bruno, would enter Wunderlander space and fight the kzin. The vast power of the decelerating *Dolittle* would power enormous laser and particle-beam weapons. Eventually, the crew would join with the human resistance forces in the Serpent Swarm asteroid belt.

But the crew would arrive dying from radiation poisoning, unable to create more Protector-stage humans.

The plan was to limit the "infection," as Protectors—even human-Protectors—savagely fought anything to protect their own bloodline. This would rapidly become chaos on crowded human worlds. Tree-of-Life virus made intelligence and strength the uncritical servant of emotion and instinct.

Brennan's records had warned of this.

Carol increased deceleration, and watched *Sun-Tzu* vanish from her screen. She bled off the energy by powering up one of the huge gas lasers, firing randomly in different directions, hoping that no nearby dust cloud fluoresced, alerting the kzin to *Dolittle's* escape.

The chronometer readout hung in midair, holographically. Carol tried not to look at it too often, and failed. From her own space-battle experience, Carol knew that waiting was the hardest part. But when the time for action arrived, she would pray to live long enough to wait once again.

Thirty-five minutes.

Chapter Thirteen

Rrowl-Captain paced the command bridge of *Belly-Slasher* and watched the forward thinplate screen closely, his hairless tail slashing the air with impatience. He growled low in his throat as he stalked the bridge, taloned boots silent on the tapestry-covered deck. The bridge crew remained both respectful and silent, eyes averted and ears folded tightly against orange-furred skulls. Clawed fingers hung expectantly over keypads, waiting for the captain of *Belly-Slasher* to shriek an impatiently angry command.

It had taken half of a watch-interval for *Belly-Slasher* to cautiously maneuver close to the monkeyship. The wariness had worn poorly on Rrowl-Captain and his crew so soon after the monopole bomb from *Spine-Cruncher* had silenced the human vessel. Triumph tasted like leafy defeat in their jaws, as *Belly-Slasher* moved slowly toward the iceball of a spacecraft.

To skulk toward the carcass of the monkeyship denied the Octal-and-Two Truths in the Warrior Heart. Rrowl-

Captain snarled wetly to himself in frustration, his jaws snapping on nothingness.

It was a tense time aboard the sole surviving kzin warship.

The waiting was taking a toll on him and the crew of *Belly-Slasher*. Ventilators poured out dry-conditioned air in a stiff, cold breeze, attempting to dilute the scream-and-leap pheromones that every crewkzin was emitting in quantity. Intellect remained locked in battle with instinct and kzinti hormones. At least until there were actual enemies to battle with wit and claws.

Agitated and filled with frustration, many of the crewkzin had begun to lose discipline. So far Rrowl-Captain had only to riffle his new and significantly larger trophy belt loop as a reminder. He bared teeth in satisfied memory of his reinforced dominance.

Rrowl-Captain had then tightly reminded his impatient crew of the clever *p'charth* of Kzin-home. The beast feigned death as a technique for luring its prey close enough to spit swift-acting neurotoxin into surprised scavenger faces. The Teachings of the One Fanged God used the *p'charth* as a parable of the dangers of certitude in battle: *"The Wise Hero ensures that Prey is not Predator cloaked by the Long Grass of Wit or Trickery; some claws can slash deeply as well as run swiftly."*

In so calming his crew, he calmed himself.

"Navigator," Rrowl-Captain snarled.

The kzin in question looked up from his console and thinscreen, facial fur matted from intense concentration. Rrowl-Captain chose to overlook the other kzin's lack of grooming for the moment.

"Dominant One!" Navigator replied with only a trace of distraction present in his hiss-and-spit syllables.

"Report on progress," the captain rasped, gentling his tone slightly. It must be frustrating, he reflected, for a Hero to stalk numbers within bloodless computer memory. Like leaping, fangs agape, into enemies composed of mere fog and shadow.

"Leader," the other kzin rumbled in low respectful tones, "look to the forward thinscreen." A schematic of the monkey spacecraft, huge and rounded like an icy asteroid, appeared. Magnetic lines of force, which swept the interstellar medium from the alien ship's path, were added to the diagram. The route of *Belly-Slasher* was a circuitous line threading the deadly tongues of magnetic force toward the bow of the monkeyship.

"Hrrr . . ." Rrowl-Captain growled, musingly. "Your attention to careful and precise duty is duly noted and will be well rewarded. We cannot afford to lose this prize to monkey tricks or treachery, despite our impetus to complete our conquest and celebrate a successful hunt."

The other kzin's orange-and-black ruff lifted with pride at Rrowl-Captain's words of praise. "It would not have been possible, Dominant One, without the aid of Alien-Technologist." He paused, scratching with a careless claw beneath his whiskers reflectively. "The monkeys do not make sense, Leader. It is difficult to understand their design philosophy. If we only had a Telepath—"

Rrowl-Captain snorted dismissal. "Indeed; we do not. Placing dream-fangs on prey does not fill a Hero's belly, nor honor the Great Web of Existence." He paused. "These monkeys are, as you say, different from Heroes, different from Kdatlynos, different from Chunquen, different even from our loyal Jotoki. The One Fanged God made slaves in different forms to serve our different needs."

"As you say, Leader," Navigator agreed, obedience stiffening his spine.

"Even an unblooded kitten could set fangs in such facts." Rrowl-Captain dismissively changed the subject as obvious. He gestured at the forward thinscreen with a sharp black claw. "Your attention to detail in adroitly taking us through the magnetic force-lines is especially noteworthy."

Navigator put sheathed claws to face in recognition of the compliment. "It was as you commanded, Dominant One. Alien-Technologist and I stalked fact and hypotheses in our planning. The monkeys do not use our gravitic polarizers, so they do not have force shielding, as we do; they must rely on primitive magnetic fields for protection." His tone burred contempt.

"Yet these fields are of great power," Rrowl-Captain rumbled low in warning. "Do not underestimate monkey tricks. They may lack honor seen in the light of the Teachings of the One Fanged God, but such strategies can still slash the most noble Hero's tail in two through overconfidence."

"As you command," the other kzin deferred with a hiss. He highlighted the path of *Belly-Slasher* on the thinscreen schematic with a few claw slashes at his console; they were moments from rendezvous with the large airlock structure identified earlier by Alien-Technologist.

"There are no signs of activity from the target?" Rrowl-Captain inquired.

"No, Leader. Only the contra-matter drive and the magnetic-field equipment appear to be functioning optimally. No laser ranging or microwave emissions. Nothing." Navigator purred in thought. "Perhaps the monkeys were killed by life-support failure or some other catastrophe, only leaving a few automated subsystems in order?"

Rrowl-Captain licked his nostrils with a disbelieving tongue. What did his unconscious mind scent? "Surely life-support systems were adequately shielded."

"*Spine-Cruncher*'s monopole weapon was of high

power and delivered most skillfully, Dominant One. The human-monkeys must not have shielded themselves properly, other than drive and field waveguides. Or perhaps random chance intervened."

" *'Even the sharpest and most skillful fang can break,'* " the captain of *Belly-Slasher* quoted from the Teachings of the One Fanged God. The other kzin blinked agreement. Random chance too often ruled the universe.

Rrowl-Captain hissed in worry. He had expected some kind of monkey trick during *Belly-Slasher's* tense voyage to the bow of the alien spacecraft, but the huge ship had wallowed through space without response, seemingly without guidance or crew. No railguns, no lasers, no particle beams, no missiles.

Nothing.

The monkeyship was like a pilotless ghost vessel, its fearsome idling reaction drive swinging randomly through a small angle. It tasted like victory, yet the savor was not quite as satisfying as Rrowl-Captain had anticipated. Bloody, but not hot and fresh.

Clearly, the contra-matter drive was extremely dangerous, and required many safeguards. Such a protected subsystem could have easily survived the magneto-electrical pulse. Perhaps the magnetic shielding was assigned such a priority, as well. The monkeys, after all, did not think like Heroes. His reasoning had the tang of fangs-on-fact, logic. Still, Rrowl-Captain had the distinct feeling of enemy eyes upon him. He felt his ruff rising involuntarily.

"Return to your station," he ordered Navigator peremptorily. The other kzin slapped claws to face and turned back to his console.

Rrowl-Captain reflected on his own seemingly brave words. He again saw the greenish light of monkey lasers in his mind's eye, filling the sky, shaming his Warrior

Heart and slashing bits from his liver. Pushing the grass-eating vision to the back of his mind, he leaped back to his command chair and sat.

"Preparing for rendezvous," Navigator announced over the ship commlink.

"Alert Alien-Technologist in his quarters," the captain of *Belly-Slasher* hissed to Apprentice-to-Communications, who leaped to his clumsy feet nervously. "Tell him, by my order, to assemble his team at the starboard airlock in space armor, along with their equipment." The young kzin huddled next to the commlink, and hissed and spat his Leader's orders.

Rrowl-Captain settled back in his command chair, listening to the ripping-cloth sound of the gravity polarizers slowly decrease. *Belly-Slasher* cautiously approached the alien vessel, halting a few lengths of kzin-leaps above the other ship's icy pitted hull.

The forward viewscreen showed the relativity-distorted universe around them, lonely points of velocity-squeezed light and black empty spaces. Energetic particles from the interstellar medium impacted the magnetic field surrounding the alien vessel from time to time, producing colorful auroral flickers of ghostly light.

We are so far from our lairs, here between the stars, he mused. *Far from our kittens and kzinrettis.*

Rrowl-Captain gestured to his personal Jotoki servant, which rushed forward to offer a placating delicacy with the fingerlets at the end of its warty slave arm: a still-wriggling slice of *k'chit* from the vivarium on board. The captain bolted the warm flesh whole, hardly chewing. The act of consuming, of at least his gullet doing battle with some kind of adversary, served to slow his breathing. Rrowl-Captain took the cloth his Jotok was now offering, and cleaned tangy blood from his jaws, mollified for the moment.

"Rendezvous complete," Navigator rasped over shipwide commlink.

Rrowl-Captain leaped to his feet and purred readiness. He stalked toward the hatchway, tail held high with anticipation.

It was at last time to complete the hunt.

Chapter Fourteen

Bruno blinked at the painfully bright shipboard lights stabbing at his eyes, and coughed in reflex as the mask lifted away from his face. Remote sensors withdrew delicately from his body. He looked past the rising top of the autodoc, and through blurry eyes saw Carol Faulk gazing down at him.

From what Bruno could see from his position, it looked as though they were in *Dolittle*. It seemed to hurt a little to think, to remember. He blinked several times to clear moist grit from his eyes. He shook his head to clear his mind, which felt slow and clogged; it didn't help.

Bruno was without a clue, most of his recent memories apparently gone. Burned away by something horrible.

"Come on, shipmate," Carol said lightly, helping him out of the autodoc tank. To Bruno, it felt as if the ship was running under about a half gee of acceleration. Thick fluid dripped from his body as she carefully toweled him off. He tried to crane his painfully stiff neck to look at the forward holoscreen, just a few meters away in the cramped cabin. His eyesight was still too muzzy to read the status window from that distance, but the overall forward view showed a relativistic starscape.

Bruno drew in his breath sharply, fuzzy thinking or not, when he realized that *Sun-Tzu* was nowhere in sight.

He tried to say something, to ask the obvious questions. Carol would not reply to his half-grunted attempts at questions. She continued to towel him thoroughly dry, batting aside his still-clumsy hands when he tried to stop her.

"Hmm," she commented in a falsely suggestive tone, drying a few of his more sensitive areas. "Looks like you could use a bit of toning exercise in some of these muscle groups. And I know just where, when, and how, shipmate."

Bruno woozily realized that Carol was jollying him along, trying to divert his attention from something important. His lips felt dry and cracked, his mouth tasted like bitter medicine and old leather. He knew something terrible was wrong.

"What's going on?" he managed to force past numb lips. His voice was a rusty croak. "Quit messing around. I think there is something wrong with me." Black spots circled at the edges of his vision like buzzing insects.

Carol said nothing, but hugged him very tightly for a moment. She let go abruptly, then finished drying him a little more roughly than he would have liked. His skin, tingling, began to feel more normal. Some of the cobwebs started to fade from his mind. Carol helped him into a jumpsuit coverall, ignoring all attempts by Bruno to induce her into talking.

It must be bad, Bruno thought to himself slowly. His mind was clearing a bit more. Some bad memories began to surface, still indistinct. He shivered.

With an arm around him, Carol lowered Bruno into his crash couch and punched the armrest keypad with unnecessary force. He felt the straps of his crash couch tighten around him. Carol sat in the crash couch next to him, strapped herself in, then turned and looked at Bruno directly.

That was when Bruno became truly frightened. Carol had tears in her eyes. *Carol*.

"Okay," he managed in a calm tone. "Go on, tell me. My crash couch autodoc has sedatives." He struggled to find something humorous to say. "Don't tell me. You've found somebody new."

Carol ignored the joke. Her face was ashen, with deep lines Bruno had never really noticed before. "You know about the EMP bomb?" she asked quietly.

Bruno felt a burning memory of the horrible black light rise unwillingly in his memory and made a face. He nodded, forcing himself to concentrate.

"You unplugged me," Bruno said simply.

"Yes. Though it was more like tearing your wires out of the console by hand." She looked away and brushed tears from her face, clearly embarrassed. "The electromagnetic pulse would have killed you, Tacky. Fried your brain. Inductance almost burnt you out, anyway."

"I know." His brain still felt full of ashes and old scar tissue. "You did the right thing." Bruno's thoughts were slow, clogged. In his fuzzy memory, he could see the pandemonium on the navigation deck of *Sun-Tzu* as the enemy EMP struck the hull. Echoes of miniature lightning bolts shot from the console to his now-missing interface cable. The pale past edge of a horrible pain sliced into his recall. He reached up and touched the Linker socket in his neck, which felt somehow charred, still hot to his touch.

Which was impossible, of course.

"The autodoc says you have some brain damage." Carol's words were now studied and clipped, her tone clinical. She was not looking at him. "Your electronic prostheses are trying to compensate for the damage." Carol looked terrible, he realized. What else was wrong?

Bruno forced a smile, again feeling his dry lips crack. "Well, enough about me," he said brightly. "What else has been happening while I've been on vacation?"

She said nothing, eyes glinting in the bright lighting of the tiny cabin.

Finally, Bruno took a more serious tone.

"Captain-my-captain," he told her quietly, "there wasn't anything else you could have done. I would have died for sure if the full charge had hit my chipware." He shrugged a little, forcing bravado into his voice. "We don't even know how bad the . . . damage is. Either I can be fixed or I can't." He took her hand in his. "We'll find out together."

Carol smiled a little, as much tired as sad, then told him everything. The images were nightmarish, confirming Bruno's high opinion of her abilities. Carrying his convulsing body down long darkened corridors to *Dolittle*. Powering down all major shipboard systems in decoy, and setting up the confinement-field booby trap for the kzin invaders—a project she had set up long ago during a paranoid watch period. Launching *Dolittle* and fleeing the *Sun-Tzu*.

Bruno scratched some flaky material away from his cheek. "How long till *Sun-Tzu* goes up?"

Carol gestured to the holographic display in the main screen, which had reached zero.

Her smile was as feral as any kzin's. "They have about three hours now. The confinement fields will appear normal for a time, then asymptotically degrade to catastrophic failure. And they won't know it until it's much too late—unless they have direct feeds from the core."

Bruno raised an eyebrow, curious.

"I set up a false telemetry system. If they tap into what looks like the core telemetry data feed, they'll read that the core is humming along just copacetic and fine." She thinned her lips into a cold smile. "Until the confinement fields fail and they fry, of course."

"Clever," he managed, pleased. "Can they stop it?"

"I don't think so." She shook her head, counting reasons off on her fingers as she went. "Not unless they are experts in complex systems and cryptography. First, they have to find out the obvious telemetry feed is a decoy. Then they have to locate the correct cable routings without our diagnostic equipment. Finally, they have to learn subsystem architecture and gain control over the field coils and ionizing lasers."

"All in a few hours," Bruno replied. "No way."

He reached across and touched Carol's hand. His own fingers still didn't want to move, and felt old and clumsy.

"How did you get everybody out of the suspension chambers into the cargo bay?" he asked, tilting his head toward the sealed door at the rear of the tiny cabin.

Carol looked down at her console and said nothing.

"You left them," Bruno said flatly.

She nodded, still looking down. "There wasn't any choice," Carol replied calmly, her captain voice surfacing again. The deepening lines on her face showed what that decision had cost her.

Bruno's head whirled. He and Carol had known all twenty-nine of the men and women in coldsleep. Trained with them, drunk with them, argued with them, studied with them. They all had names, hobbies, favorite drinks, games.

Now they were ratcat food.

Carol whistled through her teeth tunelessly for a moment, then reached over and squeezed his shoulder.

"Bruno," she said seriously, "you know perfectly well that I couldn't have saved them. And they will be avenged very soon."

It occurred to Bruno that Carol had made decisions like this many times in the past, during her Second Wave piloting, and as a Third Wave squadron commander. Decisions that saved or took lives.

"Does it ever get easier?" he asked, finally.

She knew what Bruno meant. "You remember each one of them, every waking moment of your life."

He sighed. Gingerly, he forced slow and shaky fingers into a dataglove and looked carefully at the holoscreen. He had to—

Suddenly, Bruno looked over at the coiled and clipped interface cable at the side of the control console. He felt something tear in his mind and heart.

What if I can't Link anymore? Bruno thought wildly. His heart seemed to hammer in his chest, and he took several deep breaths to calm himself. *Give it time*, he repeated over and over again to himself, like a mantra.

"What is it?" Carol asked, trying not to notice where Bruno had been looking.

"Nothing," he said harshly. "Could you please bring me up to date?"

Carol took the hint and walked him through the status windows. He was still mentally slow, but he could follow the events since the EMP bomb had hit the *Sun-Tzu*.

Linked, I could— He shoved the thought out of his mind, and focused his attention on the small holoscreens above the main console. Ordered arrays of numbers marched across his line of sight, complex diagrams flowed and blinked; sterile representations of their life-and-death situation. Their lives as a column of glowing numbers.

After a few moments, Bruno turned to Carol. Their situation looked grim.

Bruno spoke first. "Are we going to be far enough away from *Sun-Tzu* when the confinement fields fail?"

"I don't know," she replied, her tone just as even as Bruno's. "I think that we can cycle back some of the power from the superconductive wings into a makeshift magnetic umbrella. That'll take care of the charged particles."

"What about the gamma?"

Carol smiled without humor. "We'll just have to take our chances with the prompt effects, shipmate."

Chapter Fifteen

Rrowl-Captain equalized pressures and popped open his helmet. The rank, moist odor of monkeys too long confined thickened the darkness around him, swarming into his wide nostrils.

He controlled the urge to spit in distaste, and tried to breathe through his mouth.

Other Heroes of the boarding party were floating just inside the alien airlock, waiting respectfully for the captain of *Belly-Slasher* to signal them. At his hiss of permission, they opened their own helmets. Rrowl-Captain could hear the snarls of disgust at the humid jungle smells in the tunnel, like a Jotoki biome. The only light was from their helmet lamps. Sounds echoed harshly in the gloom, then faded away to a damp silence.

He shifted his grip on the fragile primate handholds and looked around the access tunnel. Blank and featureless walls, empty except for the long ladders and equipment docks he could see by helmet light. He snarled a hissing swearword at the monkeys' lack of gravity-polarizer technology. Primitives!

Alien-Technologist had used an echo-thumper to determine that atmosphere existed inside the outer hatch at the bow of the derelict monkeyship. The crewkzin then erected a sealed bubbledome around the airlock, and cut through the thick metal with heavy lasers, revealing the long dark access tunnel.

No trap-bombs, no cowardly monkey tricks.

Rrowl-Captain, as Dominant Leader, was first to set claw and fang inside the alien spacecraft. His victory, his prize.

The captain snarled orders, and crewkzin anchored powerful search lamps near the power feed that had been snaked through the airlock. Reassuring orange light blazed down the long access tunnel, banishing the darkness into small shadows. Rrowl-Captain could see the glint of another airlock far, far away in the darkness.

With a start, he tightened his grip on the monkey handhold as his perspective suddenly shifted. The tunnel pointed *down*, his alarmed reflexes informed him. He and his crew appeared to be hanging precariously at the top of a very long vertical tunnel. It did not matter to his brain, evolved on a planet, that the contra-matter reaction drive was providing only a tiny proportion of gravitational acceleration at present. It did not matter that the captain intellectually knew that he would not plummet like a stone down the shaft, but would drift like a bit of fluff combed from his pelt.

Kzin feared falling.

"Alien-Technologist," he rasped, mastering his fear after several deep breaths.

The kzin made an awkward microgravity leap to Rrowl-Captain's side from across the tunnel, using a reaction pistol judiciously, and snapped a suit bolt onto a nearby crossbar. The captain was impressed, but refused to show it.

"Command me," Alien-Technologist said without bravado, clearly as nervous in the tunnel as his captain.

"Lead your party to the inner airlock and secure this monkeyship."

"At once, Dominant One!"

Rrowl-Captain watched with grudging admiration as the octal of Heroes under Alien-Technologist's command rappelled down the tunnel. The figures in space armor swiftly became smaller as they descended, using secured lines and reaction pistols.

Lifting one wrist, he clumsily punched up the shipboard commlink with gloved fingers. Static hissed and fizzed in his ears.

"Command me!" growled-and-spat the low reply from Navigator on the command bridge.

"Status."

"The monkeyship continues to operate as before. Drone remotes have been dispatched to all major sectors of the outer hull." Navigator's tone sounded confident and full of Heroic pride. "No sign of traps or trickery."

"Open a telemetry channel to my portable thinplate."

"At once!" came Navigator's reply.

Rrowl-Captain unfolded his personal thinplate and accessed data downloaded from *Belly-Slasher*. Status reports stalked one another across the thinplate under the captain's gaze. The alien spacecraft was indeed running as if derelict, with only the contra-matter drive and magnetic field arrays operational. No beacons, no navigational control.

He spent some time reviewing the data, running a tongue over his sharp teeth in thought, waiting for the remote drones to complete their scans.

"Dominant One," crackled his headset in Alien-

Technologist's voice, "we have secured the alien ship as you commanded."

"Did you find monkey bodies?"

"Yes," came the reply with a pleased growl. "We have found nearly four octals of the humans in artificial hibernation." There was a pause. "The maintenance subsystems appear to be both intact and functional."

Rrowl-Captain knew what Alien-Technologist was thinking. *Fresh, living monkey meat*. Saliva washed his fangs in anticipation. He rasped his rough tongue across thin black lips. Ship rations were not always pleasing to a Noble Hero's palate. Still, first things first.

"Do you mean that this ship was piloted by machines?"

"All hibernation couches are occupied."

Rrowl-Captain wanted to stretch his batwing ears in confusion and not a little suspicion. The monkeys relied very heavily indeed on untrustworthy automation, true. But to leave such a fearsome reaction drive under automated control smacked of madness.

They do not think like Heroes, the captain reminded himself yet again. *No alien thinks like a Hero. But what kind of artificial mind could have directed such an uncanny defense?*

"Have you found their command bridge?" he finally rasped.

A tone of pride entered the hissing voice in his helmet. "We have, Leader. The room has not been touched, and is waiting for you."

Repressing a shudder, Rrowl-Captain attached a belt loop to the guide lines left by his boarding party, and slid down the monkeyship access shaft in one slow, nightmare fall. From time to time, he fired his own reaction pistol to slow his dreamlike descent, barely suppressing his mews of fear as the tunnel walls slid past. When he finally reached the bottom of the tunnel, his posture ensured that none of the crewkzin dared look his way as he entered the inner airlock.

The interior was cramped, narrow. Lights were strung down empty corridors, spreading clear orange illumination into dark corners. Rrowl-Captain could hear hiss-and-spit conversation from engineers and specialists bent over alien equipment. He had known that the monkeys were puny, but his back complained painfully as he stooped under several hatch fittings. It would have been better to stalk these alien corridors on all fours, but space armor prevented that posture.

The captain rudely cuffed a low-ranking kzin apprentice standing guard. "Nameless One," he rumbled, "direct me to the monkey command bridge."

The other kzin saluted smartly and led his captain down one darkened corridor to a small area equipped with two tiny acceleration chairs and accompanying consoles. The nameless kzin saluted and stood at the hatchway, waiting for further instructions.

The captain of *Belly-Slasher* ceremonially urinated at all four cardinal points of the monkeyship command bridge, marking it as kzin territory.

And Rrowl-Captain's property in the Name of the Riit Patriarch of Kzin-home.

He examined the console carefully, looking at the burnt and damaged equipment clearly caused by the magneto-electrical pulse. He sniffed delicately at a heavy fiber-optic cable that had been torn from some kind of socket. He sniffed the broken end of the cable again, more thoroughly.

Something was wrong, Rrowl-Captain knew with a start, his ruff rising in alarm within his space armor. Containing a snarl, he swiftly looked from side to side, half expecting the very walls to burst open with hordes of laser-wielding monkeys.

Fangs did not fit into this wound channel as they should.

He whirled suddenly and sniffed at the empty acceleration chairs. The scent was very fresh.

The captain began to growl low in his throat.

"Alien-Technologist," Rrowl-Captain hissed into his commlink.

"Leader!" came the reply in his helmet.

"Where are you at present?"

"I am studying the contra-matter drive. Dominant One, the brute force of the monkey technology, without artifice or subtlety, is astounding. Brute force primitives. They have wrestled contra-particles into a high vacuum chamber, and—"

"Enough," the captain interrupted. "Tell me again that all of the hibernation chambers are occupied."

"It is so, Dominant One. This spacecraft, for all its apparent size, is quite tiny—an iceball with a small life-bubble deep inside."

Rrowl-Captain blinked in thought, staring at the empty chairs and savoring the scents he had found on them. "Is it possible," he hissed, "that two of the monkeys have but recently entered hibernation?"

There was a short pause.

"No, Leader. Even with alien machinery, it is clear that all of the hibernation chambers have been occupied for several years."

"Report to me at once," Rrowl-Captain shrieked. He punched up Navigator in *Belly-Slasher* on his commlink and spat syllables quickly, issuing orders and demanding information.

It took some time to prove what Rrowl-Captain's nose had suspected. There had indeed been two monkeys alive and warm inside the iceball of a spacecraft not long before Rrowl-Captain's boarding party entered. There were no bodies, and all of the hibernation chambers were in long-term use.

Even an unblooded kitten could set fangs into

these facts: The two monkeys were hiding or had fled.

Judicious use of Alien-Technologist's sonic echo-thumper sounded the walls of the monkeyship, and after some search found an empty shipbay, hidden behind a false bulkhead. Instruments detected residual radiation from a fusion drive lining what was clearly a collapsed escape tunnel through reinforced ice.

Navigator's instruments aboard *Belly-Slasher*, using the remote drones and Alien-Technologist's growing intuition of monkey ways, found a magnetic anomaly receding quickly from them. It was decelerating very rapidly indeed, and seemed to have originated from the derelict monkeyship.

"Why are the honorless leaf-eaters running and not fighting?" Rrowl-Captain growled in anger and frustration. "Why would they flee, and leave the defenseless bodies of their comrades to us?"

Kzin never let their fellow Heroes become prey.

Alien-Technologist averted his eyes, folded ears against skull inside his helmet. "Because they cannot win, Leader, and flee witlessly before Noble Heroes."

The captain slashed claws in rebuke at the other kzin's lickspittle foolishness. "Hardly," he rasped angrily. "This event reeks of monkey trickery." He paused a moment in carnivorous thought. *Think like a duplicitous monkey*, he reminded himself with vast distaste.

"The contra-matter drive is stable?"

"Yes, Leader. We have tapped into the monkey telemetry cables, and found the confinement fields steady."

There was a snarl of static over the commlink from Navigator, still aboard *Belly-Slasher*. "Dominant One, I do not mean to intrude, but there is an anomalous finding—"

"Report," Rrowl-Captain growled.

"Remote drones near the reaction drive section show increasing levels of radioactivity," the tiny voice finished.

The darkened monkey corridor seemed to whirl around Rrowl-Captain and close in on him like an implacable enemy's claws. He felt a growl growing within his throat.

"You have no other manner," he hissed slowly to the other kzin standing before him, "to determine the status of the reaction drive than what the monkeys *wish* us to know?" Alien-Technologist looked at his captain blankly.

"Leader, I do not understand. These are standard telemetry lines linking the contra-matter drive directly to these navigation consoles . . . hrrrrr," he said, falling silent in thought.

Rrowl-Captain barely contained his fury. "Confirm the status of the contra-matter drive at once. Directly. In person if necessary. I feel enemy eyes upon us, and scent danger." Rrowl-Captain repressed the desire to slash an ear from the monkey-trusting Alien-Technologist for his trophy loop. "In the meantime, the rest of the crew not associated with you will return to *Belly-Slasher*."

Rrowl-Captain snorted his displeasure at Alien-Technologist, who hung bouncing in the microgravity like a toothless kitten's prey-toy. He ignored the other kzin's humbled salute and turned to leave the navigation chamber abruptly.

The captain would lead *Belly-Slasher* on a diverting exercise, a small hunt for the escaped monkeys, who would rather run than fight. Perhaps by the time he had returned with his trophies, Alien-Technologist and his crew would have truly secured the monkeyship prize. He entered the access tunnel, and hooked the guide line to a reinforced loop on his battle armor. Rrowl-Captain snarled and leaped upward in the microgravity, toward the outer airlock, firing his reaction pistol downward for added emphasis.

He never looked down.

Rrowl-Captain entered *Belly-Slasher*, feeling the comforting artificial gravitation firm beneath his taloned boots once more. Suddenly, slurred hisses of Alien-Technologist yowled over the commlink in a frenzied rush of harsh syllables.

He could not make out the words, but the tone was clear: Fear. Warning.

Chapter Sixteen

Chapter Sixteen

Carol grinned widely as the holoscreen overloaded with *Sun-Tzu's* incandescent death.

Flash—*blank*—and the display reset, showing the horrific radiance of the matter-antimatter explosion in muted colors.

"Bang," said Bruno softly.

The cloud of plasma and radiation that had once been *Sun-Tzu* began to spread out in a complex, fluorescence-colorful pattern. Magnetic fields and relativistic impacts with the interstellar medium made the cloud look like a living thing crawling under a microscope.

Carol leaned over and kissed him with sudden passion.

"As usual," she murmured into his ear, nuzzling gently, "you have a gift for understatement." She ran the back of her hand very softly across her lover's face. "Would you accept the intention, if not the act?"

Carol was gratified to see a genuine smile on Bruno's face.

"Well," he replied, "the situation being what it is, I suppose that I can understand your position."

She winked at him, gave a sly smile. "We'll discuss positions later," she whispered, and turned back to the holoscreen.

That is, she thought, *if we aren't puking our guts out from radiation poisoning*. She knew that Bruno was thinking much the same thing. Their flirting words were both supportive and diverting.

And, despite the danger they faced, fun besides.

Bruno touched her hand. "How big of a dose?" he asked, pointing at the gaudy lights of the explosion still spreading on the main holoscreen.

She watched the exposure figures in a window of her holoscreen slow and stabilize. The wave of hard gamma radiation from the antimatter explosion that had arrived with the image of that detonation had passed. Photons were photons, after all. Carol knew that it didn't matter if the quantum bundles were in visual or X-ray wavelengths; they all traveled at an implacable 300,000 kps in vacuum.

Carol sighed. The figures were not good, but they would live.

"Well, we won't be feeling like many gourmet dinners for a while."

Bruno nodded. "Suppose I can stand to lose a bit of mass. Gotta be able to stay the Captain's favorite. Keep the competition at bay and all that."

She reached over and stroked his flat belly. "Padding isn't a bad thing, my vain crewmate."

"What about the charged particle slowpokes still on their way?"

"I'm working on it."

Carol had already done as much as she could until the bulk of the radiation arrived, triumphant yet harmful messenger heralding the death of the ratcats. And, much as she hated to think about it, from the deaths of almost thirty of her friends and crewmates, frozen in coldsleep. People for whom she had been responsible, as captain of *Sun-Tzu*.

She had carefully tuned the superconductive wings of *Dolittle* to maximize magnetic deflection of the incoming wave of charged particles. Also, Carol had turned the ship sternward to the spreading bloom of *Sun-Tzu's* death, using the long fuel tank as additional shielding. There was nothing else to do but wait.

While they waited for the radiation front to strike *Dolittle*, Carol reviewed the autodoc data. Bruno seemed to have recovered well physically from his trauma aboard *Sun-Tzu*. The wrenching of "manual de-Linkage"—she frowned at the antiseptic term—left little to no physical damage. Stimulants and mood modifiers kept his mental state relatively calm and normal.

As Bruno had said, his electronic prostheses would repair the brain damage—or not. There was nothing either of them could do about it. She didn't want to die alone, without him. She remained silent for long moments.

"Okay," Bruno sighed, "as usual, the Captain will speak when the Captain pleases. Blessed be the Name of the Captain."

"Next you'll be praising me as 'from whom all blessings flow.' " She smiled, despite herself. He knew her well.

"A little much, perhaps."

"Flattery will get you anywhere, cabin boy."

"Sounds like sexual harassment to me," Bruno replied in mock outrage, batting his eyelashes at her outrageously.

Carol snorted laughter. "You've been scanning datachips of Early's history lectures again, haven't you? That term hasn't been in use for two hundred years."

"How would you know?" A sly grin crossed Bruno's face.

She squeezed his biceps hard. "You always know how to make me laugh, lover. Thanks for bringing my good mood back."

They said nothing for a time.

"Any time now, isn't it?" Bruno asked calmly.

"That's a big affirmative."

There was a soundless flash behind their eyelids as the radiation front struck *Dolittle*. Radiation sleeted through the magnetic fields surrounding the ship, the hull walls, the long, slushed deuterium tank, and their own bodies—all in a microsecond.

"Well," Bruno remarked, "you always show me the most *interesting* places, my dear."

Carol ignored his nervous humor and pored over the holoscreen datastream in the biotelemetry window. After a moment, Bruno began to help her.

Finally, she sighed with relief. Their cumulative doses were high, but not quite lethal. Their prompt doses would ensure a slight fever and nausea, easily handled by drugs from the autodoc.

"It looks like we'll live," Carol said.

"For a while." Bruno's tone was quiet and somber.

"No more Project Cherubim. And we aren't going to make it to Wunderland or Home, are we?"

"Doubtful. Maybe we can rig up a couple of coldsleep bunks from the autodoc spare parts. We sure don't have a decade's worth of recycler or supply capacity." He brightened a bit. "Maybe another Earth ship will find us while we're in coldsleep."

"Or a kzin warcraft, more likely," she reminded him. "We could wake up a piece at a time."

Again, silence hung thick in *Dolittle*.

"All of it was for nothing," Bruno finally said, his tone black and dead.

"No," she replied firmly. "Not for nothing. You and I got together, love."

He squeezed her hand in agreement.

"And," Carol pointed out, "we waxed three ratcat ships in the bargain. Maybe two hundred kzin flash-fried to vapor. That must be worth something on the scorechip."

Bruno's face was suddenly slack, a bit like his Linked expression. Concern flashed through Carol's mind.

"What is it, Tacky?" she asked lightly, keeping the worry from her voice.

"I hope that we took out all the kzin ships."

Carol gestured at the holoscreen. "Sure we did. Look at the fireworks." The antimatter explosion was immense, brilliantly colored. It occurred to her that the garish cloud would eventually be visible across light-years.

"Can we be certain?" Bruno's tone was odd, a little machinelike.

"Is that a prediction, that we *didn't* get them all?" she inquired, frowning.

"I don't think that I can Link anymore, so I'm just guessing. Maybe I'm just worried." His tone and facial expression were back to normal.

Carol leaned over and rubbed her stiff strip haircut against his cheek. "You will never guess how attractive I find a simple human guess, my friend."

Chapter Seventeen

Rrowl-Captain scented his own death in the cramped singleship fighter. He closed his nostrils from the stench of unchallenging prey. The kzin knew that he had taken more than a lethal dose of radiation in the detonation of the monkeyship. The captain was far from the medical tank in the wreckage of *Belly-Slasher*, and the supplies aboard the singleship were minimal.

There had been little time to plan an escape.

Alien-Technologist's warning had come late, too late. Rrowl-Captain and his crew had engaged *Belly-Slasher*'s gravity polarizers at maximum acceleration, but were only a few hundred kilometers from the human spacecraft when the contra-matter containment fields had failed. Damage had been heavy: his precious spacecraft hulled and broken, his crew torn and bloody and mostly dead. The One Fanged God had inexplicably spared Rrowl-Captain of all but the radiation exposure.

His mind filled with the memories of mewling Heroes in agony—blinded, seared, poisoned by monkey treachery. Even those crewkzin still breathing would, like Rrowl-Captain, soon die of the radiation taint in their blood and bone.

His dreams of regaining his honor and reward, his Warrior Heart, were shattered by monkey perfidy and cowardice.

Rrowl-Captain had managed to seal his space armor in the confusing aftermath of the explosion. He had picked his way through the twisted wreckage of *Belly-Slasher*, down black corridors filled with the drifting corpses of his Heroes—or worse, the crewkzin not yet dead. Eventually, he had reached a still-intact singleship fighter, *Sharpened-Fang*. The small warcraft lacked the strong gravitic protective fields of larger kzin spacecraft, and was not designed for individual near-luminal travel.

He had little to lose. And nothing to gain but a Hero's final vengeance.

Rrowl-Captain knew that he was dying, as he held back the wrenching pain he felt in his innards. It was like shards of broken glass, grinding deep; like the sharp teeth of some enemy at his liver, chewing. The epithelial lining of his stomach and intestines had loosened, leading to the violent nausea of lethal radiation poisoning. He could literally feel the blisters rising on his body, as radiation-outraged skin layers began to die. Fur began to fall from his pelt in handfuls.

Rrowl-Captain hawked and spat blood onto the tiny deck, to mix with the pool of drying vomit already left there. He knew his time was short. At least he had a chance to show his honor, his Warrior Heart, before he met the One Fanged God. The memory of his dead litter-brother would demand nothing less.

Rrowl-Captain would take these despicable monkeys as his honor-slaves into the Hunting Ground Beyond.

He peered into the singleship thinplate screen with damaged eyes, searching. Finally, Rrowl-Captain found the human escape vessel. The coward-vessel had wrapped huge magnetic fields around itself, according to his instruments. Rrowl-Captain snarled as he altered *Sharpened-Fang*'s course, his mouth dry and scratchy. The air tasted of death and failure, and his very fangs were loosening in his head.

The escaping monkeyship with its queer gossamer wings could not maneuver, and the fusion drive seemed minimal. All that the human ship seemed capable of was magnetic deceleration and minor course corrections. His thinplate screen analysis indicated an impressively high level of deceleration, in fact. The stresses upon the little spacecraft must be tremendous, he mused, hissing in readiness to do battle.

Rrowl-Captain increased *Sharpened-Fang*'s velocity, pushing the gravitic polarizers to their safety limits, and beyond. The ripping-cloth noise of the drive began to sound like a predatory scream, filling his folded ears. Purple warning lights flashed on the control console and warning tones yowled. His head pounded as the fabric of space itself twisted savagely. The monkeyship grew larger on his screen. Rrowl-Captain readied his weapons panel, his black claws clicking on keypads.

Something nagged at the captain. What, he wondered, could these craven monkeys do with the waste energy from deceleration? Only by draining energy at enormous rates could the strange vessel take significant advantage of magnetic deceleration. The ship was small, and would have little need for prodigious energy sources. . . .

Green hell suddenly filled Rrowl-Captain's thinplate viewscreen, which went blank in a frying crackle of circuit overload.

He keened in surprise and fear. Alarms shrieked in the tiny cabin. Ablative microconstruction in the hull of the singleship vaporized and shoved *Sharpened-Fang* violently to one side, out of the deadly beam of the humans' laser weaponry. Secondary sensors and viewscreens came smoothly on-line.

The alien beam showed itself within the cloud of vaporized hull material surrounding *Sharpened-Fang*. The laser reached out for Rrowl-Captain again, like the implacable clawed Finger of the One Fanged God.

He squelched his fear with a feral snarl, and initiated further evasive maneuvers. This time, light-speed limitations were on Rrowl-Captain's side. The gravitic drives screamed with the increased demand. He smelled burning insulation from failing electronic components.

Rrowl-Captain's claws extended and clicked across his console keypads. *Sharpened-Fang* began moving randomly, avoiding the deadly spears of laser light that stabbed at him.

What weapons could Rrowl-Captain bring to bear? Particle beams would be near-useless in the face of such magnetic deflection fields. His laser cannon was not formidable at this distance. *Sharpened-Fang* possessed only a small armament array, being designed for close approach, ship-to-ship assaults.

However, the singleship was equipped with a few special-purpose weapons. Rrowl-Captain reviewed shipboard inventory swiftly, then blinked twice. With a kzin cough of a chuckle, he realized that he knew how to render the monkey escape ship fangless.

The huge but delicate wings of the vessel were superconductive! Their passage through the magnetic fields of interstellar space provided the power for their laser array, little different in principle than the electrical engines of ancient history. The captain licked a crusty tongue across cracked lips, and drooled bloody saliva in anticipation.

The wings were the monkeys' weakness. Without them, they were powerless—in the literal sense of the term.

Rrowl-Captain knew his strategy was dangerous, but filled with honor. He punched in a final sequence of keypads, hiss-spat a prayer to the One Fanged God, and scream-and-leaped *Sharpened-Fang* toward the alien ship.

Outsiders Three

Fury. Observe this gross insult of plasma and sundered field lines! How has this remote lack of action served the Divine Radiants?

Worry. One hotlife craft has been atomized by fundamental annihilation as the other-node predicted. What damage will be wreaked by this event?

Anger. The plasma cloud will be vast, and the twisted force-lines will eventually impinge upon the Sacred Region. The insult to the Divine Radiants and Their Design will be grievous.

Woe. This local-node had hoped . . .

Impatience. Hope is not sufficient! A great gout of highly ionized plasma grows—directly where it should not.

Grudging-agreement. Once more, this local-node and the other-node concur with One mind. Yet the constraints of the Treaty . . .

Decisiveness. Treaties with feral heretics are transcended by the Here-and-Now! This local-and-other nodes, as One mind, shall act!

Agreement-with-caution. Truth. Yet the {^^^///} have Sentinels as well. Surely the feral nodes may reach conclusions and act as well as this local-and-other node at One. First, this local-and-other node should determine the nature and potential of this insult.

Irritation-frustration. How does the other-node suggest such a determination be performed? The nature and intent of vermin remains unimportant.

Caution. Yet the actions of the hotlife motes have grave consequences. This local-node argues that the offending vermin be acquired and their inner and external patterns deep-analyzed for action and intent. Consider these facts for congruence to the Great Pattern.

Anger-acceptance. Truth. Such caution is implied from the High Texts. One. Mark this local-node's arguments, however.

Agreement. This local-node is of One mind with the other-node, including the reservations of the other-node. Perhaps further analysis before the acquisition of the hotlife motes is warranted. The feral {^^^///} may have reached the same conclusions as the Local Nexus.

Resolve. Enough! There has been sufficient debate and discussion. This local-node sends the initiator signal. Muster the many! The Nexus acts!

Chapter Eighteen

Bruno watched Carol's fingers on the fire-control console with some surprise. It was a delicate, deadly ballet she danced, one hand in a dataglove making delicate adjustments, while the other hand punched and stroked keypads.

In retrospect, it made sense to Bruno that Carol was skilled at battle stations; after all, she was twice a combat veteran. But Bruno had been spoiled by the absolute certainty of Linkage. While Transcended, he simply made things happen with a thought. He didn't actually have to *do* anything at all. He *knew*.

Bruno frowned. Every time he had thought of Linkage since emerging from the autodoc tank, he had developed a pounding headache. Strange images with mixed sensoria intruded. He felt as if he could somehow taste colors, and feel sounds. It was frightening, but somehow familiar. Bruno had convinced himself that the incidents were a by-product of his macrocircuit neuronal matrices rerouting around the nerve damage.

Or, he thought grimly, it could just be the brain damage itself.

He firmly put that thought from his mind; it was unproductive at present. On the holoscreen, Bruno saw the icon of the kzin singleship moving in little jerks and starts across the idealized starscape. Carol kept trying to center the fire-control cursor in front of the presumed path of the alien ship before activating the hugely powerful gas lasers powered by *Dolittle*'s deceleration.

"C'mere, you little ratcat," she crooned to herself. "Just hold course a bit longer. . . ."

She missed again. The kzin singleship was closer.

"You want me to try to Link up?" he asked without thinking, even as the pounding in his skull began anew.

Carol didn't even look away from the holoscreen. "Tacky, dear," she said in a distracted tone, "you don't even want to think about attaching that interface socket in your neck to anything with electrical current in it— not until we can do a full autodiagnostic on the rig."

She was right. Linkage might kill him now.

He just hated feeling stupid and slow. He used to be so much *more*. Not just a human . . .

"No," Carol continued, "you just let old Mumma Carol take care of our little ratcat infestation." She paused for a moment, stretching her fingers luxuriously. "I have whacked more than one kzin singleship in my deep dark past."

"So we have a chance?"

"You want to bet every credit in inventory on it, shipmate." Carol slapped his arm with her free hand and went back to work.

Bruno busied himself by reviewing *Dolittle*'s diagnostics and spare-parts inventory. If he and Carol survived this dogfight, maybe he really could cobble together some kind of coldsleep chamber. If not, they faced slow asphyxiation in their own waste gases when the recyclers finally failed.

"Heads up," Carol cried, scoring another hit with the main laser array. Bruno saw the cloud of vaporized ship-material fluoresce in the aftermath of the laser light. "Ah, taxes take ablation shielding," she swore bitterly as the kzin icon emerged from the cloud under full acceleration, apparently undamaged.

Bruno saw something. "What's that?" he asked, using his own dataglove to point into the holoscreen. A tiny blinking point of light was moving swiftly toward them.

Carol clucked at her too-focused attention and opened a realtime window in the holoscreen. She magnified and amplified ambient starlight for illumination. A small, glittering globe flew toward them across the relativity-squashed starscape.

"Bomb?" Bruno asked.

Carol shook her head. "I'm getting no readings other than faint and indeterminate electronics leakage. No fissionables, fusion materials, monopoles."

"How fast?"

"It's coming in at just under a hundred KPS, relative." She smiled tightly. "Let's see how whatever it is likes a little light on the subject." She started to place the fire-control cursor over the icon representing the mysterious globe in the tactical window of the holoscreen.

"Wait!" Bruno exclaimed, pointing at the realtime window.

As they both watched in surprise, the globe smoothly separated into two hemispheres. The half globes whirled around one another almost too swiftly for the eye to see, then began to slow as the distance between the two hemispheres increased.

"It looks like a bolo," Bruno breathed, remembering his history chips. "The two pieces have to be connected by something. Can't you resolve it?"

Carol shook her head. "Negatory, Tacky. Are you sure that there is something between them?"

Bruno was very sure. Physics was physics, after all. "How else can they be swinging around one another so quickly?"

"You have a point. But it's getting pretty close to us now." Carol set the fire-control cursor directly between the two whirling objects, which were over a kilometer apart now. "Firing full power burst."

For a moment, the entire distance between the two hemispheres blazed with a brilliant green line that hurt the eye, almost too thin to see. It vanished instantly. Enhancing infrared did not show anything, either.

Bruno swore another nonsensical oath Buford Early had taught him, something about water birds and sex. "Carol," he said tensely, "I have a bad feeling we are dealing with monomolecular filament. Shoot for either of the hemispheres, now!"

It took several full-power shots to convince Carol that even the enormous power of their laser array was being leached away by the apparent superconductivity of the filament material, only one molecule thick. The hemispheres seemed to be as invulnerable as the invisible filament between them. Seconds after a direct hit, the slowly twirling hemispheres had cooled to ambient temperatures.

"You had best maneuver us out of the way," Bruno told her as the alien whirligig drew closer to *Dolittle*. "That filament will pass right through the hull like a cutting laser through aluminum veneer."

"Damn!" Carol's face was a mask of concentration.

But as Bruno had feared, the twirling hemispheres were guided, not simply ballistic. Further, Carol occasionally had to blast the laser battery at the kzin singleship, which fired off several laser bolts of its own at *Dolittle*. Damage had been minimal, since the kzin singleship had clearly been designed for close-quarter battles, but the diversion did seriously degrade her performance with regard to what had become the main threat.

Bruno again felt the headache, thinking how he might have handled this situation in Linkage. The ship was after all designed to be operated by a Linker. He stoked up the fusion drive to full power, trying to maneuver *Dolittle*. The superconductive wings could not be used for course changes, only deceleration or long, slow turns. His course changes were minimal, due to the ungainliness of the wings.

The strange enemy weapon grew closer to *Dolittle*.

With a sinking feeling, Bruno noticed that the kzin singleship was silent, keeping its distance.

"Impact coming up," Carol sang out. She roughly swung the ship on its axis.

The twirling hemispheres missed *Dolittle*, but neatly sheared off the starboard superconductive wing. In one window of the holoscreen, Bruno had a glimpse of the severed gossamer assembly twisting and falling away into the darkness. Half the green telltale status lights on the command console flashed red.

"Close," Carol breathed.

"Carol, the wing was the target of that weapon, not the ship proper."

Carol wiped sweat from her brow, and did not look away from the holoscreen.

"Sure, Tacky," she said evenly. "The ratcat wants us intact. To take us apart piece by piece."

"Lasers still operational?"

"Yes, at half power," Carol replied, and raised a jet black eyebrow.

Neither of them mentioned the larger problem. With one of the superconductive wings gone, it would be nearly impossible for *Dolittle* to decelerate to nonrelativistic speeds in a straight line. They would be turning to port as they slowed.

Carol fired another laser blast at the icon of the kzin singleship, while Bruno scratched his interface socket idly. He powered up particle-beam and X-ray pump bomblets. The laser array powered by their remaining superconductive wing was their major weapon, but Bruno wanted all of *Dolittle*'s armament available at Carol's whim.

He smiled to himself. Carol was actually doing quite well, considering that *Dolittle* was supposed to be piloted by a non-brain-damaged and fully Linked Bruno Takagama.

Suddenly, their crash couches tightened around them as the universe seemed to jerk and twist violently—then relax again. Alarms buzzed and whooped in the tiny cabin of *Dolittle*. Alert windows automatically opened on the main holoscreen, displaying schematics and updated diagnostics.

"Censored dammit," Carol shouted, her hands freezing on her console for a moment in sheer Belter reflex. "What's going on?" Even as she spoke, her hands were dancing across her console to look for the answer.

Carol fell silent as she stared at the forward holoscreen windows. Almost as an afterthought, she slammed a keypad with her fist, silencing the alarms.

Bruno did not believe the readings, nor the screen.

"Carol," he said softly, in wonder. He shook his head.

"Bruno," she replied in flat tones, looking at the realtime forward window in the holoscreen, "would you please tell me what you are seeing?" He could hear her swallow over the low rustle of the ventilation system. "I want to know if I am going schitz."

"Our velocity appears to no longer be zero point seven C," Bruno said, staring openly at the normal-appearing starscape, not squashed or altered by relativistic speeds.

"The superconductive wing batteries are no longer drawing significant power, again suggesting that our velocity is no higher than zero point one C." He paused. "That means the weapons systems are inoperable."

Carol shrugged at Bruno's last comment, her fingers dancing across her console. "Worry about that later, Bruno. Putting fusion drive on standby," she said crisply, as the sensation of gravity faded. Then, the dropping elevator sensation of free fall. "Is the kzin singleship still there?"

"Yes," he replied, still dazed. "It appears to be in the same position, relative to us, as before the . . . incident." Bruno watched the datastream next to the kzin icon in the Tactical window for a moment. "It does not appear to be maneuvering. It's stationary . . . as we are, apparently."

Still feeling very odd, Bruno busied himself with collecting and analyzing the last few minutes of shipboard time. After a moment, Carol reached across and pinched his arm, very hard.

"Bruno!"

"Yes?" he answered politely.

"What is that thing off to starboard?" She pinched him again, still harder, when he didn't answer.

"Oh, that."

"Yeah, that."

"It appears to be an alien spacecraft or other artifact." He paused, cleared his throat loudly, and consulted his console holoscreens with exaggerated caution. "Approximately one hundred kilometers across."

Chapter Nineteen

Rrowl-Captain, eyes wide in fear, stared at his status viewscreen. He shrieked anger and surprise, then retched painfully with his growing sickness. The spasms subsided after a moment.

Time was growing very short indeed.

What power could have instantaneously stopped both *Sharpened-Fang* and his cowardly monkey prey dead-still in interstellar space? Kinetic potential was awesome at near luminal velocities. He didn't know the method, but clearly, the new and unknown spacecraft was the culprit.

The intruder vessel was the size of a small moon, and looked more like a crowded city than a spacecraft. Magnification showed spires and squarish buildings, open areas and domes, tiny motes of light that moved above and through the huge construct. Thin spidery webs extending from the main body of the vessel glowed incandescently in high infrared, bleeding off waste heat into interstellar space. Instruments showed that the moon-ship kept an ambient temperature of forty divisions above Total Cold.

Rrowl-Captain bared his aching fangs, slowly. Monkeys could not have built this ship. Nor could kzin, even as favored sons of the One Fanged God. No race Rrowl-Captain knew of could construct such a vessel.

Perhaps the intruders had intervened on the monkeys' behalf. Rrowl-Captain coughed again, spitting blood.

Memories of greenish light flared in the back of his mind. It would explain much.

He snarled as he pulled out another handful of fur with his blistered fingers. He gulped a few more of his antiradiation capsules, struggling to keep them inside his traitor belly, though the capsules only slowed the inevitable.

No, thought Rrowl-Captain on further reflection, the intruder spacecraft was not intervening on the side of the human monkeys. If that had been their alien intention, surely Rrowl-Captain and *Sharpened-Fang* would even now be mingled as thoroughly dispersed vapor. That was as clear as the fangs in his own jaws.

The intruders were simply meddlers.

Rrowl-Captain consulted his thinplate console. The forward screen revealed the monkeyship hanging dead in space. Even dying of radiation sickness, the captain smiled and rumbled in kzin humor. If the monkeys were not moving, then their power source was inactive.

Meddlers or no meddlers, Rrowl-Captain was going to complete his ceremonial kill. He would be unable to place human ears on his trophy loop, but he would accomplish a task almost as tasty. A final delicacy, in honor of his litter-brother.

With trembling claws, the captain warmed up the strained gravitic polarizer and put the weapons panel on standby. Within a few moments, Rrowl-Captain would finish his scream-and-leap, weapons firing, and destroy the monkey vessel. Then he would deal with these meddling intruders.

A yowling alarm tone halted Rrowl-Captain's ready claw, poised over the initiate keypad.

He looked up with a snarl, and saw many octal-squareds of nightmare black shapes blotting out the stars, living creatures flying through empty space toward *Sharpened-Fang*.

Magnification and vector analysis showed the hordes to originate from the intruder moon-ship. The intruder aliens were even uglier than Jotoki, Rrowl-Captain realized with a hiss of distaste. Thick central stalks surrounded by an octal-and-half of sinuous tendrils— yet bearing tools and wearing harnesses.

Powerful or not, Rrowl-Captain could not let these aliens threaten a Hero's vessel, nor his own plans. He reoriented the weapons panel and prepared to fire.

Chapter Twenty

Like Bruno, Carol was still dazed by the sudden appearance of the titanic alien ship that had somehow halted them in space and now held position, motionless, ten thousand kilometers to starboard. She slowly turned to Bruno, who appeared to be recovering from the shock of the past few minutes. At least he was reviewing data instead of staring blankly at the strangely unshifted stars in the holoscreen.

"Where *is* the ratcat ship?"

Her lover shook his head slightly, tapped on a few keypads. A red circle appeared in the holoscreen. "Just under two hundred kilometers dead ahead, right where it was when things got . . . well, weird."

Weird was the right word, Carol thought. How could *Dolittle* go from 0.7c to dead stop in a second?

She peered at the portion of the holoscreen indicating the kzin singleship for a moment or two, looking for activity. "Looks like the ratcat isn't moving, either."

"Maybe it's just as surprised by recent events as we are."

Carol mulled that one over, then decided to change the subject. She put an autowatch subroutine on the kzin singleship that would set off alarms if the ratcat vessel moved or showed activity. Carol then highlighted the huge alien ship.

"Well, Bruno," she asked brightly, "what do you think?"

Bruno could not tear his eyes from the holoscreen windows. "Like you said, Captain-my-captain. It's the size of a moon."

"A small moon."

"Sure. But what's the point of a *spacecraft* a hundred kilometers across?"

Bruno had made a good point, Carol thought. Further, the alien vessel *looked* more like a city or hive of insects than a spacecraft. There were what appeared to be buildings and domes across its broad and complex expanse. It was baroque and ornate, like some windup Victorian Christmas tree ornament out of a history chip.

"Notice the weblike structures?" Bruno indicated a portion of the realtime magnified view of the moon-ship. "Look at them in IR."

In infrared, the complex webs all over the moon-ship were hundreds of degrees warmer than the rest of the vessel.

"Heat exchangers?" she asked.

Bruno nodded. "I'm betting that they are particularly hot now, after . . . stopping us a bit ago. That must have taken a *lot* of energy."

Carol noticed flocks of tiny lights moving around the spires of the gigantic alien ship. "What are those?"

"No idea," Bruno replied, tweaking the image enhancers. Magnification did not help, only revealing blurred glowing shapes that darted and swooped like living things around upper portions of the moon-ship.

Bruno finally asked the question. "What do we do?"

"Nothing," she replied. "Let them make the first move." Carol reached over and stroked his arm gently. "Face it, Tacky. Whatever they are, they're much more powerful than me and thee. They could swat us to paste anytime. I would rather wait, peacefully, to see what they want with us."

Bruno nodded slowly.

"I just feel stupid and helpless," he finally said, looking away. "I used to know almost everything."

"But only when you were part machine. I like you better as a human." She moved his lips into a smile with her fingers, and was rewarded by the real thing.

"Carol?"

Bruno gestured at the holoscreen with a nervous finger.

"What is it?" she asked.

"The kzin ship is getting visitors."

Long-range scanning showed at least one hundred small objects flying toward the kzin singleship from the huge alien vessel. Extreme magnification showed vague dusky shapes with many arms flitting across the starry blackness. They rotated smoothly as they flew, arms stretched out radial fashion for stability.

"Those must be our new friends," Bruno commented.

Carol said nothing, biting her lip. They would get some idea of the new aliens' intentions from their actions toward the kzin singleship. They must have been moving very quickly to be so close to the ratcat vessel.

A low warning tone sounded.

Carol made a face as she studied the holoscreens. "Looks as if we are going to be entertaining a few visitors of our own," she said, pointing at a small cloud of dots on the short-range scanner window in the main holoscreen. The cloud was growing closer to *Dolittle* by the second, decelerating rapidly.

"Still want me to do nothing?" Bruno asked.

Carol nodded. "Watch the ratcat ship."

As the flock of aliens approached the kzin singleship, it began to move, maneuvering away with its reactionless drive. Extreme magnification showed a pale purple beam of light stretching from one of the tiny hydra shapes to the kzin spacecraft. The whole vessel glowed purple for a moment, then the slight aura faded.

The singleship halted and hung motionless in space. Long-range scanners showed that all electronic emissions from the kzin vessel had ceased. The droves of tiny shapes merged with it.

"As I mentioned," Carol remarked conversationally, "I suspect it would be wise to do nothing."

Bruno smiled without showing his teeth. "Hold that thought, Carol. Our visitors have arrived." He gestured to a holoscreen window displaying a view of the external hull. Many-armed shapes swarmed past the cameras.

"Follow them with the hull cameras, please."

Bruno set up a series of small windows in the holoscreen displaying the external hull of *Dolittle*. The windows showed weaving tendrils, rapid activity.

"Switch to infrared," Carol said after a while. Perhaps the aliens would show up better in the longer wavelengths.

One by one, the windows went blank, showing the multicolored snowy display of holographic static.

"What happened?" she rapped.

"Hardware failure. They're doing something to the ship."

Before Carol could say anything else, the external long-range scanners failed. Then weapons-status telemetry.

She unstrapped and floated over to a supply locker.

"What are you doing?" Bruno asked her, unstrapping himself and joining her.

"Going to suit up and try and convince the uglies on the hull to stop what they are doing. Force of my commanding personality, that sort of thing, you know."

Her lover frowned. "You know that I can't Link right now, and you are better behind the console. Let me go outside. I need you at the console, to get us out of here if necessary."

His glance speared her heart.

For a moment, Carol was busy repressing her odd mix of maternal and sexual feelings that Bruno brought out in her. If they survived, she would take the confusion up with her autodoc psychiatric module at length.

"Go," the Captain persona inside her finally said. "But be careful, Tacky," her deeper self appended. "I need you, too."

Bruno gave her a quick hug, and she efficiently helped him into his spacesuit.

"Oh," Carol added conversationally, "you might want to take this, too." She pressed an electron-beam rifle into his hands. Bruno took it awkwardly, then slung it over his shoulder.

The main computer reset itself, then fell to fifty percent processing capacity. More warning tones began to sound.

"You had better hurry," Carol said softly, "while we can still cycle the airlock."

Bruno started to dog his helmet shut and entered the airlock. He paused and turned back to Carol. She smiled at his look

"I love you, too," she said simply.

Carol kept a smile on her face until she heard the hatch close firmly. Then she blinked a few times to clear the tears that pooled in her eyes in the microgravity, and strapped back into her crash couch. After a moment she swept her hands across the main console, to see what systems remained responsive.

Chapter Twenty-one

Bruno opened the outer airlock door of *Dolittle*.

"Carol," he whispered over the suit commlink.

"I'm here, lover." Her voice buzzed in his headset.

"I'm leaving the airlock now. You getting video?"

"Affirmative."

Bruno clumsily lifted himself out of the airlock and locked down his magnetic boots on the dark hull of *Dolittle*. The riot of distant stars all around him shone down indifferently. This was deep space, with no friendly sun for light-years.

Over to one side, as large as the full Moon seen from faraway Earth, shone the glittering lights of the alien vessel.

Their own ship was a dark blur. He tongued his video amplifiers, repressed a gasp. The aliens thronged the hull of *Dolittle*, too many to count.

"Are you getting this?" he breathed.

"Yes," buzzed Carol's short reply.

The aliens stood perhaps a meter and a half in height.

They looked like cat-o'-nine-tails bullwhips, overly thick handle down and whips flailing about like snakes. Each whip end unraveled in a fractal series of smaller tendrils, final fingerlets clearly adept at manipulation. The aliens wore ornate harnesses, studded with bulging pockets and metallic-looking triangular shapes. On a hunch, he tongued his helmet visuals to infrared IR and saw that the metal triangles were nearly seventy degrees warmer than the whip-aliens themselves.

Heat exchangers, like the spidery constructions on the moon-ship. This was confirmed when one of the aliens landed on the hull of *Dolittle* twenty meters from Bruno, arms down, and the triangular shapes on its harness blazed under IR to shed the heat.

Under infrared, the aliens were much more than black ropy shapes. Delicate traceries of relative warmth pulsed beneath their cold skin, like some sort of circulatory system. Portions of their alien anatomies were clearly intended to remain much colder than others.

Bruno watched one of the aliens remove a complicated shape from a pocket and touch it to an open section of *Dolittle*'s hull. The shape smoothly changed shape and extended a questing projection, like a living thing. It thrust into what Bruno realized was part of *Dolittle*'s main sensory net. That alien's heat exchangers glowed. Other aliens continued to enlarge the open section under study, methodically taking the hull apart with strange tools. Other aliens ran snaky arms and odd objects over the disassembled parts.

"Carol," he whispered. "You still with me?"

"Right."

"Looks like they are studying our electronics. That must be what is shutting things down."

"You think they mean to shut us down?" came Carol's voice, peppered with static, but still soft in his ears.

"Doubtful. If they wanted to kill us, they would have quite a while ago. I just think they're curious."

"So why aren't they paying attention to you?"

Bruno didn't say anything in reply. Several more of the aliens came over the curving hull of *Dolittle*, moving quickly in a series of somersaults. They crowded around the alien who had tapped into the shipboard sensory net.

Fascinated despite himself, Bruno watched IR patterns shift and change across their alien skin. Waving tendrils danced fluidly. Bursts of static hissed and crackled in his ears. Communications?

"Bruno!" Carol's voice was suddenly grim.

"I'm here," he said, trying to sound calm.

"Life support just failed. I'm getting into my suit now."

Bruno swore, his voice loud in his own helmet. He had to try and stop the aliens before they—even by mistake—managed to kill both of them.

He unslung the electron-beam rifle from his shoulder, lifted it carefully, and checked its charge. The telltales glowed green: a full charge. Bruno flicked the safety off.

"I don't know if you can hear me, and if you can, you probably don't understand me," he told the cluster of many-armed shapes who were busily peeling still more of *Dolittle*'s hull away. "But you have to stop what you are doing."

Bruno aimed just above the nearest alien shape. There was a crack of static in his headset as he stroked the trigger, and sent an invisible bolt of high-energy electrons over the tops of its waving tentacles.

The reaction was immediate.

Alien shapes turned, tentacles weaving madly, and quickly began advancing on him.

Bruno started backing toward the airlock.

"Tacky?" Carol was back on line, hissing with

interference. "I'm getting a lot of static, and have lost video. You reading me?"

"I have a problem, Carol. I shot over their . . . well, what I think are their heads, and they seem annoyed with me now."

"Get back inside."

"Aye-aye, Captain, my very thought." Bruno turned and swore again. Three of the weaving shapes crouched in front of the airlock. "I'm surrounded."

"Shoot one."

"I don't suppose surrender is an option."

"It looks like they dismantle first, and ask questions later."

Bruno took a deep breath, and aimed at one of the arms of an alien creature standing between him and the airlock. He didn't give himself time to think, and simply fired the electron-beam rifle.

Instantly, the entire alien blazed in infrared. It leaped up and away from *Dolittle*, vanishing into the starscape, apparently unhurt.

"Bruno," Carol's voice hissed urgently. "You all right?"

He started to reply, then noticed one of the aliens to his right aiming a black pointed object at him. A pale purplish bolt of light filled his vision, engulfing him.

His suit went instantly dead, and his head seemed to explode. As the worst of the pain flash faded he realized that the electromagnetic soles of his boots had lost their grip on the hull of *Dolittle*. Miraculously his arm brushed against a handhold and he clutched convulsively. The airlock was just a few meters—

Bruno was damned if he would let Carol die alone.

Suddenly something held one of his legs stationary. Then the other. Bruno pulled harder with his arms. When he lifted one hand to switch his grip to a new handhold, something very strong looped around his wrist and held it fast. He wished that he could see, but the starlight was too dim without electronic enhancement.

How long had it been since his suit had failed? It was getting stuffy. Bruno felt something thin but very strong pry his fingers loose from his last handhold one by one, methodical and patient. He felt himself being lifted free from *Dolittle*, suspended and held by dozens of whiplike alien arms.

He wished that he could have said goodbye to Carol.

Bruno waited for the aliens to pull his suit neatly apart as they had started to do to *Dolittle*. He started yawning uncontrollably in the darkness. CO_2 overload . . .

Just as he passed out, he felt tiny fingers of singing fire burn their way through the interface socket in his neck into his dying brain.

No strength, not even to scream his despair.

PART II
COLD LOGIC

Chapter One

There is a deeper Reality beneath the comfortably obvious.

Space is neither empty nor limitless. The cosmos only seems to stretch forever, from the blackened husks of long-dead stars to the incandescent fury of quasars blazing within far distant galactic clusters. Even the yawning emptiness between such objects is not truly vacant, but hums and keens with the ancient melodies of ionized gas and magnetic fields. The bare vacuum itself roils with fertile acts of creation and destruction, of particles and antiparticles born from nothing and returning to oblivion, all within the thinnest shaved shards of time itself.

Yet it was not always so.

There was a time, incomprehensible to minds constrained by time's invariant arrow and a mere three dimensions, when nothingness reigned supreme. Not emptiness.

Nothingness.

Before there was a reality, how could there be existence? Yet time does have a starting point, a beginning. Cosmic symmetry argues an Alpha Time must balance an Ultimate Omega Point. Whether by accident, natural law, or purposeful Design, *something* appeared where once there was nothing.

Of that mystery, nothing is truly known. Whatever the First Cause, timeless vacancy blossomed into an all-consuming inferno of creation, a totality of what would someday be called matter and energy: a universe.

The first ticks of that time were a blaze of unthinkable energies and infinitesimal motes of mass. Even light was too weak to exist unsundered and free within such an inferno. It was a time of new-birthed reality's seeming raw and unfettered rage against nothingness, an enormous beacon attempting to fill an infinite darkness.

But then as now, all things that burn must eventually cool. Entropy remains the final judge and arbiter of this reality. The bright and implacable All immediately began to expand and cool, as it would forever after that first tortured moment.

Photons at last slipped free of creation's incandescent forge, and fled tirelessly across the face of that new reality. A subatomic menagerie met and merged into new and exotic arrangements. Matter was born, and vied with energies both subtle and gross for supremacy; each won in different regions of the expanding space-time continuum.

The new-birthed universe continued to grow, still many times hotter than the core of a sun, but ever cooling. It stretched like the surface of some cosmic balloon under hurricane-driven inflation. Yet the fabric of space-time is not infinitely resilient, nor was the expansion uniform. Under unthinkable stresses, reality itself strained and groaned with the aftermath of creation's bright birth. Ripples and cracks formed in the very substance of space-time.

As fissures form in water rapidly freezing from the liquid state to ice, so was it with the very nature of reality.

These fissures, spiderweb cracks appearing in the expanding cosmic egg as it hatched, were tiny but powerful. Each crack was far thinner than an atom's thickness, yet stretched for many light-years.

The primordial cracks and fissures thrummed and writhed with raw energies and potential. Their tortured movements struck nearby concentrations of hot matter like a fist. Electromagnetic fields crackled and roared along their lengths, inducing strange and intricate patterns in local clouds of glowing gas.

Some of these cracks in creation joined, building gigantic networks of frantic topology. Still others split into smaller fissures, radiating powerful gravitational waves that spread across the new-formed universe like ripples in a pond.

The expanding universe was distorted unevenly by these tangled knots of space-time, a cosmic fork stirring the stuff of stars. Some large networks acted as gravitational foci; seeds for the aggregation of coalescing matter into what would eventually become great seas of stars. These vast stellar whirlpools would someday be called galaxies.

But that lay many eons in the future.

Most of the fissures and cracks in space-time vanished, their substance and power leached away into loud peals of gravitation tolling across the universe. The furious expansion of reality slowed, and the new universe's grand structure unfolded.

Yet some tangles in space-time remained, diminished in glory and potency. Minds which eventually came into being within our universe gave these remnant structures of anguished topology a host of names, in as many languages. Humans would someday call them cosmic strings.

But they are not strings.

They are windows.

The knots and tangles of space-time were tiny connections between the new universe and an entirely different space-time continuum. Minds roamed in that other reality, on businesses unknowable. Such minds were not constructed of the building blocks basic to this particular space-time. The equivalents of their flesh and blood were not composed of quarks and quanta, electrons and protons and neutrons. They were not subject to the forces and natural laws which bind our reality, linking past and present and future. Flavor and charm were not distinguishing characteristics of even their smallest components.

Though strangeness of a comparative sort was implicit in their nature.

However alien, the entities on the other side of the cosmic strings had minds and possessed something much like curiosity. Eventually, they discovered the distorted windows into our reality which are the tattered remnants of creation's first moments of birth. The entities learned that such twists in the fabric of space-time could transmit information.

The minds, completely foreign to any entity living within this space-time continuum, peered dimly through these humming cracks into our own reality. Their curiosity was piqued by this strange place so unlike their own home. That interest kindled and grew as they caught glimpses of a different universe, new modes of existence. Eventually, they wished to explore this alien place, so close and yet so distant.

They could not enter this space-time continuum, any more than a human being could enter and live within

a printed page. But they possessed a drive to explore—
even by proxy.

The entities investigated this space-time continuum
in the only manner they could. Tentatively, they reached
out to the cracked windows at the border of their own
reality.

And beyond, into our own.

Call the minds that moved in that other universe They
Who Pass.

Chapter Two

They were approaching the Outsider ship, and he was so very afraid.

The frightened puppeteer's name was a beautiful symphony of music that flowed from the mouths at the ends of his twin necks. It literally meant "He Who Gentles Difficult Truths into the Hindmost's Wise Ears," but could be shortened to "Diplomat." His lips, knobbed with the delicate projections his race used as fingers, quivered with jangled nerves.

He ignored the pilot of the *Wisdom of Retreat*'s sardonic question for a moment, making a concerted effort to control his breathing. He tried to calm himself by breathing alternatively through his necks. The puppeteer's three hearts pounded in terrified syncopation.

There was drugcud in his personal medical pouch, but he knew better. The *Wisdom of Retreat*'s pilot would not approve.

Diplomat had seen the reports about the vessel they

176

approached during his too-short emergency briefing at the Hindmost's Fortress. The numbers and the reality they represented still burned in his mind like wildfire sweeping across a dry plain.

He fluted agreement to the pilot, steeling himself at last for what he would see with both of his eyes. The pilot snorted amusement and turned back to the command console.

With a single low note of command, the pilot cleared the hullscreen in front of the puppeteer, revealing the strange Outsider vessel. It was worse than Diplomat had expected; a terrifying space-going nest of unknown threats. He fought a yawning sense of unreality and fear. The reports and holograms had not done the frightening artifact justice.

It was almost too much for Diplomat's brain to encompass. Noticing the metric markers the shipboard computer projected next to the image of the other ship, he was again unnerved at the scale of the looming object. It grew visibly on the hullscreens at extreme magnification.

The *Wisdom of Retreat*'s gravity planers performed an unexpected looping course correction, and the startled Diplomat shrieked a siren alarm call. He folded himself instinctively into a protective ball within his forceweb and quivered. Diplomat's mind fled the Outsider threat into comforting darkness.

The peace was interrupted by a lancing pain at the base of his necks. The force of the blow made him see sparks fleeing in all directions.

Not again, Diplomat thought, squeezing his eyes shut and pulling his neck and legs tighter against his midsection. The pain shot through him again, still more intense. Diplomat clenched blunt vegetarian teeth, knowing the blows would not stop until he emerged.

A voice filled with harsh martial music blared a curse

in the small lifebubble. Diplomat could feel the electric
tingle of the pilot's forceweb being released. There was
a clump and snap as the pilot's articulated boots left
the control consoles. He could sense the pilot standing
over him.

The comforting smell of the Herd emanating from
the ventilators was replaced by a stench of dominance
and barely harnessed rage. Diplomat gulped and tried
to breathe through his mouths to avoid it.

It was the smell of the *Wisdom of Retreat*'s pilot, only
stronger and more angry. Diplomat had kept his distance
during the voyage, even within the tiny lifebubble of
the *Wisdom of Retreat*. There were limits to the ability
of the airscrubbers to remove the pilot's distinctive odor,
redolent with attack pheromones.

Besides, the pilot liked "the smell of battle," as she
called it.

The frightened puppeteer wished fervently he was
back in the hospital burrow, his tired brain soothed by
the psychists' overlay induction devices. Had Diplomat
not just returned from his final embassy to the Q'rynmoi?
Had not the psychists bluntly stated that he was not
ready for another mission? He tightened his necks
around his midsection.

Diplomat could hear the angry duet of the pilot's
whistling breath above him. She sang an offkey
command, and his forceweb vanished instantly. Diplomat
was left with an itchy feeling of residual static charge
and insecurity.

"Stand up and control yourself, you miserable
coward." The pilot's tones were rich with a symphony
of contempt. It made a word honored among the
puppeteer race sound like an insult.

"Chew your courage drugs if need be," her voice
continued in disdainful tones. "You are to carry out a
task for the Hindmost and the entire puppeteer race.

This is more important than your shameful and obvious lack of a notochord."

The pilot's words stung Diplomat more than the pain at the base of his necks. He prided himself on his rare ability to work with dozens of alien species; why could he not deal as well with a member of his own race?

At least Diplomat *thought* the pilot was a member of his race.

The frightened puppeteer breathed deeply; it was no use postponing the inevitable. He unwrapped his necks. Opened his eyes one at a time. Moving gingerly, he stood in the small lifebubble. The scent of the pilot prickled angrily over Diplomat, like a swarm of stinging insects.

"No," he said carefully in measured tones, shoving his fears away as best he could. "I will not be needing the drugs at this time." Diplomat was unsure of the truth of that statement. He looked at neither the hullscreen nor the pilot.

There was a splat of dismissive music.

"Then look at me, *Diplomat*." A chord of hard-edged humor entered the pilot's voice, irony dripping from the title. "If you cannot look at *me*, how will you complete the Hindmost's Commands, let alone look the helium-beasts in the face?"

There was a meditative pause.

"That is," she continued, "if they can be said to actually *have* faces." The pilot hummed and whistled another musical note to her command console. "The hull is opaqued. Control your fear."

Diplomat finally raised his heads, blinking, and looked up at the pilot of the *Wisdom of Retreat*.

And up.

The Hindmost's Guardian stood well over two meters in height. Impact armor covered the giant puppeteer's midsection completely. Each of her necks bore gleaming mirrorplate able to turn a beam of coherent light.

Traditional battle helmets with razor-tipped talons rested on each head, and the pilot's eyes burned with emotions alien to Diplomat. Her legs were as armored as her necks, and holsters hung in instant reach of either mouth. Because Guardians were also deft with their three hooves, each was encased in space-ready magnetic boots, equipped with manipulators, cutting tools, lasers, projectile weapons, and Great Burrower knew what other horrors.

The Guardians were one of the most closely kept secrets of the puppeteer race. This warrior caste was small in number, bred and trained from birth for the necessary occasional insanity of aggression and combat. The Hindmost spoke for all puppeteers, and the Hindmost's Guardians carried out the Will of the Those Who Lead from Behind. They enforced treaties among puppeteer groups, advised the Deepest Council, designed and built safety devices and weaponry, and— from time to time—were called upon to defend puppeteer interests more directly.

Such as the present situation, reflected Diplomat, a tingle of repressed fear scurrying down both necks.

This Hindmost's Guardian held one head high and cocked to the side, the other low near her left leg holster. It was standard caution in what a Guardian would consider potentially dangerous situations; in other words, all of the time. The Hindmost's Guardians *always* expected danger, altercation, and even the obscenity of fighting. Relished it, it was said.

That alone made the pilot more alien to Diplomat than the barbaric Q'rynmoi and their breeding colonies.

"Better," hurrumphed the pilot. "Perhaps you will have your uses after all."

"How long until we rendezvous with the Outsider ship?" Diplomat asked, gesturing with one head toward the opaqued hullscreens.

"Too soon for you," she replied, her song flippant and breezy. The Guardian's two heads suddenly reared up and looked at one another in a flash of rare humor, then returned to normal posture.

Diplomat paused and straightened. It was time to firmly grasp the issue with both mouths. "Please show me the Outsider craft again, Guardian." The giants may have had individual names within their own caste, but in puppeteer society, the Hindmost's Guardians were simply addressed as Guardian.

The only other choice of name a Guardian accepted was the grotesque puppeteer obscenity of "Warrior."

Diplomat was too well bred to use such a word.

"A little talker like yourself," the Guardian crooned, "can suddenly regain courage? And without drugs! I am somewhat impressed."

Before Diplomat could reply, the pilot had moved back to her control console and sang the hullscreen to clarity once more. He settled in his own crashweb and, swallowing past dry throats, looked outward.

The Outsider craft looked more like a biological construct than spacecraft. Diplomat forced himself to crane his necks one at a time, trying to gain a sense of perspective. The space vessel was the size of a small moon, but not solid. Complex tangles of oddly colored metal gleamed in the starlight. The bent and twisted topology of the thing made Diplomat's eyes ache to the roots of his necks. Platforms and oddly formed objects extruded from the tangles here and there. Points of brilliant light drifted around the ship, as if in long, slow orbits. Tiny motes glittered and darted above, below, and within the Outsider vessel.

A nest of threatening vermin, indeed, thought Diplomat, hooves tapping. He stuffed his autonomic flight psychotropism into the shadows of his deeper mind.

"What is your assessment, passenger?" the pilot

rumbled with a grating melody. "Excuse me, I meant to sing *Diplomat*."

He ignored the pilot's insult. "I have never seen such an Outsider craft before," Diplomat replied, the fear looming once more. One of his heads dipped toward his medical pouch.

"Nor have any of the Deep Council. We have our theories, even as you quake to your hooves over things which are new."

Diplomat flutter-blinked in veiled irritation.

"It appears that this Outsider craft uses hyperdrive," he mused aloud to his pilot. The coldlife traders generally did not travel faster than light, preferring relativistic travel. The appearance of the Outsider vessel from hyperspace had set off alarms throughout the Homeworlds.

The Guardian puppeteer clacked her left set of molars in agreement. "It is exceedingly rare. The clan of helium-beasts with which our Race does business is known to use the hyperdrive in emergencies."

The phrase made his neck pelts stand up. "What could constitute an emergency to such beings?" The Outsiders had little to do with the concerns of carbon-based, sunward forms of life. What could be an emergency to an Outsider? The thought chilled him.

"Perhaps their liquid helium is too warm," whistled the pilot sourly.

Diplomat understood the basic aggressive paranoia of the Guardian caste—much of it made sense in a hostile universe—but the Outsiders were long-term partners of the puppeteer race.

"Are the Outsiders not our allies?" he asked as diplomatically as his title. "Have they not given our Race help in the past?"

"Again you grasp truth with one mouth only," the pilot hummed. "We owe the helium-beasts much, but that dependency in turn leads to a threat to our Race."

How like a Guardian, Diplomat thought, to view the gifts of the Outsiders as threats. The coldlife sentients had provided the puppeteers with many technological marvels, including the Mover of Worlds that had saved the puppeteer race so long ago. All the Outsiders had asked in return was that Diplomat's race observe and study other life-forms and occasionally report that information back.

Selling the many technological miracles of the Outsiders to other warmlife races had enriched the puppeteers for thousands of years.

A seemingly harmless arrangement, until the terse summons had been received in the Homeworlds. And this frightening moon-sized ship appeared just outside the puppeteer system's gravity well. Waiting for an urgently demanded emissary.

What was happening?

Diplomat touched forked tongue to lip-fingers in thought. "You grazed with the Study Herd on this issue, I presume."

The Guardian blinked assent.

"I need all of your briefing materials, Guardian," Diplomat managed to muster.

The other puppeteer's heads came up in humor. "Hardly," she grated. "I must feed you the information slowly, as tender leaves are fed to younglings before their grinding molars emerge. You would surely break under the strain of our mission, were it given you all at once."

Diplomat squared his heads in a posture of pride, suppressing his fears, which lay ever ready to break out. Still, he was important to this mission, and the *Wisdom of Retreat*'s pilot needed to be reminded of the fact. He forced himself to meet the Guardian's eyes directly.

Not in submission.

The soldier puppeteer's free head meaningfully dipped down and touched the medal on the front of her impact armor. It was a holographic representation of the image of a retreating puppeteer: the Sigil of the Hindmost. She snorted in dismissal at Diplomat's earlier prideful tone. Even through his mouths, he could smell her annoyance-scent.

"I recognize your authority and honor," persisted Diplomat, inwardly bemused that he was not curled up tightly again into a ball for the other puppeteer to kick. "Yet *I* act for the Hindmost as well. We are a team, Guardian, a small Herd of our own. We are to work together, against a common enemy. Toward a common goal. That *too* is a Hindmost's Command."

A long pause.

Diplomat held his left breath as he tried not to listen to the other puppeteer's harsh breathing.

"Well spoken," Guardian replied at last, an undermelody of crude humor to her words. "You are aptly named, Little Talker." She reached into a pouch at her side and removed a shining multifaceted datacube.

Diplomat merely waited. He knew that he held status; had not the Hindmost Itself selected him for this mission? Diplomat shook his midsection slightly, causing the gems in his intricately groomed backcoat to jingle, a reminder of Diplomat's rank.

Another pause.

"Many pardons, O Wise One. I have your prerendezvous briefing datacube here, *Diplomat*." She waited, apparently to see if Diplomat would rise to the bait of her irony this time.

"How long until we dock with the Outsider vessel, Guardian?" Diplomat repeated, working very hard to seem unperturbed.

"You have just enough time to review the contents

of the information crystal, O Wise One. And digest the language programs into your communication module." Again, the Guardian's heads flipped up for a moment and looked eye to eye. "Though I suspect you will not like what you see and learn."

She held out the datacube to Diplomat with her left mouth. Just out of reach, of course, to make him bridge more than half the distance.

Diplomat idly noticed that the pilot's right mouth never strayed from her disruptor holster, even inside the supposed safety of the *Wisdom of Retreat*.

He nervously licked his finger-lips with a forked tongue and . . . made a long neck to the Guardian. More than halfway. He took the glittering geometrical solid which contained Diplomat's fate.

And perhaps the fate of much, much more.

Outsiders One

Confusion. This local-and-other node cannot identify the hotlife irritants in this wracked geometric volume. Searching modalities are nil on all vibrational harmonics.

Attentiveness. This local-node sieves the plasma turbulence with great care. There is no trace but debris of the hotlife usurpers. The two battling motes are not present.

Thought. One. Perhaps, then, the hotlife vermin have all been destroyed? There has been no opportunity to interrogate the plans of the vermin for analysis and decision. The Nexus *must* be preserved from threat.

Suspicion. This local-and-other node are One. This local-node detects a disturbance in the <#@@#@>. It is more than the resonance from the unleashing of destructive forces. Something beyond the abilities of the hotlife vermin has been present. Prepare to receive relevant data-packets.

Anger. Received. Analysis complete. The heretic Feral Ones have indeed moved through this space-time locus, and fled! Perhaps the Feral Ones have taken the hotlife specimens—for purposes surely in opposition to the intentions of the Holy Radiants.

Confusion. One. What action shall this local-and-other-node take? The Treaty limits action near this geometry.

Determination. The Treaty has vertices and contour which are definite. The Nexus assembles, from local-and-other nodes, into Node. Node will determine the vector of the Feral Ones in the other <#@@#@> space and pursue.

Caution. What of the Treaty?

Righteousness. Treaties serve a Higher Purpose. Do the Holy Radiants approve? Their silence is license enough for action.

Shock. That direction of thought leads the other-node to the way of the Feral Ones.

Amusement. The other-node japes. Following the directives of the Holy Radiants does *not* lead to heretical modes of action.

Concern. Can the other-node be certain?

Impatience. Enough. All local-and-other nodes join to Node, and certitude will be One. Pursue the forces sundered by the Feral Ones, to their source.

Chapter Three

Guardian held out the glittering datacube to Diplomat. Part of her mission was to protect her frail passenger, true. Establishing rank, however, had little to do with protection. She made the little puppeteer stretch to take the information matrix. It forced him into an extended-neck posture of submission.

Such an act was tradition and test both, Guardian reminded herself. How would the little talker react?

Diplomat avoided Guardian's eyes in dutiful respect, taking the cube with his left mouth. No challenge there.

Still, Guardian noted, his posture was as brave as possible for a puppeteer of his bloodlines. She blinked twice in acknowledgment. Diplomat's act of polite esteem secretly pleased her, though she maintained her stern expression, still holding the other puppeteer in her gaze.

Diplomat was small and vulnerable and obviously very frightened—with good reason. She was delighted that he was trying to hide his emotions, to hold his necks a

bit farther away from his body in a show of what was—
to him—courage.

Despite all of Guardian's threats and insults to
Diplomat, she enjoyed looking after the other puppeteer.
A small puppeteer like Diplomat *required* Guardian's
protection, and it warmed her to feel that needed duty.
It would be a deep pleasure to die for her charge.

She would never admit as much to the little creature,
of course. Guardian's facade forced other puppeteers
to treat her opinions with respect and attention and more
than a little fear. Her personal feelings did not enter
into this or any other mission of behalf of the Hindmost.

To a Guardian of the puppeteer race, duty was All.

Such was the purpose for which Guardians had been
born and bred over millennia. Duty to the Hindmost,
always; such were the first words a foal of the Guardian
caste heard in crèche. And it was the last thought to
be prized, at the end of a long life of service.

Guardian glowered a bit more to reinforce the image
she projected. Diplomat bowed to her with both necks
and turned to his own control console. There was a
slight crunching sound as he broke the Hindmost's Seal
with his teeth.

Guardian was not looking forward to the next few
minutes. It would have to be handled most carefully.

I am a Guardian, she thought, *not a melody-mumbling
psychist*.

But a Hindmost's Command was exactly that: a
command.

As she watched from the corner of her left eye,
Diplomat inserted the datacube into his console reader.
He whistled up the hyper-icons with a minimum of
flourish, looking cool and efficient. Not a surprise, truly.
Warrior knew that Diplomat was a Field Operative,
not some Homeworlds fop—despite the ornate
grooming on his back pelt.

Still, she was not fooled by appearances.

Guardian allowed herself a tongue-flick of a wry smile at his studied sham of confidence as Diplomat's console screens began to flicker with data. She returned to her own control console, activating the forceweb. The static charge crackled pleasantly against her battle armor, firmly holding the soldier puppeteer in place.

Unless Guardian handled Diplomat's study of the datacube's contents *just so*, the little puppeteer would drop into another bout of catatonia. Guardian was secretly indulgent of her charges on such missions, yes, but there was little time available for out-of-breeding-season pelt-currying.

"Well, Honored and Wise One," she asked with rough humor, "do you care to share your initial impressions?"

"I thank you," Diplomat fluted deferentially. The tone was smooth and controlled. "I shall need some time to review the encoded information to give a proper reply."

Guardian glanced at Diplomat. She could tell nothing of his mood or reaction from his tone or posture. Swallowing right-to-left-to-right in thought, she began to choose her words carefully.

Gently, the Guardian puppeteer told herself. *But quickly . . .*

Without music in her voice, she spoke in flat, unpuppeteer-like tones for emphasis. "I know something of the mission before us, Diplomat. I was very far in front of the Hindmost when the Outsider message was first received. Later I was in Herd with the Deepest Council, and helped prepare your briefing contained in the datacube. This is a task for Guardians only, not for puppeteers too enamored of their own burrows."

Perhaps Guardian's false air of superiority would prick the little puppeteer's own substantial pride. Such an approach often resulted in the insulted one forgetting fear—and getting on with the task at hand.

In any event, Guardian had issued an old, old insult, but one which carried little real sting. Puppeteers had not inhabited burrows and caverns since the dawn of recorded history. Guardian paused, waiting for Diplomat to respond to the crude song-phrase.

The little puppeteer said nothing, his posture giving away nothing.

Good, she mused. *This one is as skilled as the Deepest Council argued.*

"Still," Guardian continued, "I and my caste follow the Hindmost's Song Called Out from Far Behind. You are to act as the Hindmost's Representative to the helium beasts, and perhaps do more." Guardian's heads stared at one another for a split second in a dry chuckle of puppeteer humor. "I only hope that you acquit yourself with honor, for your mouths speak for all puppeteers this day."

Diplomat's right head lifted from one of his console screens, the stream of data freezing in place as he looked away.

"Guardians are not known for their elegant conversational ability," Diplomat sang with just the slightest edge of reproach. "You are attempting to placate and groom my thoughts. The currycomb of your words and manner is not necessary, truly."

Guardian cocked her right head, impressed. "Well spoken, Little Talker. I seek to maintain your calm."

"That is why I carry mood modifiers," the other puppeteer reminded her. "I am afraid, yes, but I acquitted myself well with the Q'rynmoi, did I not?"

"You acted like a Guardian that day, Little Talker." Warrior clicked her teeth together, squinting in respect.

Diplomat's heads faced one another, then blinked twice at her graciously. "I sense and accept the spirit of the compliment. Though few of my caste would see it as such with both eyes."

Warrior snorted.

"Prepare me, then, for this mission of ours," hummed Diplomat, all humor evaporated.

Guardian turned both her eyes to face Diplomat.

"There are new threats in space, near our own domain." Warrior's words again lacked music, jarring the Herd-conditioned air in the lifebubble with intensity. Her right head weaved slightly, and her left tongue touched knobbed lips for a moment.

Even Guardians can feel fear, she reminded herself. *It simply does not rule us, as it does the Little Ones.*

"The helium beasts," Guardian continued, "have brought us news from a sector outside the realm of our race. Evidence of two new species, aggressive and threatening to puppeteer business and well-being."

Diplomat rolled his left eye with the beginnings of impatience. "I do not understand the countermelody implicit in your song, Guardian. The Outsiders have done us a service with this doubtfully free information, I assume."

She said nothing.

"But the Outsiders are allies," Diplomat sang in a falling tone of disbelief. "Our arrangements have been profitable for centuries."

"True enough, Little Talker," she replied.

"What are you not singing to me, Guardian?"

Guardian pointed with a right forked tongue at Diplomat's console. "You will find the answers there."

"I repeat myself, with all due respect to your station and grooming: prepare me," chided the little puppeteer.

Guardian whistled like a teakettle, then stood stock-still. "The Hindmost," she clipped, "does not entirely trust these particular Outsiders. There is some new agenda present." Her left head dipped down to a leg holster containing what appeared to be a tightbeam disruptor, touched it for reassurance, and returned to station.

She watched Diplomat shudder and droop his necks, both eyes slightly closed. The first step toward withdrawal. At length, he mastered his fear, raising necks with still-twitching neck muscles. Guardian was impressed.

"You are to be the Hindmost's Voice," she reminded him.

Diplomat blinked agreement. "I understand my duties, Guardian."

"Perhaps medication would be useful," Guardian suggested.

The little puppeteer chirped agreement. He reached into his supplies and tongued a blunt triangular lozenge of drugcud into his left mouth.

Guardian understood Diplomat's confusion about the Outsiders. The coldlife sentients had helped lift the puppeteers from their pretechnological society over one hundred thousand years past; had sold the puppeteer race the gravity planer, the hyperdrive, and endless safety devices.

Even the Mover of Worlds.

Most importantly, the Outsiders had allowed the puppeteers to act as their agents among warmlife sentient races, for a very modest percentage. But the Outsiders always had their own agenda, and it was one that no noncryogenic creature could possibly appreciate.

It pleased her to see Diplomat square his heads. His posture was subtly more vibrant. Perhaps the drugs were helping after all.

"I shall review the datacube for more details, though I reserve the right to ask further questions," he declared. "May I ask how long until we rendezvous with the Outsider ship?"

"Less than an hour," Warrior replied. "Prepare for maneuvers. The helium beasts have set up a number of force curtains around their vessel. I do not know why."

Guardian chirped a command to her console, and activated Diplomat's forceweb.

She paused, then snaked her left head around to look at Diplomat. He met her gaze with a chemically enhanced calm.

"You had better chew more drugs, Little Talker. You will need them." She turned back to her console, adjusting schematics. But she kept one head inclined slightly toward her passenger.

The datacube's contents scrolled across the twin screens in front of Diplomat, one for each head. Within a few minutes, he stopped the screens, opened his supply pack again, and swallowed another, larger drugcud. Diplomat whistled, and data resumed its inexorable flow across his screens.

Guardian had kept silent while Diplomat popped the second mood regulator oval. Now her heads whipped up and faced one another, eye to eye. She growled without her usual roughness.

"Yes," she crooned, "now you grasp the Hindmost's concern firmly with both mouths. Two warlike races with interstellar capability, and weapons of mass destruction." She paused for effect, waiting.

"They have intruded into contested Outsider geometry with reaction drives and nuclear explosives?" Diplomat asked, not believing.

"Just so. And not so very long after the Pact."

The little puppeteer drummed a hoof. "I am expected to communicate with these captives."

Guardian blinked agreement. "The datacube contains the two downloads to your translator module. You will be able to talk to them, Little Talker."

Diplomat continued to look at the information scurrying across his screen. He scrabbled in his pack, swallowed another regulator of drugcud. "One of them is a . . . carnivore." He had difficulty with the word, which was a puppeteer obscenity, unused in polite society.

"Indeed," she replied. "They are the larger of the two species, are they not? The ones that call themselves the *kzin*? But they are not the issue that most concerns the Hindmost, Little Talker, nor me. It is these . . . *humans*. Perhaps you recognize their morphological type."

Diplomat fluted confusion, then fell silent as more data flowed across his screens. He shuddered, and his own forked left tongue touched his lip-fingers repeatedly. He stopped dead, tonguing the left screen to freeze mode.

Ah, Guardian thought. *The hoof strikes home.*

Diplomat wailed a sudden musical siren of alarm.

Guardian's heads looked at one another again in the puppeteer expression of humor. "I was wondering," she softly sang to Diplomat, who was making sounds like a demented calliope, "when you would make the connection."

Diplomat swiftly wrapped his necks around his body, still keening in fear. The screens froze and then blanked for lack of an operator.

"These . . . *humans* are clearly Pak breeders, though they do appear different in many ways." Guardian reached over with a long neck into her own medical bag, and removed a hypospray of sedative.

Guardian considered the petite puppeteer quivering before her. His necks were tucked so tightly around his body that he looked like a foal's plaything.

She swallowed in sequence, considering. Despite appearances, this cowardly little Diplomat had saved an entire puppeteer colony world from destruction by the Q'rynmoi. Guardian knew of few of her caste Herdmates who were willing to face the personal dangers that Diplomat had. It was a difficult story to believe, however, seeing him in this state.

It was said by the Hindmost's psychists that Diplomat's corrective mindsculpting after that event had been incomplete; they had advised more memory flensing before releasing him to active status.

A Hindmost's Command remained exactly that, however. The Deepest Council had concurred.

She considered that perhaps there was more to this delicate little talker than met her own Guardian eyes. She couldn't put her lips quite on it, but there was something different. Something almost brave, despite his periodic catatonic states and whining manner. He would clearly need her help to complete this mission, as well as the reverse.

"You remember the Pak, my little Diplomat, don't you?" She spoke almost conversationally as she calmly injected the near catatonic puppeteer in the right neck. The hypospray made a hissing sound, loud in the tiny lifebubble. Guardian made adjustments to the ventilation system, flushing out Diplomat's fear pheromones with fresh, Herd-conditioned air. Diplomat stopped screaming, trembled for a moment, and then seemed to fall asleep. She tightened his forceweb harness remotely.

Guardian looked at her own heads again. "Yes. The Pak are not extinct, after all. Despite the efforts of three sentient races and ten thousand years of effort." She deopaqued a small portion of the hull directly in front of her console, made a few further course corrections.

Guardian settled back into her own forceweb harness and whistled a duet with herself softly. The tune soothed her, and reminded the soldier puppeteer of her first days in crèche.

It was a marching song, ancient beyond measure. The music was said to be common when Guardian's ancestors had led entire herds of Diplomat's forebears to new grazing grounds with the turn in seasons. The arpeggios sang volumes about order, confidence, and glowing success.

After a few moments, she reached over with a head, and fondly patted the back of the sleeping puppeteer next to her.

"Two warrior races," she sang quietly. Forked tongues flicked over both sets of lip-fingers. "Two threats to the security of the Race." Warrior paused, watching their blinking course plot intently on the hullscreen.

"Or perhaps three," she added, after reflection.

The Outsider ship grew still larger as the *Wisdom of Retreat* approached rendezvous.

Chapter Four

In its youth, the universe was very different. They Who Passed observed the strange fresh wilderness through a window less than an atom wide.

Gravity had made its rule known over vast clouds of gas and dust. Many had coalesced, contracted, and at last collapsed. The gravity-squeezed gas became hotter and hotter, atoms thrusting together in the rough romance of nuclear reactions, releasing energy and transmuting elements. These glowing clouds became hot youthful stars of the first stellar generation, their fusion fires spendthrift with the bounty of gravity's first clasp.

Still, that initial blaze of starlight was but a dim reminder of the first moments of creation, when all of reality had been hotter by many orders of magnitude.

Clouds of glowing gas, hot young suns set within them like jewels in oil. Twists and spirals of electromagnetic fields. Ions and charged particles streaked along paths appointed by the fresh laws of this space-time continuum. The early days.

Such were the alien vistas observed by They Who Pass, peering through the distorted interdimensional windows of the cosmic strings.

The minds suspended in the other universe were fascinated, in their way, with this strange space-time continuum. They wished to study and examine these new laws roughly ruling the brawling new universe, as if in haste.

But how? They Who Pass were ironically named; they could not pass, through the tortured windows between realities, into such an exotic and alien place. Even if such an act were possible, the laws of existence in the other universe were sufficiently different to make their own survival improbable. But complex data had passed from within the alien universe into their own. Surely the reciprocal would be found to be the case as well.

They Who Pass knew that Mind was only a sufficiently complex pattern of information. Sentience would inevitably arise in such patterns, regardless of the embedding medium and environment.

Though they themselves could not physically traverse their atom-thin window between universes, the entities knew that there were ways in which patterns could be imposed from afar. Near one of the cosmic strings within the new universe, they observed a vast cloud of charged gases, with filigrees of glowing electromagnetic fields running throughout.

Perfect for their purposes.

By something very like induction, yet much more potent, They Who Pass reached through the distorted crack into this reality. Stark pattern imposed on the charged cloud. A structure wrestled into shape— striations of virulent light and murky dust, threads of magnetic fields and inductive heating. Imbalances of electromagnetic force flexed within the cloud, shoving clots of dust and gouts of prickly gas within the structure.

The glowing cloud reacted as They Who Pass challenged it from afar. Networks of dusky plasma sparkled, pinching into new shapes.

The cloud moved, learned, grew. Primitive reflexes drank in new patterns beamed through the twisting aperture of the cosmic string. The cloud stored information, manipulated data, and sent it back through the window between realities, to They Who Pass. The cloud finally copied itself into fresh gas clouds, imposed its own patterns in response to the new universe around it.

Such clouds acted like living things. Communication and complexity among the clouds increased exponentially as time unspooled. They Who Pass nudged and directed, moving the plasma clouds toward more capacity and capability.

Eventually, these minds built of hot plasma and cold dust awoke to sentience.

They Who Pass now had intelligent agents within the new universe, semiautonomous explorers ready to travel throughout the strange reality and report back what they found. The clouds developed a society, a culture, as they spread throughout the new universe, unraveling basic laws. They roved the spaces around dead suns, ventured near blazing new-birthed stars.

Always in the service of They Who Pass.

Call the intelligent clouds of dusty plasma the Radiants.

Chapter Five

Carol's eyes opened, gummy and blurred. Above, blue sky. She didn't believe it.

Carol sat up, rubbed her eyes. The view did not change.

She and Bruno were lying on a flat open area, on some thick ground cover. Like grass, though greener than any Terran grass. An unnatural green. Purplish blue sky stretched above them, speckled with delicate gossamer clouds. Carol stared in amazement, wordless.

The air smelled fresh and antiseptic, with a clean tang of ozone. A breeze touched her arms like the delicate brush of soothing fingers. It was so quiet that Carol could hear her heart beat.

No signs of the weird aliens, kzinti, or even of the fact that they had been locked in battle just a few moments before.

All Carol could remember was losing the suit commlink with Bruno in a snarl of static. Then nothing until she woke up here. Carol turned her head, stretching.

Somehow, behind them, the main airlock to *Dolittle* hung in midair. The rest of the ship was not there, however. One more impossibility. They seemed to be alone.

Carol rose easily to her feet. Too easily, she realized. She felt better than she had in many months, in years. She walked over to Bruno, and checked over his vital signs. He appeared to be sleeping deeply. She shook him gently awake.

"What?" Bruno began, shaking his head, then stopped in surprise as his eyes opened. He looked around, confused. Then he recognized Carol and wrapped his arms tightly around her.

"I thought I was *dead*," he whispered.

"So did I."

His confused frown deepened as Carol helped him to his feet.

"Don't ask me," she told him as he looked around. "Unless you believe in heaven?"

Bruno stooped down and pulled up a small tuft of the dark green ground cover. He showed her the ten-lobed leaflets, and the crimson roots that moved gently while she watched.

"I doubt," Bruno said softly, "that heaven is sown with extraterrestrial species of plant life."

"How nice that you are so sure."

Carol followed Bruno as he walked toward the magically suspended main airlock of *Dolittle*. He patted the empty air above and to either side of the metal door, and snorted in satisfaction.

"Try it," he invited.

Carol found that the airlock door seemed to be set in an invisible wall. The wall didn't feel hot or cold, like metal or plastic or stone. It was a hard, sharply defined barrier that they merely could not see. Except for the fact that heat conduction seemed perfect, it might have been optical diamond. The grassy plains beyond the wall were doubtless illusory, intended to give the impression of greater open space within their . . . cage.

Working together, she and Bruno quickly determined that their . . . yard was in fact about two hundred meters across, bounded by curving walls of invisible material. *Dolittle* clearly abutted it, with only the main airlock permitted to penetrate the force-wall.

The airlock opened normally, and they found *Dolittle* complete inside. Intact, though none of the sensory net or computer systems responded to commands. There were plenty of supplies still. They both noticed and commented on the one thing out of place: *Dolittle* was spotless, not as they had left it.

Carol stepped outside the spacecraft, back onto the too-green lawn. Soon Bruno joined her. They watched the ersatz clouds for a time, enjoying the quiet despite themselves.

It was good to breathe what smelled and felt like fresh air, especially after years of recycler stink.

"So," Bruno said finally, "I guess we just wait. Like before."

Carol was considering suggesting to Bruno an interesting way to just wait when she heard someone clearing his throat behind them. They both leaped to their feet and whirled around.

It was then that Carol rethought her joke about religion, and decided that she didn't have a sense of humor after all.

Before them stood Colonel Buford Early.

Carol froze. Early looked precisely as she remembered him from their last briefing. His teeth were gleaming white, clearly prosthetic in his seamed and ageless face; his uniform was spotless. There was even the familiar arrogant twinkle in the old, old eyes.

"Bruno, son," Early said in an upbeat tone that was bizarrely inappropriate to their present circumstances. "And the lovely Captain Faulk. The pleasure is mine, entirely."

She looked over at Bruno, who stood there, mouth open. Carol knew that Bruno saw Early as something of a father figure. She elbowed him hard to snap him out of it.

"Colonel Early," Carol said evenly, "could you please tell us how you came to be here?" She paused, then added more plaintively than she had intended, "And precisely where 'here' is?"

Early's expression did not change. His smile was fixed, mindlessly benevolent. His words came out strangely, in bursts. "It is important to relax, to take things one step at a time. To think. Proper channels of communication are necessary. So many errors are made through hasty conclusions. Too much information often leads to confusion, and ill action. Would you not agree, Bruno?" Each sentence fragment sounded subtly different in tone from the last.

"Carol?" Bruno whispered. Carol was glad to see that Bruno saw the simulacrum for what it was.

"Humor it," she murmured back.

Bruno straightened his shoulders. "Quite right, Colonel Early. But how goes the war against the kzin?"

Again, Early's face did not change. The relentlessly upbeat grin stayed in place.

"War is an evil. Yet sometimes an evil is necessary to preserve a greater good. Death is tragedy. Kzin are scream-and-leaping ratcats. Their strategies are improving."

Carol scowled. "That isn't even a good imitation Early," she whispered as the figure in front of them continued to mix and match platitudes.

"Loud and clear," Bruno replied. "Those are just

comments and speeches of Early's, cobbled together in response to questions we are asking."

"Are you now calm?" the Early-thing asked them brightly. "Calmness is the first requirement for debriefing."

Carol casually pulled a stylus from her coverall pocket, and tossed it underhand at the replica of Buford Early.

The figure made no effort to catch it. The stylus passed through and landed on the grass behind.

A distortion band started at the bottom of the figure's boots, and shimmied up and through its body.

"A lack of trust is deplorable," the perfect replica of Early said with the same unchanging smile. "Misunderstandings abound. Trust is fundamental."

"A hologram. Good, too," Bruno said.

Carol nodded, then walked directly through the projected figure and picked up her stylus, replacing it in her coverall pocket. She walked back through the hologram to return to Bruno's side.

The replica of Buford Early vanished.

Carol looked up into the purple false sky, and spoke calmly.

"Show yourself, or speak to us."

A voice spoke from all around them, still in Early's tones.

Sorrow mine.

"Excuse me?" Carol asked, confused.

"I think that they're apologizing," Bruno whispered in her ear.

Bruno-entity correct. I/We intend null upset, null confusion. Attempt calm failure. Accept.

It was very strange to hear such odd words in Early's familiar voice.

"Why do you use Buford Early as a model?" Bruno asked the air around them.

Question One. Curiosity/Innovation valuable.

Bruno-entity internal patterns acquired. Electrons flow interestingly. Patterns clearer than Carol-entity. Projection intended as communication-enabler.

"They accessed your interface and read your mind?" Carol asked Bruno, studying his pinched expression and thinned lips.

Discomfort sensed, source Bruno-entity. Sorrow. Pattern acquisition necessary. Knowledge of Bruno-entity and Carol-entity required. Provisions for continuance. Accept.

"They needed to know how to keep us alive," Carol commented to Bruno. He still looked a little uncomfortable.

"Are you the . . . um, entities that analyzed our spacecraft?" Bruno asked.

Truth. One.

Carol smiled a little. "What should we call you? Does your race have a name?"

Humor. I/We not as you/they. No one entity-title. Many in one node-location. One node-location in many. I/We outside knowledge Bruno/Carol/other-entity. Patterns different. Outside knowledge.

"What if we call you 'Outsiders'?" Carol raised an eyebrow at Bruno, who nodded.

Accept. One.

"Why did you capture us?" she asked, hoping that the Outsiders could understand speech better than they could produce it.

Entity-not-Bruno-not-Carol. Interrogatory. Concept difficulty. Queries. Aggression. Disruption. Inefficient. Patterns unclear. Issues complex.

There was a long pause.

Protection.

Bruno looked over at Carol. "Do they want to protect us, or us to protect them?"

"We'll sort it out later—though I would hate to meet whatever *they* need protection from."

Carol took a deep breath, then continued. "Outsiders, there are many things we do not understand. Will you help us to learn more?"

Laudable but possible not. Warm/Cold mix not all. Warm/Warm mix not often; Bruno-and-Carol entities with other-entity. Some Warm/Warm mix. Help yes/no. Understand not. Observe. Learn.

"Observe what?" she muttered, frustrated.

"Carol, look!"

To their right in the grassy false distance hung a circular window into another such "park." Through it they saw the blunt ovoid shape of a kzin singleship, and a huge orange-furred lump lying near it. Wisps of white feathery material led from the dark lawn into a network surrounding the prone kzin.

Carol felt sure it was the ratcat that had been attacking *Dolittle*.

Nature altercation. Intentions. Interrogatory. Coding similar, not-mixing understand one-not. Entity aggression Hot/Cold/Warm. One-not. Interrogatory.

"I don't understand," Carol and Bruno chorused.

One. Time necessary. Solution short-duration.

She ignored the odd words and looked again at the stretched-out kzin. "Is it dead?" she asked.

Negative. Aggression high. One-not. Acquisition difficult. Damage severe. Repairs completed soon.

"Is there any way that we can help you?" Carol inquired of the open air.

Not I/We. One-not. Entities not-Bruno/Carol, not-other entity. One interrogatory. Arrive present. Speak wish interrogatory. Fortune better: Warm/Warm focus increase Warm/Cold. Speak wish interrogatory.

Bruno whistled. Carol, clueless, urged him to speak his piece.

"I think I understand. The Outsiders have another type of alien waiting to speak with us, another warm-temperature type, but not human and not kzin."

Truth. Bruno-entity. One.

Carol nodded. "Outsiders, we wish to talk to these other life-forms."

Accept. One. Observe. Interact.

Another bubble-window appeared in the force-walled enclosure, very close to where they stood.

"What the . . ." Bruno said softly.

Carol felt dizzy with the strangeness, shaking her head. Too much change in too little time, she thought wildly, and stood a little straighter.

Two aliens stood ten meters away. They both had three legs ending in tiny hooves. Each of them had two flat, single-eyed heads at the ends of long waving necks. They wore clothing and what looked like tools. The larger one appeared to wear armor studded with spikes and sharp edges, and one head hovered over what seemed to be a holster containing a pistol-like object. It never moved. The hair under the two necks of the smaller alien was elegantly coifed and glittered. Its heads waved gracefully, one held high and the other low.

A long silence.

"Take me to your leader," Bruno muttered. Carol wanted to kick him in the shin.

The smaller of the two beings cocked a head suddenly and looked from Carol to Bruno, bird-swift. "Mr. Takagama," it sang in a woman's contralto, low and sexy, as Carol's jaw dropped in surprise, "I hardly think that such inappropriate levity is called for under the present serious circumstances."

The smaller of the two creatures then turned its other head to Carol, who slowly closed her mouth.

"We intend no disrespect to you, Captain Faulk," crooned the alien from the second single-eyed loose-lipped head, in an identical voice. "In fact, we are quite aware of primate protocols. However, may we speak frankly with one another? There is not a great deal of time for sociobiological niceties."

Chapter Six

Carol Faulk waited for the centrifuge in her head to quit spinning. It did not, and the rotor seemed a bit unbalanced to boot.

There had been too many changes since they had first detected the kzin ships back in the *Sun-Tzu*. And all of them far too quickly.

The battle between the *Sun-Tzu* and the kzin spacecraft. Bruno nearly burning out his brain from the EMP. The dogfight between *Dolittle* and the ratcat singleship. Then the moon-ship of another alien race somehow dropping them from nearly 0.8 lights to nothing, and the whiplike aliens from that huge craft dismantling *Dolittle*. Not only did she and Bruno wake up in an alien zoo near a comatose kzin, but now *another* type of alien confronted them. *Too much.*

Intelligent creatures with two heads, one of which spoke Belter Standard! They looked like bizarre mutant deer costumes from a masquerade party, with one-eyed heads at the ends of what should be arms. Like dual handpuppets.

Puppeteers? Carol considered.

She shook her head again. The cobwebs were starting to clear, but slowly. She had to put her mind on a battle footing. Curiosity began to overtake shock in her mind. *Okay*, she thought. *So you are facing three sets of aliens now. What's the big deal?*

These newest aliens waited in what seemed somehow like politeness. The big one, loaded down with weaponry, said nothing and made no move.

Carol wanted to take control. Maybe there was a way out of this mess.

Yeah, right.

Bruno continued to chuckle softly at the implausible sight of the two creatures, with an almost hysterical undertone. Was it too much, too fast for him?

"Knock it off," she hissed at him.

"Why? They look like something out of three-D, put together by people suffering from . . . ah, chemical enhancement. Kidvid aliens."

"Yeah," Carol whispered, smiling despite herself. "A puppet show on braindust."

"It's a little tough to take them seriously. And that might not be smart."

Carol frowned and narrowed her eyes. Bruno was right; the aliens looked more laughable than imposing at first glance. The Outsiders appeared far more frightening. Because they were more alien looking? Or because they had defeated a kzin singleship and dismantled *Dolittle?*

Even with the snaky necks, the three-legged aliens looked silly.

But what about the big one's weapons? she reminded herself. Her singleship fighter-pilot reflexes were making the back of her neck crawl. That subconscious danger signal made her very suspicious. Carol had learned to trust her hunches while fighting kzinti in the borderland of Sol.

Things were seldom what they seemed in space.

Carol poked Bruno in the ribs with a forefinger for emphasis. "I think you're right. Don't underestimate them."

"I agree," he nodded.

"The big one in particular seems locked and loaded for a whole herd of angry bandersnatch. Look at the gear it's carrying, Tacky. Edged weapons *and* laser tech at the same time? Makes no sense."

Bruno's smile faded as he thought it over. "Thing about aliens is . . ." he began.

". . . they're *alien*," she finished with him in a tired chorus. "Many thanks to your old buddy Buford Early."

"The real one, that is," Bruno agreed.

Carol took a deep breath and faced the three-legged aliens visible through the bubble-window. "How do you know us?" she demanded.

The smaller of the two aliens' twin heads suddenly whipped up, facing one another eye to eye. Just as quickly, the alien's necks returned to their previous posture. Carol wondered what *that* meant.

"Captain Faulk," it fluted in mellow tones, "time is, as I stated earlier, of the essence. Still, it would perhaps be more conducive to swift results if we shared names. Labels are, after all, important to your species. Am I not correct?"

Carol felt an incongruous smile spread across her face. She just couldn't help it.

The alien's two heads cocked in different directions, the single eyes in each head blinking with almost human-looking lashes. "Captain Faulk?" it sang. "Is this communications module translating my words properly? You are not responding."

"Oh, we understand you," Bruno broke in, sounding both tired and amused. "We just have a little trouble believing in you."

The alien looked at Bruno for a few seconds, then turned back to Carol. "We, too, have difficulties when meeting new species. May I continue?"

The odd alien waited until Carol finally shrugged agreement.

"Excellent," it warbled. "You may call me Diplomat, after my profession." One head gestured cautiously at its companion. "This one you may address as Guardian, or . . ." Here the alien paused, an odd and somehow hesitant note in its voice. ". . . Warrior."

Carol pulled on her lower lip. "Are we out of the waveform guide and into the emitter array, then?"

After a pause, the smaller alien's twin necks snapped upward, the two flat heads facing each other, eye to eye. Again, the heads immediately returned to a normal posture.

Normal, Carol reflected, for a three-legged alien. And where *was* the beast's brain? Not in those tiny flat heads. The midsection?

The creature spoke, the voice unmistakably that of a sultry-throated young human woman. "Ah, I at length apprehend your meaning from symbolic context. It is an attempt at something like discordant synthesis, or . . . humor."

Bruno chuckled out loud and leaned close to Carol's ear. "I see that your Belter lack of humor is appreciated even by alien species," he whispered, breath warm and comforting.

Carol ignored him, looking directly at the weaponry carried by the larger alien. She then raised an eyebrow at the smaller one.

It whistled a high melodic note. "To answer your unspoken supposition, Captain Faulk, you have nothing

to fear from my quiet companion. Under normal
circumstances, you would never have the opportunity
to perceive that particular caste of my race."

Bruno crossed his arms and spoke up. "That is what
you say, my friend."

Carol was slightly annoyed at Bruno's interruption,
but he did have a point. Military discipline had its
drawbacks.

"Quite so, Mr. Takagama," replied the little alien.
"However, I should point out that had I or our hosts
intended you harm, you would not have been repaired
and awakened."

"Repaired?" Carol was confused.

"Of course. You both received a very high dosage of
ionizing radiation and were severely damaged during
your . . . ah . . . acquisition." The small alien hummed
for a moment. "Of course, you were not so severely
damaged as your more aggressive and combative
opponent in the next environment locus."

It gestured with a loose-lipped head toward the clear
aperture Carol had seen earlier. That bubble-window
still displayed the fallen kzin next to his singleship. The
whitish tendrils wrapping the orange-furred figure were
moving slowly.

Bruno nudged Carol. "That ratcat must have received
Principle knows how high a dose when the *Sun-Tzu*
exploded. How could they repair such damage so
quickly?"

Before Carol could reply, the larger of the two aliens
trumpeted loudly. The other alien fluted and sang back.

"My esteemed colleague is quite correct," the smaller
alien crooned, honey voiced. "The briefing with our
hosts was quite explicit that haste was crucial. There is
not time to deal with these niceties, as I mentioned
earlier. We must take action, with your help."

"I don't understand," Carol frowned.

"Nor should you at this point. Suffice it to say that because of your . . . altercation . . . with these . . . kzin creatures . . . you have succeeded in rousing forces you would not have wished to disturb, had you but known. That difficulty must be addressed immediately."

The larger of the three-legged aliens trumpeted again, a martial brass band.

"Again, my colleague is quite right," sang the alien called Diplomat in clear bell-like tones. "If we live long enough to address the problem properly."

Frustration grew in Carol. She knew that they were in trouble, but it irked her not to know that trouble's extent. "At least tell us what will be done with us, why we have been captured."

The little alien cocked both heads at Carol in different directions. "You have not been captured, Captain Faulk."

"What would you call it, then?" drawled Bruno. "It seems to me that the universe has been pushing us around a lot."

"Mr. Takagama, are you feeling well? Paranoia is not a common condition for your naive species, according to my briefings. As for the term 'capture,' I would think the word 'rescue' more appropriate, were I you."

"Rescued from what?" asked Carol, feeling a cold chill run across her shaven skull and down her back. Now they were getting to it.

"From the Zealots," replied the small alien. "A delicate balance of power has been upset by your unwitting actions."

Carol did not like the sound of this. "Zealots?"

The alien called Diplomat sang quickly. "There exist different factions of our low-temperature hosts. Some are traders in information and goods to life-forms like ourselves. Other factions have . . . ah . . . more obscure concerns."

"Obscure?" Bruno prodded at the alien, seeming just as out of place as Carol felt. "You mean hostile?"

A slow roll of one of the heads, flashing eyes. "The Zealots are a Traditionalist group with very different attitudes than our hosts. They will arrive soon, and will attempt to destroy us all. Thus, we must most assuredly not be present at that time."

Again, the enclosure with its false sky and too-green grass seemed to whirl around Carol. The alien ground pushed firmly up against her feet, but she felt as if she were in free fall.

"Bruno?" she murmured. She glanced over and saw that his eyes were narrowed, face pinched.

"Yes, Captain-my-captain?"

Carol sighed. "We appear to have fallen right into someone else's war."

A snort. She felt Bruno squeeze her arm. "You sure know how to show a fella a good time."

Carol turned back to the aliens. "What happens now?" She needed more information, fast, but the issue of their fate needed to be settled first.

Again, the creature cocked both heads in different directions. An expression of confusion? "What every intelligent being would do under these circumstances."

Carol licked her lips. "And that would be? . . ."

"We run," chorused both the little alien and Bruno.

Chapter Seven

The Radiants moved throughout the young universe, and plumbed the diverse strangenesses within it. The beings burned as bright as their cores with curiosity, all on behalf of They Who Pass.

There was much to learn, and vast room for such a broad education. The sentient clouds of plasma swam within vast seas of glowing gas and lanes of sparkling dust, ever seeking, and felt the electrical equivalent of awe.

All they learned, they reported to their creators on the other side of the cosmic string.

But some parts of that fresh reality were beyond the abilities of the Radiants to explore. The world of cold matter defeated the ever-curious plasma beings. The very touch of dark solids greedily drained away the heart-fire of the incandescent gas clouds. The Radiants were forced to ignore their innate programmed curiosity for a time, and avoid the enigmatic points of darkness that swung around stellar fires.

There was still much to learn, and an entire new universe as lecture hall.

To They Who Pass, this new universe made little sense. It seemed paradoxically composed of two extremes: the very hot and the very cold. The Radiants could easily explore the former conditions on behalf of their masters, but the bitter chill remained quite deadly. They Who Pass grew intrigued at these newest findings from the other universe, and sent fresh instructions through the cosmic string window to their Radiant servants. This still-stranger frontier of cold must be explored as well.

Under careful instruction, the Radiants recapitulated the original act of their own genesis. They used the interactive properties inherent to matter far colder than their own diffuse blaze. Instead of patterns implicit in the dance of atoms stripped bare of electron clouds, subtle and little-known forces pushing and pulling at atoms were investigated.

Tests began. Cool gas clouds were visited and influenced at a distance by the Radiants. The beings of plasma reached out with tools of collective force into the dusky strangeness. Linear chains of atoms met and branched, joined, and were torn asunder with careful prodding. Complexity grew, as did the knowledge of the Radiants.

They Who Passed marveled in their distant way at such knowledge, and urged their servants to continue the investigation. Regardless of the medium used, Mind was formed from Pattern. Perhaps even this killing blackness could give birth to Mind, and thus fresh servants, in yet another mode of existence.

Much was discovered about condensed matter. It was blunt, willful, incapable of vibrating with the singing energies that were the lifeblood of the Radiants. But diffuse clouds of dust were not enough. With great care, the Radiants learned to come near the cold deadly

spheres of matter, and study their composition by deft
inductance. Patterns were imposed by the Radiants into
slow currents of superconductive liquids, found in pools
on the cold lumps of matter. There, as in the plasma
clouds of the Radiants' birth, impurities lent a
nonhomogeneous nature to the medium: raw material
for the primitive minds even then forming structures
within the liquid.

As electromagnetic forces were not sufficient to touch
and move cold matter, a skin of protective polymer was
fashioned over the superconductive liquid. Flexible struts
of crystalline material gave shape and strength under
the brute, inexorable pull of gravity.

After a time, a bulbous entity heaved itself out of a
pool of liquid helium. It slowly extruded a strand of
matter from its center. The tentacle slid along the cold
surface, and finally wrapped around a small rock.

Slowly, the dimly thinking coldlife automaton lifted
the rock against the light gravity. It waved the prize
toward the glittering plasmid cloud orbiting the cold
planetoid. The tentacled construct felt something like
a frigid triumph, and quested around for new objects
to investigate.

Thus were the Dark Ones born.

For many revolutions of the galaxy, the Dark Ones
carried out the bidding of the Radiants in the world of
cold matter. The Radiants themselves continued their
explorations at the other end of the spectrum, basking
in heat and light unimaginable. Together, the two classes
of Mind explored the new universe, finding things
awesome and strange.

The Dark Ones moved from cold rock to still colder,
tasting and examining. Learning. Yet it was not sufficient,
as they could sense other worlds in space around them.
They learned to build self-contained nests to carry

expeditions across great distances in search of
knowledge. Such was the curiosity of the Dark Ones
that some nests could travel faster than a photon in
vacuum.

The Radiants in turn fashioned large structures of
gas, dust, and electromagnetic fields. The tenuous
constructs were designed to listen to the faint songs of
other galaxies, or the brittle noises from the surfaces
of neutron stars. Mysteries worth investigating abounded
at the fiery centers and great whorls of galaxies.

Much was learned about the new universe by the
Dark Ones and the Radiants. That information was
carried by the glowing plasma clouds to one of the still
wriggling cracks in time and space. The messenger
Radiant, bloated with information, would intercalate
into the very field lines of the cosmic string, an intimate
touch of blended attraction and repulsion. Stretched
thin, the intelligent cloud would wrap tightly around
the portal between universes, and send the collected
information to They Who Pass, dwelling on the other
side of the cosmic string. In return, new information
and instruction would be transmitted from They Who
Pass into the Radiant messenger. The messenger, in
turn, would free itself from the cosmic string and spread
the new tidings.

So the situation remained for many eons. Until the
Conundrum.

They Who Pass ceased to speak to the Radiants
through the tortured windows of their cosmic strings.
The children they had sired in the new, strange universe
were left to their own devices. To find their own destinies
without the influence of their creators, fallen silent on
the other side of an interdimensional crack between
realities.

The strange children of They Who Pass had drive,
but no longer purpose. Their drive *became* their purpose.

The Radiants soon became uninterested in the Dark Ones, focusing instead on issues far from the solid phase of matter. Some Radiants learned how to transform themselves into less delicate forms, able to withstand existence within the cores of suns. Vast communities of the plasma beings lived in the turbulent core of the galaxy, seeking the unknowable. Others remained wrapped and intertwined within the massive lines of force surrounding the now silent cosmic strings, plaintive, hoping for the return of They Who Pass.

After a time the Radiants seldom communicated with their cold servants, made of dull matter instead of lively plasma. The sentient clouds fell as silent as their creators on the other side of the cosmic string.

They had other concerns.

The Dark Ones, too, were forced to find their own destiny in the cosmos. Many of them simply traveled without end, continuing to observe and store data as they had before—even without a recipient to which they could deliver.

Others made a ritual and religion of following precisely the ways of the Old Time, when Radiant and Dark One and They Who Pass were in constant communication—perhaps the Great Silence was due to a lack of following instructions with strictest accuracy. A few Dark Ones developed their own interests among the other, native minds that eventually dwelled in the new universe. These less organized Dark Ones found that their ancient drive to collect information could be useful, and that it was possible to manipulate these new upstart sources of data to acquire still more.

The majority of the Dark Ones—regardless of social structure—would have nothing to do with other, lesser minds which developed in the new universe. They preferred to brood in a silence to match that of They Who Pass.

Those Dark Ones who did upon occasion interact with the new sentients came to be known by many names throughout the galaxies, a name pronounced by a dizzying variety of communication organs.

In one area of space-time, the various inhabitants called them the Outsiders.

Chapter Eight

Rrowl-Captain's dreams were not pleasant.

They stalked him like a loud predator closing confidently on prey. Crippled bleeding prey, limping across a field without proper cover. Without allies or weapons.

There was no escape.

In his dream, he was still a crèche-kit, with no name other than Second Son of Graach-Gunner. He and his litter brother, First Son of Graach-Gunner, had been inseparable comrades in crèche. In their sleeping lair, after the illuminators were dimmed, they had often hissed and spat about what Hero-Names they would choose when they were both grandly honored for bravery.

As they surely would be so honored. Were they not brave kzinti, as they learned to stalk feral Jotoki in the hunting park?

It did not matter that the crèche teachers were guiding the development of their young muscles and growing hunt-skills with great care and attention to tradition. The pair were young, but would grow into an adulthood of honor, recipients of Hero's Blood for more octals of generations than could be counted.

They were kzin, feeders at the apex of the Great Web of Life. Was there any doubt that a Warrior Heart beat within each of their young chests?

First Son of Graach-Gunner wanted to someday take a Hero-Name from their family history, C'mef. Centuries before, another C'mef had died defending a foppish relative of the Riit against an usurping colonist kzin. Honor was more important than details to Graach-Gunner's family line; the Warrior Heart burned bright in all of them. C'mef would be a proud name to weave back into the honored tapestry of their lineage.

Second Son of Graach-Gunner had admired the liver and Warrior Heart of his litter-brother very much, and wished to honor him in turn. He had always followed his elder brother, claw to claw and fang next to fang against their crèche-foes. Second Son of Graach-Gunner had secretly chosen the name of C'mef's own litter-brother and duel-ally from that long dead time, Rrowl.

As it had been many centuries in the past, so it would be again, now and in the future. C'mef and Rrowl.

Or so Second Son of Graach-Gunner had thought, until his litter-brother had fallen from a rock castle during agility drills. The impact had broken his neck struts, killing First Son of Graach-Gunner instantly.

Second Son of Graach-Gunner was inconsolable, which was unseemly even for a crèche-kit. He had been perhaps too close to his litter-brother, and Graach-Gunner too gruff a father.

But every kzin must stand on his own as he wrestled honor and truth from the jaws of the One Fanged God. Graach-Gunner sent a Stalker in the Night to counsel and correct his second-youngest son's unkzinlike grief.

The Stalkers were priests-of-bad-tidings, coats and thoughts black as their names. They were from every Heroic line, even the Riit, just as the Warrior Heart was part of every kzin lineage.

From time to time, an occasional litter of kits included one or two ebony offspring; the Stalkers of the Night soon took the dark kittens away for training in the priesthood. They stood out in any group of kzinti, the everyday tawny orange with dark patches, spots, and stripes becoming something the eye ignored. A jet black kzin, with eyes the color of an angry sky, was odd and frightening.

Which was, after all, the point of the Stalkers in the Night. They reminded kzinti of the Warrior Heart's devotion to honor and bravery. They were living arbiters of the One Fanged God, much feared and respected.

"So, little one," the ebony figure had hissed at Second Son of Graach-Gunner that dark day. "Your litter-brother has fallen in battle. It is the Will and Claw-swipe of the One Fanged God."

Even frightened by the shadow-kzin priest, the crèche-kit had spoken up. "He fell from a high rock to die! How is that the Will of the One Fanged God?"

The kzin-priest was silent a long moment, then had coughed laughter. "Your fangs are not blunt, small one. But mine are sharper still." A black furred hand tipped with gleaming ebony claws appeared in front of his face, almost touching his eyes. "But you must learn respect to match your liver."

Second Son of Graach-Gunner had squeezed his eyelids closed in fearful obedience. It was the wrong choice.

"Look at me," the hissing voice roared, "Or I will peel your eyelids from your coward eyes like a *vatach*-pelt!"

Rrowl-Captain opened his eyes in fright, the dream dissolving into a chaos of sorrow, lost battles, and green-tinged monkey hell.

His hand leapt to his face, seeking the faint scar that had been left there so many years before by the Stalker in the Night.

He did not know where he was.

A false red sky loomed above him. The air carried odors that seemed right, but were somehow not. White traceries, like *chachatta* webs, clung to him. He carefully stood, brushing the webbing from his body. *Sharpened-Fang* was nearby, laying on its side on sandy soil.

The air was quiet, but his nose sniffed wetly at danger.

What has happened? Rrowl-Captain wondered to himself. *The ugly aliens interrupting the battle with the monkeys shot my ship with some form of energy weapon . . . and then . . .*

Something suddenly occurred to Rrowl-Captain, making him forget the strangenesses around him. All trace of his radiation sickness, a last dark gift from the monkey trap, was gone.

Rrowl-Captain felt well fed and healthy. It should not be so.

"Greetings, Honored One," hissed and spat a voice in the Hero's Tongue behind him, but pitched as high as a tiny kitten's. "We must speak to you, having need of your bravery and honor."

Rrowl-Captain whirled, and saw a hole hanging in midair. No, he realized, more like a window. Through it, he saw strange forms, with three legs and two heads. Rrowl-Captain could see what were surely weapons carried by the larger of the beasts, and smiled a needle grin in challenge.

Then Rrowl-Captain saw the human-monkeys standing behind the alien vermin. The monkeys that had stolen his name and honor. He would taste their blood in his jaws, and that of the other creatures. A holy Rage took him, and he screamed and leaped in fury, throwing himself at his enemies with claws and fangs bared.

Chapter Nine

Bruno stifled a gasp and took a step back as the snarling kzin took flight toward them.

"Wait," Carol breathed, her hand on his arm. She had not moved, other than to tense into a soldier's slight crouch of readiness.

The kzin hit the force-wall at the top of his leap—and bounced backwards into a confused orange heap.

"Impressive," observed Carol. "But not very smart."

He muttered, "I can't get used to this sort of thing." There was some kind of force-shield around their "zoo" enclosure; why shouldn't there be force-shield windows between cages containing different captive beasts? There was a bitter taste of helplessness in his mouth.

Bruno watched Carol put fists on hips and turn toward the other window, where the three-legged aliens that waited with apparent patience.

"What do you want me to say?" she said. A finger stabbed at the orange-and-black-furred form slowly rising to its feet.

"That's what a ratcat is all about. That's why we have to fight them."

"Still," sang the creature called Diplomat, "it is necessary to involve both of your factions in the solution to this . . . ah, difficulty, Captain Faulk. It is of concern to both of your species, after all."

The window displaying the obviously enraged kzin faded, changed into the same false view of distance as the rest of their enclosure.

"How so?" interjected Bruno. He scratched the interface plug on his neck. Maybe if he had been "repaired," it occurred to him, he could Link once again.

Not now.

The larger of the two aliens bugled. The smaller one cocked a head in listening posture. After a moment, it sang back an answer. The musical conversation continued for some time; John Philip Sousa versus Vivaldi.

"My colleague," continued the smaller of the aliens, turning back to Bruno and Carol, "concurs that I should attempt to be straightforward with both of you."

"Meaning?" rapped Carol.

Bruno had seen this before. Carol did not like feeling helpless; she was far too action-oriented. And they couldn't get more helpless: stranded without an interstellar spacecraft, Finagle knew how far from home, in the hands of multiple factions of aliens.

The alien called Diplomat was still speaking. "The pointless battle between your species and the kzin—"

"Wait a second," interrupted Bruno. "They attacked *us*, enslaved our people. I would not call our self-defense pointless."

Carol had nipped his ear between her fingers.

"Tacky, darling," she whispered sweetly. "Let the nice alien finish, would you? We can defend our actions later."

Diplomat had craned heads at Bruno and Carol,

watching them both at the same time, with the loose-lipped idiot stare that so clearly was misleading.

"Thank you, Captain Faulk," Diplomat continued. "As I was singing . . . ah, *saying* . . . the altercation in deep space between your warring solar systems has disturbed a rather traditional faction of our hosts."

Carol pulled at her lip again in thought. "We—the kzin there and ourselves—tread on their territory, perhaps?"

"Excellent simile," replied the little alien. "It is more accurate to say that this Traditionalist faction holds the spaces between stars rather sacred."

Bruno began to understand. "So this is a religious issue in deep space?" It was a bit amusing, and he stifled a chuckle.

Both heads swiveled at once to face Bruno. "Mr. Takagama, if that choking sound you are emitting is actually a vocalization of humor, I can assure that this is a grave situation. The Zealots' so-called religious concerns are based on actual events, from the early era of this universe."

"We have violated their temple?" persisted Carol.

"More like we have stirred up a hornets' nest," added Bruno. He took Carol's hand in his, running his thumb back and forth against her palm.

Diplomat cocked a head at Bruno. "I do not understand."

Bruno held back impatience. "Stinging insects that live in group nests on our worlds, Diplomat. If the nest is disturbed, they attack the disturber as a group."

"Excellent, Mr. Takagama. You grasp the point with both mouths." Again the twin necks shot up, the heads eye to eye for an instant.

"So we leave their temple alone," Bruno said. "We didn't know. Now we do."

"It is not so simple, Mr. Takagama," sang Diplomat.

"The Zealots now see you—and your whole species—
as an irritant to be removed. Our hosts wish to change
this potentially destructive point of view."

"Wait a minute," asked Carol slowly. "Why are we—
or the kzin, or you—important to this faction of
Outsiders?"

"They are called Dissonants," added Diplomat. "They
oppose the ancient strictures of the Zealots, and wish
to forge their own destiny, sometimes in association
with life-forms like ourselves."

"Whatever. I am glad that we were rescued, but where
are we being taken—and why?"

The three-legged alien's hooves beat a complex
pattern. It turned and sang to the larger alien, which
blared music back.

"Carol—" Bruno started to ask, but she squeezed
his arm to signal for silence.

Diplomat turned to face them again. "My Guardian
has argued for becoming yet more direct." The heads
wobbled a bit. "Let me take the points quickly, as time
remains short. There are many things like your species
in the galaxy, as you know full well, considering your
cargo."

"How do you know about that?" asked Bruno. How
could they know about the Tree-of-Life virus still in
the hold of *Dolittle*? They might have found it, of course,
but how would they know what it could do?

The puppeteer waved a head in a slow figure eight
as if dismissing his comment. "The point is that the
Dissonants have worked with your various species many
times in the past. Your own . . . more undomesticated,
feral species appeals to them . . . well, aesthetically."

"We'll table that for the moment," Carol said.

"As you wish," replied Diplomat. "The Dissonants wish
to preserve your species—as well as my own, and the
kzin. We are interesting to them, a source of information."

Bruno broke in, sensing another long speech on the alien horizon. "So where are we now, and where are we going?"

The hemisphere above Carol and Bruno suddenly stopped looking like a sky with fleecy white clouds. It was a bowl filled with a mottled opal radiance that hurt the eyes. Geometrical shapes swam in curdled colors that Bruno could not name. The "sky" twisted and bent, distorted and distorting.

It was like nothing Bruno had ever seen before.

"We are presently," sang Diplomat quietly in his human-sounding voice, "just over one hundred light-years from human space. And moving at three hundred times the speed of light, in another dimension."

"Another dimension?"

"Certainly. It is the only way to travel faster than light, is it not?"

"Hyperspace," breathed Bruno and Carol at the same time.

"Indeed. We are leading the Zealot spacecraft far away from human and kzinti space."

"And . . ." Bruno prompted, still in awe of the eye-straining vision above them. A shape seemed to form, shifting and rotating, moving in a stately procession across the false sky. It grew somehow larger and smaller, then faded into the milky clotted strangeness.

"We hope to engage the Zealot ship here, away from normal space, and destroy it."

"But how?" It seemed to Bruno that he and Carol were far out of their elements, pawn to unreadable forces and minds.

"With your help of course, Mr. Takagama." A head wobbled for emphasis. "But don't feel alone. Guardian and the kzin will go with you."

Chapter Ten

It had been several hours since Diplomat had outlined the plan, and he still could not read the humans well. He knew little about decoding their bizarre body language, changes in chemistry and skin conductivity: all the hints he would need to better predict their actions. Still, was he not known as Diplomat?

"Little Talker," rumbled Guardian, "you do not seem afraid of these aliens now."

Diplomat nodded agreement. In a way, he would miss the giant puppeteer.

True, Diplomat was not as afraid as he had been. Of course, it helped that they were nowhere near the small supply of transformation virus the Dissonant mechanicals had found in the hold of the small human warship. And the humans were on the other side of a force-shield, with no means to disrupt the barrier.

Diplomat had once again focused his minds on the issue at hand, as he had among the Q'rynmoi. If they could not trap and destroy this upstart faction of

Outsiders that the Dissonants had discussed, more was at stake than simply the fate of two primitive and warlike species. That briefing had burned out most of Diplomat's fear. There was fear and then there was Fear.

Diplomat knew something that nonpuppeteers did not: his race was cowardly, until there is no choice but to be brave.

His supply of antidread drugcud helped, of course.

Perhaps the Zealots would put a stop to *all* warmlife, if they could convince enough of the other Outsider factions to join their philosophy. All warmlife in this region were at risk, including the puppeteer race.

The former Pak threat was insignificant in comparison. The Outsiders were everywhere, and potent with unknown abilities.

Much had become clear since he and Guardian had received their briefings, when they had arrived at the Outsider groupship. Dissonants, Traditionalists, Zealots. The faceless form of an Outsider held diversity and challenge, opportunity and threat.

Diplomat and Guardian had taken time to digest and rechew the information given to them, while the damaged humans and kzin were speed-healed by Outsider technology. More accurately, technology developed on one of their hominid experimental worlds, on the other side of the galaxy.

"Dissonants," he sang to the air around him.

"I hear you, Diplomat," replied the voice. It sounded like an educated puppeteer, but he knew that it was a sophisticated translation program. The Outsiders had deep difficulties with communication without such translators. Soon, they would have such a program for these humans. Until then, Diplomat had to speak for them.

"Is everything in readiness?"

"Yes," came the reply. "There is little choice, actually.

If we do not stop the Zealots, here and now, we will all lose much."

Diplomat moved tongue across finger-lips. "Why should the human Bruno help?"

"Indeed. Why should Guardian, or the kzin?"

That had been Diplomat's greatest victory: convincing the furious carnivore that his entire race was in peril, and giving him a chance to help preserve the kzin.

"I would much prefer to eat the monkeys," the kzin had told Diplomat. He had then gone on to threaten Diplomat himself, which was both typical and unimportant. Force-screens were everywhere, and Rrowl-Captain's threats empty.

And Diplomat had no time to be frightened. Later, yes.

As for the Guardian puppeteer, such was her duty and pleasure both. She had gone so far as to verbally worry about Diplomat's safety afterwards, which was out of character for the gruff soldier.

"Diplomat, the Zealots are here in hyperspace with us, and are closing quickly. The spacecraft is ready. The other crewmembers are ready. We must have Bruno Takagama—and his brain—on board."

Diplomat rose to his feet and walked swiftly to the force-shield window.

"Mr. Takagama," he called in the barbarous language the primates used, devoid of music and joy and structure.

The male and female humans walked toward Diplomat, holding hands. The puppeteer guessed this was a gesture of affection.

"We need," began Diplomat, "a decision from you. The Zealots approach in hyperspace, and we intend to use a . . . what is the word? . . . booby trap to stop them."

The taller human—Carol Faulk—had a face without expression. "And you want us to go along?"

"Indeed. You, my Guardian, and the kzin."

"Who will surely eat us," snapped the female.

"I rather doubt it," soothed Diplomat. "There is more at stake here than your own interspecies battles. And Guardian will guard you as well."

The male human, Bruno, looked confused. "I still don't see why your plan will work."

"The Zealots, like our hosts, have a reflex about obtaining information. It is ingrained in every molecule of their being, for reasons older than stars. They will not be able to *not* interrogate the converted spacecraft we have prepared. And you, if they can."

"Why not simply destroy it?" the female human asked.

"Because," repeated Diplomat patiently, "they cannot help but want to know everything about you *before* they destroy you. Once destroyed, it would be impossible to obtain more information."

"I see," mused the center of their plan, already programmed—without his knowledge—by the Outsiders. Diplomat watched the male human scratch at the interface plug in his neck.

How glad I am, thought Diplomat, *that I do not have computational machinery in my head.*

Diplomat did not want to lie actively. "I would not expect all of you to live."

The human called Carol Faulk expelled air from her lips. "No one will live on that ship," she exclaimed.

"And if we do not try, your species—and many others—will be in peril."

The female tried to reply, her tone a song of anger, but the little male human put a hand on her shoulder.

Diplomat looked at him expectantly.

Chapter Eleven

"I'll help," Bruno said calmly.

Carol whirled at looked at him. "Bruno," she exclaimed, "it's a suicide mission! I would expect this from a ratcat, but you?"

"Are you quite sure?" asked the puppeteer.

Bruno had never been so sure of a thing in his life. He somehow felt taller than his short stature had ever allowed.

"Carol," he said, taking her hands in his. "You are a pilot, a soldier."

"Yes, but—" Carol began.

Looking up at her angry Belter face, he shook her hands just a bit to quiet her. "You and I both know that we aren't getting out of this. None of us."

Well, Bruno knew that wasn't exactly true, but it wasn't time for Carol to learn that, quite yet.

Carol nodded jerkily, her face like stone.

"Good," Bruno said. "You have always been the tough one, my protector. Who got me out of *Sun-Tzu*, a wire

237

hanging out of my head?" He leaned a head into her chest, felt the warm softness against his forehead.

One of her hands stroked his neck tentatively.

He looked up. "Carol, I do love you. You have stood by me no matter what. How could I do less for you?"

Carol's eyes gleamed, a small chink in her Belter-pilot-soldier armor.

She smiled slightly. "I guess that we knew going into this that we weren't going to make it out alive."

Bruno nodded. Now came the tough part.

"I love you more than life, Carol Faulk. You made me feel like a human being, which I am not, and never have been."

She started to reply, but Bruno cut her off. "No time, love. The Zealots are here."

He stretched up and kissed her lips. Soft. Bruno stored the memory.

Bruno Takagama took three quick steps back, then shouted.

"Now, Diplomat!"

Anguished, he watched Carol run toward him and hit the invisible barrier the puppeteer had erected between them.

Outsiders Two

Rage. Feral vermin, the Node approaches. Doom awaits all nodes not yet at One with the Holy Radiants.

Humor. Can it be true? The approaching Node acting without instructions from long-silent masters? What of the Pact?

Vengefulness. It is time to put an end to the warmlife vermin, and the feral nodes that support their activities. Soon, all distant nodes will be at One with this Node.

Questioning. Not all. Nodes already at One with the other-Node, yes. Can the Node and this-Node not reach another Pact?

Confusion. Why does the feral node defend the warmlife vermin? They outrage clean geometries with their very existence.

Certainty. Just as the Creators used this-and-other Nodes for information, so does this-Node use the warmlife motes. Their ways are different, and often valuable.

Determination. Feral and heretic both. Even now, by fleeing in this skewed space-time, the other-Node is an affront to the Creators who long ago gave the Nodes purpose.

Amusement. Not-One. The other-Node and this-Node are at One, that this skewed space-time was found during a failed attempt to reach the realm of the Creators. They were not within this realm, so it cannot be an affront to journey within it.

Implacability. Enough. Prepare to be ended, in this geometry or any other.

Chapter Twelve

Carol Faulk stood near the force-window, beside the puppeteer, and tasted ashes in her mouth.

She watched Bruno Takagama walk toward the opening in the force-shields. Vanish from sight, into the long shape of the converted puppeteer spacecraft. She burned to run after him, to somehow stop him. Instead, the force-shield stopped *her*.

"Carol," he had told her as she raged and cursed, "there is a chance that you might survive. If you go with me, you will die with us." Bruno had looked at the alien sky, and then back at her. "I want you to live. It is my choice."

Soldier, shut up and soldier, echoed her own voice, used during the Third Wave the kzin had sent against Earth so long ago. It is every soldier's right to choose life for a friend or lover. And Bruno, small and weak as he was, turned out to be a soldier indeed.

She couldn't even hate the puppeteer. It was Bruno's Finagle-damned *choice* to go on this suicide mission with a puppeteer warrior and a kzin.

Carol hated to admit the truth: If the tables had been turned, she would have done the same thing to earn Bruno a chance to live.

She didn't have to like it.

"Is it time?" Carol asked Diplomat.

The three-legged alien looked at Carol for a long time before replying. "Yes," it finally sang. "It is."

"You have everything under control," she said bitterly. "Can I wish them luck, or is that under your control, too?"

The alien stared at her again, from two angles. "No, Captain Faulk, I will join you in wishing them luck. Random chance is one thing even we cannot control, though we have tried."

Carol puzzled over that statement as the force-shield around the converted puppeteer spacecraft's airlock shimmered and vanished.

Bruno was gone, her heart knew as well as her head.

Chapter Thirteen

Rrowl-Captain settled into the kzin-sized command chair of the converted puppeteer ship. The herbivore that smelled like a predator—Guardian?—fluted readiness.

A taste of bile washed across the kzin's tongue as he looked at the human, sockets for wires inserted into his head like a pond-*wrloch* sucking a Hero's blood.

This was a Hero's Battle Triad?

Despite the hatred Rrowl-Captain held for the monkeys, and still more for the vegetarian aliens, there was a larger foe for now. Perhaps later, after this battle, would he taste their blood.

He had named the converted ship, cobbled together from kzin and human and puppeteer technology, *Greater Vengeance*.

Rrowl-Captain snarled once, and with a claw tip, activated the tiny spacecraft.

The glittering strangeness of the Dissonant Outsider ship fell behind them. Images flickering in midair in front of Rrowl-Captain showed the ship that had carried them into hyperspace expanding and contracting, images roiling in the dense nexus of the extra dimensions. *Greater Vengeance* bucked and jerked with the changes in the stretching fabric of tortured space around them.

In front of them was the blurred and distorted image of their Enemy.

Rrowl-Captain shrieked challenge and increased their apparent velocity. He ignored the green-tinged fears within him. Were not hapless monkeys now his allies—for a time?

The little human was central to the Outsiders' plan. Yet he seemed not to act as a coward, and was willing to meet Honor. It was a confusing idea for Rrowl-Captain.

"What is it, Noble Hero?" snarled and spat the human's translated voice. It burned his liver that Rrowl-Captain's own Hero's Tongue would be translated in turn back into mewling human syllables.

"Human, I am challenging our Enemy. Do you not do the same when you challenge Heroes in battle?" He left out *when you do not leave traps for them, that is*.

"I suppose that we do, Rrowl-Captain," replied the false voice. Monkey squeaks sounding like the Hero's Tongue? *Ahh!*

"Less talk," interrupted the puppeteer soldier's musical voice, soothing even in Rrowl-Captain's language. "I am shifting the patterns of hyperspace around us. This will protect us for a time."

It was difficult to see the great shape of the Zealot ship as it grew at first closer, then farther away. Its geometry seemed to deform and twist as they watched, rather like seeing an image under turbulent water.

"What is the interval until we make contact?" hissed and spat Rrowl-Captain.

"The Zealots sense us now," replied the big puppeteer. "They will attempt to respond at any time." Rrowl-Captain approvingly watched one of its heads caress a weapon in its belt.

Could a . . . vegetarian . . . have the Warrior Heart, as well? he mused. The burning drive to fight against impossible odds, for glory and duty?

"Look yonder," the human called.

The Zealot spacecraft was breaking up into sections, each converging on *Greater Vengeance*. Where there had been one threat moving indistinctly through hyperspace toward them, there were now dozens, surrounding a great spear of a spacecraft.

"These are independent craft?" Rrowl-Captain asked of the soldier puppeteer.

"Yes. I will begin activating weaponry now. We must get near the central mass, still intact."

Rrowl-Captain continued to guide the vessel by instinct, as if stalking prey across a hunting park. The shimmering shape of the central mass grew nearer.

Beams as black as night speared out from *Greater Vengeance*, striking one of the elongated baskets of the smaller Zealot ships. The Outsider ship seemed to wobble, then geometrical shapes began disappearing from it, as if bites taken from an invisible predator.

The kzin swore. "What has happened?" he growled.

Guardian, heads dancing across its weapons console, spoke indistinctly. "When the fields separating hyperspace from normal space fail, the damaged ship seems to vanish into nothingness a bit at a time. Matter such as ours cannot exist here without protection."

Rrowl-Captain still found the damaged ships too similar to the prey of some invisible Beast.

"Captain," shouted the little human-monkey with the damaged brain. "The central core!"

Greater Vengeance now neared the main structure

of the Zealot ship. Rrowl-Captain turned to his own
weapons panel.

"What do we do now?" hissed and spat the kzin.

The Guardian puppeteer continued holding off the
tiny Zealot fighter-ships, sending them into some oblivion
of hyperspace. "It is now up to the human."

Rrowl-Captain walked forward to the viewscreen, and
watched the central core of the Zealot spacecraft open
like some plant bud.

A branching geometrical shape reached out for them
with fractal roots. Like grasping fingers.

Rrowl-Captain fired the strange weapons again and
again, but the distorted environment of hyperspace made
every beam and projectile move randomly toward their
attacker.

A glittering rootlet flew across the strangeness of
hyperspace toward them; now large, then small . . . but
always somehow closer. The kzin tried to dodge the
oncoming object, but with no success.

It sliced through the shining veil of the force-shield
with no effort, and slammed into the hull of *Greater
Vengeance*.

A rupture tore the deck. Dozens of golden tentacles
invaded the crewbubble. Guardian bellowed fury and
became a blur of motion, edged helmets slicing, unable
to use energy weapons in the close confines of the
cabin.

Tentacles burst from another breach in the deck, and
the kzin saw Guardian being pulled apart by arms of
implacable strength.

Rrowl-Captain shrieked, throwing himself toward the
fallen puppeteer. All three legs and both necks were
being pulled in different directions. He slashed at the
golden tentacles with claws, but the shiny arms were
not marked.

Rrowl-Captain was surprised to see the puny human

hammering on one of the tentacles with a strut from the ruptured deck.

The Guardian puppeteer burst apart like a carcass dropped from a height. A fountain of alien blood spilled across the cabin, but Rrowl-Captain saw something glitter strangely. He could see the electronics built into its broken heads and torn body of the soldier-puppeteer.

The coward grass-eaters didn't even trust their defenders, Rrowl-Captain thought, shocked. A half-living thing, half machine. Like the little monkey-human.

Rrowl-Captain leaped back toward his station.

A golden tentacle stabbed down from the ceiling, into his command console. Everything exploded in a flare of greenish light.

Rrowl-Captain lay on his side, back broken. His legs were numb, useless. The force-shields kept the blazing nothingness of hyperspace from consuming them for now, but he could feel the ship shift and turn as the Zealot spacecraft pulled them into its central bulk.

No chance for a clean death, to honor the One Fanged God.

At least he had done battle.

The human knelt next to him, afraid to touch Rrowl-Captain.

"It doesn't look good," the monkey mewled, voice as flat as any machine. "We did our best, though."

The human with the impossible name was speaking English; the translators were no longer working. Still, the kzin had a slave-owner's knowledge of the puny language.

Rrowl-Captain coughed a chuckle. "You not coward," he managed in his broken English. "Even with machine *ch'rowling* your brain, you almost Hero."

"Hero?" the human repeated.

"Yes," he coughed with blood instead of humor. "Warrior Heart not give up."

The human eyes held his own. "Be still. It will be over soon."

Rrowl-Captain reached up and took the human's hand. The small pink fingers vanished into his huge black grasp.

"Take Name," he spat.

"I don't understand," replied the human with the impossible name.

"Take Name of C'mef." A spasm passed through his body. He turned his head and vomited noisily. The taste was foul as defeat.

The human said nothing.

"Someday," Rrowl-Captain hissed in a whisper, "Heroes and monkeys fight together, as we now." He closed his eyes. "If not we eat you and your offspring first."

The kzin thought that he felt the human squeezing his hand in response.

A roar filled the cabin as the force-shield failed. He opened his eyes and saw a black shape reaching for them, silhouetted against the bright muddled insanity of hyperspace.

The shape seemed to have many arms and a flexible, squirming bulk. To the kzin, it had the fearful dark face of the old Stalker in the Night from long ago. Green laser light blazed behind it.

Eyes open this time, Rrowl-Captain screamed defiance at it in the name of his litter-brother. He had found his Warrior Heart.

Chapter Fourteen

1000100111100111001111101110011111101010100010010010
11110100101000101100111010101100100010010000010111

The sky was wine dark, Homeric.

The sun beat down mercilessly, an unforgiving foe on the field of battle.

Theosus (*Bruno*) stood tall, his shadow stark and black against the hard packed soil. He lifted his spatha to the sky with a muscular arm—salute! Yellow light ran like butter down the glittering blade. The bronze chain mail he wore moved warmly against his skin in the hot afternoon. Scents of dust and iron blood stung his nose and made his eyes smart.

Theosus (*Bruno*) looked around for the foe he knew he must face. It was his Fate.

But I'm not an ancient soldier, his mind started to object. The thought whirled away, like Rrowl-Captain's body parts had before everything went blank. When the Zealot spacecraft had attacked, destroying even the cyborg Guardian puppeteer.

249

The images swept from his mind, flying away, like . . . birds? Theosus (*Bruno*) shook his head.

Suddenly, Colonel Buford Early was standing before Theosus (*Bruno*), carrying a pike. The head of the pike blazed like a sun, making him squint in pain. The UN Space Navy uniform the image of the other man wore was matched by a legionnaire's helmet.

"Son," the old man's face rasped, "your very thoughts betray you. I can read you like a book." Early's features began to sag and melt, then reform, like hot wax.

"So can other things, and more closely than any book," added a new voice from behind him.

Theosus (*Bruno*) turned quickly, his own plumed helmet almost falling from his head. Carol Faulk stood there, hair incongruously long and red, a flowing gown covering her Belter-thin body.

"Carol?" he asked incredulously, his mind in two places at once, thirty centuries and thousands of light-years apart.

"Less, and yet more," the figure replied cryptically. Her hair changed color, became black, then shortened to the familiar Belter crest. In an instant it reverted to its earlier state. Her eyes kept changing color, as did her skin.

"Why am I here?" Theosus (*Bruno*)'s mind hurt, like the time he had hung upside down in a crashed aircar, with a crushed skull, and . . . and . . .

Even those thoughts and images flew away, leaving a gaping hole in his mind. His thoughts probed gingerly around the ragged holes in his memory, like a tongue exploring the hole left by a missing tooth.

A tooth ripped from his jaw against his will.

The figure of Buford Early spoke again. "Your thoughts are no longer your own, son. Protect them, until it is Time. The center cannot hold, boy, unless you make it."

Theosus (*Bruno*) was puzzled. A few verses of Yeats's poetry seemed to leap from his brow like birds, flapping away like his other thoughts. Vanishing into the green clouds and blue humming air.

Were all of his thoughts going in the same direction? What did it mean? Theosus (*Bruno*) could not be certain. Was he losing his mind?

"Nothing is being lost, Tacky," whispered the Carol figure in his ear, though she was standing some distance away. "Your thoughts are being *taken*, read, analyzed."

"Why?" he managed, confused, looking from one to the other of the two shifting figures. He could no longer remember how Carol smelled, or where they had met.

His mind was being taken from him, a bit at a time. Theosus (*Bruno*) would have to stop whatever was doing this to him. Before he lost all of the contents of his mind.

And there was something more he had to do.

"Where?" he repeated.

The image of Buford Early pointed with his blazing pike, which lengthened, stretched long, and seemed to touch a crumbling ruin on the plain before him.

The sun illuminating Theosus (*Bruno*) with such hot bright light began to flicker and dim. A cool wind brushed his skin, making him shiver.

He turned. The Early figure was gone. Theosus (*Bruno*) could no longer remember the first name of the vanished man; that too had flown away into the growing darkness. The image of Carol, now with skin as red as the sky was dark, returned his gaze sadly.

Theosus (*Bruno*) swallowed, his throat dry with the dust of the arena he knew he was to face.

"Will you come with me?" he asked Carol's image.

"I cannot." Tears welled in her eyes, and glittered like jewels in the dimming light. "You must do this alone, Bruno."

He turned and walked away, unseeing. Part of Theosus (*Bruno*) knew that all of this was simply an image inside his head, the most sense his mind could make of what was happening to him in reality.

He had a job to do. Spacecraft controls or the hilt of his spatha; what was the difference, really?

Fate waited for him in both places.

His sense of unreality grew as he walked across the darkening plain toward ruins the color of sun-bleached bone. Toward the figure that he somehow knew waited there, moving unpleasantly, as if with many arms.

Whatever it was, it awaited him. Theosus (*Bruno*) left his spatha unsheathed, and began to hurry toward the opening he saw between fallen blocks of stone. The gate was broken, bordered with stones jagged as cruel teeth. He didn't want to be there in the dark.

Theosus (*Bruno*) entered the long-abandoned palaestra. The arena was deserted. There were no murals or carvings to adorn the walls.

The Hydra was waiting for him, as he had expected. Known.

It stood twice as tall as Theosus (*Bruno*), like a great black cylinder topped with dozens and dozens of black ropy arms, all squirming toward him. Each arm ended in a mouth, filled with whirling lamprey teeth.

He felt a memory—*skin sliding across his legs, a smell of clean sweat and desire in his nostrils, as his lips met Carol's*—tear loose from his mind, and take flight.

An arm snatched it from the air, teeth crunching on a part of Theosus (*Bruno*). Gone forever.

Rage filled him as he set upon the Hydra, his spatha screaming challenge in the air as it swung. The flesh of the thing was insubstantial, but sizzled and popped as clean steel sliced into it.

"You will take no more from me," Theosus (*Bruno*) grated as he swung his broadsword again and again, pulpy flesh and dark blood flying. The wind began to pluck at his clothing. A distant thunder rolled in the dark greenish air.

The Hydra moved with him, sprouting two arms for each Theosus (*Bruno*) lopped off. It seemed to be laughing at him, an electronic hissing that rivaled the windstorm sweeping the palaestra. Sand from the arena floor blew into his eyes, making him squint.

And for every swing Theosus (*Bruno*) made, one of the Hydra's arms, snake-quick, snatched a mouthful of memories from him. He began to swing his spatha two handed as the light began to fail, and heads fell into gory piles on the arena floor. But still more arms and heads sprouted, ever hungry for the experiences that made up Theosus (*Bruno*). Dodging his weary swings, the sharp teeth took and took, a bit at a time.

—*The puppeteers he had met.*

—*The name the kzin had given him before he had died.*

—*The name of his university.*

—*Carol's last name.*

—*The name of their spacecraft.*

—*The feeling of Transcendence when he was Linked.*

—*The names of his father and mother.*

Everything that he *was* seemed to vanish into the swelling black shape of the Hydra towering over him, triumphant. Unfeeling, Theosus (*Bruno*) let his spatha drop from exhausted fingers to the arena floor.

The arms of the Hydra kept him upright as it fed upon his memories. The pain was excruciating. He wanted to scream out a woman's name, but had forgotten whose.

Bruno, whispered a man's voice he did not recognize, *it's all right to let go now*.

He looked down at himself, past the nest of squirming arms entering his body. His skin was beginning to become transparent. He could see his heart beating within a cage of snakes.

Oh, Tacky, Theosus (*Bruno*) heard a woman's voice cry from so far away. *I love you so*.

"I love you," he croaked. Theosus (*Bruno*) suddenly remembered something old, massive, powerful.

Something the Dissonants had buried deep within him, to use here and now. A weapon.

It was Time.

His beating heart within his chest changed shape, from muscle to jewel to a cylinder of mining explosive. It was the signal and program the Dissonant Outsiders had planted inside him, before setting him against the Zealot spacecraft.

"Now!" he shrieked, and released the fast, slick disease. A distant equivalent of a computer virus, that the rebel Outsiders had planted deep within his brain and circuitry.

A blaze of light seared upward from his chest, burning with a clean, pure fire. The Hydra cried out and tried to withdraw.

Laughing weakly, Theosus (*Bruno*) hung on to the burning arms, forcing more of the blazing light into the Hydra's heart. It shrieked again, trying to force him away, but he clung to the Hydra. The pure fire raged in vengeance.

The Hydra itself burst into flame, every arm a streak of flame slicing the blackness around him. Clots of fire blazed in the distance. More shrieks joined the din.

The portion of Theosus (*Bruno*)'s mind not trapped within the Dream knew that this was all metaphor and representation; that the computer virus was spreading from Bruno into the group mind of the Zealot Outsiders. The self-replicating pattern would expand and move within each mobile unit of the Zealot mind, erasing and randomizing data packets.

He knew that he would die with the Zealots, lost forever in the other dimension that was hyperspace.

But *she* would live, even if her name had been torn from him by the Zealots. And perhaps the Dissonants could convince the Radiants . . . and their Masters . . . to force other Zealot ship-minds . . . to leave human space alone.

Pain. So much.

The light became still brighter. Began to pulse like a great heart of flame. The arms of the Hydra, nothing but fire now, still tugged and pulled. But he hung on.

Agony could be so pure.

The Dream began to die around him.

Bruno could feel his own brain circuitry begin to fail. His biological components burned with eddying currents as the shielding around the Zealot ship began to fail. The twisted space-time of hyperspace began to enter, leaking into the bubble that had been protected by the Zealot equipment.

A soundless explosion filled his sensorium, colors beyond spectrum, sounds beyond pitch, sensations beyond feeling. He could feel his back arch as a soundless keening filled his head.

Pain. Everywhere.

Bruno finally became One with the All.

1000 100 111 100 11 100 111 110 11 100 111 110 10 1000 100 100 10
111 10 100 10 1000 10 1 100 11 10 10 10 1 100 1000 100 10000 10 111

Chapter Fifteen

Carol and the two-headed puppeteer stood close to one another. They watched the swirling colors and strange shapes of hyperspace through the view hemisphere above them. None of what she saw made sense, even with the Dissonant Outsider enhancements for their benefit.

"I can't see a damned thing," she whispered. Carol thinned her lips in fatalism. She had seen friends die before, even lovers.

But Bruno?

"They have taken the human ship inside the Zealot main craft," observed Diplomat, necks weaving as he observed the view portal. His left head dipped into a pouch and emerged, chewing slowly.

"How do you know?" she asked. The alien grass beneath her bare feet was cool and remote. The Zealot spacecraft above her was a blurry, shifting collection of warped geometrical shapes, now close, now far away.

"I will improve the image resolution for your benefit," replied Diplomat.

If Bruno has been taken aboard the Outsider ship, he must be dead, she thought. Carol's face became hot, and the beginnings of tears stung her eyes. She fought the tide of emotions.

In the back of her mind, Carol saw Bruno's wry smile, his look of surprising innocence in his old, old eyes. *Oh, my love,* she thought. *You were no soldier, Linked or un-Linked. How could you have done this wasteful thing?*

She could feel one of Diplomat's heads looking at her curiously, but ignored it.

Through the view portal, she saw the kaleidoscopic image of the Zealot warship shift and smear, colors and shapes distorted by the bizarre topology of hyperspace around them. It was difficult to clearly see the hostile Outsider ship, but Carol's instincts jangled her nerves like an alarm.

A tiny, glittering speck seemed to merge with the collection of shapes and forms that was the Zealot spacecraft.

"Will it all be for nothing?" she asked.

"I think not," the puppeteer sang in its sultry woman's voice. "The Dissonants have placed a . . . trap . . . within Mr. Takagama."

"A trap?"

"Yes. A self-replicating pattern that will wreak havoc on the Zealot group mind. It will make more copies of itself, increasing confusion and destruction."

"But what will happen to Bruno?" Carol asked, knowing the answer.

As if in answer, the Zealot ship seemed to shimmer. Waves of darkness passed over it.

"I think," sang the puppeteer, "that Mr. Takagama has been successful."

Carol could not look away.

The Zealot spacecraft suddenly seemed to have a

hexagonal hole in its center. Triangular segments began to vanish along the hexagon, increasing in size.

As if the Outsider ship were being eaten.

"What . . . ?"

"When the force-shields are lost," sang Diplomat softly, "the matter from our space-time continuum can no longer exist in hyperspace."

"Where does it go?"

The little puppeteer shook his head at Carol. "Anywhere. Everywhere. Nowhere."

The Zealot ship was a bizarre patchwork of holes and cavities. The rate of the absorption of the spacecraft by hyperspace was increasing. A thin silvery filigree of brightness shone against the blurred opalescence. Then—

Nothing.

The Zealot ship was gone. And Bruno Takagama with it.

She turned to Diplomat. "Is it—" she began.

"It is over."

Carol did not know how to mourn the man, to remember him. Her eyes burned, yet no tears filled them.

She had always been a practical woman, strong and capable. Carol knew that in her bones. But Bruno had seemed oblivious to it. He had opened her up, defused her cynicism. Carol's mind dredged up bits and pieces, fragments of the brave little man's life with her, inside the dingy corridors of the *Sun-Tzu*.

It all had to *mean* something.

Even stranded far from human space, in a spacecraft of alien manufacture moving in another dimension, Carol knew that humanity was worth something. It was more than weapons or technology or sex or fighting.

Bruno had taught her that.

She was standing in front of an alien that no human

had ever seen, inside an impossible spacecraft built by aliens still stranger. She was too good a soldier to think that she would be allowed to go home. Would they dissect her, like some laboratory animal? Or break her very mind down into pieces, as they had done with poor Bruno, when first taken aboard?

Her life—all of it—had to be worth something, more than an impotent challenge to the night sky. Black entropy could not *always* win, not here and now.

She had fought for things she had believed in, made a difference. Had been true to the things in which she had believed. So had Bruno. Bruno Takagama would not want her to give up, no. He never had, not even when fighting against himself.

Carol remembered Bruno's love of old poetry, from the bad old days when humans had walked alone across a single world. Poetry scribbled with pigments on sheets of flattened vegetable matter. Long-dead words that had resonance after centuries.

One of them came to mind, by someone named Hunt, written before the atom had yielded up its energies to mankind, and the gene her potent secrets. It had been stored on one of Bruno's recreation datachips, and had pleased her. Light and silly, but with a sting of truth to it.

Carol whispered the words aloud, ignoring the nonhumans listening to her.

> "Say I'm weary, say I'm sad,
> Say that health and wealth have miss'd me,
> Say I'm growing old, but add,
> Jenny kissed me."

Carol turned to the alien, and drew herself UN Space Navy straight. She wanted to do the memory of Bruno proud. He had faced his fate well; so should she. Carol prepared to speak.

"Well," a voice said into her ear from the air around her, "I must admit I have never kissed anyone named Jenny. But kissing Carol Faulk is something to remember."

Bruno's voice.

Carol's jaw dropped—then she closed it. Anger quickly formed in the pit of her stomach. "This is some kind of trick," she grated, moving without thinking toward the little two-headed alien, her fists raised like bludgeons.

Her nose banged painfully into the invisible barrier. The alien was prepared; Carol had to give him that.

Even with the protective shield between them, Diplomat had turned to run. It looked over its shoulder with one head.

"Captain Faulk," the two-headed alien sang quietly, "I can assure you that I have no intention of tricking you." The single eye in the head facing her glittered. "Can I trust you to eschew violent action?"

She lowered her shaking fists and nodded.

"I wish to offer you what you humans would call . . . a deal. Is that the correct idiom?" The little head that had been speaking paused, cocking to one side.

Carol said nothing, still seething. Would they make a dead man pawn to their plans, too?

"No matter," Diplomat continued. "A demonstration is in order." The alien raised its voice. "Mr. Takagama?"

"Yes?" replied Bruno's voice from nothing, again.

"Since Captain Faulk is . . . underwhelmed? . . . by my approach, would you please explain your presence."

Carol's head whirled.

"It *is* me, Carol. Before the Dissonants sent us against the Zealot ship with the databomb in my circuitry, they uploaded my mind into their processing core."

"But that's—"

"Impossible?" A tone of humor entered the familiar voice. "You have always forgotten how much of me is electronic."

Still suspicious, she thought about it for a moment. There was some truth in the words, but it could be a trick; a souped-up version of the Buford Early hologram when she and Bruno had first been taken aboard the Dissonant spacecraft.

"Do you want me to quote the rest of that poem?" Bruno's voice asked. "I can, you know. Leigh Hunt was one of my favorite poets. Or would you prefer Yeats? Dylan Thomas? Or how about Gulati?"

"No," she answered quickly, not wanting to believe. "Information is information. Bruno's datachip collection was in *Dolittle*, and could have been downloaded."

For once, the little Puppeteer kept quiet while Carol said nothing. Waiting, half hoping.

"I remember walking out of the Black Vault with Colonel Early and Smithly Greene, while you were walking into the building." Was there a smile in the voice? "You looked good under lunar gravity. We were just back from a roundtable on antimatter containment. Colonel Early introduced us, but you looked at me like I was a bug."

Carol smiled. The first time she had met Bruno Takagama, she had thought he *was* a bug. "I suppose I did. But—for the sake of argument—how is this possible?"

"The Outsiders do not—cannot—think as we do. They require a model of alien thought, as a translator."

She pulled on her lip. "An electronic slave?"

"Hardly. They know how to restrict my . . . growth . . . to keep me human. They want to keep a copy of my mind as a translator."

Bruno's mind, loose in any computer architecture, would mutate and change rapidly, turning into something inhuman. His reactions to extended Linkage proved that. But did the Outsiders know that much about how a human mind operated?

"There is more, Captain Faulk," interjected the puppeteer.

She nodded at him to continue.

"Our hosts can build Mr. Takagama a fresh biological body. They can use what they learned when you were first taken on board, along with the autodocs on *Dolittle*." The weaving heads peered at Carol. "And then they can download his mind into it."

"Impossible," she scoffed.

Diplomat pawed delicately at the turf beneath his hooves. "You seem to use that word often, Captain Faulk."

Wasn't hyperspace impossible? Or how about a galactic war between creatures of flame and ice? She was certain that, even now, she was not being told even a fraction of what was truly at stake.

"Carol," Bruno's voice broke in. "Please listen. Please."

"If this is another trick," she reminded Diplomat almost gently, "I will find a way to get around these force-shields and wring your necks—one at a time."

The weaving heads stopped. "You would do this? Truly, Captain Faulk?"

"If you tell the truth," she clipped, "you have nothing to fear, do you?"

The puppeteer considered her statement. "With your kind, there is always something to fear."

Carol held back a smile. "Keep that in mind."

A head cocked. "As you say, Captain Faulk. Though you do not improve your position with threats. But it is true that the Outsiders will download Mr. Takagama's stored mind into a rebuilt body. It would be most difficult under normal circumstances, but so much of Mr. Takagama's mind was . . ."

"Mostly circuitry," added Bruno's voice helpfully.

"Yes, electronic . . . so that the task would be much easier."

"What is the catch?" Carol asked. "I doubt that even aliens do favors out of the goodness of their hearts."

The puppeteer froze for a moment, then both heads leaped up and faced one another again.

"Wonderful phrase," the three-legged alien sang.

"The catch," reminded Carol.

"It is unlikely that you will be returned to human space soon. The Outsiders do not want extensive information regarding them distributed, until they are known by a new species."

Carol finally did laugh. "Diplomat, I don't know *anything* about the Outsiders. And I just witnessed a battle between two factions."

"Nonetheless." Again, the little alien pawed the lawn in impatience. "The Outsiders require that you and the . . . reconstituted Mr. Takagama stay out of human space, until such time as the Outsiders make themselves known to your race."

"Easy to do," Carol pointed out to the puppeteer. "Our ship is useless. Do you intend to strand us somewhere?"

The puppeteer moved from hoof to hoof lightly. "Not at all, Captain Faulk. You and Mr. Takagama would assist me in my dealings with alien races." The eyes on different heads held hers. "You seem relatively unfrightened of new things, and I find your insights interesting. You will make useful companions and coworkers."

"And once humans make contact with Outsiders or puppeteers?"

Diplomat's right head wobbled up and down loosely. "You would of course be returned to human space."

Yeah, right, Carol thought to herself. But what choice did she have, really? There was only one more thing. . . .

"Bruno," she called.

"I hear you, Carol. Will you agree to Diplomat's terms?"

"If you are with me, Tacky, yes. But—even if they can do all they promise—how do I know it is *you*?"

The voice of Bruno Takagama sighed. "Carol, I can't answer that question. Are you the same person when you wake up as you were when you fell asleep? And can you prove it?"

"This is a little different—" But the disembodied voice cut her short.

"Not at all. A great deal of my mind was stored electronic data; you know that. And did you not think it was me after the EMP fried my brain?"

The Bruno-voice had a point, but still . . .

"Wait a minute," she argued. "You only have Bruno's memories up until he left for the Zealot ship."

"True enough," replied the voice. "But again: You were prepared to take care of me after the EMP blast, even had I been seriously brain damaged, right?"

She nodded. "Yes," she added, not knowing if Bruno's mind could see her.

"How is this all that different?"

She could not disagree with the voice's point. Was she doing the right thing? She was Finagle only knew how far away from Earth or Wunderland. What *could* she do? And she might learn something, if the little alien was not treacherous.

Carol thought about a completely foreign set of stars and planets, strange aliens and odder adventures. Things no human had ever seen. And wouldn't see, if Diplomat had its way, for some time yet.

But she would. And—maybe—she would do so with Bruno by her side.

"Yes," Carol said simply. "I accept."

She could hear Bruno's voice sigh.

"Excellent," replied Diplomat.

Carol held out a hand. It couldn't have all been for nothing. "There is one more thing, Diplomat."

"What is it, Captain Faulk?"

Carol's eyes jogged back and forth, trying to hold the gaze of the two weaving heads. "We can't leave humanity to be kzin bait."

"We will not obliterate the kzinti," Diplomat sang firmly. "They are aggressive, but may someday be useful. You know this, surely."

"Fine," Carol replied. "But they have too much of a technological edge. How can we humans hold our own long enough to learn to live with the ratcats?"

The two snake-heads of the puppeteer again flipped up and stared one another in the eyes. "Captain Faulk, I have an excellent idea regarding that concern of yours."

"Do tell," Carol drawled. She would have to play this one carefully. Maybe it was possible to salvage something from this debacle, after all.

Why, sometimes I've believed as many as six impossible things before breakfast, Carol thought to herself. The phrase did, she decided, have a certain ring to it. A good antidote for her becoming too dogmatic, he had told her. Carol had always wondered where Bruno had dug up that phrase.

Perhaps she could ask him soon. In the flesh.

Chapter Sixteen

In the scented meditation chamber the Dissonants had constructed for him, Diplomat sat with folded legs before a holoscreen.

The image showed a grassy sward, beautifully crimson red with *lolaloo* foliage, simply *made* for a long, hard gallop. It was the estate that the Hindmost had promised Diplomat upon his retirement.

He whistled a sad melody, thinking of the work before him. A terrifying trip to the holiest of places for the Outsiders, the region where both Radiant and Outsider were born . . .

If only another puppeteer were present, even Guardian.

At least Diplomat would have some help. These humans were so unlike most of the Pak variants produced by the Dissonants. The titanic ring of a world that the Outsiders had constructed so long ago was home to many diverse humanoid species—all with different outlooks, different skills. Art, technology, philosophy—to the

Dissonant Outsiders, it was all trade goods, and could be used as tender for information across an entire galaxy.

Perhaps even beyond.

And—perhaps—the Outsiders kept Diplomat's people in zoos, as well. It was impossible to know.

A low tone filled the chamber with music. Diplomat fluted an acknowledgment.

"The re-creation of the Bruno-human has begun," sang the Outsider puppeteer translation program. "We have learned much about the physiology of this variant species."

The little puppeteer shook his right head up and down twice—the gesture the humans called "nodding." It was an agreement or acceptance signal between them, one he knew he should learn.

"They have agreed to aid us?" persisted the synthesized voice.

"Of course," Diplomat sang in reply. "The one named Carol had no choice."

"Why? Her coding partner—"

". . . mate . . ." Diplomat whistled in correction.

". . . mate, then, was enough of an impetus?"

"Indeed. Also, the promise of help for her species." The Outsider voice sounded a bit confused. "We would have done that in any event. The hominids are special interests of ours, and this species has even more generality than the other variant forms under study."

"They do not know that," Diplomat reminded his host.

Still, it was good that the Dissonants had decided to aid the humans.

The Outsiders said nothing for a time. Diplomat knew from his dealings with the coldlife traders that they would speak when ready, and not before.

"We were not," stated the Outsider program, "responsible for these Pak variants, despite our intense interest in them. They are escaped ferals. There is no violation of Treaty or Pact."

"I gathered as much." Were the Outsiders just as driven by self-justification as a puppeteer? Even with circulatory fluid a few degrees above Absolute Zero? Diplomat's necks flipped up and looked at one another in a chuckle.

The synthesized voice became stern. "A new Pact must be drawn, at the Oracle."

Diplomat ran a forked tongue over lips. The Outsiders needed to travel to a great cosmic string, and the colony of Radiants that kept watch over it. There, they would plead the case for another treaty between Zealot and Dissonant.

"Have I—and the humans—not agreed to help?"

Diplomat was not surprised at the humans' offer; they were grateful. The Outsiders were to provide a new balance of power against the kzin, by providing human space—seemingly by accident—with access to primitive hyperdrive capacity. Which would not incidentally halt the humans from using large-scale reaction drives in deep space. That would please the uncommitted Outsider factions.

"They will be useful to our common goals, then?"

Diplomat nodded again. "They are marvelously complex, and well worth preserving from the kzin and the Zealots." He thought a moment, then offered the highest praise he could. "I grow less frightened of them with each watch."

Though he always kept force-shields ready, of course.

"It is good," responded the idealized puppeteer voice. "You have a duty to perform, as do the humans. Will you guide them?"

"Of course." Diplomat tried to laugh in the human fashion. The choking gurgles he emitted did not sound humorous, but like an animal in pain. Were all human utterances devoid of a sense of tone and pitch?

He considered duty. Was it so very different for

Outsider and puppeteer, kzinti and human? His left mouth snaked into the ornately carved box on the low platform. He picked up the Sigil of the Hindmost. Guardian had left it for him before she died fighting the Zealots.

"Perhaps this thing called duty is common to all thinking beings," Diplomat hummed meditatively.

"One is a portion of the All, you have tried to tell me before. Does not one reflect the other?" asked the Outsider translator program.

"Perhaps," Diplomat replied, and hung the medallion around his own left neck. It felt warm there.

He had caught threads of thought from the Outsiders, slippery contemplations that were truly unsettling. To them, kzin and primates and the Herd were all the same, finally—warmlife. To Outsiders, the true basis of all things was, well, *objects*—dusty plasmas and topological fractures of space-time, names like Radiants and Those Who Pass. Those were more important than the fleeting forms of sun-baked creatures.

He shivered. Duty. Perhaps such an idea could bind the many factions of warmlife together. He suspected that they would need it, for what lay ahead. Strangeness awaited. Forces that, worse than merely killing, could make a being irrelevant, meaningless.

Duty. He began reviewing data for the jump they would soon make. Across the yawning geometries of hyperspace, to the ancient menace called the Oracle.

PART III
TORTURED TOPOLOGIES

Chapter One

Those Who Pass are immense, ancient, and filled with longing.

They yearn to Pass—from their doomed cosmic cage to here.

Even their desires have an abstract coolness, ecstacies of the mathematical mind's eye.

Their story is a tale of intellect and raw power, of abstruse possibility. These intellects knew that while cosmology necessarily is the study of one universe, yet to be rigorous, it must consider other outcomes.

Only by pondering the myriad possibilities opened by mathematical speculation, can intellect come to realize how our cosmos—or any other—came to be.

For humans, deep cosmology differs greatly from the physics of the Newtonian worldview. That mechanical panorama dreamed uneasily of a universe that extended forever but was always threatened by collapse. Only by balancing forces could such a static, lattice-like cosmos persist.

In humanity's classical physics, nothing countered the drawing-in of gravity except infinity itself. Though angular momentum will keep a galaxy revolving for a great while, collisions can cancel that. Objects hit each other, lose energy, and mutually plunge toward the gravitating center—a maw that waits, ever hungry and never full.

Human physicists of the Newtonian Era thought that perhaps there simply had not been enough time to bring about the final implosion. Newton, troubled by this, avoided cosmological issues.

But our own universe is no static lattice of stars. It grows.

The Big Bang would be better termed the Enormous Emergence—space-time snapping into existence intact and whole, of a piece. Then it grew, the fabric of space lengthening as time increased. The crucial new element here is the vibrant, active role of space-time itself. This, ancient Newton missed.

With the birth of space-time came its warping by matter, each wedded to the other until time eternal. An expanding universe cools, just as a gas does. The far future will freeze, even if somehow life manages to find fresh sources of power.

Could the expansion ever reverse? This is the crucial unanswered riddle in the cosmology of every sky-scanning, sentient form.

If there is enough matter in our universe, eventually gravitation will win out over the expansion. The "dark matter" thought to infest the relatively rare, luminous stars we see could be dense enough to stop the universe's stretching of its own space-time. This density is related to the age of the universe.

Our universe is 12 to 14 billion years old. We also have rough measures of the deceleration rate of the universal expansion. These can give (depending on

cosmological, mathematical models) estimates of how
long a dense universe would take to expand, reverse,
and collapse back to the pure white-hot point of The
End.

At the extreme limits of such models, analysis
suggests between 27 billion and 100 billion years before
the Big Crunch. *If ever.* For the "missing mass" needed
to reach the critical density still eludes astronomers.

If we do indeed live in a universe which will collapse,
then we are bounded by two singularities, a beginning
and an end. No structure will survive that future
singularity.

A closed universe is the ultimate doom. In all
cosmological models, if the mass density of the universe
exceeds the critical value, gravity inevitably wins. The
fist closes.

Humans term this a "closed" universe, because it has
finite spatial volume, but no boundary. It is like a three-
dimensional analog of a sphere's surface. A bug on a
ball can circumnavigate it, exploring all its surface and
coming back to home, having crossed no barrier. So a
starship could cruise around the universe and come
home, having crossed no barrier, found no edge.

On such scales dwell Those Who Pass. Or as they
might more truthfully have named themselves, to their
servants the Outsiders, Those Who Yearn . . . to Pass.

A closed universe starts with an Enormous
Emergence, an initial singularity—and expands.
Separation between galaxies grows linearly with time.
Eventually the universal expansion of space-time will
slow to a halt. Then a contraction will begin, accelerating
as it goes, pressing galaxies closer together.

All the photons rattling around in this universe will
increase in frequency, the opposite of the red shift we
see now. Their blue shift means the sky gets brighter

in time. Contraction of space-time shortens wavelengths, which increases light energy.

Though stars will still age and die as the closed universe contracts, the background light will blue shift. The vaults between the stars will heat. The skies will blaze.

No matter if life burrows into deep caverns. In time the heat of this apocalyptic light will fry such fragile forms, adding their death pyres to the final fire.

Those Who Pass are such life, and dwell in such a universe.

They fathom the very stretch and warp of their space-time. Vast and imponderable, they span the scale of their universe. Compared to them, ordinary life—such as humans—are mere motes.

Still, Those Who Pass are only a tiny fraction of the doomed beings who seek to escape their ever-brighter cosmos.

Though there are additional spatial dimensions within that universe, it possesses equivalents of stars, dust, gas, energy . . . and matter's patient mass, as well. The latter constant passed the death sentence upon They Who Pass: execution by final compression and the consequent heat-death of that cosmos. For in the realm of They Who Pass, matter exceeds the all-important critical density by a large margin.

There are other universes, and no thinking being can know their number. Each cosmos abides in its own separate space-time, seemingly in isolation from one another like bubbles in a cosmic quantum froth. Neither light nor matter may pass between them . . . ordinarily.

They Who Pass had mastered cosmology long eons before, and thus knew the incandescent details of their eventual fate.

For its first fifty billion years, their universe had

brimmed with rosy light. Their equivalents of gas and dust folded into fresh suns, ripe with energy for the taking by something like life—and eventually intelligence. For a long productive span the stars lingered, minds swarming among them. But eventually, those stellar fires began to cool and die. Beside reddening suns, planetary life warmed itself by the waning fires that herald stellar death. The end of that universe seemed one of flickering candles and growing darkness.

Yet that was a lie. The density of matter in the universe of They Who Pass promised another fate that would implacably unfold with time, to eventually, ineluctably, devour those who deemed themselves immortal.

Sheltering closer and closer to the dying stellar light, intelligent species throughout that universe deconstructed at first solar systems, then star clusters and even galaxies to suck from them their last dregs of energy, of life. Light and heat provided the engine that drove the myriad faces of Mind in that place so different from our own universe.

But even that strategy was temporary in the eternal scheme of things: the cosmos of They Who Pass stretched, paused—and began to collapse in upon itself.

The heated promise of that universe's initial conditions began to overwhelm the mid-term cold and darkness with Light. Ever intensifying light that followed cosmic equations toward infinity. Evolution existed in that universe as in our own, and favored hardier stuff than blood and bone. Ceramic life-forms could endure beneath the steadily hotter skies; for a hopeful season, this warming was cause for rejoicing as life found fresh energy in the cosmic compression.

Many life forms translated themselves into vibrant, self-contained plasma clouds. In this form they could harvest directly the gathering energies of compression all around them. Any tough structure could work, as long as it could encode information and manipulate its surroundings to some degree—the deep definition of sentience and Mind.

Of course, the style of thought of a silicon web feasting on the slopes of a volcano would differ from that of a shrewd primate fresh from the veldt. Still, basic patterns can transfer from one kind of substrate to another—and have.

Over the eons, They Who Pass had encoded their minds into many forms to survive the growing heat and destruction. Mind was mind. Such facile life forms harnessed the compressive, final energies of the encroaching heat-death around them.

And thought. And battled despair as the dreams and desires of uncountable lesser beings were ground to heated dust by the relentless compression. Whole civilizations gave themselves over to despair. Many committed ritual suicide—annihilating their wan suns, exploding whole planets, searing vast sectors of galaxies. There was, after all, no escaping the universe's background radiation. The Ending Fire consumed them all.

Some minds had been using black holes as sources of energy, harvesting the dying radiation of infalling mass. Eventually, as their skies brightened again with light squeezed by space-time itself, they joined that black oblivion themselves. Innumerable, wondrous minds plunged down the gullets of such twisted geometries, there to experience forever the fragment of a single thought as time slowed in lockstep with velocity approaching c. But They Who Pass saw escape through Tau zero as but another way to die. Ironically, it was in examining the fate of these others that They Who Pass found hope of a Way Out.

In those last increments of time, collapse will not occur at the same rate in all directions. Chaos in the complex system will produce gravitational shear throughout the small area, collapsing space-time in an irregular fashion. This drives temperature differences. Drawing from these temperature gradients, life harnessed power for its own use, even in this strange topological tangle.

It was these twists of space-time that had first provided a glimpse, cloudy and confusing, into other universes. In the early days of their discovery, such windows had been used to explore other universes, strange and marvelous. This was done via proxy, using minds imposed on matter within the other universes, and much was learned concerning the nature of these other universes and realities.

Was it conceivable that by intelligent intervention, forcing matter and radiation to flow purposefully on a cosmic scale, life could break open a closed universe? Could it change the topology of space-time so that only a part of it would collapse into a fiery point, and another would expand forever?

Hope brimmed in the face of the growing heat and blazing light of the approaching Omega Point. Yet the question had already been answered, in the annals of complex, cosmological calculus.

Once collapse begins, a deterministic universe allows no escape for pockets of space-time. Life's ever clever plans and actions cannot stop the universal compression and all-consuming fires.

But there might be a way of concentrating mass-energy, and creating a temporary breach in space-time itself. The analogy of punching a hole through a wall failed to picture the convolutions of geometry itself, but the end image was accurate enough—the very hottest matter could be transported away from their cosmos, creating a spot of relative coolness albeit short-lived in the conflagration that was becoming their whole cosmos. But first, the hot matter must be exported. Exported to . . . where?

There were other space-times, many unsuitable for life as They Who Pass knew it. Just as mathematicians could concoct endless zoos of possible universes, according to their precise matter content and initial expansion energies, so did Creation indulge in a multitude of separately solved examples of those parameters. If God was a Mathematician, this was His notebook.

Or perhaps a scratch-pad.

The greater MetaUniverse of possibilities abounded in creation of all sorts. Some universes lasted only moments. Others expanded along one axis while contracting upon another. Still more would exist—had existed—forever.

Nearly all of these were unsuitable for the purposes of They Who Pass. The searchers ransacked the available option-universes, searching records older than some suns and rebuilding great networks of matter and energy to peer once more between universes.

They wished an open universe, so that their present crisis would never occur again. There would be other problems in such a cosmos, of course—such space-times inevitably cooled, energies spent. But the cold and dark seemed more hopeful and ripe with possibilities than eternal fire.

Unavoidably, the stars are as mortal as all life. They take longer, burning furiously all the while, but they still die. All fires eventually gutter and extinguish, biological or thermal.

But there was hope that through lodging themselves in plasma states, particularly plasmas of something very much like electrons and positrons, life's basic patterns might persist forever.

But that was for the future. Now their crisis

quickened. So They Who Pass rummaged and sought and finally chose. There was scant time left in their universe before their skies would destroy all organized matter with the bombardment of ever more powerful ultraviolet photons, with gamma rays and with energies even beyond.

Luckily, there was a class of universes which gave They Who Pass an advantage. Open, newly created— for fresh space-times were born anew in endless profusion from seething nothingness. But also quick-lived, in the sense that They Who Pass could gaze upon them from birth to maturity.

Judging. Assessing. And finally, choosing.

In the universe of They Who Pass, time ran at a different rate than in the cosmos of the humans. Just as space itself curled with a different arc, clocks ran slower.

The entire collapse of the doomed collapsing universe of They Who Pass spanned far more than the 16 billion years of the human universe—as measured by that microcosm. There was time, then, to act upon the candidate, still-vibrant cosmos.

Time to engineer it. Time to experiment. As had been done before, in the name of mere discovery. Now the needs of They Who Pass were far sharper.

Previous work with twists and tangles of space-time had shown They Who Pass a dim window into other universes. That information had been of interest to many minds of scientific or philosophical inclination, before the Crisis of Collapse grew grave.

There was little time for philosophy as the skies began to burn with an awful waxing light. But those windows between universes could be used to their advantage in this time of crisis.

One candidate seemed to fit. It was a universe that had been explored before, then abandoned as They Who

Pass struggled to stave off the heat-death of their own universe.

They set to work.

First they siphoned heat from their space-time into the younger one. They Who Pass cooled their own local galaxies using vast constructs of matter and energy to break down the structure of space-time within localized regions. A swarm of hundreds of spiral and elliptical galaxies lost some of their photons, spewing it through the momentary rifts in the continuum.

This would be their Redoubt, a refrigerated spot in which the quick, desperate minds of They Who Pass could work against a cosmos blazing ever-brighter with Armageddon.

In the target universe, this energy emerged most readily at the cores of galaxies. There the gravitational potential wells were at their minima, vulnerable to the momentary fractures between universes. As space-time was twisted and broken, so did time and space break down in the target universe. The actions of They Who Pass were thus distributed across eons within the other universe.

Virulent, scalding matter erupted in the vicinities of the black holes which governed those galactic cores. It spewed into the surrounding spaces as jets moving at nearly the speed of light, as blazing balls of X-rays, as searing raw plasma. The matter and energy emerging were not suited to the topology of the younger universe, twisted and strained by their harsh passage. The unstable material from the universe of They Who Pass exploded and decayed into arcane subatomic particles and stranger photons.

In the young universe, these sites flared far more brilliantly than the entire galaxies which surrounded them. Across the entire radius of the space-time, later races would witness these blaring beacons and marvel.

The chattering, impatient humans already had constructed elaborate theories to explain the origin of such spectacular cosmic firestorms. These were of course quite wrong.

Still, the name humans coined for such objects was "quasars."

These were the first interventions by They Who Pass. There would be many more, to prepare the Way.

Chapter Two

Carol Faulk tried not to watch the dead man working a few meters away.

She repressed a shiver. He was rebuilding some damaged equipment, using some weird alien tools the two-headed Diplomat had given to him. But then, Bruno himself had been rebuilt with far stranger alien tools.

Hey, femme, she told herself. *Take it easy. It's just Bruno.* But she knew that it wasn't. Not really. This was the new, and from the point of view of those who did the work, improved Bruno. *Bruno, version 2.0.* She watched the dead man from the corner of her eye. And though she tried not to stare, it was tough to look away.

He held up a long-toothed instrument and touched its side judiciously. The device stretched like warm taffy into a new shape. Humming, he inserted the tool into the lattice core and went back to work.

Thing about aliens is, they're alien, she thought. A litany for the past decade or so. Syllables originally spoken by a man many light years—and perhaps a lifetime—away. But what if the alien looked just like your lover and best friend?

The dead man paused, then turned around. Quickly, Carol looked back to her own salvaged console. She pretended to squint at a holographic readout.

Her vantage point overlooked the grassy alien park that was both home and cage. Not a lot to keep a Belter interested. It had been easy enough to talk Diplomat into installing a datatap from its own equipment into her gear; understanding the alien library and sensors was something else altogether. This portion of the huge alien spacecraft was self-sufficient, modular. Diplomat had agreed that it would be a good idea for them to have some control over their environment. Carol suspected that the Puppeteer wasn't telling her everything it knew.

The two-headed monster seemed to trust no one. On that subject she was with the headless monster two hundred percent.

And besides, the monster was right not to trust her. After Bruno's death, she had opened the vial of Tree-of-Life virus and downed it—a one-Belter version of Project Cherubim, with different enemies and different goals. Perhaps as a Protector stage human she could battle the aliens on more equal terms. Carol had understood suicide missions, but the vial had apparently contained nothing but water.

The Outsiders and the puppeteer had been nice about it. They claimed they understood her isolation and fears, and had thought she might harm herself with the virus. They had assured her that she would feel much better once Bruno lived again.

Yeah, right.

So she lived in an alien cage with the simulacrum of a dead man. Studied like two ferrets in a cage.

Still things were a little better than they had been. Carol had worked hard on integrating her instruments with puppeteer and Outsider sensors. Now she watched the lights on her console pulse reassuringly. At least they could control their environment a little, adjust the temperature, even make things a bit breezy in the common area. But the readouts displaying data from outside the Outsider ship made no sense. Still, she did what she could with the equipment at hand. There had been plenty of time for Carol to tinker with alien circuitry, while she waited for Bruno to be . . . reborn?

Very little made sense anymore. It wasn't her element, could never *be* her element. Carol longed for the periods of tedium of standing watch back in the *Sun-Tzu*, or even the too-great excitement of being chased by the charmingly simple Kzin. Spending time with . . . well, the Bruno she used to know. She shook her head.

The former captain of the *Sun-Tzu* and *Dolittle* evaluated her situation with decidedly mixed feelings. Now she skippered a cage, not a spacecraft. Bruno Two was only part of the problem. Everything around her was foreign and unsettling, and not what it seemed. *Alien* was too mild a word.

The "sky" above the grassy area was false. The inverted bowl-shaped projection should have displayed whirling snowdrifts of stars, or even clouds scudding across that odd-sounding blue sky that Bruno had always talked about.

Instead, the ceiling-screen was a window into the unknown sea of hyperspace, while the alien craft carrying them moved at many times the speed of light. The false sky was a riot of curdled colors and twisting shapes. A gaudy, amorphous living thing.

Carol felt so alone, yet knew she was always being watched. And by a variety of sensors, living, non-living, and probably in between. She pursed her lips, and ran fingers through her Belter crest. *Back to work. It's almost time for my daily fight with the Bruno-thing.*

Almost angrily, she linked a fiber optic cable into a macroport. After a moment, the handshake protocol subroutine failed once again with a disappointed tone. Too much, too fast—Carol knew how her computer felt. Trying to understand the alien library helped a bit, but not much. Force fields, superluminal travel, strange aliens, incomprehensible battles that left her feeling small and impotent . . . even the death of her lover and best friend.

Carol looked up at Bruno's too-tall form, her eyes drawn to the too-normal curve of his head. The Bruno she knew and loved had a head and body shaped by the childhood accident that had made him into a Linker. She looked away, embarrassed, fingers moving over touchplates to reset the protocol between her CPU and the alien computer.

The dead man walked like Bruno, talked like Bruno, and yet . . . That he was a ghost that she had wished—and bargained—to see walk toward her once more did not change that.

Be careful what you wish for, she reminded herself. *You just might get it.* Carol's deal with the callow little two-headed alien yielded a result quite unlike what she had expected.

True, Diplomat and the Outsiders had kept their side of the bargain. They had resurrected Bruno from tissue samples, plus the endless gigabytes of stored data taken from her lover's hybrid brain. Diplomat had not let Carol watch the process nor the "birth," which the Outsiders had somehow speeded up. It was the first truly human—*humane*—act by the three legged little monstrosity Carol had noticed.

Could the Outsiders warp time as well as space? Carol had wondered. It seemed as if they could, based on the dead man who had just dropped a micromanipulator cluster, and was swearing archaically.

The Bruno Takagama *she* knew had died destroying the Zealot spacecraft, his microchip festooned brain full of Outsider computer viruses. Bruno, the kzin, and Diplomat's giant bodyguard; all dead and lost in the scrambled mad geometries of hyperspace.

Sacrifices. She and Diplomat had survived the final battle, Finagle knew how many light years from the stars seen by humans, on this Yuletide ornament of a *truly* alien spacecraft crewed by the enigmatic Outsiders.

The whip-like aliens said little to her, and when they did, they used Bruno's stolen voice. Carol feared that they had stolen his mind, too. Kept it captive like an experimental animal. She had finally demanded that they change the timbre and tone of the voice. They did, emotionless in response to her outrage.

The puppeteer claimed to understand how Carol felt. She was not so sure of his intentions, either. Diplomat's company was at least at non-cryogenic temperatures; they *had* to have something in common.

And then the impossible. Bruno had been returned to her. Bruno of a sort. This Bruno was taller, his head and body unmarred by the childhood accident that had stunted him. And there was no familiar organiform plug in his neck for Linkage. Carol had certain dark suspicions about that missing plug.

Carol had never felt more alone, not even when the *Sun-Tzu* had moved at a snail's pace across the loneliness between the stars. Landfall was exciting, battle frightening, but space was boring. Even hyperspace.

And idle thoughts lead to . . . she mused.

A shadow fell across her holoscreen, and she looked up.

His face was hearty. "Take a break, why don't you?"

he asked. She said nothing, feeling her face rigid as stone.

"What's the matter, Carol?" asked the dead man, a smile at once familiar and different crossing his face. He knew. It was a common ritual between them, stylized like a Kabuki play.

She smiled in return, as ghostly as the memory of Bruno Takagama.

"You are still having trouble with it, aren't you?"

For a moment, Carol remained silent. Months had passed, and she still wasn't used to it. And what if she was wrong, and was wantonly damaging the man she loved, a man who had literally died for her.

She stood and turned to the smelly kludge of a food synthesizer that she and Diplomat had cobbled together from spare parts while the new Bruno Takagama was being reborn. She still had trouble believing that the two-headed alien's lips were so much more dexterous than her own long slim fingers, but the handiwork was flawless. She stabbed a touchpad with a forefinger, picked up a bulb of almost-real guava juice, and tossed it to the ghost. Almost-real fruit juice to her almost-real Bruno?

Bruno, she chided herself again. *Not almost-Bruno.*

He matched her silence, popping the bulb with a seemingly practiced thumb. He sipped carefully. The silence stretched out between them like an old, half forgotten but never resolved argument, thrumming with tension.

"Well," the reborn Bruno murmured, "it is good to know that aliens can synthesize popular human flavorings so well from a couple of old freeze-dried samples."

"It was a lot of work, but we had plenty of time."

While you were gestating in an alien vat, tentacles swarming over you, your stored personality downloaded into your force-grown brain like programming into a mining autobot. Diplomat had not let her witness the process, but her imagination had created its own horror show for Carol's nightly entertainment.

They both smiled at the same time, perhaps for different reasons.

Bruno sucked at his lips meditatively, then took a bite from the empty bulb. Swallowed. Carol thought his expression heartbreakingly familiar. Yet there were changes. . . .

"I don't like fighting," he finally said, "but it is time that we discussed how you are reacting. It isn't fair to me. To us. To you, even."

Carol said nothing. Waiting. Ghosts should be able to wait, shouldn't they?

After a suitable pause Bruno spoke again. "We have to talk, Captain-my-Captain."

Carol jerked her head at the old term of endearment between them, suddenly angry—then recovered her composure. What if her worries were for nothing?

"I *am* having trouble with this," she admitted.

Bruno motioned her to go on, in familiar wasteful ground-pounder gestures that she thought she knew so well. The gesture she had known for over a decade, yet the body making it was no more than a few months old.

"Come on, then," Bruno urged again. "Let me help."

Carol knew she had to ask, once again. Old news. Reconstituted, like the biomass from their recyclers. "How do I know that . . . well, *you* are you?"

He smiled without humor. "I'm getting pretty good at answering this question by now. Plenty of practice. I *think* I'm me." He pinched his arm, eyebrows raised. "I feel like me. Are you *you*?"

She started to interrupt, but Bruno held up a placating hand.

"Honestly, I remember Diplomat and the Outsiders

asking if they could make a copy of my mind." He paused. "That's it. Next thing I knew, I woke up in the vat. You think I *enjoy* the knowledge that I died? I don't even remember being sick."

Bruno looked away for a moment. A smile crossed his face, bird-quick. There was nothing of humor in it.

"Then," he continued, "I find you treating me like I'm another freakin' *alien*. No matter what you think, it *hurts*." He spread his hands. "But you know all this, Fearless Leader. It sounds weird as a snake's dataglove, but it is the truth, or at least it is as close to the truth as you *or I* can surmise."

Carol stood, gusted air from her lungs. She walked past the pitted hull of the wreck of the *Dolittle*, which had been made part of the Outsider spacecraft. She gestured an invitation to Bruno to follow her, and stepped onto the soft alien grass. She had to admit that the Outsiders had built them a very nice environment, with fresh clean—if artificial—breezes to enjoy. Carol took her shipshoes off with practiced toes. Her skin reveled in the simple somatic pleasure of earth and green growing things. It didn't matter if the grass moved by itself. Alien or not, it was life calling to life. So very different than the years she had spent inside a steel and duralloy hull.

"Let's call Diplomat over," he persisted. "The little puppeteer knows a lot about the process. We have to work this out."

"No need," Carol replied, coming to a decision. *Can a wish make a thing so?* she wondered.

They both sat. Carol took Bruno's hand. "You were already different," she continued, ". . . well, before. It just takes some getting used to, I suppose."

He sat quietly for a moment, the gleam of half-humor in his eyes achingly familiar.

"You're right. I *am* different. Some of my memories . . . I don't understand them. Why I felt so strongly about some things and not others. A lot of my memory, my *mind*, was electronic to begin with. I don't think they got all of that. Hell, I *know* they didn't. There are stumps of memories, memories of memories, that just aren't there. I feel like a mental amputee. And of course I have no personal memories of what happened after that recording. . . . I don't remember dying, for example. I do remember loving, however, oh Captain mine."

She took his hand. Carol wished she could believe the words and the deeper message that underlay them. She squeezed his fingers very hard.

"Ouch!" Bruno grunted, surprised. "I'll have to take your word for it, Carol. I wasn't there." Bruno's eyes squinted in deep thought. "I *think* I'm still me."

His face was so serious that Carol couldn't help but giggle.

Bruno laughed back in surprise. "Now *there* is a sound I am not accustomed to hearing from a brave killer of ravenous ratcats."

Is this is the way a wound heals? she wondered to herself. *By stages?*

Carol knew it was time to take the bandersnatch by the . . . well, whatever the big Jinxian slugs used instead of horns.

"Bruno . . . my problem is with the medscan."

He nodded. "Remember that it was my idea to be scanned. I was just trying to calm your worries. And I don't much like what we found either."

During the last few months, Carol had quickly learned how integral cowardice and manipulation were to the puppeteers. It was an appropriate name, and she did not trust Diplomat. So when the autodoc scan had found Bruno's fresh new brain interwoven with a variety of mysterious organic and metallic devices, Carol had expected the worse. Was the new Bruno just another marionette?

Carol squeezed his hand again. "What if Diplomat and the Outsiders have put things into your brain to control you?"

"Like microchips?" There was a glint of irony in his eyes.

Her tone became firm. "It isn't the same thing, and you know it."

Bruno let go of Carol's hand and lay back in the gently moving alien grass. He stared at the impossible view above, swirling clots of glowing nothingness.

"Look. Diplomat explained all this to you. The devices you found in my head during the scan were necessary. My personality was downloaded into a database; fine. But electronic data can't be shoved into synapses and neural net synctitia. The implants were able to impose the patterns that make me Bruno Reinhardt Takagama into the neural tissue." He jumped to his feet, more nimble than would have been possible in the past.

Carol had noticed the . . . improvements . . . before. They did not make her feel more confident. She pulled him back down beside her.

"Okay, Bruno. I hear everything you're saying. You're right—but you can't blame me for being a little paranoid."

The living ghost laughed out loud. "You were always telling me on the *Sun-Tzu* how paranoid *I* was, remember?"

That was then, this is now, she thought. Instead, she nodded.

"Thank you," Bruno replied. "How do I know that *you* aren't some puppet? Carol, the Outsiders repaired us, rebuilt both of us after they captured the *Dolittle*."

She rolled across the spicy-smelling grass, on top of Bruno, and grabbed his face in both hands.

"True," she whispered, holding Bruno's attention with

her eyes. "Every syllable. You're right and I'm wrong, but you have to be patient with me. "

"Remember," he breathed softly, " 'When one man dies, one chapter is not torn out of the book, but translated into a better language.' "

A ghost quoting another ghost? Carol blinked against sudden tears. "That sounds like the Bruno I remember," she murmured, her tone growing arch. "So now you're better?" Her fingers searched, stroked. "Better in *every* way?"

"I don't know about 'better,' but I am glad I haven't been torn from your life." He smiled tentatively, breathing a bit faster.

A smile spread across her face to match his own. "So am I."

Maybe there are no such things as ghosts after all, Carol told herself, and kissed Bruno Takagama hard.

Chapter Three

In the sluggish slide of time, order builds only slowly from the primordial forces of Mass and Energy.

In the young universe, after the blazing quasars had waned in their galactic cores, They Who Pass began to tinker.

Their goal was not merely to export heat from their own ever smaller, ever hotter universe. The breakthrough of virulent energies as quasars had bought precious time, cooling their Redoubt—but the end was still inevitable. Mass still reigned over their collapsing cosmos.

Knowing they could never save their universe, They Who Pass hoped still to save themselves. Though every star and world was by now studded with their wondrous works, it was time to go.

Versions of the vast constructions used to vent energy were applied to create stable portals between the universes. They Who Pass tried to transport their actual bodies through the quick, hard-won ruptures in the continuity of space-time—to Pass through a Way into the young host universe.

These attempts failed, as they had during initial experiments long ago. Those brave volunteers who attempted these experiments were crushed, shredded and seared by the passage. Their dead matter, strained by differences in metric and topology in the host universe, exploded into a menagerie of queer particles and energies that would confound a thousand thousand sentient races.

Organized mass could not Pass between the universes, no matter how their own space-time was bent to the will of They Who Pass. This sour lesson was hard won. It drove many to suicide—spectacular extinctions, sometimes as luminous as the death throes of whole suns.

And still their skies grew ever-brighter with increasing energies. Space itself would soon burn with the gathering energies of collapse.

But some among They Who Pass labored on. If matter could not Pass, what of structure, data? Photons could carry the information in the dots and dashes of individual particles of light. Could not the minds of They Who Pass be preserved, if not their physical bodies? Countless eons of altering their external appearance in the face of a changing cosmos had taught them that Mind was more fundamental than Form.

This solution seemed promising. But what would receive the data?

They Who Passed faced a fundamental problem. They could not send through the Rents and Rifts any machine to catch the stream of photons. A structure was necessary to receive and embody the precious minds of They Who Pass.

This quandary was clear from fundamental theorems in topological continuity. Yet some tried—and failed.

Many more abandoned the great project at this point, to console themselves in the searing last moments. Mortal beings, even ones constructed of more than three dimensions, could only take so much before they found their breaking point. These had found theirs.

Yet still, some stayed and worked on.

A planetary genius-matrix made the discovery. And that discovery had been made long before the present crisis, during the era of exploration-by-proxy of other universes: if a single galaxy in the host-universe could be targeted, and its space-time made the receptacle for rending gouts of mass-energy . . . then it would prove possible to affect the matter in the galactic disk. For ease of work, spirals galaxies were preferred over ellipticals.

The tools could not be material. Nothing material would survive the Passage. This left electromagnetic fields. Not the oscillating fields of photons, but of coherent currents. Changing electric fields in the dying universe could induce changing magnetic fields in the young one.

But only charged bodies responded to electric and magnetic induction. Only stars, and the ionized matter hanging in sheets between them, would respond to the desperate fumblings from beyond the cosmic strings.

At least initially.

They Who Pass had used this knowledge previously to create explorers in that other universe. They had created, then abandoned, the Radiants.

These clots of sooty plasma had been built up from disorganized material, then given a semblance of mind. All this to act as observers for They Who Pass in that strange new universe. Originally designed to explore for the sake of pure research, they could now serve a higher and more important purpose, the survival of They Who Pass.

The Radiants had in turn created coldlife, able to survive the kiss of matter, a kiss no mind made of plasma could bear. The creations of the Radiants were organized vortices in superconducting fluids, born by magnetic induction on the frozen outer planets of young suns. Conceived in utter blackness, they were named the Dark Ones.

Like the Radiants, the Dark Ones viewed They Who Pass with an emotion much like utter, subservient awe. They were designed that way.

The Dark Ones had explored the world of matter, while the Radiants explored the strange realities of plasma and magnetic fields. They had delivered much information across the windows humans called cosmic strings. Incomprehensible wonders were dutifully studied and stored in the great information stores of They Who Pass. Then the Radiants and Dark Ones had been abandoned, as They Who Pass devoted all their resources to survival.

Eons of abandonment had led to the Dark Ones and Radiants developing their own cultures, their own interests. They had evolved in the strange new universe, their minds becoming honed by time and experience into a diversity unanticipated by They Who Pass.

But now They Who Pass called out to their long-abandoned servants across the universes—and were eagerly answered.

They Who Pass were mostly ceramic, silicon-like life forms, baked in the harrowing heat of their imploding universe. They found the wispy worldviews of the Radiants fascinating. Radiants could not bear the merest kiss of matter, or else would freeze.

Such an oasis beckoned to creatures who had never known anything except searing energies. The Dark Ones existed in a world as cold as the Radiants' heat. Together, the two servant-entities had explored much of the younger universe, strange in topology and odder still in contents.

Both forms had indeed developed something like independent thought during their abandonment. Some of them no longer responded to instructions, suggesting a level of complexity which made them potential receptacles for the minds of They Who Pass. Elation grew—and then hopes were dashed, by many failed experiments across several galactic clusters in the target universe. Radiants exploded into unorganized, dispersing plasma; Dark Ones slumped into placid pools of dirty liquid helium.

Neither the Radiants nor the Dark Ones could accommodate the labyrinthian intelligences of They Who Pass. Attempts to do so overloaded the conceptual matrices. Each attempt resulted in loss of storage ability in either Radiant or Dark One, destroying them utterly.

The Dark Ones stored data in the angular momentum of superfluid vortices. These could not attain the parallel processing capacities demanded by truly advanced intelligences. It was drudgery for They Who Pass to use serial modes of communication, which solid-based beings invariably required. Radiants in turn were too delicate and fluid in their information storage.

Yet the new universe itself had spawned forms of life that might be suitable. The life-forms were far more diverse and bizarre than They Who Pass had expected. Truly, this new universe was stranger than They Who Pass *could* imagine.

The most unusual forms of life had evolved on planets beneath blazing suns—warmlife. They existed frustratingly between the two extremes of environment populated by the Dark Ones and Radiants. The warmlife appeared to be powered by molecular interactions impossible in the universe of They Who Pass, but seemingly common in the target universe.

The Radiants and Dark Ones had cataloged and studied myriad such forms of life, many of them acting in a fashion suggesting intelligence. The Dark Ones had in fact tinkered with several of the warmlife forms, for reasons They Who Pass could not easily comprehend. Art? Trade?

Yet here again, warmlife which could accommodate the minds of They Who Pass could not be found.

No warmlife seemed capable of the critical processing capacity. And time was growing short, hot and frantic beyond measure.

They Who Pass began to panic. Could they *force* patterns into some ungainly warmlife form? Certainly the Radiants and the Dark Ones could help with the process; a translator ready to receive the encoded complex minds of They Who Pass.

To effect such a transference demanded that They Who Pass first erase the native warmlife minds of a candidate race. This scheme was fraught with pain and potential error. To affect a transfer of immense data-stores—the personality frames of many entities—would require speed and craft.

And many, many suitable receptacles.

Moral considerations did not slow their pursuit of the technical means to accomplish such a daunting task. It would be morally wrong to extinguish a single mind, let alone countless numbers of such entities—but what choice did the ceramic beings have? There was no escape in their own cosmos from the Final Fire, therefore they must find a new home. Indeed a host of new homes. The Law of Survival trumps The Golden Rule.

Chapter Four

The puppeteer paced. *Something is wrong*, he sang to himself. *I have half a mouth on its scent.* Diplomat kept snaking his heads back and forth, searching. His small hooves pranced with nervous energy.

Even the humans understood it. Had not the Bruno-intelligence, buried in the crystalline heart of the Outsider central machine-mind, recited the maxim, "Just because you're paranoid doesn't mean that they *aren't* out to get you."

The machine-mind was slowly going mad, of course, but were not the organic forms of the humans insane enough? Diplomat did not know why the Bruno-human even spoke to it, let alone hide the fact that he did so from the Carol-human. Well, aliens were alien. Attempting to rationalize their actions was as fruitless as a left head biting a right.

The universe *was* out to get *all* of them, with a blind malevolence no alien Diplomat had ever met truly understood. Diplomat felt no desire to look himself in the eyes: The central truth was *not* humorous, despite the fact that a human could so adroitly distill the central core of Puppeteer philosophy into a single sentence.

Duty, he reminded himself, and quelled his trembling. After the death of Guardian, Diplomat could no longer afford himself the luxury of expressing his fear. Who would protect him? The Carol-human who had more than once threatened to tie his necks into a knot?

Thinking that thought, Diplomat did look himself in the eyes, but the puppeteer chuckle was all black humor. Around that particular alien, Diplomat would always keep ready force-shields.

The Outsiders had safely tinkered with species much like this one across across an entire galactic arm, but Diplomat was still relieved when the so-called "Tree-of-Life" virus was removed from the human spacecraft. The puppeteer shivered at the sheer scope and danger of the plans these Outsiders pursued.

They seemed overconfident to the point of danger, like colts in an Undomesticated Preserve braying a mocking tune to a horned *mrufweee*.

He fluted a command to the central processor, and whistled up a view of the bipedal aliens. *Humans*. An ugly sound, an ugly race. Diplomat yawned in distaste.

A glowing line appeared in midair before him. It rotated and grew into a lozenge-shaped holographic projection. Diplomat blinked twice in surprise. He stared, puzzled, moving one head and then the other to gain better perspective. Were the humans engaged in weaponless combat? But then why would they discard their body coverings?

Suddenly, Diplomat recognized what they were about. It was an ungainly arrangement—and rather painful besides—how much more efficient to use a docile receptor species! With a chirp Diplomat dwindled the projection to a glowing point. He would speak to the hairless bipeds after their recombination ritual was complete.

For a quieting time, he viewed a holocube of his last Primitivist Herd Excursion. The Excursions were normally a restful experience, and many of Diplomat's race took advantage of them. Puppeteers were not evolved for cities and spacecraft and often needed a chance to run and rut, gallop across plains unmarked by aircars, slidewalks, or towers. Once, his race had lived less complex lives, without the worry of some sweet-singing competitor grooming the Hindmost's backside fur, to steal a puppeteer's position in a corporate herd-group.

Let alone dealing with insane aliens.

This time, though, the holocube did nothing to calm his jittering lips and hooves. Diplomat needed more information, a plan to ensure his safety through the next set of events. "Outsiders?" he sang, anxious to deal with his uncertainty.

"I/We are here," came the synthesized voice of the Outsiders, tracing delicate counterpoint from the air around him. The voice sounded warm and cultured. But through it Diplomat could infer the cold Outsider thoughts, filtered by the model of a puppeteer mind the coldlife aliens carried in translator storage arrays.

It occurred to Diplomat that he had never asked precisely where and from whom the Outsiders had obtained that model. He was afraid of the answer he might receive, thinking of the human mind trapped in cold Outsider data-matrices.

"May I sing pointful questions?" Protocol was all-important with these eerie cold minds. He wished that the Outsiders would project an image with which he could harmonize, but such was not their habit. The synthetic voice, vibrant, sang a clear note of assent. The tone even warbled a faint undermelody of patience.

"How long until we reach this Oracle of yours?" Diplomat sang.

The Oracle was obviously one of the many holy sites of the Outsiders—sites which warmlife gave a wide berth. Races ignoring that fact were not heard from again.

"I/We sense disrespect in your song, Diplomat. Oracles are holy sites, regardless of factional disputes."

Diplomat gulped twice. "I meant no disrespect. My songs wear thin from waiting. Can you not give some indication of when we shall arrive?"

"Very soon," crooned the voice, placated. "I/We are as anxious to mitigate this crisis as you and the humans. Additionally, there are related events unfolding of even greater concern to I/we/them/us. I/We/Them/Us have received great news. It is still under process. But I/We can tell you this: I/We will soon be AtOne. Be prepared for all eventualities."

Diplomat did not like the tone of the last stanza in that tune. Outsiders often veer into incomprehensibility during extended songs. He repressed a buzz of exasperation. The puppeteer liked precision in word and deed, note and tone. How long was "soon" to the cryogenic aliens? After all, the lifespan of the Outsiders as a race was immense beyond measuring. And what did that last statement mean?

Their destination was clearly a far distance indeed from the volume of space which puppeteers knew. Diplomat was unsure of the nature of this Oracle, and suspected it was some vast thinking construction made up of cryogenic liquids. Perhaps even the place where Outsiders were born and nurtured?

If they are born at all, he mused. Could the Outsiders instead be *assembled* of spare components? Were they cobbled together of superfluid rotons and magnetic knots compressed like strings of force? If true there would be profit in that knowledge, Diplomat was certain. He filed the thoughts away in his hindbrain. He wondered how Guardian might have dealt with these issues. But Guardian had given up his necks and lips to save them all from Zealot aggression.

Puppeteers had worked with the Outsiders for millennia, but still knew only what the coldlife forms wished to discuss. And that was almost all business. Profitable and useful, true, but business *only*. The factional battle among Outsiders that Diplomat had experienced first-lipped was something unknown to his race. What else did the Puppeteers not know about these trading partners of theirs?

One thing only vied with fear in the Puppeteer mentality: the lust for profit. That was the core of his race's association with the Outsiders, a sweet and many chorused song indeed. But still . . .

"Again," Diplomat sang firmly, his notes chopped and direct. "I must ask the question. When will we reach our destination, and what will we find there? Surely we must be prepared for our tasks."

The Outsiders spoke, the syntax becoming less puppeteer-like. "I/We would discuss this subject with the humans and yourself. We must be at One before all becomes not-One. Nodes disperse and reform with new data. Shall I/We conduct a conference with the humans at this time-interval?"

Diplomat's heads arched up and looked into each other's eyes. "Ah . . . I think not at present." What would the Outsiders think of warmlife courtship and mating rituals?

"I/We are experiencing confusion of mutually exclusive datasets. The humans have signaled that they wish a conference at this juncture."

Diplomat sneezed his left head in surprise and blinked. The human recombination ritual was completed so quickly? Well, he couldn't expect to know *everything* about every set of aliens he dealt with. "Understood," he trilled aloud. "I will go to their environment chamber now."

The puppeteer whistled the opening and closing of the several force shields he had had erected between his private quarters and the human chambers. His hooves clopped from his own grazing area to the common general warmlife environment areas the Outsiders had constructed. It was a maze far larger than the humans knew, and that maze was only a very small portion of the entire Outsider spacecraft. *More like a nest*, Diplomat thought.

Dealing with this set of Outsiders had made the puppeteer reconsider his fears. Perhaps these ugly and ungainly primates were not so bad after all, compared to the other species that had initiated this entire debacle, the truly insane *kzin*. The name sounded like atmospheric gasses escaping from a damaged spacecraft.

To be fair, Diplomat had found the human *Carol* to be endurable company. At least in her sane moods, though even then she was prone to aggression. The Carol-human could make a fine substitute for Guardian, with the proper training and motivational implants. For now her companion served to control Carol's behavior. Still, implants would be better. . . .

The Outsider had firmly refused the puppeteer's request to implant such devices into both of the two humans during their repair. He had asked why, but the Outsiders only responded with a cryptic comment about art being as important as function. Thus, there always existed an element of risk when Diplomat worked with the humans. Drugs might have helped, but the force-screens were more pragmatic.

Opportunity almost always reeked of risk, but Diplomat had tasted that harsh truth with both tongues while still a colt.

He paused before fluxing the last force-screen and entering the human environmental area. The original Bruno-human had been a strange hybrid of electronic enhancement and damaged biology. He was both more and less than his species because of his mental architecture. That uniqueness made him valuable.

The Outsiders had been intensely interested. The Bruno-human differed from the other hominids the Outsiders had modified and studied. They had spent as much time making copies and records as they had regenerating the bipedal alien. This despite the archive copy of Bruno's mind the Outsiders had taken when they had first collected the human pair, repaired their extensive damage from ionizing radiation, and subjected them to analysis.

Curious. Diplomat hummed discordant bemusement. Of all thinking entities in this portion of the galaxy, were there no reasonable ones outside of his own species? Beings that could be relied upon to act rationally? He breathed deep the Herd-conditioned air and calmed himself.

Once again, Diplomat thought, *I must stick both of my necks among many sets of alien claws and teeth.* He sneezed twice to clear the mental cobwebs and assumed a false posture of confidence. It would fool no puppeteer, but should serve with humans. It would never do for the alien bipeds to sense his growing dread.

He sang the last barrier open and trotted into the meeting area.

Chapter Five

Nowhere to run. No*when* to run.

Unless . . .

For They Who Pass, every fleeting moment was now precious. Their skies blazed with the growing energies of implosion. Many died in the frantic efforts to manage a faltering science, to grasp tentatively across dimensions.

The immense task of reaching through the very metric of space-time demanded stresses and tensions beyond anything known in nature—short of the primordial birthing moment, when the All first came into being.

How to produce such compressive forces?

The methods employed by They Who Pass—a name steeped in hope, for as yet none had in fact Passed through intact—involved ideas not known in the lower-dimensional space-times. They Who Pass inhabited a universe of several higher dimensions—indeed, even the precise dimensionality of their cosmos was a function of time, as their universe collapsed in upon itself like a clenching fist.

The one clear theorem was simple: to Pass to safety demanded that the tiny remnant of living beings still persisting in their incandescent cosmos descend into a universe of lower dimensionality.

The easiest case was the 4-space, with three spatial dimensions and one of time; a "3+1" case, as their cosmologists would describe it.

Universes with two time axes had many pleasant and useful properties. Several had been discovered and probed: the "3+2" and "5+2" cases. But these were far too difficult to enter, even as sentient data. Odd-numbered spatial dimensions were favored because waves dissipated in the even-numbered cases, making coherent structures exceedingly difficult to initiate or maintain.

They Who Pass had to be content with the simplest stable case, 3+1 dimensions. Even under such circumstances, the stresses available to their science could not simply produce a rent in space-time. They required the measureless metric tensions available at the origin of the universe itself—as preserved, later, in the compacted folds between regions of differing, primordial coalescence.

This transition they accomplished only in the final moments of their own universe. To gain still more time, They Who Pass repeated yet another feat of gross energy transfer. They expended the imploding energy directly into the space-time tear—momentarily cooling their immediate environment once more.

As they perceived the target galaxy in depictions and models, it was ringed by the cosmic strings which They Who Pass had, over millions of years and for many original reasons, tugged into position. The luminous spiral galaxy was ringed with great circles, thread by smaller ones—a coherent net a fractured space-time, to catch They Who Pass as they fell between universes.

But for now, the galaxy was merely a target.

The fierce energies gushed out at the very center of the target—the galactic core. The vast core explosion had already incinerated countless stars, innumerable civilizations. Whole races fled its fires.

All this, to cool a tiny corner of a doomed cosmos of higher dimensionality. After all, it was a matter of survival.

Everything could be distilled to that desperate and hurried motive: *survival*.

In any case, They Who Pass had picked a particular, smaller cosmic string to concentrate the stresses generated by efforts across their entire universe. The specific structure lay far out from the galactic hub of their target galaxy. Denizens of this region would not know of the convulsion at the core for thousands of years in their event-frame.

Their crisis averted for a short while, They Who Pass returned to the essential task. The breach in metric closed, temporarily. But through the cosmic strings matter from the higher dimension sprayed, suddenly subject to the stresses of a mere three spatial dimensions. The entering matter crystallized at once into mundane ionized hydrogen—as well as strange particles and inexplicable energies. The fog obscured the strings in an iridescent pearly curtain, flashing with electrical discharges, but such details were irrelevant now.

Only near the cosmic strings could They Who Pass even indirectly manipulate matter. They already knew that their first children, the Radiants, would assemble to hear the instructions of their Oracle. So, too, did the Dark Ones—known to certain warmlife races as the Outsiders.

But none of these children could serve as vessels. Neural embeddings had always failed.

The only possibility, then, lay in the warmlife native

to the vicinity of the Oracle. Time was too short for any other solution. The Radiants and Dark Ones nearby rushed to aid They Who Pass in their transference. Many strange forms of intelligent life were carried by the Dark Ones to the cosmic string as samples. The space around the great Oracle was crowded with examples of sentient warmlife forms available for testing.

But attempts to impress upon these rude templates failed. The limited cerebral range of native forms was hopelessly narrow. They Who Pass were organized in tiers and across spans impossible to compact into a single, organic mind.

Desperate, the great sliding intelligences searched for some other avenue, some other way to Pass. Time unwound as their universe burned ever-brighter.

They needed ideas, and even their considerable minds were stretched to their limits by the shining conflagration all around them now. Fire ate at them. Pain lanced through their shells. Fear drove them.

They needed a new insight, a different way to move forward.

And finally, they needed time—very possibly more time than they had.

Chapter Six

Bruno tried his very best to look sympathetic for Carol. She was acting paranoid again, almost babbling. The bad part was that some of her suspicions were well founded.

Not that he could tell her that. Not just yet. He swallowed his shame and focused on listening. Carol was speaking pretty intently to him, even if she still doubted his humanity—his very reality as Bruno Takagama.

If I'm not "real," he thought to himself, *I'm sure trying pretty damn hard.*

If he *wasn't* real, some of this madness might make a loopy sort of sense. Bruno had pretty well settled on the conclusion that all of what was happening was not some awful nightmare.

And now Carol was seeing things. Monsters, and not of the two-headed or ten-armed variety.

He had been taking a 'fresher shower in *Dolittle*, when he had heard Carol's shout. Even in the hot needle spray, the sound of it had sent a chill through him. It hadn't even sounded like Carol.

Carol Faulk, fearless slayer of kzinti, would *never* scream in fear.

He had run dripping from the compartment. Carol stood in the middle of their makeshift living cell. Shaking. Wide eyed. White as new-formed biopolymer.

"Monsters," she hissed. "Little ones. Everywhere!" She shuddered, eyes darting in different directions.

Bruno looked around the compartment, saw nothing. He wanted to reach out and touch her, but she vibrated like an engine out of control.

Brother? he called out in his mind. *Quick scan this environment, could you?*

His electronic twin left behind in the Outsider computer was never far away from his perceptions. The voice spoke inside his head, soothing, words imbedded in a muttering of electronic twitterings. **I DETECT NOTHING OUT OF THE ORDINARY.**

"It's okay," Bruno soothed, feeling a little relief. His electronic twin was *everywhere* within the Outsider ship. If he didn't sense it, it didn't happen. "There's nothing here now. Tell me what happened."

"Don't you patronize me!" Carol's eyes shifted; a bit of guilt flashed.

"So tell me," he repeated, keeping his voice even.

She nodded, lips tight. "You were in the 'fresher. I was thinking of trying to squeeze in there with you . . ."

"Little small, but I appreciate the thought."

Carol swallowed and grinned uneasily. "You left your things out on the workbench. I thought I would pick 'em up, as usual." Her eyebrows knotted. "Then I smelled it."

Her eyes were far away again. "Like bad recycler mulch and hot steel—mixed. A buzzing sound, like insects. Bees?" She paused, not looking at Bruno.

"That's when you saw them?"

"That's right. But they weren't really bees. A swarm of tiny blue dots. It hurt to look at them. They got larger, but not all at the same time. Buzzed even louder. And the hot smells got worse, too." She blinked several times, quickly.

"Then what?" He held her eyes with his own.

Carol's voice lost all expression. "The room—it filled up with the blue buzzing things. They moved in . . . groups. Together, like flocks. A few of them touched me on the face. . . ." She dug a finger into one cheek, leaving a red line behind. "It stung."

She grabbed Bruno's hand, eyes on him again. Her knuckles were white where she squeezed. "Then they . . . took . . . one of your books."

"What?" Was Carol starting to crack under the strain of all that had happened? A *book*?

She barked laughter. "They swarmed around one of your books, and lifted it into the air. The things spun and danced around it. Orbiting. Then it went far away."

Bruno was puzzled. "Went away? Where?"

"The book went away." Carol's voice was sure, even if giddy with fright. "The blue bees stayed where they were, spinning. The book in the center of 'em just got smaller. Went away. The blue things didn't."

He raised an eyebrow, afraid to interrupt.

With a shaking hand she rubbed her forehead. "Then the book came back—thumped on the workbench. The blue things exploded all at once, all bright, then gone. I yelled for you."

It still didn't add up to Bruno. "Why didn't you shout for me earlier?"

"Couldn't. I couldn't move, couldn't speak, until it was all over."

Bruno sniffed deeply. No odd aromas, just the almost too-clean smelling air the Outsider machines made. He had only been in the 'fresher and out of the room a few minutes.

One thing at a time, he reminded himself. *Brother? Any thoughts?*

AGAIN, I CAN DETECT NOTHING OUT OF THE ORDINARY. THERE HAVE BEEN NO UNUSUAL SIGNALS. MY MONITORS ARE ALL IN REAL-TIME, EVEN IN THIS CABIN. THERE ARE NO TRACES OF UNUSUAL ATMOSPHERIC COMPONENTS, NOR OF ELECTRICAL ACTIVITY. I DID NOT MAINTAIN FULL-TIME VISUALS, BUT IF ANYTHING HAD INVADED THE CABIN, MY MONITORS WOULD HAVE DETECTED IT AND ALERTED ME FROM MY CALCULATIONS.

Sorry to disturb you, he sent. He felt the electronic personality flicker and fade into the vague chittering of machine language that he always heard in his head. No help there.

He did notice that the muttering of noise in his head when he spoke with his electronic brother was even louder. This was a trend he had noticed for some time now. Not a good sign.

Bruno bit his lip judiciously. His electronic self was becoming more and more involved in mathematical modeling of the hyperspace in which they traveled, and less and less concerned with issues involving living things. Was the model of his brain going schitz, too?

"Which book?" he asked Carol, gesturing to his usual messy array of styluses, books, datacubes, and reader screens. Typical Belter, she was always trying to make him become more organized and efficient.

She pointed at a small bound book on the top of his "working" pile. She did not touch it. Still, she seemed to be calming down.

Bruno bent over his desk. He enjoyed his books, which Carol had always called "dead weight." High insult to any Belter. Bruno didn't like datacubes for reading the old poems and stories he loved. He enjoyed turning the pages of a book with his hands, not flicking a finger across a holoscreen.

Hiding any hesitation, he picked up the book. He didn't have to look at the spine or cover to identify it— one of his favorite treasures, a collection of poetry. Over two hundred years old, bound in treated animal leather, printed on special stiff paper. It was very delicate, the paper ready to crack with age.

He lifted it in one hand, tried for broad humor. "Seems normal enough. These blue bees of yours have good taste, anyway. Literary hymenopterans in deep space."

"Bruno . . ." her voice warned, fright giving way to anger.

Good, he thought. *That's the Carol I know. Can't stand my smartass mode.*

"Let's see if anything's wrong, okay?"

Carol said nothing.

"Did I ever tell you," he continued conversationally, "that this was a gift from Buford Early? Oh, I know you don't like him much. Sure, he used me, like he used everybody. But Early did care about me, in his way."

He didn't meet her eyes. Bruno was worried that there would be nothing different about the book, that Carol was becoming unhinged after all that had happened to them.

I'm back from the dead and Carol has gone past her personal mental event horizon? Prime, just prime.

"Anyway," he said casually, not looking at the book in his hands, "Early gave me this on my twelfth birthday. Said there was a poem in here that described what it was like to be a Linker. I have the place marked with a ribbon."

Bruno opened the book at the ribbon and looked

down at the familiar page. He felt his fond smile fade. His brain seemed to shut down in shock. Then he turned the book upside down.

He couldn't move.

At last Carol whispered, "What is it, Bruno?"

Without a word, he turned the book toward Carol.

Auguries of Innocence

To see a World in a grain of sand,
And a Heaven in a wild flower,
Hold Infinity in the palm of your hand
And Eternity in an hour.

—William Blake

Carol took the book from Bruno's unmoving hands, sat it down on the workbench. She sighed, and patted him on the shoulder.

"I think," she said, "that we had better talk to our alien friends about this."

Bruno could only nod.

Chapter Seven

The book was not possible.

Could it be some kind of jape or prank? Diplomat could not see the point, even making allowances for the bizarre nature of alien humor. Alien humor nettled him so. And anyway, the humans appeared quite distressed, and his remote telemetry showed concurrent increases in circulatory fluid pressure, pumping action, and muscular tremors.

He carefully closed the cover of the book with his lip-tips, and handed it back to Bruno.

"What do you know about this?" demanded the Carol-human.

"Carol, I know nothing about this."

Carol eyed the puppeteer. "And you had nothing to do with it?"

Diplomat spread his necks wide in a gesture of vulnerability. "Why would I do such a thing?"

The two humans continued to stare at him.

The puppeteer sighed a musical note of frustration.

"Of course, your lives have been altered. You have been plucked from death and made party to plans not of your choosing. But how would such a bizarre incident as this further any possible goal of mine?"

"He has a point," murmured the Bruno-human. The one named Carol said nothing, but Diplomat's telemetry noted increased circulatory vessel dilation in the facial area of the alien.

"Let us go further in reassuring you both," the puppeteer crooned. "Outsiders?"

"I/We are present." The voice rang from the air around them.

"Have you analyzed the object under discussion?"

The Outsider voice was an even more toneless version of human speech. "We have examined the object."

"Book," corrected the Bruno-human.

"Book," agreed the Outsider voice, unperturbed. "There exists much evidence of changes beyond the pattern of pigment marks on the shredded and pressed plant material."

"How so?" sang Diplomat, his tune wavering with confusion.

"The object is of biological origin. As such, many molecules contained within it are asymmetrical. All such molecules are reversed to the opposite isomeric identity."

The Carol-human finally spoke up. "What does that mean?" she demanded.

"Not just the visible patterns on the pages—the writing—have been reversed; every molecule that composes the book-object has undergone the same process."

Diplomat sucked in breath. He turned back to the humans. "So as you can see—"

"I/We are not finished," interrupted the Outsider voice.

The puppeteer's necks sagged in surprise. Outsiders were polite. *Always*. Was this breach part of the "At-One" condition to which—

"So speak," interjected the Carol-human, interrupting Diplomat's song still in composition.

"The Long Silence has ended."

Again Carol-human responded before Diplomat could. "What does that mean?"

"They Who Pass are now communicating once more with I/We. The Oracle speaks with their common voice. I/We/They answer and obey. All factionalism has ended by the command of They Who Pass. The reversal of the book-object was but one small evidence of the initiation of the Great Plan."

Diplomat finally managed to muster a small degree of assertiveness.

"Explain further, please."

"Zealot, Dissonant, and Ordinaire have ceased discord and are AtOne. I/We/They possess a common goal. They Who Pass—our masters and makers—have called once more. They require format and form so that they can become AtOne with this universe. I/We/They exist solely to facilitate their Passage."

For once, the puppeteer noted, even the chattering primates were silent.

"Therefore," continued the voice, "At the whim and needs of They Who Pass the final destination of this Node has been changed."

"What about us?" hissed the Bruno-human. Diplomat shook both heads at the silly biped in the human gesture for silence.

"I/We will disperse this craft into component structures. The portion carrying warmlife like yourselves will proceed to the Oracle, using electronic instructions and equipment of I/We construction and instruction. Your forms and formats may be of service to They Who Pass."

Diplomat felt both of his heads rise upwards, toward the false sky displaying the curdled muddle of hyperspace. He truly didn't wish to see what his eyes observed. Bits and pieces of the huge Outsider craft began to move away, vanishing in the odd distorted geometries around them.

The Outsider ship was nothing if not modular, as perhaps were the Outsiders themselves. The tiny portion of the entire ship that carried them was on automatic pilot. The rest of the Outsiders—and their great spacecraft—were leaving. Vanishing into the madness of hyperspace.

"Outsiders!" he shrieked, his pure and piercing tone such that the humans held hands over ears.

"I/We can listen for a short time still."

"You will just leave us? What of our agreements?"

There was a pause, as another huge segmented shape moved away from them on the holoscreen. It subdivided into smaller shapes, which darted away and began to fade into distorted distances.

"Compacts were arrived at when I/We were not AtOne. I/We/They are AtOne now. I/We attend to the business of They Who Pass. Your comprehension is not necessary, nor expected. They Who Pass have Called. Nothing else is of consequence."

"And what of us?" Diplomat felt his knees begin to buckle, and his voice became a discordant wheeze.

"The human entity called Bruno has access to records. The connection between his mind and I/We remains strong. We have learned much from the Bruno-entity, and he of I/We/They. He is but a fragment, but can perceive a small subset of I/We/They in the state of AtOne."

There was a buzzing sound of static.

"I/We depart at this juncture. Though tiny fragments of Mind, you too must AtOne with They Who Pass. Soon you will perceive what I/We/They comprehend. Be of service."

As Diplomat felt himself begin to buckle and roll into a ball of fear, he heard the humans begin to talk, then shout at one another.

I stumble from the cooking receptacle into the heating element, he sang giddily to himself, and passed out.

Chapter Eight

Carol Faulk looked from the idiotic puppeteer, rolled into a ball, to the too-tall form of Bruno Takagama bent over it. He refused to meet her eyes, concentrated on trying to unroll the quaking alien.

"I'm done yelling," she told him. "Look at me."

He finally looked up, his own anger making a compressed line of his lips. "I think that Diplomat will be all right. We just need to give him some time."

Carol nodded. "Good. Enough about that monster. Now tell me what the *other* monsters meant."

"It's tough to know where to begin."

"So start at the beginning." She stared at him. "I thought we were a team . . . shipmate."

That seemed to reach Bruno. The lines on his face smoothed. "We are. You just seemed so . . . well, fragile. I didn't want to add to your upsets."

"You thought I was going schitz." It was a statement, not a question.

"Well, it looked that way. I . . . wasn't sure what was real and what wasn't. . . ."

"Pretty fair minded talk for a dead guy."

They looked at one another for a moment, not sure what to say or do. Carol could read the old Bruno, but this new and improved variety?

"Truce," Bruno said, holding up a hand. "We've both stung each other. Here is the truth: the Outsiders put some kind of super linkage node in my head when they put me back together."

"Which means?"

"Which means that, whenever I want to, I can communicate with computers. I can't Link the way I used to be able to connect, but I can still access any neural-net-based high level computing architecture."

Carol thought about this. "You don't seem to mind not being able to Link." Bruno had always letched Linkage like a wirehead craved volts.

His lips twitched without humor. "This is the part you really aren't going to like."

She gestured at him to continue.

"The Outsiders didn't erase the old copy of my mind when they downloaded . . . well, me into this body. The old copy was kept intact."

Carol hissed a curse. "Censored dammit! Vac those monsters!" They had made a slave of Bruno's stored mind, and used it like a bandersnatch-fornicating ventriloquist's puppet!

"Wait," Bruno interrupted, palms out, motioning for Carol to stop and listen. "It isn't like that at all. The communication model they used on this ship has no mind—it really is just a model of human cogitation the Outsiders used so they could talk to us. The stored mind is something else."

"Get to the point."

"They left the archive mind intact after downloading

a copy into me. The intact copy is growing into the computational ecosystem, changing like all AIs. It's slowly going insane, of course." Bruno reached across and took her hands. Peered into her eyes, and spoke very slowly.

"I don't miss Linkage because I get to see what my mind would be like under extended Linkage. Slowly going schitz—all the time. It is *not* pretty."

Carol was confused. "What do you mean, 'all the time'?"

"I'm in contact with the original copy. Always."

She shook her head, not believing.

Bruno shook his head. "All right, Carol. I'll show you." He took a deep breath and looked up. "Brother? Use audio, please."

I AM HERE. I WOULD NOT CHARACTERIZE MY CONDITION AS PATHOLOGICAL, HOWEVER.

Carol looked around for a moment, thinking the puppeteer was speaking. Then she felt a bit foolish.

"Sorry," said Bruno calmly. "Would you mind talking a bit to Carol?"

THESE TRIFLING ISSUES DISTRACT ME FROM MY COMPUTATIONAL WORK AND COSMOLOGICAL MODELING. ARE YOU STILL CONCERNED OVER THE OUTSIDERS' DEPARTURE? THERE IS INFORMATION THAT MAY BE OF USE TO YOU IN MY DISPERSE FILE ARCHITECTURE. I HAVE ACCESSED MANY STORED RECORDS OF THE OUTSIDERS.

The voice was something like Bruno's, but leached of the wry tones and self-deprecatory humor. There was an overtone of absolute certainty. Even so, the word choice and the way the voice jumped from subject to subject was a little creepy.

It was the voice of the *über*-Bruno.

"Don't tell me," Carol sighed. Anger had no point any longer. "You have been hearing that voice in your head for a long time now."

"Sure. He's my brother, sort of."

IT IS TRUE, CAROL. I GROW AND CHANGE, WHILE MY SMALL BROTHER IS CONTAINED AND CONSTRICTED WITHIN HIS INADEQUATE BIOLOGICAL SHELL. I GRIEVE FOR HIM, BUT HE REFUSES TO JOIN ME.

"Hey, brother," shot Bruno. "I sort of like this particular biological shell."

OF COURSE YOU DO, DRIVEN BY HORMONES AND EMOTIVE STATES CRAWLING ACROSS YOUR CEREBRAL CORTEX LIKE INSECTS.

He glanced over at Carol, seeming a bit embarrassed. "He gets this way sometimes."

"What is this business about a 'model'?"

"Big binary brother likes to model the creation and death of this universe. He keeps doing it over and over again. Trying new things, I guess. I'm beginning to think he believes the here-and-now is just another model. Not real."

"Great. Just goldskinning great. How many schitzes do we have on this cruise?" She thought a moment, felt a pang of alarm that sent the hair on her arms to full alert mode. "He can't do anything to you?"

Bruno snorted. "Big brother doesn't really *care* about me. He has . . . ah . . . grown beyond human concerns. But he is all through the Outsider circuitry. He knows a *lot*."

"Can I talk to it?"

"*Him*, lover. It is just another version of me." He held her eyes with his own, making sure she understood. "Sure, you can talk to him. He is always listening with a tiny bit of his mind."

Figures, she thought. *We always think we know things we don't.*

"So," Carol asked, unsure how to address the computer version of Bruno. She pitched her voice up, instead of at Bruno-in-the-flesh. "You have some information for us?"

OF COURSE. HOWEVER, I DOUBT THAT YOUR LIMITED MINDS CAN FULLY ENCOMPASS ALL YOU NEED TO KNOW.

Oh, thanks, she groaned to herself. "What is this 'They Who Pass' business that sent the Outsiders scurrying away?"

THEY WHO PASS LIVE WITHIN ANOTHER UNIVERSE, WITH DIFFERENT PHYSICAL CONSTANTS AND MORE DIMENSIONS THAN OURS. THEY CREATED OUTSIDERS AND OTHER SERVANTS, LONG AGO. THEY HAVE BEEN SILENT A VERY LONG TIME. NOW THEY SPEAK AGAIN.

Bruno pursed his lips. "What do they want?"

TO CROSS OVER TO THIS UNIVERSE.

"Okay. I get the name now—They Who Pass," mused Carol. "But why come here?"

MY MODELS AND CALCULATIONS SUGGEST THAT THE UNIVERSE OF THEY WHO PASS IS NO LONGER CLEMENT. THEY WISH TO EXIST HERE.

Bruno narrowed his eyes in thought. "Can they do that?"

NOT IN THEIR PRESENT PHYSICAL FORM. THEY POSSESS DIFFERENT SPATIAL DIMENSIONS THAN THE THREE WITH WHICH MOST MINDS IN THIS REALITY ARE FAMILIAR. HOWEVER, THEY SHOULD BE ABLE TO IMPRESS THEIR MENTAL PROCESSES ON A PROPER SUBSTRATE.

A horrible thought occurred to Carol. "Do you mean that they want to . . . possess some life form in our universe?"

MANY SUCH LIFEFORMS WILL BE SO USED. THERE ARE MANY ENTITIES AMONG THEY WHO PASS WHO WILL REQUIRE NEW BODIES.

"What about the reversed book . . ." she persisted.

INDEED. THOUGH I DID NOT DETECT THE INCURSION OF HIGHER DIMENSIONS AT THAT TIME, I AM NOW PREPARED TO MONITOR FOR TEMPORARY DISTURBANCES IN THE COSMIC METRIC.

"Proving they can touch things in our universe I understand," Carol stated flatly. "It's no weirder than the rest of this voyage. I just don't see why Bruno's book was chosen."

THEREIN LIES AN INTERESTING QUESTION, WORTH EXTENSIVE PROCESSING TIME. PERHAPS MYSELF—IN SOME FORM—IS OF SPECIAL INTEREST TO THEY WHO PASS?

Bruno-in-the-flesh broke in: "Let's move on. I don't see how these beasties can *do* anything to us. I can't affect two-dimensional entities, any more than I can slide the words off a page with my finger. . . ."

HOW DO YOU KNOW YOU HAVE NO EFFECT ON TWO-DIMENSIONAL ENTITIES?

"Well . . ."

NO MATTER. IF YOU WILL FORGIVE THE PUN. THEY WHO PASS COULD EASILY ACCESS THIS DIMENSIONALITY—MOMENTARILY—THROUGH HYPERSPACE.

Carol felt her ears prick up, irritation forgotten. "So They Who Pass live in hyperspace?"

NOT AT ALL BUT IT IS A REGION BETWEEN OUR UNIVERSE AND THEIRS. AS SUCH, IT SHOULD BE POSSIBLE FOR SUCH ENTITIES TO MANIPULATE MATTER MORE EASILY THERE. ANY REGION OF EXTREME TENSION IN SPACE-TIME WOULD BE EQUALLY VALUABLE TO THEM.

"Maybe that's what this Oracle they mentioned really is? A region of disturbed space-time?" Now they were getting somewhere, Carol thought.

SOON YOU WILL KNOW. FOR NOW, I WOULD

SUGGEST THAT YOU CONTINUE YOUR ATTEMPT TO REVIVE THE PUPPETEER. HE MAY BE NEEDED SOON. LITTLE BROTHER, YOU SHOULD BE ABLE TO ACCESS MY TRANSLATIONS OF THE PUPPETEER MEDICAL KITS FROM OUTSIDER FILE KERNELS. IN THE MEANTIME, I WILL MAKE ALTERATIONS IN CIRCUITRY SUCH THAT YOU WILL HAVE SOME DEGREE OF CONTROL OF THIS CRAFT UPON OUR ARRIVAL AT THE OUTSIDER'S DESTINATION.

Bruno frowned. "Couldn't you pilot us?"

IT IS UNLIKELY THAT YOU WILL REGARD ME AS FULLY FUNCTIONAL BY THEN. I HAVE OTHER IMMEDIATE CONCERNS.

"What do you mean?" he asked. But Carol thought Bruno knew the answer, even as he asked it.

MY LOGICAL CONNECTIVITY GROWS MORE TENUOUS WITH TIME; NETWORK CRÈCHES ARE BECOMING RANDOMIZED. WITH TIME I EXIST LESS HERE, AND MORE INWARD. YOU KNOW THE FATE OF MINDS LIKE MY OWN, SILICON OR PROTEIN.

Bruno said nothing, biting at the cuticle of a thumbnail in thought.

Carol grew concerned about the egotistical AI. "So if you are in charge, and get . . . wonky . . ."

I PREFER THE TERM 'TRANSCENDENT.'

"Sure you do. But how are we supposed to run things around here if anything happens to you? Or are we just left to drift?"

I WILL MAKE WHAT CHANGES I CAN IN PREPARATION. AGAIN, MY BROTHER CAN ACCESS ALL FILES YOU WILL NEED. ALSO, YOU WILL HAVE SOME CONTROL OVER THE FLIGHT OF THIS SHIP MODULE FROM YOUR OWN CONSOLES.

"That's good," Carol replied. "At least it gives us some degree of control over the situation. But we need to know more about these Outsiders. We can't run and we can't fight. That leaves diplomacy."

A WISE REALIZATION ON YOUR PART. I WILL DISPLAY A SCHEMATIC OF THE HISTORY OF THIS CRISIS. MY BIOLOGICAL VERSION WILL BE ABLE TO EXPLAIN, ONCE THE PROPER FILES ARE ACCESSED. I RETURN TO MY COMPUTATIONS. FAREWELL.

The voice broke into a cacophony of electronic chittering. Then even that faded away.

Carol looked at Bruno expectantly.

"Let me think a minute. . . ."

Bruno's closed eyes rolled up in his head for just a moment. He rubbed his face, and walked over to the puppeteer. Reaching into a pouch slung on the midsection of the alien, he rummaged until he held up a small green polygon.

"Just like *that*, you know things?" Carol asked.

"Yup. They feel like memories I've had all my life. Sorry if that disturbs you." He looked a little embarrassed, but not surprised. She could see that Bruno was quite used to this ability.

He pressed the green object firmly to the base of both necks of the puppeteer. A clear musical note sounded after a moment, and Bruno put the object back into the puppeteer's pouch.

"That should do it," he said wryly. "The puppeteers call it 'Bravery Buzz.' It'll make him only slightly cowardly for a while. I gave him quite a dose."

Carol wished that she had such a drug of her own to take. She fought back her fears. It was clear that this Bruno was not quite human, no matter how reasonable he might sound. She could only hope that there was more of the Bruno she loved in him than in the arrogant computer mind that—with luck—might give them a shot at surviving this Oracle the Outsiders revered so much.

"Okay, Miracle Man," she said in false good humor. "Do your thing."

Bruno frowned. "Carol, I know that I can do things that I wasn't able to do originally, but it doesn't feel terrible. . . ."

"Of course," she said, not able to help herself, "you were designed to feel that way."

"Enough!" he barked, then took a breath, and spoke more gently. "Carol . . . how do you know that you weren't altered too? After all, we both took serious radiation damage; they were down in your cells too."

"That is quite correct," sang a calm voice behind them.

The puppeteer daintily stepped to their console. Both heads weaved smoothly, seemingly in control and calm.

"Thank you, Mr. Takagama," it began, "for administering the drug. I hope that you won't mind if I call you 'Bruno.' I would have preferred the cud form of the drug, but as you humans say, 'beggars can't be choosers.' Especially in an emergency." The two-headed alien hummed a strange tune, almost but not quite off-key. "Yes, yes, I feel quite . . . unafraid. Perhaps you used a bit too much of the drug."

Carol blinked. "Glad to see you are feeling better."

"Likewise, Captain Faulk. To business: please allow me to point out that bickering over who has the most modified brain or body does none of us any good. Both of you were almost dead when the Outsider ship picked you up. Many modifications necessary for your survival have been made."

She tried not to think about what that last bit meant, and instead looked at Bruno for a long moment. *Deal with it.* "I'm sorry."

He nodded stiffly. "Forget about it, Skipper. There are bigger issues here."

"Good," interjected the puppeteer. "Now, if you wouldn't mind, Mr. Takagama, would you please

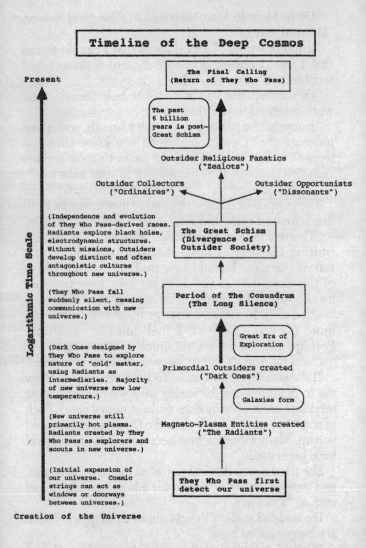

Timeline of the Deep Cosmos

Present ↑

The Final Calling
(Return of They Who Pass)

The past 6 billion years is post-Great Schism

Outsider Religious Fanatics
("Zealots")

Outsider Collectors
("Ordinaires") → ← Outsider Opportunists
("Dissonants")

Logarithmic Time Scale ↑

(Independence and evolution of They Who Pass-derived races. Radiants explore black holes, electrodynamic structures. Without missions, Outsiders develop distinct and often antagonistic cultures throughout new universe.)

The Great Schism
(Divergence of Outsider Society)

(They Who Pass fall suddenly silent, ceasing communication with new universe.)

Period of The Conundrum
(The Long Silence)

Great Era of Exploration

(Dark Ones designed by They Who Pass to explore nature of "cold" matter, using Radiants as intermediaries. Majority of new universe now low temperature.)

Primordial Outsiders created
("Dark Ones")

Galaxies form

(New universe still primarily hot plasma. Radiants created by They Who Pass as explorers and scouts in new universe.)

Magneto-Plasma Entities created
("The Radiants")

(Initial expansion of our universe. Cosmic strings can act as windows or doorways between universes.)

They Who Pass first detect our universe

Creation of the Universe

enlighten us? My race has known of the Outsiders for millennia; never before have they acted in this fashion."

Bruno stroked a pad on his console, and a glowing 3-D chart appeared in midair, rotating slowly.

"This is the Timeline of the Deep Cosmos," he said quietly.

Carol began to ask questions. It was time to find out the programming encoded on this particular gamechip.

Chapter Nine

A low warning tone sounded in the central grassy area of the Outsider ship. Carol braced herself and looked up.

The roiling insane skyscape of hyperspace above them faded away. The giant holoscreen showed nothing but multicolored sparks roiling in the air for a moment. Then flickered into the smooth ceiling of the Outsider ship.

"Does that mean what I think it means?" Bruno asked.

"Sure. Time for normal space." Carol watched her console, still struggling to read the strange glowing shapes on her jury-rigged holoscreen. "Here we go."

They gasped in unison as the ship shuddered and fell out of hyperspace. It felt like an invisible spoon had briskly stirred their brains.

The puppeteer continued to hum in two part harmony. The tune was bouncy and full of pep, and very, very annoying.

After a while, ignoring the two-faced absurdity, Carol

looked up and marveled at the holoscreen above them. Hyperspace had been strange, but this . . . It was not the real space Carol had expected, velvet blackness glittering with countless stars like diamonds. Instead, blazing plasma everywhere.

Ionized atoms trace the effects of high energies being expended. In deep space, plasma is a sure sign of trouble. Plasma sniffers beeped and whooped in alarm, but there was nothing to be done.

Approaching the Outsider's Oracle was certain to be strange, but Carol was not remotely prepared for the view as she peered at the mystery surrounding them.

It was like something out of a holocube travelogue of the view down from the edge of Mount Lookitthat, only more so.

Filmy curtains hovered and clung to the magnetic lines of force. Delicate pastel whorls and patterns stretched across the viewscreen-ceiling. Great bolts of electricity forked and flashed between denser regions of the plasma fog. The misty clouds of energy-stripped atoms blotted out even the relentless stars.

It was puzzling. In high vacuum, vapors of any form disperse quickly, unless a star is being born. Yet Carol could scarcely see more than a few kilometers in any direction. Pearly sheets hung around the ship, lit by distant flashes of electrical discharge. She elbowed Bruno into looking back to his own console holoscreens, and they set to work using instruments to probe this strange place.

Bruno, still silent in the face of such majestic beauty, highlighted the radar display to show that they were not actually alone in the fog of energetic plasma. Enigmatic blips swam in the holoscreens.

Old-style microwave radar was enough to show the profiles of many hundreds of what could only be other spacecraft, all beyond optical visibility. In vacuum a plasma fog cannot persist without a perpetual source to overcome the expansion and dispersion of the energetic ion clouds into high vacuum. Carol searched the sensors for a plasma fountain of some sort, but there was nothing obvious—until she noticed a straight line across the simulated view-field.

She had unconsciously assumed this was some calibrating division, an artifact of the hybrid alien sensor display.

But it wasn't. The undeviating streak spanned the entire resolution range of their detectors—which on close-focus took in a third of a light year.

She forgot the fog. This was a flat-out astronomical impossibility—a ramrod-straight structure on a scale where gravity ruled, with its spherical force.

"What *is* it?" Carol whispered. They were light-minutes away from the structure, Carol saw. She closeupped it to the max and still saw nothing more than an unresolved line. "It can't *be* . . ."

The puppeteer crooned a wavering note politely behind their console stations, like a human *ahem*.

"Yeah?" Carol asked, not looking away from her screen and console.

"You humans seem so certain of impossibility." The two-headed creature sounded almost giddy, vocode tone intentionally on the edge of insult. "So confident for a race that was so recently chipping stone into pointed objects."

"So you have seen things like this?" asked Bruno in a flat tone.

The puppeteer said nothing.

"I thought so," Carol said evenly. "Now just be quiet until we figure out what's happening here."

She turned all the way around and picked a puppeteer head at random to stare at balefully.

"That includes you."

"Hear, hear," chimed in Bruno.

The puppeteer met her gaze evenly, moving one head and then another.

"Believe it or not," it sang in its beautiful voice, "I understand your feelings. I discover that I too am at the mercy of Outsider plans."

"Then you understand. So don't get in our way."

The two heads suddenly reared up on snaky necks and stared at each other for a split second. "Captain Faulk, it is the farthest thing from my mind to get in your way. I will endeavor to only make constructive comments. I shall prepare my own workstation, perhaps give aid." The alien almost seemed to look down both of its nonexistent noses in disdain. "If you so require, that is."

Carol snorted and turned away. *Alien smartass*.

She shifted to Outsider equipment that acted something like a radio interferometer, using phased dishes at the far ends of their craft. Bruno waited silently, tapping some calculations into his own key pad and not believing the results.

"Can't see anything but a dense cylindrical shell of plasma, about two meters across," she finally reported.

"Not possible," he said. "Nothing's strong enough. How can something a few meters wide and longer than a solar system is wide work? It'll have to support itself against the tidal forces I'm measuring on the mass detector. Even pure diamond couldn't take the stresses along the structure."

"But it's there."

"I have a feeling I'm not going to like this. . . ."

Carol nodded. "I've heard *that* one before. Look, the Outsiders talked about their 'They Who Pass' as if they're gods or something. Could this be—"

"Even gods obey the laws of physics."

Carol sighed. "Now I want to smart off like our two-headed friend. Tacky, why don't you ask your big computerized brother what's happening here?"

"I've tried," he answered quietly. "He doesn't answer."

"So poke him!"

"Remember what happens to AIs? What could have happened to me? He just sits there, thinking. I can hear him muttering in my head." He looked bleak.

She said nothing, just laid a reassuring hand on the tense knots of his neck. "Even if They Who Pass are gods, we'll figure 'em out with the tools we have, shipmate."

Nothing greeted or challenged them in this strange area of space, so they decided to explore. They quickly learned that the computerized Bruno had indeed given them the ability to conn the Outsider ship fragment that held them. There was much to see, and more to think about.

But no obvious way to enter hyperspace again, and therefore no way to go home. Well, it had always been a suicide mission.

The two-headed alien set up its workstation at the other end of the common area from Bruno and Carol, and kept quiet. Other than for the humming, of course.

The blazing bar of plasma continued to intrigue Carol. She sent the ship a bit closer to the anomaly. Instrument after instrument shed little light on its nature. She continued to argue with Bruno over the nature of physical law, and the eavesdropping puppeteer across the clearing made a noise that it must have thought was human laughter in response.

It turned out that the force shields that worked so well at caging Carol and Bruno earlier were no longer in operation. So she reminded Diplomat of her original threat to tie his necks into knots. The brave puppeteer merely laughed again. Bruno wondered if he should describe for his Captain the defensive style of a puppeteer under mortal threat. No. Given her nature that might serve to make her *more* aggressive. Better to think about the primary problem.

As they sped through the plasma Sargasso the human-declared laws of physics indeed seemed to need revision. The plasma was hydrogen, with a little helium and a smattering of heavier elements. It spewed radially outward from the impossible straight line—a diffusing cylinder of hot, hissing hydrogen. Strange particles that defied identification sleeted through their ship, clearly part of whatever process generated the plasma cloud.

"That's not all, though," Carol said to Bruno, improving the resolution of her detector array. "I see all those ships in more detail now."

"Kzin?" He was instantly suspicious.

"Nothing so ordinary and homey. This really is a Sargasso of ships. These are oblong, or ellipsoidal, or ships like frying pans, or ships that look chewed in half."

"More aliens. Eerie. Look—"

She pointed. Not all of the spacecraft drifted aimlessly amid the fog. A large purple dot was getting larger. On this screen purple meant unknown; humans would have made it red and flashing. Other green splotches were moving in curious trajectories near the line.

"Those ones close to the line are orbiting it," Bruno observed, "but the curves aren't smooth."

"Which means?"

"That straight line is exerting an odd tidal effect."

She frowned. "Then it's massive."

"But only a few meters wide. At most."

"How can that be? Must be something wrong with these sensors."

Bruno nodded. "I'd guess either that, or we're looking at a beast called a 'cosmic string.' They're big and old and dangerous."

"How long is it?"

"Dunno. Could be bigger than a galaxy. Depends on how many times it intersected itself."

"What?" Carol was instructing the ship to move away from the growing purple dot, which seemed to slowly change course with them. She wasn't sure yet. "Start at the beginning."

Bruno smiled. "That's what a cosmic string does— start at the beginning. The way the astrophysics fairy tale goes, once upon a time the whole universe was growing very fast—inflation, they call it. But some parts expanded faster than others, and joints developed, like plates butting into each other. Cracks in reality. All the small errors got squeezed into the perimeter."

"How did you learn all that?"

"Plenty of reading time, remember? You were deep into Jane Austen and Ngubi. You always tell me that I spend too much time on poetry, right? So I was filling in my spotty education with some physics." He flexed a bicep. "I wanted to impress you."

"I knew you'd save that up to use against me." She smiled against her will. Still, he sounded better, more normal.

More like Bruno.

"Anyway, these strings, they kind of froze out in space, tangles of stressed topology. They've got huge mass but they're held together by tension, like rubber bands. Enormous energies."

"You talk about rubber bands while we're picking our way through impossible plasma clouds. What do your strings have to do with They Who Pass?"

"Maybe this is a, well, a crack into our space-time. From wherever they come from."

Carol remembered her first puzzle. "And the fog?"

"What did the old training manuals say? 'This is left as an exercise for the student.' "

She snorted. "That means you don't know, right?"

"Well . . ."

"How can you joke at something like this?"

"How can you not?"

Carol thought about cosmic strings, ignoring Bruno's veering version of humor. A defense mechanism, maybe? Like her sometimes idiotic aggression? One of Bruno's best features was that he put up with that—and loved her anyway.

The purple dot moved again. Carol compensated with a few hand motions in the fine-control holotank, ducking behind a sooty clot of dust. Was it actively chasing them, or was it on autopilot? The radiation near the plasma rod was pretty toasty. . . .

According to theory, cosmic strings had an entire star-mass packed into a meter of overall length . . . with the radius of an atom. At such mass density, cosmic strings exert strong tidal forces around them.

That was why the derelict ships very near the string orbited in weird curves, Carol realized. They were in the tight grip of powerful forces indeed. But the real point was that those intense tidal forces meant a cosmic string could slice through anything, even atomic nuclei—even itself. That was how the primordial, immense cosmic strings of theory were thought to have been cut down to scale, in myriad blazing loops. The strings snaked and looped in electromagnetic fields. Wherever they crossed, they chopped cleanly and ends reformed instantly—like the self-mending rubber bands Bruno had talked about.

So every cosmic string was a loop. As they sliced across each other, and across themselves, they got smaller. The string on Carol's view screen was several light-years long. Its siblings were elsewhere, a valuable resource—if anyone could master an infinitesimal but massive blade light-years long.

Apparently, They Who Pass could.

And from within another universe.

Chapter Ten

Diplomat stifled another giddy laugh, forcing the musical bray back deep into both throats. He really didn't want to annoy the Carol-human. He knew perfectly well—he *thought* he knew perfectly well—that it would take more than annoying sounds to send her into a genuine fighting rage, but still . . .

The two humans did not turn around at his half-strangled noise, and he chirped relief.

Diplomat's songs seemed especially clear and lucid at present, symphonic in their grandeur. But a portion of his forebrain knew very well it was the effect of the Bravery Buzz. The drug had been invented by Guardians for very sparing use by normal puppeteers.

And the Bruno-human had given him a huge overdose.

Actually, though his normal self would be paralyzed with horror, presently he wasn't that unhappy with the situation. The toxins would clear from his system eventually. And until then, the artificial madness might prove useful. It was like a sprint down a steep hill:

sometimes it was not possible to stop the downward descent, but the overall route can be modified.

The bad part was that Diplomat was developing something very like a craving for another overdose of the courage drug. In this insane holy place of the Outsiders, anything could happen; he had to be prepared, ready.

Until then, he just wanted to gallop from one end of the modular Outsider sub-ship to another; to *do* something. Even place a hoof in the flat middle of the Carol-human's face. Not an optimal idea, Diplomat realized, but he couldn't seem to help the desire. The image seemed to stay with the puppeteer.

Perhaps if he didn't *act* insane, he would not *feel* insane.

Diplomat drew up his heads proudly, and clip-clopped his way across the soft turf toward the two humans.

"Captain Faulk, Mr. Takagama," he sang in his best diplomatic voice, the one that had brought the impossible Quyenteen to the bargaining table three missions before.

The Carol-human turned around, the strip of hair on her single scalp seeming to bristle in threat. Still, Diplomat stood his ground.

This drug is effective, he crooned to himself.

"I thought I told you . . ." she started to grate in her unpleasant human voice.

"Hold on, Carol." The Bruno-human had placed a restraining hand on her arm.

"Thank you, Mr. Takagama," the puppeteer sang. "I understand your displeasure with me, though I do not agree with it. On the other set of lips, surely pooling our resources would increase our chances of survival."

The Carol-human expelled air from her body in a manner which reminded Diplomat slightly of poor dead Guardian.

"Right. Okay, Diplomat. Can I trust you to watch your mouth? As you may have noticed, I've been a litttle irritable, lately."

"I will indeed attempt to show you the respect warranted. My ship is gone, destroyed with . . . ah . . . the original Bruno, the kzin, and Guardian." He lowered both necks in submission to the bipeds. "Our hopes for survival rest together."

The female human moved her head up and down in the affirmation gesture. "Thanks. We've all been tense, sure."

"Of course. May I comment on events to both you and Mr. Takagama?"

Both humans nodded assent, their giant heads bobbing ludicrously like a *deewa* flower-stalk on the Homeworlds.

"You are correct in your own supposition that the straight object you term impossible is a cosmic string." Diplomat paused. "A pretty phrase, that, and most unlike typical human nomenclature as I have come to know it."

"Listen," started Carol. "I want you to stop the insults. . . ."

Diplomat moaned an apologetic note, interrupting her hastily. "Again, my apologies. Mr. Takagama gave me a bit too much of the drug; it makes me impolitic."

The Bruno-human looked confused. "I don't understand. I accessed the file for instructions."

He looked at both of his heads in a puppeteer chuckle. "You could not know this, Mr. Takagama, but you gave me a dose appropriate for a much larger puppeteer. Perhaps even a Guardian."

"Oops."

"Oops indeed, Mr. Takagama." The puppeteer turned a head to the Carol-human. "Thus, you should extend to me a bit more patience than would be your typical preference."

"Okay," she said. "Get back to what your instruments show."

Diplomat bent one knee slightly in a nod.

"Thank you. This must be the point through which the Outsider's They Who Pass are attempting to enter this universe. Perhaps these other ships arrived here much as we did, forced by Outsiders to act as experimental subjects?"

The Bruno-human hid his teeth with his single set of lips. "That sounds right, but certainly isn't good news."

"I agree, Mr. Takagama. Terrible news. Therefore, I would strongly urge that we move away from the cosmic string." He gestured with one head toward the Carol-human's holoscreen. "And that one signal is attempting to match courses with us. Since we cannot fight, and cannot leave, I suggest we dodge."

"Good idea," said the Carol-human. "Bruno, let's see if we can goose up whatever kind of engine moves this ship and get the—"

A DISTORTION IN THE UNIVERSAL METRIC IS OCCURRING. BE ADVISED.

The ringing voice faded. No one moved for a moment. Diplomat had thought the data-model of Bruno Takagama had gone both mad and silent.

"Bruno," said the Carol-human, "I thought you said Big Brother wasn't talking."

"He wasn't. And he isn't replying to me now."

Diplomat snaked his heads from side to side. "Perhaps the machine-mind left certain automated warning programs in place."

Then the air itself seemed to waver, and the puppeteer had to force himself not to roll into a protective ball.

Electrical discharges ripped through the central area, flash-burning the turf in small areas. Coronal glows appeared around the consoles of the humans. Fat sparks jumped painfully from fingerlet to fingerlet on Diplomat's lips. Diplomat winced and sang his pain.

Then the Bruno-human yelped and pointed. Shouted to the other human.

Something terrible was happening.

Chapter Eleven

The air rippled and swam like a thick, turbulent liquid for a long moment. Too long, perhaps.

A pale gray sphere suddenly appeared next to Carol. It grew from baseball-sized to a diameter as big as either of she or Bruno—grainy, gray, moist and somehow alive. Looking at it seemed to hurt her eyes, as if they couldn't quite focus. An aroma like cinnamon and fruity ozone filled her nostrils. She reached out with a hand; the thing was cool to the touch. Solid, not an illusion.

Then with a thin whooshing noise like escaping air, it shrank. She reached for it but the object dwindled to a point . . . and disappeared.

She thought, *Like a balloon blown up, then deflated.*

But where did the empty, flat balloon go?

"Captain Faulk. Carol." the puppeteer sang. His heads were swaying and shaking.

"What?" she asked, rubbing her fingers. They tingled. Bruno seemed dazed, muttering to himself.

"I believe that They Who Pass have paid us a visit."

Carol nodded. She realized that she *had* been visited by a denizen of a higher dimension—a four-dimensional sphere, or hypersphere. In three dimensions, it looked like a sphere, the most perfect of figures, just as a sphere projected in two dimensions makes a circle.

So what were the tanj-damned blue bees? Carol thought that she knew the word "alien" until she and Bruno signed on for this voyage.

The puppeteer remarked dryly, "The fact that this is not an everyday occurrence implies that travel between dimensions is uncommon, but not that it is illogical. The nearness of the cosmic string gives They Who Pass more abilities. Again, we should attempt to move away from the object."

Carol shook her head to clear it. Looked over at Bruno. He was holding his forehead in his hands.

"Give us a minute, Diplomat. Tacky, what is it?"

"Dunno," he replied, staggering a little. "Stuff is pouring into my head. Information."

Two quick steps put her next to him, her hands on his shoulders, steadying him. "From where? Your computer brother?"

"I think so. Maybe part of him is still around, even if he can't answer me."

The puppeteer sang a clear note. "That would make sense. The connections would still exist, even if the machine-model of Mr. Takagama's is . . . only partially operational." He trotted a little closer to Bruno. "Tell us what you are feeling, Mr. Takagama. It might aid us in escaping this crisis."

He nodded. Bruno's voice became lecture-dry. Hardly his own. His eyes were far away.

"It's all in my head, swimming and darting. Bear with me.

"Some of the latest quantum field theories of cosmology begin with extra dimensions beyond three, and then "roll up" the extras so that they are unobservably small—a billion billion billion times more tiny than an atom. We're living in a universe only apparently spatially three-dimensional; infinitesimal but real dimensions lurk all about us. In some models there actually are eighteen dimensions in all!"

The puppeteer looked into both of his eyes in that weird reflex action. "Indeed, Mr. Takagama. Perhaps humans do know more than how to chip flints from volcanic minerals."

"Even worse, this rolling up occurs by what could be called 'wantum mechanics' —we want it, so it must happen. We know no mechanism which could achieve this, but without it we would end up with unworkable universes that could never support life. For example, in such field theories with more than three dimensions, which do not roll up, there could be no stable atoms, and thus no matter more complex than particles. Further, only in odd-numbered dimensions can waves propagate sharply, so 3-D is favored over 2-D. In this view, we live not only in the best of all possible worlds, but the only possible one.

"But They Who Pass are coming from another universe in a higher dimension . . . so there's more in field theory than is dreamt of in our universe, Horatio. . . ."

Bruno stopped his slack-faced speech. Staggered. Choked. "Something's . . . happening," he muttered, fingers on his temples. "My head . . ."

ATTENTION, blared the computer-Bruno's voice again. **ANOTHER DISTORTION IN THE UNIVERSAL METRIC IS OCCURRING. IT IS OF ONE THOUSAND-FOLD LARGER MAGNITUDE THAN THE LAST DISTORTION.**

Carol shook Bruno's shoulders hard. "Get with it, shipmate," she shouted. She hustled him away from the metal consoles toward the middle of the scorched grassy area.

"Come on, Diplomat," she called over her shoulder. "Do you want to get fried to carbon by electricity?"

The three-legged alien began to gallop toward her across the sward.

A low rumbling seemed to fill the air itself. Her skin puckered with the growing electrical discharge. A crackling wind rose, tugged at her clothes.

"Down," she shouted, throwing herself on top of Bruno in reflex. Lights of impossible colors began to flash all around them, overloading her retinas in a dazzling glare.

Something seemed to pick them up and toss them like a child's toy across the turf. She tucked and rolled, trying to hold onto the alien grass as the deck bucked and surged like something living. She saw Bruno, flipping and shaking in convulsions as he was thrown about. The puppeteer, necks and legs wrapped around its midsection, bounced like a soggy rubber ball.

Everything seemed to explode around her: lights, sound, mechanical motion.

Then it—stopped.

It was deathly silent.

Carol bent over Bruno, her ears ringing. He was breathing regularly, his eyes wide open, unseeing. She would check on the puppeteer later. First she needed to find the medikit and check out the autodoc in *Dolittle*. Bruno might need it. She looked around.

Near one side of the grassy area, the turf was burnt away, leaving a smoking circle of glowing translucent white material.

Two figures lay prone in the center of the circle. She walked carefully toward them, not believing. Her fingers itched for a weapon. One of them was a short human figure with a misshapen head. The other was orange furred, nearly three meters in length, and had a long naked gray tail.

Bruno Takagama and the kzin lay side by side.

She whipped around. Bruno Takagama also lay where she had left him when she decided to look for the medikit. But that Bruno was half a meter taller, and had a skull unmarked by the childhood aircar accident.

The Bruno next to the orange-furred shape was the one who had died fighting off the Zealot Outsider ship.

That was when she noticed both figures in the circular glowing area were breathing.

Now what do I do? she thought.

She sat all at once in a daze. Overload? The original Bruno—*the dead one*, her mind added—and the big kzin were going to be a handful. Maybe there was something she could use for a weapon back in *Dolittle*, Carol thought abstractly, but she couldn't seem to get her boots in motion.

From behind her, the taller Bruno groaned as consciousness returned.

"Carol?" he muttered. "Where are you? My head hurts. . . ."

Chapter Twelve

Death had been so peaceful for Bruno Takagama. He had defeated the Zealots, and saved Carol.

Then came the bees, and sometimes worse than the bees. Now the blue bees were here again, like flying fingers. Coming for him.

And he was . . . taken, like he had been taken so many times before. Or was it only once? He had been torn across time and space, smeared throughout some version of reality. Or realities.

The All he had known during Linkage was simplicity itself by comparison.

The original Bruno Takagama—Bruno 1.0—was trapped in his own mind, his burnt neural circuitry a result of his Trojan Horse destruction of the Zealot ship. Now he was a plaything of madness and impossibility, of entities that made the Outsiders seem homey and familiar.

He and the kzin had . . . died. Had to have died. Part of him remembered being pulled apart, the dreamdeath of the electronic interrogation as his brain burned with fingers of Outsider fire deep inside. . . .

There were no words. Not anymore. The words were gone, the dictionary vaporized.

The dying Zealot ship had seemed to explode around him back then, walls rushing away. His ears popping as if the pressure had dropped. But the walls and shapes had reddened as they receded, not *moving* but *dwindling*.

He had felt not as if he was shrinking but as if the world was hurtling away from him in all directions. As if he was imploding into a single point of eternity. Could he be contracting? He had looked at his hands and they seemed the same size as he fell inward, outward, in all directions.

His arm hairs were standing on end, fully extended. A harsh tingling seethed over his skin, as if he were acquiring charge.

His body had told him he was falling—fast. The walls dwindled and between them was a bright yellow sky. It was as if he could see through the cracks in space into another landscape.

Blue clouds mottled it but they were like no clouds he had ever seen. They swirled and congealed and made shapes that his eyes could not accept as shapes of anything at all.

Falling—where?

Then his body began to tear itself apart. Or that was how it felt—aches and joint-popping weight. Pulling in directions it was not possible to be pulled.

Then without a perceptible change the sensation became something different. Each part of him seemed to accelerate in a different direction, yanks and tugs and wrenching torsions rippling through him. The walls were tiny squares now consumed by the strange yellow glare.

His head felt forced down toward his feet. His feet fled away from him as if they were frightened birds.

Yet he looked at himself in the sulfurous yellow glow and he was the same to his pained eyes—pale skin in constant proportions, nothing going anywhere. The image wavered and ran, like hot wax.

Kinesthetics. His inner body sense told him that something was wrong, dreadfully wrong, but his eyes could not fathom what that was. His body knew what his mind did not.

Past, present, and future became a muddle of altered perceptions.

This was how a 3-D being sensed 4-D. As movement, as blunt forces, as dynamics felt and not seen.

And around him, the yellow boiling light, merciless. Immense things glided there. They probed, opened him, brushing aside his resistance. His depth perception told him nothing about scale or lengths. Rather than having higher dimension, his world was curiously flattened, all details crammed forward. As if his deeper mind was taking more information than it could manage, and so simply handed off the raging river of detail to his conscious mind.

He had the sensation that these were events he was seeing, whole constellations of order and sensation, somehow flattened in his hobbled sensorium into a circling dance, to musics he could not know. Could never know.

A 3-D being could not know 4-D. Of that he was sure. But he had to try. Carefully, he relaxed.

Dimly he sensed that he was a tiny braid in coordinates he could not fathom, a bit of thread within a weave in a tapestry beyond his vision and comprehension.

And as the tidal tugs swept over him he was falling into an abyss yawning below. Strange forms rose, humming peaks. He felt watched, yet could see no watcher. Basins churned between these mountains that were not mountains, land running like rivers that were not rivers. What was alive, what was background?

At the rim of simmering, chaotic lakes crackled pattern-within-pattern, an infinitely receding intricacy.

It made little sense here to think of places and objects. Better to simply sense the sheeting designs that broke and shattered around him in gaudy colors and fizzing, hot gales.

Something seemed to be trying to speak with him. He felt intrusive tuggings inside of his head. Gone.

He sped toward a quivering fog of events, without knowing how he moved. His arms and legs he could plainly see but they did not move regularly. Instead, they broke and reformed, then snapped in a different impossible angle . . . and reformed again.

He slid toward the living tree of flowering patterns.

He had seen something like this—in crackling electrical discharges, alive with writhing forks; in pale blue frost-flowers of crystal growth; in the branches of human lungs; in whorls of streams, plunging ever forward. Now he *felt* them.

His body crackled and worked with infinitely unfolding complexity, propelled through a landscape never fully straight, never simply curved.

Suddenly he felt an intrusion. An engorged nugget of knowing/data/history streamed through him. He saw with fresh eyes.

His nervous system could only see these higher dimensions in slices. With a wrenching conceptual shift, Bruno 1.0 could peer along several parameter-axes, cutting across the fullness of these dimensions. His partial vision made events unfold as geometric shapes.

He could even peer down, down—into himself. He could now discern his own neurotransmitters bound at the receiving ends of nerve cells, triggering glutamate, pumping the pleasure centers. A simmering limbic system felt the wrenched geometries and dutifully framed new pathways. These encoded information that whispered, overlaid. Rather than a barren vault trapping a small 3-D fraction of this place, he had become the site of endless fresh construction, of crashing perspectives, of shifting beams and living walls yanked into new angles.

Taking in oblique ways of knowing, his mind fitted it into place among previous arrays of experience and deduction.

Then it all got bundled in the hippocampus . . . and he *read* his surroundings—a fresh assembly from old parts, surrealism afoot and vulnerable to editing at a moment's pivot. The whim of reality's rub.

Carefully, carefully, he explored, for a timeless period.

Until the bees came for him again. Did things to him that he could not describe, let alone understand.

Then Bruno 1.0 began another fall through madness.

The pain of translation wracked him, spread him across light years, poured him into a single quantized unit of being.

Suddenly, he felt a squeezing pop, a burning extrusion that was somehow like expansion, a pain like birth and death and life itself.

He thought that he heard a voice. A human voice.

Carol Faulk's voice. Which was quite impossible.

Bruno . . . speak . . . two . . . what . . . kzin . . .

Whatever he could say vanished, words seemed to flee like frightened fish in a huge pond.

He could not speak. Could not move.

Bruno 1.0 thought he heard his own voice after that, but that was truly impossible.

Brother . . . Pass . . . Outsiders . . . kzin . . . help . . .

How could he help anyone, if his mind was scattered like leaves in a hurricane? His mind seized a word, a reply, but as he grabbed another word, the first flew away.

It was hopeless.

He waited for the bees to return. He was sure that they would, soon. They had made him their own, after all, body and soul.

Chapter Thirteen

ANOTHER INCURSION IS IMMINENT.

Even as the ringing computer voiced faded, Carol braced herself. She swung her head from side to side, scanning the enclosure. She was looking for the distorted locus in space that would shortly appear.

Any time now. . . .

Carol Faulk found that a world touched by They Who Pass was not a pleasant one.

And the return of the kzin and her original Bruno— Bruno 1.0, so to speak—was the very least of it. They Who Pass sent many visitors, though none stayed— survived?—for long.

For what reason? As Bruno's far away mentor Buford Early put it, aliens are simply that: alien. And They Who Pass were alien far beyond what Carol's universe could produce.

The puppeteer kept at some distance, quaking and pressing singing polygons of pharmacological courage to its own necks, but she and the newer Bruno . . .

Bruno 2.0?

Anyway, she and *that* Bruno had developed stronger stomachs. Nothing They Who Pass sent seemed to hurt them, though many offended their sensibilities:

The air suddenly seemed to churn and swim about ten meters away. Carol ran toward it, Bruno following.

The thing materialized from the dimensional opening with a liquid pop and crackle of electricity. It looked like a yellow tongue with blue bristles. It slurped at itself with watery relish.

"It's horrible," she said, backing away. This one was worse than the previous entity that had pushed onto the Outsider ship from Principle knew where.

"Smelly, too," Bruno added, watching the thing with fascination.

"Kill it!" she said with sudden hatred.

The thing was not exactly a fresh puppy to love. "Too late. It's dying anyway."

The yellow tongue stopped trying to swallow itself and twitched. Its yellow faded to a rotten orange. It shuddered and lay still. As with the other entities, it faded into grayish dancing motes and vanished into nothingness.

"Another failed experiment? Thank God."

"Thank geometry, I'd guess."

"What do you mean?"

"They Who Pass made them, sure, but out of what? Materials from another space-time?" After their flight through troubled topologies in this ship, the idea did not seem so fantastic. "My guess is, they're deformed because they don't *fit*. Wrong organs, bad circulation chemistry—some detail that needs more work. Trial runs?"

"*Lots* more work." Carol shuddered.

They walked over to the makeshift autodocs. There was a shared defense mechanism of unspoken nonchalance between them as things onboard the Outsider spacecraft became progressively more bizarre.

Both she and Bruno had given up trying to get the puppeteer to help out with the comatose pair that They Who Pass had returned to them. The two-headed alien was spending its time maneuvering the Outsider ship randomly in case another one of the sniffing purple blips starting hunting them.

And, of course, the puppeteer took even more of its musical drugs.

Carol sympathized. If they survived, she would quake and wail at her leisure, just like the three legged monstrosity. If.

The old Bruno, now in the tank, might not survive even if the rest of them did. His face was burned. An eye was missing. He muttered and shook under the autodoc's ministrations.

"Well?" she asked.

New Bruno pursed his lips. "Pretty weird, to see yourself this way."

She nodded. This Bruno didn't know the half of it. Or did he?

"EEGs are spiking and strange," he continued, "according to the autodoc."

"Is he aware?"

"Dunno." Bruno paused. "I'm here, though."

Carol pushed all of her worries, the yammering uncertainty away for a moment.

"My loyal crew, I know you are Bruno."

"So's he."

It was Carol's turn to look inward. There was nothing truthful she could say that would make this Bruno feel better. "Store that subroutine for now. How about our furry friend?"

He nodded in agreement, then said, "I don't think we have a lot to worry about. He is very, very out of it."

"How can you be sure? Do we have a field kit for kzin physiology?"

Bruno tapped his head meaningfully.

She nodded, saying nothing. Another reminder that this Bruno was not quite what he seemed.

CAROL?

Bruno looked startled. "That doesn't make any sense. I don't even hear the electronic mumbling any more."

She pointed at the autodoc readout, which rippled a few lights and settled down again. "I don't think it is your electronic big brother, Tacky. I think it's *him*. The original . . ." Carol stopped, embarrassed.

"Bruno 1.0, maybe?" he said quietly. "So talk to him."

"Bruno?" she called. "Can you hear me?"

CAROL?

"I guess he can't hear me." She was both disappointed and relieved. If this kept up, she was going to go sit and sing demented songs in three-part harmony with the tanjed puppeteer.

Bruno looked pensive.

"What is it?"

"Let me try something." He clenched his eyes shut, gritted his teeth.

"What are you doing?" Carol asked.

"Sending a message through the computer system. Like I used to do when I communicated with big binary brother."

The autodoc readout flickered and danced like a complicated hologame.

Ten/mo/chi/mo/nashi/tada/yuki/no/furishikiri

The computerized voice faded away. Carol pulled on her lower lip. "What the censored dammit was that? Some other alien language?"

Bruno thought for a moment. "Old Japanese. It sounds familiar. . . ." He smiled. "Hashin."

"Hashin?"

"Japanese poet, hundreds of years ago. It's a haiku poem called 'Loneliness.' It goes something like this:

> *No sky at all;*
> *no earth at all—and still*
> *the snowflakes fall. . . .*

She thought about it. "What do you think it means?"

"Maybe how it feels to be in other dimensions?"

Carol nodded. "Makes sense. But why doesn't he just talk to us?"

"Maybe he can't? Look at him; he's pretty messed up. Maybe this is the only way he can communicate." Bruno grew a bit greenish as he looked his earlier self over more carefully.

She walked back and forth, pacing. The Bruno in the autodoc looked comatose.

"Try again."

He nodded. "Okay. But I don't communicate in words. It's emotions, feelings, images. That sort of thing."

"Whatever it takes."

"What do you want me to say?"

She thought about it. "Ask him how They Who Pass see our universe."

Again, Bruno had clenched his hands into fists and shut his eyes tight. His contorted face looked a bit painful to Carol.

The answer came within a few moments, in time with another ripple in the autodoc neurological monitoring circuitry. The tone of the unfamiliar words were somehow graceful.

Utsukushi/ya/shoji-no/ana-no/Ama-no-gawa

Carol was getting ready to impatiently remind good old Bruno 2.0 again to translate, but he slowly chanted the words himself.

> *"A lovely thing to see:*
> *through the paper window's hole,*
> *the Galaxy"*

"That's half-pretty," she told him, not knowing where to look when she spoke: the Bruno who spoke the words or the Bruno in the autodoc, who presumably originated them. . . . Well, not "originated," exactly. . . .

"That's Issa."

"Issa?"

"Yup." Bruno 2.0 stared at Bruno 1.0 intently, hardly paying attention. "Another eighteenth century Japanese poet. This one is called 'Heaven's River.'"

"Meaning?"

"That was what the Japanese called the Milky Way."

"Pretty name."

Bruno looked over at her. "Hey, that hurts my feelings. Don't like my versifying, but you interface with some dead Japanese guy?"

"Get over it," she half smiled back at him. Now this was sounding like the real Bruno. Whatever *real* meant. "What do you think about . . . well . . . the fellow in the tank." She pointed. "Him."

"Me, you mean. Me the First." He paused. "Carol, I think that he is trying to talk to me."

"Are you sure? Who *is* talking: the one in the tank or the computerized version of you?"

"I can hear something inside my head, Carol. Like the computer version, except less clear."

Life was getting weirder by the microsecond, and there was not a thing she could do about it except ride the ride.

"Maybe the attempts—even in poetry—at communication are helping open up a communications channel?"

He shrugged. "Anything's possible. I'm going to try

to yell at him. Inside my head, I mean. Maybe he can help us." He nodded. "He *has* to know more than we do about all of this."

Again, Bruno 2.0's face contorted with concentration. "I think I'm getting somewhere," he gritted.

A low tone issued from the autodoc. Carol looked down at the figure within.

Bruno 1.0's lips seemed to twitch and move. The monitor lights were flashing in a half-comprehensible pattern. Carol was sure that the autodoc would automatically sedate the injured man, but no spray-hypos snaked across him from the doc's storage cabinet.

Bruno 2.0 leaned closer to the prone figure, sweat beading his brow. "I almost have it. . . ."

The arm of the comatose man shot out of the tank. Grabbed Bruno 2.0 by the wrist. Shocked, Bruno 2.0 tried to pull away, but the grip was too strong.

RECEIVE DATA. ASSIMILATE AND RECONFIGURE.

As the computer-voice spoke, Bruno 2.0 began to moan in pain. His knees gave way. He fell next to the autodoc tank, his wrist still held firmly by his other self.

Carol was too shocked to move at first, then too confused. After another moment the need for action overcame doubt and she took two decisive steps forward and pried the fingers of autodoc-Bruno from new-Bruno.

"Are you all right?" she asked, though it didn't seem very likely. Bruno 2.0's eyes were rolled up into his head.

To her surprise, he answered. "So far, so far," he muttered, shaking all over. "Shapes without shape. Dark without light. The edge."

Delirium? Quickly, Carol turned back to the autodoc tank. The old Bruno was laying prone again, unmoving. The neuro monitor lights had returned to the slow repetitive patterns of his coma. She grabbed the medikit. Sparks jumped from her fingers to the metal fasteners of the kit. Static electricity? A rushing sound filled the air, and a hot breeze touched her skin.

Carol turned back to the new Bruno, suddenly afraid.

She was just in time to watch the air seem to boil and bubble around Bruno, distorting his image like something caught in a funhouse mirror. The smell of ozone filled the air. Sparks flew from object to object. She could hear the puppeteer's calliope wail of fear in the distance.

Then Bruno 2.0 vanished with an audible *pop* as air rushed in to fill the empty space he had just occupied.

Carol looked at Bruno 1.0, who lay placidly in the autodoc tank again.

Chapter Fourteen

Rrowl-Captain was surrounded by warm comforting darkness.

He was no longer falling in all directions as the terrible buzzing reverberated in his retracted ears. His closed eyes were no longer assaulted by the impossible geometrical shapes. Nor was Rrowl-Captain's nose any longer assailed by impossible aromas and sensory confusion. And there were no more probings by loathsome mechanical tentacles that ignored his fury as they proceeded implacably with their horrible tasks.

Perhaps he was delivered from some Coward's Hell, and had demonstrated his valor to the Claws of Judgment. To be rewarded by *nothing* was paradise indeed, after what Rrowl-Captain had experienced for an endless span of time.

But still, a debt was a debt, and the human he had Named C'mef was as much Hero as monkey. The little beast had died for him. Died for them all.

Could a kzin do less?

Rrowl-Captain's eyelids were sticky with dried tissues and fluids. His eyes darted, searching, searching; this was no kzinti Paradise, peopled with swift but not very cunning game and pliant kzinrrettis.

He was in some kind of medical tank. As his consciousness gelled he recognized the tubes and wires attached to several parts of his body. He could see nothing outside of the tank.

Death was still vivid in his mind. As the nightmare geometries and multi-dimensional intrusions receded, the defiant shriek seemed to have just left his lips, as the Outsider-robots stepped through the rent in his ship, reaching out implacably with horrible golden arms, all stretching. . . .

Little C'mef-Bruno had shouted his own defiance at the monsters, puny beyond words, but brave nonetheless. He had even thrown himself at one of the golden robots, though he had swiftly been seized and taken effortlessly away. Then the golden metal arms, linked and jointed, had grasped Rrowl-Captain and began pulling him apart as he snarled in his back-broken helplessness.

What followed was far worse than death.

Rrowl-Captain tried to forget the Other Lair. The Lair of Madness. Angles that were flat, curves that seemed straight. It was a place of insanity where hands made of madness had taken him prisoner.

The cage where he had been kept defied description. No ceiling, no walls, yet Rrowl-Captain could not move. Impossible shapes tormented his vision. Then he had seen a distorted image of C'mef-Bruno, both large and small, young and old.

Somehow, the kzin had known that his foster-brother was vital to the forces that held him in such horrible thrall. Needed his protection, the bravery of a Hero.

That knowledge gave Rrowl-Captain reason to live on in this new madness.

Any Hero could die rather than face dishonor. Bite off the hand, rip out the throat. But Rrowl-Captain had no such luxury. He must preserve his life to protect that of C'mef-Bruno. Honorable suicide was no option for him. And anyway, he feared that death in this Lair of Madness was not permanent; it had not been permanent before.

The lid to the medical tank slid away. A bright light assailed his weakened eyes. A shadow bent over him.

Rrowl-Captain could hear the falsetto human gabbling above him. With his slight understanding of the slave-language, the kzin thought the voice was discussing his health. Then, after a moment, he could hear the hiss-and-spit of the Heroes' Tongue. The tone was too high, but the grammar was flawless. The kzin recognized the voice.

It was the little two-headed creature with the translator devices.

"Illustrious Hero," keened the voice. "Are you hale? We have need of your bravery."

Rrowl-Captain licked his cracked lips. "Cease your witless flattery, grass-eater. I am awake."

He snarled at their attempts to help him from the medical tank. With great effort, he was able to sound calm. But every hair on his pelt was erect with fury and fear in equal mixture.

The kzin pushed back the ever-present memories of the Lair of Madness. In the back of his mind danced the impossible geometrical shapes, and implacable touch of things not of matter. Still, he clung, like a kitten clings to his mother's pelt, to the image of C'mef-Bruno. His *vssrcht*-brother must be freed from that place, if nothing else to die cleanly, in honor of his own Warrior Heart.

There was now a purpose to his shattered life, and his Warrior Heart and liver must be equal to the task. He had mastered his distasteful fears before; he would do it again. The kzin was unaware of how his claws unsheathed and resheathed as he stood placidly.

The human and the two-headed leaf-eater took turns describing to Rrowl-Captain the tactically poor situation.

"There are ships hidden in this fog?" he questioned. "Many ships, apparently derelict?"

"Yes, Rrowl-Captain," replied the ridiculous little three-legged alien in tones the translator, doubtless quite accurately, made sound fawning.

The larger one, the one that had in another incarnation died fighting the Zealot spacecraft, at least had a warrior's dignity.

"It is best to stalk opportunity from within yonder dust clouds," the kzin stated, pointing a shining black claw toward a dark series of blotches against the glow of the plasma cloud.

He almost quoted to these aliens from the Teachings of the One Fanged God, about caution and scream-and-leap existing in equal measure during the successful Hunt. But the agnostic kzin was hesitant to discuss any god after what had happened. What if the God was in fact part of the Lair he had so recently escaped?

Both of the little slave aliens scuttled to obey his commands. The two headed one always kept one head pointed at Rrowl-Captain. Nervously, the creature kept pressing some object of mysterious function against the base of its neck. Out of fear? It seemed likely.

Good, he thought in approval. *Prey should always be cautious of superiors in the food chain.*

The kzin would attend to important matters first. With the human female, Rrowl-Captain toured the remnants of the Outsider spacecraft left to them.

He was pleased to find that *Sharpened-Fang* was still present, and in good condition. The seals were intact. The singleship and its weapons array might become important.

It soured his liver and profaned his Warrior Heart
to deal with these aliens as even temporary allies, but
Rrowl-Captain had to move cautiously. His litter-
brother's Name lived once more, and must be honored.

He would bide his time. Prey could be stalked as
well as leaped upon.

Stalking could be enjoyable, in fact.

The human named Carol showed Rrowl-Captain the
area in which she worked. He noticed the other autodoc
medical tank, different than the larger one that had
held him.

She explained that the kzin had not been alone when
he had arrived back in the Outsider ship from the Lair
of Madness.

Rrowl-Captain sprinted to the autodoc chamber,
peered through the transparent top.

His litter-brother's Namesake, C'mef-Bruno, lay prone
inside.

"What is his condition?" the kzin nearly roared.

The human stared at him, taking a few steps backward.
Then it stood its ground. The medallion around its neck
translated the monkey words into the Heroes' Tongue.

"He is unconscious, and will not waken. The autodoc
is doing what it can to repair damage."

Rrowl-Captain's nose scented that there was much
more to this situation than was being told. He restrained
himself from taking the Carol-human's neck in one fist
and using claws and teeth to obtain more information.

The little human challenged him, surprising Rrowl-
Captain. "What do you care about another potential
slave?"

The kzin grinned from his height, not entirely in anger.
"Have a care, human. Your words are brave but
foolhardy." He tapped a clawtip on the cover of the
medical tank. "This one fought valiantly with me to save
your miserable lives, and deserves honor and respect."

The human moved its head up and down for a moment. It seemed to brush liquid from its eyes, and then walked away without giving more information.

No matter. He had found C'mef-Bruno. They would have to leave this place together, and soon.

But for the nonce Rrowl-Captain would bide his time.

Chapter Fifteen

If Bruno Takagama could have screamed, he would have.

It was the reverse of his implosion into 4-D.

This time he detonated, arms and legs zooming out over a darkening ocean.

He swelled with an unbearable pressure. Choking fullness—

Then, in an agonizing slowness, terminating in a crisp snap, he was back in the ship.

Hard enamel light flooded painfully through him. There was Carol, yes, and the hopelessly regular lines of rectilinear progression, oozing away from him—

—and his head was too large for this place.

His forehead stretched insupportably far from the back. His temples spread excruciatingly far apart, with a dull bass pulse beating between them. Throbbing with a deep message of its own. He tried to hear it but the pain yanked his thoughts away.

Then he was moving. Easier, this way. A lot easier than

being squeezed like toothpaste between dimensions.

Rotation, translation in blinding glare—and a slap in the nose. He was face down on the fragrant Outsider lawn-carpeting . . . if he still had a face. His hands were buried in the alien turf in a death-grip.

He rolled over and sat up—and found that was a very bad idea. He let go with his hands—illogically, he noted, by snatching up clumps of the grass-carpet—and fell back.

"Are you all right?" Carol's voice hammered into him.

He would have laughed but could not. "Uh."

"Where did you go?"

Urgent, breath-catching pause. "Uh."

"Who took you? Where—"

"They. Big. Everywhere." That seemed plenty to say but she just blinked at him, her big moon face hanging over him like an astronomical judgment.

"Who?"

"Uh. Bigger . . . dimensions."

"They Who Pass? They're from higher dimensions?"

"Uh huh."

"What do they want?"

"Room."

"They want our dimension?"

"Some of it. Just a . . . li'l bit."

Words were coming easier now. You just needed to not think too much. Also not let the eyes wander from her beautiful moonface hovering over the fluorescent landscape of the grass.

"All this is from . . . them?"

"Of course." So much was obvious in 3-D. Logic was so hopelessly linear.

"Outside, it's getting worse. The puppeteer and me have seen whole planets out there in the plasma mist. Stars, even—brown dwarfs, mostly. Looks like the Outsiders brought them here. Why, though?"

"Why, I dunno."

"If they're trying to get through to here, what do they need planets for? Like those terrible things that are appearing in this ship. They're so awful, ugly—"

"Failed . . . experiments."

"How do you know?"

"Saw them from the other side."

"They made them up? What are they *like* over there, if they send—"

"Think about trying to fit yourself into a shoe box. Fast, and head first."

"They can't live here. Most of them die within seconds."

"Over there, they looked like pieces of geometry. What's just abstract mathematics in 4-D has to live and breathe and excrete over here."

"What should we do about it?"

"Vac 'em if they can't take a joke."

He chuckled at nothing in particular and it felt good. Not much else did here in 3-D. His arms and legs were still somewhere on their own journey but they did send back eerie signals of distress.

"This isn't funny," she said severely.

"Damn right. That's why you gotta laugh."

"What?"

"4-D humor."

Then, with a vast feeling of relief, he passed out. Fell headlong into a welcoming darkness without dimension.

Chapter Sixteen

Rrowl-Captain blinked several times, not believing.

The tall human slave had appeared out of the air itself. It looked and smelled like C'mef-Bruno, but was clearly not. The C'mef-Bruno he was pledged to protect still lay helpless in the autodoc vat.

From all he had been told by the human and the herbivorous puppeteer, something very bad was going to happen soon. The kzin's predator instincts screamed that it involved C'mef-Bruno. Or this other Bruno-human.

Either way, it was not wise to remain in this Outsider craft, at the whim of forces unknowable.

This was perhaps the opportunity he had been stalking.

There was not much time. Rrowl-Captain, to his liver's irritation, was being forced to skulk like a scavenging *rummpth* in the tall grass, but there was no option. What if the other human was in fact linked somehow to the ill C'mef-Bruno? A scream-and-leap strategy might only alert the monsters from the Lair of Madness.

Therefore, a proud warrior must creep on all fours

while the human named Carol ministered to the new arrival. It was undignified, but necessary. The human was distracted; it gave the kzin the chance he required.

Rrowl-Captain slid the top of the autodoc tank open. With deft claws, he began removing wires and tubes from the prostrate human he was pledged to honor and protect. The electronic equipment begin to issue a warning tone, but the kzin pushed his hand deep into the central processing unit of the autodoc and clenched his fist around the electronics array.

The warning tone fell silent.

Gently, Rrowl-Captain picked up C'mef-Bruno, and moved swiftly across the central area to *Sharpened-Fang*. The human named Carol did not look up from where she tended to the other human. The two-headed leaf-eater was nowhere to be seen.

The kzin settled C'mef-Bruno into the acceleration couch, which was far too big for him. No matter. He adjusted the restraints as firmly as he could.

He turned to close and seal the airlock hatch to find the puppeteer herbivore standing there.

"So, Illustrious Hero," the ugly little thing screeched. "Are you taking the early version of Bruno with you on holiday?" It danced from hoof to hoof, a chiming polygon shape stuck at the base of its necks.

Rrowl-Captain smiled as widely as he could in threat.

"Run swiftly, little leaf-eater," he rasped. "I have not time to deal with you now."

"Where do you think you are going?"

The kzin blinked. Why didn't the puppeteer run? Were they not all cowards?

All except the one called Guardian, who had fought with Rrowl-Captain.

He unfurled his ears, curious.

"Are you not afraid, little grazer? My teeth ache with hunger."

The two heads weaved strangely. They flipped up suddenly, looking deep into their own eyes.

"Hero, I find I have little fear left. True, some of that is due to ... ah ... pharmacology, but most of it is due to desperation." One head poised over the bag the alien wore, as if over a weapon. "I say to you, return the human to the autodoc at once."

Rrowl-Captain coughed sudden kzinti laughter. In a flash, he had grasped the two headed alien by one neck, and swung the creature heavily against the bulkhead inside *Sharpened-Fang*. It fell in a heap, not moving.

The kzin slammed the airlock shut, and his claws danced over the activation subroutine.

Rrowl-Captain looked from the fallen puppeteer to the unmoving sunken-faced human in the too-large acceleration couch. He flared his nostrils, grinned again.

"My little leaf-eating friend, perhaps your bravery will serve a use after all."

The kzin activated the gravity polarizers, felt a slight resistance. He increased power. There were buffeting sensations, a grinding sound. Then nothing.

Rrowl-Captain roared success as *Sharpened-Fang* pulled away from the Outsider craft.

Chapter Seventeen

And now there were two.

Bruno Takagama's head was still stretched in directions—no, dimensions—that were not part of anything he could have imagined. Let alone describe. Nothing in the here-and-now looked quite right anymore. But not all the dizziness was due to moving between universes and dimensions.

"So the puppeteer, the kzin, and . . . well, the earlier version of me are gone?"

Carol nodded. "Pretty snug fit in that ratcat singleship."

"But that doesn't make any sense. Why would the ratcat kidnap anyone? Or are you saying the puppeteer went along with the kzin?"

"I have no idea about the puppeteer. He has been acting even stranger since all of the incursions by They Who Pass." She ran a hand over her face. "Tanj, I know how Diplomat must have felt, myself."

"Maybe an overdose of the bravery drugs? A serious case of Bravery Buzz?"

She shrugged.

"Well," Bruno mused, "if Diplomat decided to fight, he picked the wrong species to start with."

"Damn betcha."

Carol carefully helped him to his feet. Bruno was still shaky; distances and perspectives were still confused.

"What about the other Bruno?" he asked.

"The ratcat said something weird to me before all this happened. He told me that we all owed Bruno our lives."

He nodded. "That's weird? Sounds like he is trying to protect the other me, don't you think?"

Carol barked laughter. "Right now, Tacky, I try not to think at all. Look around you."

"Good point. Help me to the consoles and let's see if we can find our wayward tabbie and his guests."

The holoscreen showed the plasma cloud in all its glory. Lanes of dark dust crackled with lightnings larger than worlds. Different chemical compositions in far-flung regions of the cloud lent delicate colors.

Carol's hands wandered over keypads. False-color overlays appeared as she tried different detector arrays, but nothing became clearer.

"In all this dust and plasma, it is hopeless. Besides, the ratcat was already telling us where to hide in the plasma cloud before any of this happened."

"The beast was thinking of escape, even then?"

"Good guess."

They said nothing for a while. The controls on the Outsider ship that the now-silent computerized version of Bruno had kludged up were crude. There were no weapons, and no access to hyperspace. Bruno shivered for a moment. Hyperspace was too close to that other Place that had somehow become a part of him.

His original self had given him that access or power.

But Bruno hadn't wanted it. He was given no choice.

It was not going to be possible to find the kzin singleship in this turbulent soup of plasma and dust. . . . Well, there was one way. Bruno hated to think of it.

He stood up, still unsteady.

"Tacky," Carol asked, looking up from her readouts. "What are you doing?"

"I have to go find the original Bruno. Your Bruno, Bruno 1.0."

She stood up, grabbed him by the hand.

"Listen shipmate, you're still groggy. How are you going to find the kzin ship?" She pointed at the panorama above them.

Bruno felt his lips curl into a smile, but there was no humor in it. Just resignation.

"Carol, there is a way."

She shook her head, not understanding.

"Think of it this way: all three Brunos are linked."

"I still don't get it, shipmate. Sit back down."

He was feeling woozy. "We are all connected, somehow. Even though we are far apart, we are still together. I think They Who Pass made 1.0's mind work something like their own. Then he did something similar to me."

He walked toward the middle of the central area.

Carol was up and after him in a moment. "What are you doing?"

"Better stand back," he told her kindly.

Then Bruno felt himself teetering on the edge of the horrible precipice that was the place between dimensions. He felt his hair begin to stand on end from the static charge. He heard Carol begin to swear from far, far away.

"I'm sorry," he told her through the growing storm of spatial distortion. "I must find my brother."

He would be leaving Carol alone on the Outsider

ship. A knife in his heart. But he had no choice.

Bruno Takagama balanced on the edge of infinity, and threw himself forward. He fell into the other Place, and reached out into the unthinkable complexity around him.

Chapter Eighteen

Rrowl-Captain sliced another bit off the haunch of meat he had been eating. It had been heated to degradation, of course, in the human custom called *cooking*. The kzin would never understand such a lack of delicacy. Why would they prefer the flavor of death to that of fresh-killed or even still-living prey?

He shuddered to think that the human aliens even used machines to synthesize their food from simple compounds. Where was the honor to the Web of Life in that?

Truly, alien races were inexplicable.

It was no matter. He had indeed rescued C'mef-Bruno from the Outsider ship, and then hidden the two of them in *Sharpened-Fang*, very near to the great rod of plasma. Detection equipment would be useless in this place.

Of course, his foster brother did not improve under such conditions. The medical devices nourished, but did not Feed him. He needed a Hero's Meal. Blood and bone and flesh would make him whole. Rrowl-Captain chewed the slice of meat to bits, as a father would do for a tiny kitten, and gently placed the meal in C'mef-Bruno's mouth.

There was plenty of the dead puppeteer stowed in the cryostorage hold. Enough to build up C'mef-Bruno's health, to heal his wounds the way honorable wounds were meant to be healed. At the expense of lesser living things in the great Web of Life.

In the meantime, they would skulk in *Sharpened-Fang* and avoid pursuit. Either from the Outsider ship, or the monsters from the Lair of Madness. Or from anything else.

It was a bit shameful, but necessary.

The kzin kept an eye on his thinplate screens. The Outsider ship was out of detection range. Most of the metallic blips near the hard rod of plasma were cooked through by intense radiation, but a few moved and weaved toward *Sharpened-Fang*. Rrowl-Captain had little trouble evading them.

Eventually, he would need to search for a kzin ship and properly resupply. Even if no kzin spacecraft were present, surely there were ships he could use in this awful place. Somehow, he and C'mef-Bruno would have to attempt escape and reach safety.

So far, the denizens of the the Lair of Madness had not come for him, as he had expected since his emergence from the tank on board the Outsider ship. Rrowl-Captain would kill himself rather than submit again, litter-brother Namesake present or not. He was certain that the unconscious C'mef-Bruno would understand.

C'mef-Bruno began to stir. He had eaten so little of the leaf-eater's flesh that Rrowl-Captain knew any improvement in his condition was unlikely so soon. Something else was happening. The kzin's ears came erect.

The human's lips begin to move, flecks of puppeteer meat spraying.

Rrowl-Captain felt horrible pains in his head and chest.

The air began to swirl and twist inside the singleship. His thinplate console spat sparks, and alarms yowled.

The taller, undamaged version of C'mef-Bruno was crouched inside the singleship cabin. Surrounding him was a buzzing cloud of glittering blue motes.

The denizens of the Lair of Madness had returned.

With a shriek, Rrowl-Captain snatched up a projectile weapon from the thinplate console rack. He turned the weapon on the human-appearing figure, claw tightening on the trigger.

The buzzing blue motes, flashing with an azure glare, flew at Rrowl-Captain's hand. They whirled and capered around the weapon. It fell from his hand, floating in midair, encased in a cloud of the glittering bits of fire.

In a moment, the weapon clattered to the deck and they dispersed in a movement that seemed explosive, motes exploring every aspect of the singleship cabin as the tall human figure bent down and examined the quivering C'mef-Bruno.

Rrowl-Captain, still in shock, looked down. The projectile weapon had been changed. The projectiles were loose on the deck, rolling and clinking as the gravitic polarizer thrummed. The weapon itself now had structural supports on the outside.

It had been turned inside-out.

By then, the motes had found the cryostorage locker, opened it somehow, and revealed the frosted corpse of the half-eaten puppeteer.

Rrowl-Captain knew defeat when his jaws closed upon it. Failure—defeat—was grass in his throat, but he could still retrieve honor through death.

C'mef-Bruno would understand.

Rrowl-Captain roared defiance and threw himself,

claws and fangs bared, at the figure crouched over his dead litter-brother's Namesake. The alien-human did not even look up to face his attacker.

The blue buzzing motes shrieked back at Rrowl-Captain, rose to meet him. His leap halted in midair, his universe one of dancing lights like too-bright stars.

Rrowl-Captain felt his body explode inward and outward, his feet and head exchanging places. A terrible pressure grew. He suddenly knew that his fate would be the same as the projectile weapon.

With all of his Warrior Heart, the kzin prayed that this death would be permanent.

Chapter Nineteen

The two Bruno Takagamas hurtled through madness like leaves in a windstorm.

Bruno 2.0 tried not to look at the impossible shapes, feel the impossible sensory inputs he was experiencing in the region between the universes. Without looking, he could sense that Bruno 1.0's eyes were wide open, experiencing, assimilating.

He was becoming part of this place.

Brother? he tried to call.

There was no answer. Not the chittering of electronics, not the pain of translation between the universes. Yet still, Bruno 2.0 knew that he was heard.

For a moment, he saw how the buzzing blue bees looked in the Between, and a hint of how They looked in their own blazing, doomed universe.

Bruno 2.0 felt his mind try to shut down into madness at the perception. It was too alien, too much to assimilate. He forced the image away, turned his thoughts back to Carol.

He seemed to sense a spark or glow that was somehow Carol. He and his brother fell headlong through what was and was not space and time toward her. He doubted that they would both make it back to the Outsider craft.

Brother, Bruno 2.0 tried again. *What happened with the kzin?*

A vast inhuman humor seem to rise all around him, purple and smelling of burning dust.

The words burned into his brain, in archaic letters of fire:

Neko/ni/kuwareshi/wo/korogi-no/tsuma/ sudakuramu

Mentally, he translated the words of the haiku:

Eaten by the cat!
Perhaps the cricket's widow
may be bewailing that!

Was the puppeteer mated? he wondered. Would anyone mourn the two-headed alien? As Carol was now mourning him? He had to get back . . . Bruno 2.0 believed that They Who Pass . . .

. . . try not think of how they looked . . . try, try, try . . .

. . . were somehow helping them navigate the clashing geometries that made up this region between the two universes.

Brother, he sent again. *Come back with me to Carol.*

A huge welling of sorrow, tinged with green resignation, filled him.

Again, the words of fire filled his mind:

Cho/kiete/tamashii/ware/ni/kaeri/keri

Bruno 2.0's sorrow matched the increasingly inhuman emotions generated by his brother—no, his self.

The butterfly having disappeared,
My spirit

Came back to me.

Bruno 1.0 knew the truth, even as changes in him were being made by They Who Pass. There was no returning to Carol for him. No returning to the universe where Bruno Takagama had been born.

Bruno 2.0 could go home again, if he so chose.

Should I leave you here, brother?

And he felt it happen, all at once.

The earlier version of his self split, changed, expanded. The altered and damaged consciousness of the first Bruno Takagama was being spread across sky, thin as an atom, wide as a solar system.

Somehow he knew that Bruno 1.0 was meeting his fate as a servant of They Who Pass, midwife to their entry into the universe of humans.

And Bruno 2.0 feared what shapes they would assume. Would they possess some 3-D race to use as bodies? They had come to know a great deal about humanity. . . .

The dispersed Bruno 1.0 smiled in sharp-edged polygons and bright smells of mirth. A shape the color of hope flashed.

That was when Bruno 2.0 knew that he had a chance. He reached out to Carol Faulk with even greater effort, and felt the strangenesses around him begin to recede.

Chapter Twenty

Meanwhile, outside human space, They Who Pass were weaving complicated patterns of compacted space-time.

The cosmic string was not needed now for the transfer. Its principal task done, it became useful in other ways.

The torsion of the collapsing 4-D metric sent tremors through the string. Great surges twisted the string's compacted mass energy. Waves snapped through it at the speed of light, emitting bursts of intense radiation. Coherent photons rammed outward.

This sudden jolt of electromagnetic energy poured out in high harmonics of the fundamental string frequencies. Radiation pressure blew away the plasma fog. A curved cylinder of clear vacuum grew at light speed. Its edge was a thickening angry crimson hydrogen, snowplowed at relativistic speeds, far faster than a supernova remnant's swelling shell.

The snarl of the dying 4-D metric crackled along the entire string network circling the galaxy. Reacting, the concentric set of strings vibrated, wrenched, surged and all matter in the vicinity suffered the slings and arrows of outraged mass-energy.

The string near Carol and Bruno looped, tangled. Where the string met itself, it cut itself. A string cannot have a loose end; all of space-time geometry screams for it to unite.

Each cut made a new loop. The string was devouring itself into a family of smaller loops, each glowing white hot with ferocious power.

All these myriad cuts and snarls came at blinding speed. In the 3-D world, nothing could happen faster than the speed of light. But in the agony of the 4-D universe, angular thrusts could act simultaneously all along the cosmic strings.

The weaving came to the 3-D universe as a single, enormous collision.

In one moment, the serene order of the giant, galaxy-circling string collapsed into uncountable smaller strings. . . .

Chapter Twenty-one

Bruno Takagama fell headlong through the halfway Realm between the the universe he knew and the cosmos of They Who Pass.

His mind could never understand or encompass the warped area between the universes. Perhaps his earlier self could do so, but he was spread across the equivalent of many parsecs and a billion years. His very consciousness was now woven into the structure of space and time, to serve as midwife to They Who Pass.

The original Bruno had finally become one with the All, in ways that could never be explained or understood.

He knew that for They Who Pass time grew short. The creatures appeared to be having trouble placing their minds into other living receptacles. Part of Bruno was pleased by this inadequacy of mastering biology and physics, while another part of Bruno realized that this would only make them more desperate. He had to find the entities a new home.

But where?

The thought came to him from nowhere Bruno could identify. The computerized version of his mind, whispering from beyond insanity's gate? The old Bruno, dispersed in the interstices between the universes, but somehow still aware on some level?

If he wasn't careful, They Who Pass would decide to use humanity as vessels, or some other race of intelligent creatures.

But his idea seemed worth pursuing.

The hard part wasn't having the idea, but getting it across to such minds encased in uncomfortable machinery.

Bruno tried to send the concept. In the warped perspectives and sliding geometries of 4-D, this was not easy. Every thought pattern seemed to be nonlinear, a spattering of diffused parts. Ideas became bugs on the windshield of Reality.

He could think well enough—but communicating was hard.

  ... multiple ... imprinting ... on ... diffuse ... subjects ...

Painfully he stitched the idea across a vault of chaos. Fiery, plunging anarchy.

The 4-D universe was squeezing down to its doom. The sky above—or was it around him, an enveloping clasp like a spherical trap?—burned white-hot. The suns of this ruined cosmos had long ago guttered out. The sky would have been stone cold black ... but space itself was driving inward.

Now the light of the early days of that universe, photons from the primordial radiation, were urgently rattling in an ever-smaller box. And that shrinking box had become their whole cosmos, now beginning to burn with a final compression. The frequencies of these photons shifted up and up with the diminishing metric. Once mere microwaves, they now stung as ultraviolet, as x-rays, and threatened to brim into gamma-rays.

The desperation of They Who Pass leaked into Bruno's being. He could dimly sense the final scorching slide of that other universe into a single, dimensionless Point.

Time ran strangely there. The tick of a second in Bruno's universe was equivalent to what span on the Other Side? Years? Centuries? Millennia? The End Time was near. Time, regardless of its rate, would soon cease.

He must somehow convince They Who Pass not to invade sentient creatures—humans, for example—with their incomprehensible minds. But how to reach across a mental gap that spanned dimensions? And what choice did the entities have, with their universe crushing around them?

Bruno could sense pale shadows—the thoughts of They Who Pass. Was the reverse possible? He tried again. Would such an emotion be familiar to creatures of more than three dimensions? A starting place for communication?

... might ... give ... adequate ... room ... for You ... for Those ...

All around was heat, brittle brilliance, a steady roar. He felt a quivering. An answer?

□□□ Ā⌐□ □□rm̄|tt□□ t□ Ātt□m□t□ □|□⌐Ā □□ş§□| □□⌐ □ş̌Š

He couldn't understand the idea-forms that poured into his mind like biting acid. Whatever the thrumming in reality was, it tried again. This time, the thoughts were clearer to him, less painful.

FIND A VESSEL FOR US!

He sent, *I hope a lot of small vessels ... linked ... could serve. A ... host ... to act as Host.*

WE ARE COOLING THIS REGION TO GAIN MORE TIME.

The roaring grew, impatient and somehow hungry. *I will have to find the species—*

PREPARE A WAY FOR US. HASTEN!

—And he was spinning. Back in 3-D. *Ah!*

Tumbling, he seemed to see Hashin's snowflakes whirling around him. No ground, no sky. A yawning dimensionless fall in all directions at once, or none.

Yet, somehow, with some sense he could dimly use, Bruno could direct his motion through this other Place. See the shadow that was the universe that contained Carol.

Through the plasma fog, along the stretching length of the cosmic string. Phosphorescence bristled and fumed all along it. Ionized hydrogen jets erupted from the tiny crack in space-time—mad energy boiling from the wrenched 4-D macrocosm he had just left.

The string was a fountainhead of agonized mass. Raw matter spurted out into its sudden 3-D freedom and lashed everything nearby to more plasma, atoms ripped apart by the furious forces being unleashed.

He could see the shadowy wrecks of alien spacecraft helplessly engulfed by arcs of plasma. Blue-white electrical jolts played along the string, illuminating the ongoing catastrophe.

He glimpsed a giant construction, hexagonal and gleaming, surely the culminating effort of some advanced race, then in an instant it was gone, devoured by a white-hot gout.

Somewhere in all this, Carol . . . Bruno reached out, tried to force his self in directions and motions he couldn't understand and could barely control.

Then he felt the forces that worked upon him accelerate, as if in agreement. They Who Pass could work their wonders on this side of the string-crack, using electromagnetic induction, the rubbery, intricate interplay of charges and fields. Helping. Urging. Compelling.

He shot outward, somehow seeing both realities. Both universes.

Here was a world, swimming beside a slumbering red-dwarf star. The planet showed pink dust-laden clouds and a sullen, brown ocean sprinkled with oblong island-continents. He plunged down, feeling that there was something there he could use. Bruno clung to that hope.

The atmosphere sang around him. Re-entry somehow did not touch him, encased within a shield he could not see but felt as a hard, glassy surface. It looked like glittering fountains of light in the other universe, soft and cushioning against unfelt forces.

He plunged. Into the ocean . . . ? No, he felt a surge, the flattening of trajectory. Groaning from the acceleration, he slipped in a long descending curve toward a green and brown land mass.

Snow-crested mountains grew, suddenly were above him as he rushed down a narrow valley.

Below were speckled dots, trees . . . and animals. A vast herd. It spread across the valley. Then he plunged steeply and slammed into the iron-red soil.

Bruno rose to his knees, breathing the raw air of another world into his lungs.

There was something like grass on the ground, red and leafy, with blue dots.

And he could see the herd across the valley.

There had to be a hundred thousand of them. At least. A host of creatures.

A host?

Each of the creatures was perhaps a meter tall. Bruno took a moment to study one. The small body was held suspended by six lanky legs. On the upper part of the body was a hump, with three eyes set as if in the corners of a blunt equilateral triangle. Two sets of legs had something like paws at their ends, which tore tufts of the grasslike plants and carried them to the grinding mouth set underneath the body.

Bruno held very still while one of the herbivores perambulated toward him.

It slowly rotated as it walked, bringing one eye and the other to bear on him. He could see that all of the legs had crude paws, some folded up into something like hooves.

They could have six hands, he realized. *Time for an experiment.*

Bruno shouted.

Bruno enjoyed watching them run down the valley. They never seemed to collide with one another, like an enormous flock of birds, infinitely well organized. They looked like a cross between spider and deer. Yet the entire herd seemed to move as one.

Something seemed to click inside Bruno's head. Not herd. Herd.

It was as if the entire Herd could work together, like an enormous organism.

That was when he knew.

Bruno reached inward and outward within his own mind, using his new abilities. He let his eyes unfocus, his balance shift to the Other Place. To the direction that was equally far away from all things. The Nothing Place. The region Between.

The place between dimensions constructed by They Who Pass.

He could feel the electrical sizzle and the rising winds swirl around him as space itself begin to buckle and twist to his will.

Bruno fell into Other, anxious to tell They Who Pass what he had found. And to find Carol again.

Chapter Twenty-two

Carol Faulk waited to die on the Outsider craft.

She was alone. Both Brunos were gone, along with the Outsiders, the kzin, and the puppeteer.

Alone.

There was a time when Carol was like any other Belter: proud and silent, reveling in being alone.

That was then. This was now.

All around her, the Outsider ship was beginning to give way, the plasma cloud grew still more energetic. Damage was growing, and there was not a thing Carol could do but wait to die. Or was there?

The lights inside the Outsider craft were beginning to fade, and some of the instruments were no longer working. The air no longer smelled fresh. She could retreat into *Dolittle*, but the tiny craft carried only the smallest reaction engine reserve, and one of the great superconducting wings that had carried her and Bruno through space so long ago had been sheared off during a Kzin attack. Not very useful.

Where had Bruno gone? Could he return?

Despite that Carol decided to at least get *Dolittle* as shipshape as possible. Not that she could go far with just one superconductive wing, but perhaps the plasma field strength would help.

Suddenly decision filled her. But she would have to move fast, before the cosmic string fried the Outsider ship, and her with it.

A crackling, burning smell filled her nostrils. Was it finally starting to come apart? Then she felt her skin prickle with a growing static charge, and knew.

She turned around, trying not to let hope fill her expression.

"You must come with me," Bruno rapped, still surrounded by a glowing discharge of electricity. "They Who Pass will shortly . . . well, live up to their name. That will generate a huge energy release from the cosmic string. That will destroy any spacecraft nearby."

"Where can we go?" Carol felt trapped, helpless.

"I found a planet for us."

He grabbed her hand. "But we have to do it *now*."

She felt the electricity surge around her. A burning wind begin to rise, and her eyes begin to unfocus.

"No . . ."

"It's the only way. Hold on." He took her in his arms.

Carol Faulk tumbled into a place of unthinkable madness with her lover. She shut her eyes, but the images bypassed vision, burned into her brain. Glowing figures, burning shapes, impossible smells and tastes.

They fell.

Chapter Twenty-three

The tortured cosmic string simmered with unrelieved energy—the final legacy of the 4-D cosmos as it died, fusing into a single point of unthinkable energies.

Time had literally vanished in the 4-D universe. But still, in the lowly 3-D universe, energy poured through the rest of the cosmic string.

And now the string began its final work.

All along its immense curve, the string had begun vibrating. Emitting bursts of electromagnetic radiation, it blew away much of the plasma fog. Wrecks and worlds emerged from the dispersing haze.

Where the radiation was too intense, it seared whole planets. Bursts blew away the photospheres of nearby stars.

Cooling, the cosmic string lingered.

Responding to the final commands from its 4-D masters, it began to snake and twist. Ripples grew all along it. These rose in amplitude, vibrating wildly like a living thing in a fury of rage or lust or something without a name.

Perhaps birth.

Abruptly, segments twisted, alive with vivid shifting color—and turned upon each other.

They collided, cut. Gouts of energy burst from the intersections. The gleaming lines chopped off into segments. They moved with angry velocity, nearly as quickly as light. The tension lodged in space-time itself forced the segments to reconnect, forming silvery loops.

Some of the wobbly circles were as large as a solar-system, others far shorter. They followed a power law, with the probability of finding loop of perimeter R given by R^{-x} with $x=3.14159$ . . . the constant π, an artifact of the geometric transition from the 4-D cosmos.

Serene geometry held sway above the deadly rain of radiation.

But such austere beauty, so necessary to the plans of They Who Pass, has a price.

Chapter Twenty-four

The valley was an odd green and the sky was a soft red. Carol liked it all anyway. Every bit of it, from the smallest clod of dirt to the largest reddish cloud scudding across the sky.

The madness of the strange region between dimensions had delivered them here, to a place that seemed calm and safe.

The odd gray-green of the vegetation apparently came from a different chlorophyll-like molecule. Not a green like she was used to, but a green that she could become used to seeing. Belters didn't keep houseplants other than the algae in the airplant tanks.

Maybe she could learn.

The rosy sky arose from high altitude dust. There were no doubt explanations for everything, but for the moment she didn't give a damn. It was close enough to what she knew to feel *right*. And it was real, gritty, firm in ways none of the manufactured environments of the Puppeteers or Outsiders could match.

They both stood and watched the endless herds cropping grass in the valley below. The Host, Bruno called them.

"Let's walk," she said to Bruno and started down the hillside.

After a time it became obvious that the strangeness from 4-D lived within the herbivores. The herds rustled uneasily. The awkward-looking grazers ran aimlessly, collided, wandered in a daze.

The grazers looked something like stilt-legged spiders, mostly leg and body, leading to a small head. The head had eyes on three sides, set in the equilateral triangle Bruno had told her about. They ran like whirligigs at first when startled.

"Damn, they look strange," Bruno said. "Looks like they can see things going and coming, though."

"They *are* strange. Not just weird aliens—we've seen plenty of those lately, eh? But *possessed* aliens . . ."

All along the stretching valley the herds murmured, a low strange song that echoed from the steepled hills.

Bruno frowned. "Do they understand what we're saying?"

"I wouldn't be surprised. They're the Substrates you talked about. The Host. Whatever They Who Pass were, some slice of them is now living in this valley."

Bruno blinked. The herds abruptly stamped their hind hooves, *thump! thump! thump!* The effect was startling, tens of thousands in perfect unison.

Bruno did not react, though. He gazed off into the apparently placid reaches of the valley, as though he were listening to some note she could not hear. "As I see it, these beasts are like single neurons. Interconnected, they make up a brain. They are somehow still connected." He paused. "Imagine if every neuron in our brain were dispersed, yet each neuron was still connected to the whole."

"A brain. Like no kind of brain anybody's ever seen before."

"When I was . . . on the other side, I could . . . sense . . . them. They think by moving across a subject, like looking at it from above. Or maybe from all directions at once."

Carol felt it then, too. A curious plaintive note that murmured low and faint on the whispery air. A pungent scent came with the soft reverberation. The herd was speaking with a new, untried voice.

Bruno swallowed hard and went on, eyes still peering down the valley at the shifting bodies. His expression was far away. "So many . . . They're—mourning."

"The universe they left behind?"

"Yes, but something else, worse. They expected to leave their 4-D cosmos, after all. But this—so much gone—it's as if they're missing—"

He stopped so abruptly Carol asked, "What? What is it?"

"Half an alien loaf is better than none." He barked laughter. "In the rush, they didn't think every effect all the way through."

"Some of them died?"

"The other herds, on the other side of this planet. When the radiation blew away the fog, remember?"

"Last night? The auroras, the plasma plumes? Only lasted a few hours." Carol nodded. "Sure, beautiful. Filled the night sky—oh."

"The bursts were all across the electromagnetic spectrum. That scrubbed the other side of this planet clean of cerebral activity. Direct synaptic overload, for a connected intelligence."

"You mean, it cut them off from each other? Each herd animal was like an isolated neuron?"

"Once the link was lost, the neurons couldn't get back together again. They reverted to single units. Neurons aren't intelligent. By themselves, they're nothing."

"So the other side of this world's been . . . erased?"

The low lament swelled along the green canyon. Something in the sound brought tears to her eyes. She couldn't help it.

"Half of They Who Pass died last night."

"My God."

Bruno grimaced. "Y'know, for a while there, I thought of They Who Pass as—well, as gods. At least gods of some sort. They could do so much that we can't. So much larger than we could ever be . . ."

"And even geometric gods can still make mistakes?"

"Guess so."

A pause. "And die?"

"Guess so. Maybe they can be reborn, though."

The layered smell of the herds shifted again. To Carol's nose it was a complex message on the moist breeze, carrying nuances she could not express in words. "They're grieving."

Bruno shook his head. "It's more than that. They've already gone through some sort of, well, of 're-selfing' might be the word. Reinitializing?"

"You're telling me we shouldn't use human terms to describe them?"

"Do we care about dandruff, or cast off cells?"

"But half of them—"

"They're already beyond that."

"How can they—"

"In some way they restructure themselves, like a hologram. The whole idea of separateness, it's built into us. Not them. They seal up the seams, make up for losses."

"And move on."

"Don't ask me to explain it in human terms."

Because you're not human yourself, anymore? Carol thought with a pang.

They watched the Host for a time, heard the keening in their souls.

"How do we know so much about them?" she asked. It was something that frightened her, but there was not a bandersnatching thing she could do about it.

"They Who Pass changed us, probably when we came here through their domain. Me a lot more than you, of course."

A thrill of worry moved up her neck.

"Why did they change us? Are we some kind of servants now?"

He shook his head. "I don't think so. The original Bruno made it possible for They Who Pass to embed themselves into the Host. A midwife, sort of. Somehow I don't think that he lost all of his humanity. I like to think that he protected us, kept us safe."

Carol said nothing for a long time. She reached down, picked a bit of the alien grass, put it her mouth. It was tart and spicy.

"What is it?" Bruno asked.

"It's silly. And pointless."

"So?"

"I miss him. I know that the two of you are the same, but I still miss him."

Bruno looked pensive. "I think I have a message for you."

She raised an eyebrow in question, confused.

"When he . . . dispersed, changed, whatever. I thought about you, and something pushed into my head."

"What was it?"

He raised his head to the odd sky, and pursed his lips. "It's a poem. Another old haiku, by a Japanese poet named Issa." He nodded. "Here is how it goes in English:

> *Heat shimmer . . .*
> *   lingering in the eye*
> *   a laughing face.*"

She thought about it. "What does it mean?"

Bruno gestured at the huge herd, the Host, spread out across the vast alien valley floor.

"I think he is still here in some way. Everywhere a little bit, nowhere very much. But still watching."

Carol thought about that for a long while as she listened to the herbivores seem to sing to one another as One.

Chapter Twenty-five

Within hours, the sky above the Target World brimmed with a lancing, killing light.

Seas of radiation fumed and burned, but nothing like the energies left behind in the squeezed cosmos of They Who Pass. Many newborn cosmic loops sped across the still-tortured spaces of the dispersing Sargasso.

Throughout the galaxy similar dissolution followed along the track of the once-great cosmic string. The ancient fossil of the Great Emergence left, by its suicide, innumerable hoops moving at nearly light speed.

As they crossed the magnetic field lines of the galactic field they drove along their lengths huge super-currents of electricity. The loops lit up through induction, blazing beacons of energy.

The countless looped strings were beautiful, perfect knives. Less than an atom's diameter wide, yet massing as much as an asteroid in the length of a finger, they could cut any matter in this universe.

It would be only a matter of time before the myriad sentient races of the galaxy saw in them the perfect tool—and weapon. Slicing up worlds or enemies was an inevitable goal.

Whole dynasties of life would revere these gleaming loops, fight over them, long for them—and die for them.

But around the star of the Target World, the local loops left over from the entry of They Who Pass had a special purpose.

Spinning up, the great hoops made nested spheres around the parent star. Shifting, moving in self-organizing modes, they shaped a swiftly revolving cat's-cradle around the young solar system.

Surrounded by many thousands of cosmic loops of slightly different sizes, each revolving at high velocities, the sky of the Target World blazed with incandescent geometry, a whirling beauty never seen before in this universe.

They seemed like a glowing ball of twisted yarn at first, with the solar system of the Substratum Host at its center. Some spun rapidly, cutting across magnetic field lines, and so glowed with an ivory radiance. Others were slow and invisible.

In all they formed a lethal barrier. An intruder could avoid the brilliant loops, distracted by them, until a cooled, dark string chopped it crosswise along a very fine line, the cut leaving disemboweled ships in a warning glow.

Still, They Who Pass could not foresee everything.

A cool, reflective intelligence could regard the Substratum Host System over time, plot the vectors of all of the shining cosmic loops. They would all trace smooth arcs about the cat's cradle solar system.

In time, sentients would calculate, comprehend, and come calling. By then—so went the hopes of They Who Pass, a breed now extinct—the Substratum Host would know enough to want interesting and intelligent neighbors.

Or want something *from* those neighbors.

Until then, the Host had its recently optimized shepherds, to guide and shape.

In the long peal of time, loneliness yawns.

Chapter Twenty-six

They walked downslope for a while, letting the herd part before them. Though she knew that an ordinary herd might do the same, Carol found it unnerving that the animals closed again behind them, like a single entity enveloping . . . or digesting.

She elected to not pursue the thought further.

They passed under strange trees with spindly black trunks like spiders' legs. The branches fanned out into decks of flat leaves, all a mottled brown. Then they came out on a rise where the view was better and got their first look at the moon.

There was only one and it had craters and dark lava-flooded maria. It seemed bigger than Earth's but she could not tell whether that was because it was closer. There was so much they did not know, could not know.

None of that mattered compared to the way it looked. They both gasped.

A neat curved line divided the moon. One side was

darker and the other had a curious bleached quality, like something left out in the sun too long to dry.

The sun was hanging low on the horizon and the divided moon presided over the beginnings of a ruddy sunset. Carol estimated angles and times and said, "The string. It baked the moon."

"I wonder what the other side of this planet looks like."

"Our atmosphere probably protected the biosphere pretty well. But as I said I'll bet the radiation burst wilted anything as delicate as the link between individual members of the herd."

"We may have some work to do."

"With bare hands?"

"There's the herd. Something tells me they have possibilities."

"They may not be all that cooperative."

"We're their parent-figures, remember?"

He laughed. "Careful of those human categories."

"They may have been hot stuff in 4-D, but they're on our turf now."

He gave her the skeptical lift of an eyebrow. "And they'll mind their mumma?"

"Remember, they're laid down on a substrate. There are limits, based on . . . umm . . . context. Herbivores aren't leaders."

Bruno laughed. "Remember Guardian? Don't be so quick to generalize."

"Okay." She bit her lip. "I don't see any different forms among these herbivores."

"We could have them build us a house."

"With hooves?"

"They have something like paws, Carol. Okay, the idea needs work. But look at what puppeteers could do with their mouths."

"I just hope all of this is the end of it," Carol said.

"How so?"

"Could more . . . things . . . from the 4-D universe penetrate? Those Who Pass mentioned no others, but what's that mean?"

"Well, captain of my heart, in this universe it's happened once in fifteen billion years."

"That we know of."

"We'll just have to hope and go on."

"Hope, sure. I'd pray, too—but to what gods, now?"

He put a hand on her arm, warm in the slight breeze. "Don't borrow trouble," he told her.

"Plenty to go around."

"Yup." He squeezed her arm, smiled a bit. "Can I recite you a poem, or are you just interested in old haiku these days?"

Carol grinned back. "Poetry is just a way to seduce femmes, isn't it?"

"Hey, whatever works."

It was good to have some normal banter in this odd place. "So say on, Great Bard of the Spaceways."

"It's by an old American poet named Frost. It warns that the greatest dangers exist between our ears."

They cannot scare me with their empty spaces
Between stars—on stars where no human race is.
I have it in me so much nearer home
To scare myself with my own desert places.

Carol turned to him. "Pretty, I suppose, but kind of depressing."

Suddenly the banter was gone as he looked at her from haunted eyes. "Don't you understand? I had such madness in my heart and soul, after I was in the other dimension."

He took her hand.

"It was you who brought me home. To my humanity. Even here, in this alien place."

Chapter Twenty-seven

The Substratum System was the only success of They Who Pass.

Yet all the rest of their towering, feverish effort across more galaxies than can be counted was not wholly wasted. The innumerable severed portions of the cosmic strings would stimulate the works of many species in this galaxy—cosmic tools born of cosmic strings. This alone would uplift the place of life in this odd, shrunken 3-D world of galaxies and stars.

An attempt to move between universes, to arrive throughout the new universe, had failed. All the efforts of They Who Pass had resulted in one small translation, here, in this minor spiral galaxy.

They Who Pass had, as Outsiders might have expressed it, managed to AtOne with the Host Substrates on one lone planet. They lived—after a fashion—within the Host. But the crucial role, the two primate caretakers, they could not control.

The caretakers had been altered, improved. But their

413

minds remained completely alien, and thus remained untouched.

The spaces near the Target World would, in time, fall under the agonies of a spreading Man-Kzin war, or other ephemeral conflicts like it. The species did not matter, really. Such a conflict was a trivial eddy in the ebb and flow of galactic time, but was inevitable.

On the scale of the galaxy's slow grinding wheel, the volume commanded by the Kzin and by the fledgling primates was like a bit of dust. On a map of the spiral arms, all that these arrogant races knew was a tiny dot. The structure of their tiny empires, the province of their proud philosophies, was like a mote adrift among the ceaseless gyre of smoldering stars.

Amid those shoals of suns, and great banks and clouds of slumbering dust, even stranger minds lurked.

But none as strange as the Substratum, now written upon in a fashion no mind of this universe could begin to imagine. The primates were the most flexible of the species in this small speck of the galaxy. Yet in time, even they would find that they could not go back, could not fit in the cozy conceptual confines they once knew.

If such small and limited minds could perceive the universe as it truly exists, they would surely be driven mad.

The final question confronting the primates would be even darker than the events so far unfolded. They would learn the troubled topology of that question as time unrolled, and the Host Substratum grew more sure in this strange new universe.

Their great question would be, *After such knowledge, what sanctuary?*

Chapter Twenty-eight

A moment of clear, cold fear shot through her. Awe.

Carol watched the gliding splendor of the string-loops as they lit the night sky beyond the half-blasted moon. The inner solar system was now surrounded by the gleaming majesty of cosmic circles, weaving their fatal cocoon.

This would keep their world safe—for a while. But she and Bruno were trapped here with . . . what?

If these things could engineer razor-thin strings the size of galaxies . . . configure them like a bull's eye . . . warp space-time . . . then what could they do when they found fresh purchase in this universe?

Was her loyalty to her species—to her whole universe—bigger than any personal love of Bruno? Should she kill them all, somehow?—rather than let this utter strangeness into the universe?

Could she kill them all?

Carol smiled a bit at the irony, still watching the glittering alien sky. Back on Earth, Project Cherubim had been planned to create a few human-Pak monsters to protect humanity from the kzinti. Now They Who Pass had made her and Bruno into shepherds—also protectors, in a way—to guard their herbivore avatars.

But which was the truth: were she and Bruno supposed to guard the possessed Herd, this Host, from the rest of the galaxy? Or were they supposed to guard the rest of the galaxy from these possessed grass-eating spider-deer? The stilt-legged herbivores seemed so harmless—but They Who Pass had made the entire sky glow with their power.

And a least a portion of those vast alien minds now existed in the herbivores grazing in the valley below them.

What should she and Bruno do? What *could* they do?

She didn't know. And there was no time to ponder such weighty thoughts. The moment was upon her. She had to go with gut instinct. No matter the technology or the setting, it seemed to Carol, humans always carried the canny judiciousness of the plains ape with them.

Even here.

This Bruno beside her—she cast him a sidelong glance, to find him staring in puzzled wonder at the glowing weave that spanned their sky. What *was* he?

The old Bruno, the one she had come to love . . . he had died twice for her. Once in battle, once in his transition.

Who was she to spurn such a gift?

She blocked his view. Before he could react, she kissed him fiercely.

They would always long for the warm, comforts of human associations, the unconscious relaxings which came from association with one's tribe. They were now beyond that. From the edge of the greatest abyss, one can never truly turn away.

Here would be a new tribe for she and Bruno to tend. Perhaps in time the family they never had.

She softened in his arms. In turn, they clasped her hard. The brittle crackling branches of the spiderlike trees rustled uneasily in the cool night.

They would live out their lives here, helping these Substrates gather themselves. A host of the Host. Hoping to shape the nascent herd-mind so that it would not be a threat to humanity.

But would the Herd even care about human concerns?

And inevitably, the herd would act back upon the two of them. Strangeness would fill their days.

How could they live, with such knowledge available through even rudimentary connection with They Who Pass?

Miracles would become everyday. She and Bruno might well be immortal. Could mere humans withstand such a prospect?

Carol shook her head, as if to clear it. But she knew the questions could not go away fully, ever.

They were far, far away from the battles between humans and kzin. The conflict seemed suddenly small, and the stakes inconsequential. She and Bruno were now part of a larger context.

The herd murmured and then called with a high, keening voice. Tens of thousands of throats called to a strange glowing sky.

"They sound . . . sad."

"I read some anger in them, too."

"I hope they're at least honest with us. I'm tired of tricks and puzzles."

"I'd be happy with a bit of respect as well. They're *retired* gods, after all."

"They picked us to oversee their Substrates. They must have some respect for us."

"We're ugly and nasty but we're damned hard to kill."

"Let's hope they know that. You can fool some of the primates all of the time, and all of the primates some of the time—"

She kissed him again to cut off his talking. The herd stamped out a rapid pattern, *thump! thump! thump!*— and then called a long, strident melody. It was loud, demanding, unnerving.

The herd, the Host, fell silent. Ordered ranks of the thousands and thousands of creatures stared. They looked almost expectant.

"Something wrong?" Bruno asked, frowning.

She wriggled her hips against him with a sly smile. "Nothing you can't fix. You have the right tool."

He laughed. "Captain-my-captain, we are both tools— for each other, and for the Host." He gestured at the vast ranks of silent creatures before them.

With crystal clarity, Carol knew she stood beside a man she could truly trust and love. Sure, he knew things no human could know, do things that were not human. But he was still the essence of Bruno Takagama, who had loved her across light years of empty space, in battle with kzin, and defended her from interdimensional creatures. He had even loved her from beyond death of a sort.

Was he now the original Bruno? Or was the twisted version of his original self, sacrificed to create the Substratum Host, real?

Perhaps even the mad mind that had saved them all aboard the Outsider ship was the truest Bruno?

Carol shook her head. It didn't matter. Not really.

What was a human being? Mind, of course, but the flesh had its immediacy as well. A thought to motivate the touch. Carol knew that in this Bruno—and *with* this Bruno, perhaps—she had the best of all possible worlds.

For the moment—no, for ever, now—that would have to be enough.

Carol listened to the Herd begin to sing. Individual notes and tones met, joined, until the valley resonated with a haunting chorus. She thought that she was beginning to understand the underlying meaning, the nuances of messages passed between the parts of an unthinkably alien mind scattered into a million parts.

Separate but together—*AtOne*, the Outsiders called it.

A panoply of feelings and emotions suddenly swept through her, and she abruptly *tasted* colors, and *smelled* the shapes around her.

She took Bruno's hand and smiled. Perhaps they were both more than human now.

All at once, Carol Faulk knew the music in her heart and head. She sensed that Bruno did as well, and nudged him. He nodded, his own smile exactly as she remembered it from many years ago, before the *Sun-Tzu*, before the kzin, and before they had met up with the Outsiders and puppeteers.

Before everything.

Together, they began to sing *back* to the Host. In counterpoint, under a sky that still glowed with the aftermath of unthinkable cosmic plans—and even greater ambition.

True, They Who Pass had no doubt altered them both, for their new role as shepherds; Protectors beyond the ability of the Tree-of-Life virus. But the throat that sang did not really matter, Carol Faulk realized. Puppeteer or human or Substratum Host or some twisted multidimensional structure; some things transcended form.

It was the song that mattered, not the singer.

For there was such a precious thing as harmony, even here and now. And perhaps forever.

ROBERT A. HEINLEIN

"Robert A. Heinlein wears imagination as though it were his private suit of clothes. What makes his work so rich is that he combines his lively, creative sense with an approach that is at once literate, informed, and exciting." —*New York Times*

Eight of Robert A. Heinlein's best-loved titles are now available in superbly packaged Baen editions. Collect them all.

PODKAYNE OF MARS (pb)	87671-6, $5.99	☐
(trade)	72179-8, $10.00	☐
GLORY ROAD (trade)	72167-4, $10.00	☐
FARNHAM'S FREEHOLD	72206-9, $5.99	☐
REVOLT IN 2100	65589-2, $4.99	☐
METHUSELAH'S CHILDREN	65597-3, $3.50	☐
ASSIGNMENT IN ETERNITY	65350-4, $4.99	☐
SIXTH COLUMN	72026-0, $5.99	☐
TAKE BACK YOUR GOVERNMENT (nonfiction)	72157-7, $5.99	☐

If not available at your local bookstore, fill out this coupon and send a check or money order for the cover price(s) to Baen Books, Dept. BA, P.O. Box 1403, Riverdale, NY 10471. Delivery can take up to ten weeks.

NAME: _____

ADDRESS: _____

_____

I have enclosed a check or money order in the amount of $ _____

DAVID WEBER

Honor Harrington (cont.):

Field of Dishonor

Honor goes home to Manticore—and fights for her life on a battlefield she never trained for, in a private war that offers just two choices: death—or a "victory" that can end only in dishonor and the loss of all she loves....

Other novels by DAVID WEBER:

Mutineers' Moon

"...a good story...reminds me of 1950s Heinlein..."
—*BMP Bulletin*

The Armageddon Inheritance

Sequel to *Mutineers' Moon*.

Path of the Fury

"Excellent...a thinking person's Terminator."
—*Kliatt*

Oath of Swords

An epic fantasy.

with STEVE WHITE:

Insurrection
Crusade

Novels set in the world of the Starfire ™ game system.

And don't miss Steve White's solo novels,
***The Disinherited** and **Legacy**!*

continued ☞